PRAISE F

"Laws is a master craftsman."

—*Shivers*

"Stephen Laws presents a fresh, chilling voice among the multitude of authors feverishly clawing to imitate Stephen King or Peter Straub. Laws is no imitator!"
—*Seattle Post Intelligencer*

"Laws's work typifies a new generation of horror writing: [It] inhabits the world as we know it, and is all the scarier for it."

—*Maxim*

RAVE REVIEWS FOR *FEAR ME*, WINNER OF NOVEL OF THE YEAR FROM THE DRACULA SOCIETY!

"First-rate horror. Gripping to the last page."

—*Locus*

"A sleek and sexy book, laced with horror and triumph. No other author today is writing horror as effective and as powerful as Laws."

—*Starburst*

"A big, ambitious book, eloquently written, inventively plotted, perfectly paced. Great stuff."

—*Interzone*

"Laws updates the vampire story, weaving a compelling tale that is all the more effective for ditching the standard stake-and-garlic trappings. Very well done."
—*The Times* (London)

THE WYRM

"Horror which is both truly frightening and dangerously unpredictable. A brilliant book, full of characterization, horror, and a creature so frightening that most others pale beside it."

—*Starburst*

"Laws achieves a truly oppressive atmosphere as this awesome pariah is unleashed on the town.... Unquestionably our most promising genre writer."

—*Samhain*

"Fast, clever, and full of zombies."

—*City Limits*

"Keeps the suspense gripping until the tense thriller reaches its chilling conclusion."

—*Western Morning News*

"Hair-raising horror that pulls no punches."

—*Liverpool Daily Post*

"If his first novels vibrate with dread, than his latest drips it from every page."

—*Fear*

DARKFALL

"Brilliant...one of the scariest and truly unique storylines I've read in a long time. If you miss this novel you will be missing the quintessential horror novel of the year."

—*Midwest Book Review*

"...horror afficionados will be pleasantly spooked by this impossible-to-put-down read."

—*Publishers Weekly*

THE THING ON THE BED

"Wake up…"

Yvonne did not move.

"Come on, wake up!"

Nothing.

Angrily, Satch pulled back the covers further and fell heavily into bed beside her. Her body bounced on the mattress beside him, but still she didn't wake.

"Playing dead, eh?" said Satch again, as he pulled the covers back. "Well, that won't do no good, Yvonne."

No answer.

Roughly, Satch grabbed her shoulder and pulled her over hard to face him.

Screaming, he frantically thrashed back out of the bed away from her.

The nightmare had not ended.

"Please…" moaned Yvonne. "Please…help me…" And Satch looked on in horror at her face, which had somehow aged horrifically. The face of a one-hundred-and-thirty-year-old woman pleaded with Satch from the bed as he backed off on his rump until he was stopped by the bedroom wall. "Don't let him do it, Satch. Please…help me…" The hair was white, the eye sockets sunken. The thin, ragged lips were drawn back from Yvonne's teeth, giving her the appearance of a death's head. Her sunken eyes had cataracts, and her face was a mask of wrinkled grey skin. When she raised a hand towards him, it was like a claw.

The thing on the bed said "…help me…" one last time before he slid down the bedroom wall to the floor, unconscious.

Other books by Stephen Laws:
THE WYRM
DARKFALL

FEAR ME

STEPHEN LAWS

LEISURE BOOKS NEW YORK CITY

A LEISURE BOOK ®

January 2005

Published by

Dorchester Publishing Co., Inc.
200 Madison Avenue
New York, NY 10016

If you purchased this book without a cover you should be aware
that this book is stolen property. It was reported as "unsold and
destroyed" to the publisher and neither the author nor the publisher
has received any payment for this "stripped book."

Copyright © 2005 by Stephen Laws

All rights reserved. No part of this book may be reproduced or
transmitted in any form or by any electronic or mechanical means,
including photocopying, recording or by any information storage
and retrieval system, without the written permission of the
publisher, except where permitted by law.

ISBN 0-8439-5486-8

The name "Leisure Books" and the stylized "L" with design are
trademarks of Dorchester Publishing Co., Inc.

Printed in the United States of America.

Visit us on the web at www.dorchesterpub.com.

FEAR ME

Prologue

It didn't take them long to find the car.

Black Mercedes, brand new.

And it was parked just where Leonard said it would be. Sleek, black, with the dim overhead lights making it glisten as if wet. There were no other cars parked beside it down here in the subterranean quiet of the underground hotel car park, and that had made their task so much easier.

There were three of them. Three women, standing in a concrete recess directly opposite the Mercedes. Hidden in the shadows of the concrete buttresses; feeling the dank cold creeping through their clothes, settling deep under their skin and in their bones. Three women, united in the same purpose. Three frightened women.

Waiting.

"Will he come?" asked the woman in the dark grey raincoat, one hand gripping the collar up tight to her neck to ward off the chill. She was wearing a black headscarf to con-

ceal distinctive, close-cropped blonde hair. Large eyes reflected liquid darkness.

"He'll come," replied the woman in the leather jacket and
jeans. Dressed deliberately to look like a biker, even though
she had no bike. Her words were clipped and angry—and
when she spoke, the third woman began to cry. "God,
Yvonne," snapped the leather-jacketed woman. "Be quiet, or
he'll hear." The third woman was slighter than the other two;
wearing jeans with a black blouse, long straight hair tied
back and—even here in the darkness—wearing sunglasses.
She stifled her tears with a strangled sob, but the tension of
recent events had brought her to the edge of hysteria. She
crammed both fists to her mouth to try and quell the sobbing, but it was rising and swelling within her to the point at
which she must surely dissolve into hysteria. The woman in
the black jacket pushed her back into the recess, one hand
raised to strike her across the face, trying to shock that oncoming hysteria out of her system.

"No, Bernice!" hissed the woman in the scarf, grabbing her
arm, pushing her roughly back, swinging around to face the
woman in the sunglasses, seizing her wrists now and pulling
them away from her mouth. Breathing harsh, clipped and
brutal words into her face.

"Stop it, Yvonne. Stop it, *now*! He's going to come and
we're going to put an end to it. Do you understand?"

The woman called Yvonne had ceased making the keening sound and was fighting to get her breath back.

"Do you understand?"

Yvonne whimpered and nodded her head vigorously, like
a child; the gleaming black lenses of her sunglasses like the
eyes of some terrified insect, ready to take flight.

"All of us," hissed Bernice. "Remember, we agreed. All of
us." The words were individual stabs of anger in the darkness.

"I don't know if . . ."

"You can!"

"Jacqueline, please . . ." Yvonne's shining black lenses were turned to the woman in the headscarf.

Jacqueline restrained Bernice from moving angrily on to her again. And now Bernice was sighing heavily, looking back to Yvonne. "It isn't going to work. Look at her. Oh *God*, we must be mad . . ."

And then Bernice felt the familiar stab of fear and sickness in her stomach. She felt it first, but now the others were feeling it, too.

Yvonne was shrinking further back into the concrete recess uttering a strangled gasp of despair. Jacqueline stiffened, breath hissing between clenched teeth as if someone had slid a needle-thin stiletto under her ribs.

Unnecessarily, Bernice said, "He's coming."

They strained to listen, but there was no sound in these catacombs. Just the faraway hiss of traffic somewhere above in a world that should care, but didn't. Water dripping, like water in a cave. The sounds of their own frightened breathing.

And then the footsteps.

Bernice shrank further back into the recess, next to the other two, merging with the shadows. Jacqueline twisted to see where the footsteps were coming from. They seemed close, impossibly close and drawing nearer. The acoustics in the car park made the sounds echo unnaturally. Louder, closer.

Yvonne began to whimper again. Bernice clamped a hand across her mouth. She didn't want to hear her fear, afraid lest it might completely unlock the fear that was already building inside herself.

Where is he? Where is he?!

Yvonne was trying to push past, fear overtaking her; desperate now to run away from this place for ever. Bernice and Jacqueline held her back.

Oh God, thought Jacqueline. *He'll hear, and then he'll . . .*

A figure moved into view. Walking slowly, head down and deep in thought. No more than fifty feet away. He stopped beside the Mercedes, head still down, still deep in thought. He was tall. At least six foot three, with a slender but powerful frame. And although they could only see his silhouette, they knew that it was him.

He knows we're here.

Slowly, his head turned in their direction.

He knows!

And now Yvonne could contain the fear no longer. Her screams echoed and bounced in the underground car park like panic-stricken, terrified birds. Jacqueline caught her by the sleeve as she clawed past them out of the recess and into full view. Her impetus was arrested, but now she had dragged them both out into the open. As Jacqueline struggled to control her, Bernice stepped forward, heart hammering, sick fear in her stomach.

The tall silhouette remained in exactly the same position as before, watching them.

Don't throw up! Bernice commanded herself. *Keep calm. Keep calm and remember what he's done.*

"I'm sorry!" shouted Yvonne, and then began to shout it over and over again. "I'm sorry! I'm sorry! I didn't want to do it. Honest! They *made* me . . ." And this time, Jacqueline turned and grabbed her by the shoulder. She shook her, hard. Yvonne was silent.

The man remained unmoved, his face in deep shadow.

Bernice swallowed hard, summoning her courage, and said, "You bastard."

They couldn't see his face in the shadow, but they knew that he was smiling. The same satanically handsome smile that by turns could be so inviting, so entrancing . . . and so terrifying.

"Was this all your idea, Bernice?" His light bass voice was carefully modulated, so gentle. Bernice could feel sweat beginning to trickle down the small of her back.

"No!" snapped Jacqueline, dragging Yvonne with her to join Bernice. "It was *all* of us."

"Even little Yvonne?"

Yvonne whimpered in terror and tried to pull away. Jacqueline held her tight.

"Even her," said Bernice, hands thrust deep into her pockets, fists clenched.

"I told you never to follow me." The tone of his voice was a mocking reproach. "How could you disobey me after I've been so nice to you?"

"Don't turn on the charm," replied Jacqueline. "Not now."

"The charm?" The man laughed, face still hidden; a long, slow sound. "Is that what you call it? Yes—it's a good word."

And then he stepped forward. One step out of the shadows so that the faint overhead light spilled down over his face.

"Oh Jesus . . ." said Bernice.

"Don't look," said Jacqueline. "For Christ's sake, don't look."

Instead of struggling to get away, Yvonne clung tightly to Jacqueline. The terror had risen in her throat and she couldn't speak. All she could think was: *Mother of God, have mercy on us sinners . . .*

Bernice unclenched one fist and scrabbled in her pocket.

"I told you what would happen," said the man. He began to walk slowly towards them.

Suddenly, Jacqueline could find her voice at last and screamed at Bernice, "Do it, do it! For God's sake, just do it."

And then Bernice pulled the Webley service revolver out of her jacket pocket; large, black and heavy in her hand—so heavy now that she had to raise it with both hands to get it up to arm's length, pointing at the man.

The ghastly smile that was not a smile flickered and froze on the man's face. Was that fear in his eyes? In *his* eyes?

"Do it!" screamed Jacqueline again, and now the suddenly impossibly tall shadow was striding towards her through the darkness; terrifying and unstoppable, one arm slowly raising towards her.

Can't . . . can't . . . can't . . .

With a small cry, Bernice pulled the trigger.

The gunshot was agonisingly loud; stabbing their eardrums, lighting the car park in a split-second thunderbolt of blue-white. The recoil was so unexpected, so fierce, that Bernice staggered backwards, almost dropping the gun in shock.

The man staggered to his right, his raincoat flying, as if he had been trying to side-step the bullet and someone had given him a hard slap on the shoulder. He remained frozen in that side-step position. Dark drops began to patter on the ground at his feet, and Bernice knew that he had been hit. She gave an involuntary cry as the man came on.

She pulled the trigger again.

And this time, she clung grimly to the gun as the impact hurled the man backwards. He staggered and collapsed to his knees, hugging his midriff.

Slowly, he lifted his head again to look at them.

. . . and God oh God, Bernice didn't want to see his face again. She could see his eyes, reflecting the faint light, almost luminescent—and the gun was now so heavy in her hands. So heavy that she could no longer hold it, could no longer pull the trigger. Her arms lowered.

And then Yvonne—poor, terrified, shrinking Yvonne—broke free from Jacqueline in a frenzy of fear and repressed, screaming panic.

"You can't have me!"

Seizing the gun from Bernice's lowering grasp, she swung it towards the man as he began to rise to his feet.

"You can't!"

Her scream reached its crescendo with the third, echoing, shattering gunshot. The bullet slammed the man from his feet, hurling him backwards through the air across the bonnet of the Mercedes behind him. His arms flip-flopped as he rolled from the bonnet and slapped on to the cold concrete floor.

He began to crawl. A monstrous, crawling shape in the shadows.

Yvonne flurried forward, stilettos ringing on the concrete. This time she fired directly into his back, at almost point-blank range. The body convulsed and spasmed. For an instant, there was a small gout of flame from the bullet hole in the raincoat between his shoulder blades, where the fabric had momentarily caught alight.

Then the shape began to crawl again.

"He won't die . . ." said Yvonne, as she backed away from him; sounding more like a little girl than a twenty-six-year-old woman. "He won't die."

Jacqueline was frozen. The man's hands were the only thing she could see, everything else about the crawling shape was in shadow. Spasming, white fingers clutched at the concrete as the shape slowly dragged itself hand over hand towards them.

At no time since the first gunshot had the man made a noise. And, impossibly, he was still alive. His fingernails scraped on the concrete like talons as he crawled out from the shadow of the car.

The Webley revolver clattered to the concrete from Yvonne's nerveless fingers. Her face was the colour of frozen pastry as she swayed and then collapsed to the ground.

The shape was still coming, still crawling; dragging itself by crooked white hands towards them.

Those hands took me, thought Jacqueline. *Those hands caressed me, stripped me, touched me . . .*

Bernice was retrieving the gun.

You just did what you wanted.

Bernice was moving back to the hideous crawling shape. A dark pool was forming around it as it came.

You did the same thing with Yvonne. The same thing with Bernice.

Bernice was trying to raise the gun again as he came on.

You nearly destroyed my life.

Jacqueline took the Webley from Bernice. She did not resist.

And when the man braced his gnarled white hands on the concrete and raised his blood-masked face to look at her, she stepped forward and shot him in the face.

Any further shot was unnecessary, because now the man was dead at last.

But she shot him again anyway, and kept pulling the trigger as the hammer fell on empty chambers.

Part One
Lust

Chapter One
Paul

He watched himself approaching from a distance, his reflection in the glass double doors at the other end of the hospital corridor. The sounds of his footsteps echoed as he walked: sharp, crisp . . . almost angry. And as his reflection grew larger in those doors, he found himself becoming objectively fascinated by it. Somehow, that reflected figure did not seem to be *him*; it was as if he were objectively watching a complete stranger approaching. This was not a new preoccupation, and he wondered if he was, after all, a complete narcissist.

As the stranger approached, he tried to analyse him; trying, in the way that a nineteen-year-old might, to make some sort of sense of the figure. What kind of person was he? Where was he going? What would he become?

Tallish, perhaps five foot ten, but with one shoulder characteristically bent to one side making him slightly shorter

than his full height. As he watched, the figure straightened
as it came on.

Maybe he's neurotic.

Brown jacket. Red shirt. Blue Levis. Maybe because he'd
seen Jack Nicholson wearing that in *Hell's Angels on Wheels*
and he'd looked really cool.

*So he's a hippie Hell's Angel? Hell no, haven't even got a
Harley Davidson.*

Dark hair, almost but not quite black, cut fairly short. A
sallow complexion. Dark, liquid eyes that caught the light in
a way that some women found attractive. A face unlike his
mother's or father's.

A stranger's face.

And now that stranger was reaching out to meet him. The
glass double doors banged open as Paul blended with his
reflection. He passed through into Ward 7. The smell of antiseptic and cleaning fluid was now so familiar that he hardly
noticed it any more, even though it had terrified him at first,
bringing back childhood memories that he wanted to forget.

*Paul! You've learned that bad language from the devil.
Drink this! Drink it and clean out your mouth . . .*

The reception area for Ward 7 was a little way ahead, and
just when he began to wonder whether she would be working on shift today, the nurse stepped around the corner and
saw him.

"Hello, Mr. Shapiro."

"Hi, and it's about time you called me Paul."

The smile again. The smile that was more than just a professional courtesy, that gave him a hint that maybe there
could be something for them both beyond the walls of this
hospital, but always that barrier there for some reason. Always that barrier of the person in Ward 7 who Paul visited so
frequently.

"How is she today?"

"She didn't have a very good night . . ."

"Walking around again?"

"Yes, but she's been sleeping most of the morning and she's fine now."

"No bad dreams?"

The smile again, slightly fractured around the edges.

"No, none."

What the hell else is there for me to say?

And now she was gone, into the ante-office on the side of the corridor, talking now to one of the orderlies. Paul moved on, feeling that apprehension building again as he stepped into the main ward. There were other visitors there, clustered around beds and one or two orderlies to make sure that none of the more demonstrative patients interfered with anyone. Mr. Evans was walking in circles again at the bottom of the ward by the window, wringing his hands and counting from one to a hundred over and over. The elderly woman whose name Paul didn't know shouted another expletive from her bed, to no one in particular. Sun was beaming through glinting windows this morning, casting shafts of brilliant light into the ward. Somehow, it seemed to accentuate the shadowed corners even more than usual.

He turned a bed-screen and there she was again.

Guiltily now, he realised that he had been hoping she would be sedated this morning and that he would therefore have to cut his visit short. She was lying peacefully in bed, her white hair spread out around her on the pillow. It looked as if it had been combed. Her eyes were closed, her hands crossed on her chest; rising and falling gently with her breathing. Was she asleep?

"Mother?"

"You're no son of mine," she said tightly, eyes still closed.

Paul gritted his teeth and pulled up a chair.

"How are you?"

"How old are you now?"

"Nineteen. But you know that. The nurse tells me that . . ."

"So it's just a matter of time, then." She opened her eyes now and there was an undisguised vehemence in them as she spat at him, "Just a matter of *time!*" Her eyes closed again and now she was smiling, the indignation gone. "Know about time?" she asked, almost conspiratorially.

Here we go again, thought Paul. *Another thirty minutes of riddles.*

"The nurse was saying you had another uncomfortable night."

"She doesn't know what happens in the night. She's lucky. I can hear it, though. I can hear the talking. I know what he's doing . . ."

And as she talked, Paul found himself tuning out again as he so often did on these visits; concentrating on her face as she talked, still with eyes closed again. She had been a good-looking woman when she was younger. He had often looked through the photograph album at the pictures of them both together; first when he was a baby, then a child. He had searched his mother's face as if trying to find there the tell-tale signs that were leading her to desperate confusion and eventually to this hospital bed. But the pictures revealed a perfectly healthy mother and her child.

The signs of abuse had gone largely unnoticed until Paul had been five years old. The cleaning fluid had been the first open example discovered by his father, who had dashed the bottle from her hand as she held it up to his lips. He remembered the horror of it, even though he had been so small. Not the horror of struggling to squirm away from his mother, twisting his head away to avoid the pungent, acrid liquid . . . but the horror of his father's reaction. Such a gentle man, with never a harsh word or action. It was strange.

Things had become worse thereafter, with his mother's

behaviour becoming increasingly erratic. Social Services had subsequently become involved. And then one day, his father had told him (when he was seven years old) that Mother was going away for a rest. That rest had become a long-term stay at Craigfern Hospital, and that was when Paul had first heard the term: Alzheimer's Disease.

He remembered asking his father what it was. Remembered the way that his father had looked at him for such a long time.

"They say that's what it is," he had heard him say clearly. But as he turned away, he also heard his father say under his breath, "But that's not what it is."

"What?"

And then his father had explained the symptoms of Alzheimer's Disease. Barely able to understand at that tender age, Paul was more entranced by the words his father had said which he wasn't meant to hear. They contained a depth and a resonance which seemed to register with him deeply, although he couldn't work out why.

"But that's not what it is."

His mother—Veronica—had been in Craigfern for twelve years now. Not recovering, although it had to be said—not deteriorating. Her confusion somehow remained at a constant. With two visits per week for the last twelve years, both Paul and his father had seen other patients with the same condition come, deteriorate and go . . . but Veronica remained. No pattern to her confusion, no key to the secrets she claimed to possess, no convincing her that there were no mysterious conspiracies.

And Paul had watched his father's face on the visits. He had watched his face and wondered what pain his father was masking there. She had ceased to be a mother and a wife. She was someone else. Someone they visited. But not the person they remembered.

As he watched his mother, and listened to her talking without hearing a word, he remembered all these things. When she had finally talked herself back to sleep, he waited a while longer; then carefully pushed back the chair and stood. He deliberated trying to kiss her before he left, fingering the scar on his cheek and remembering how last time he'd done that she'd clawed a hand across his face, laughing. No, perhaps not . . . and that damn awful ache in his throat had begun again. An ache that seemed to constrict his breathing, making it difficult to swallow.

The other visitors were still sitting around their relatives' beds when he left.

Chapter Two
The Women

The three women left the underground car park quickly and quietly. Bernice had taken the Webley revolver back from Jacqueline's shaking hands and had shoved it deep into her jacket pocket again. It lay heavily in that pocket; heavy as a stocking full of pennies, dragging down the hem. Bernice bundled both women into the stairwell and hung on to Yvonne when it looked as if she might run screaming away. They had to stay calm. It was vital not to draw attention to themselves in case someone was coming up that staircase towards them.

It should have taken one shot.

They had agreed that beforehand. Just one shot and then out of there as quickly as possible without being seen. But it had taken all six shots in the revolver and somehow, their luck had held out. There hadn't been another car or another hotel customer since Gideon first arrived.

"He wouldn't die . . ." said Yvonne in a voice filled with tears. Her face reminded Jacqueline of a sparrow she had once saved when she was a child. She had kept it for a day in a cardboard box after rescuing it from the family cat. She had prayed that it would get better, and it had just sat there on the cardboard floor of the box, shivering and looking at her . . . just the way that Yvonne looked now, as she said again, "He just wouldn't die . . ."

"Well he's dead now," replied Jacqueline as they hurried down the staircase, surprised at the flat and unemotional sound of her voice. "We're free of him."

"Be quiet!" hissed Bernice, and now they had reached the ground floor. Yvonne looked as if she was going to run straight at it and burst out into the street, but Bernice hung on to her arm and pushed open the door calmly. The sudden bright light from the street outside made Jacqueline wince as she followed after them.

They kept walking down the side-street which abutted the car park, glancing nervously over to the loading bays and back entrance of a department store. There were men working back there; they could hear the crash and clatter of crates and fork-lift trucks, but they were too far away and too involved in their own business even to notice three women passing by. At the top of the street was a main thoroughfare and now they could see a two-way flow of pedestrians. As they drew nearer, Jacqueline expected to hear cries of "Stop!" or "Murderers!" But there were no voices; no sounds other than the ever-nearing sounds of street traffic and crowd bustle.

When they reached the main street, Jacqueline searched each face that passed for a sign that they had been discovered. But the faces were unconcerned, intent only on their business and their destinations.

And then the crowd swallowed them, and they became a part of it.

Jacqueline cast one look back at the hotel's car park, strained to listen for the sounds of police sirens. But there was nothing. She wondered if she could ever live with herself after what they'd done.

But Bernice was looking at her now, and somehow seemed able to read her mind. "It's over, Jacqueline," she said. "We had to do it. He would have killed us. You know that, don't you?"

"God, Bernice, we've just *killed* someone . . ."

"What we killed wasn't human. And if he wasn't human, then it wasn't murder, was it?"

"What *was* he?" said Yvonne, more to herself than to the others.

"I don't care," replied Bernice. "I don't want to know. All I do know is that we're safe now that he's dead."

"What about the police?" asked Jacqueline.

"We weren't seen. And no one can trace this gun."

"And now?"

Bernice stopped. She let go of Yvonne, who now looked too exhausted, too drained to dash screaming into the crowd. All three women looked desperately tired now, finally awoken from a living nightmare.

"Now," said Bernice, "we go back to our lives."

"Should we meet again? Do we need to . . . ?"

"No," said Bernice simply . . . and walked away into the crowd.

Jacqueline watched her walk away, watched as Bernice casually glanced at shop windows as she moved off; looking just like a well-to-do upwardly mobile local media personal-

ity out shopping and not wanting to be recognised. Not
someone who'd just killed a man.

"Are we free?" asked the sparrow.

"Yes," replied Jacqueline as Bernice vanished into the
crowd.

"Goodbye, then." Yvonne looked at her for a long time,
squeezed her hand and moved off into the crowd, walking
slowly in the opposite direction to Bernice. Her head was
lowered, and she didn't look back. Jacqueline felt inex-
pressibly sad for Yvonne as she walked away. What kind of
freedom had she had before this nightmare had been visited on them? Soon, Yvonne was also absorbed into the
crowd.

Jacqueline thought of home.

Brian . . . and the kids.

She wondered if the fear, guilt and sadness would dissipate or remain with her for ever.

The nightmare was over. She had to keep telling herself
that.

At last she surrendered to the crowd.

Chapter Three
Veronica

The trees were singing.

And she knew that no one else could hear that singing;
knew that to the others it would simply be the wind in the
branches. But they were singing nevertheless; it was a

lament, a keening, crooning lament. Sometimes it was comforting, at other times deeply unsettling—as if they were trying to give her a warning. Today, she could not be certain what the trees were trying to tell her. There was a difference in their song; an urgency which was new. For a long while, she lay there, trying to decide whether she wished to listen to what they had to say or not.

Dimly, she was aware that a nurse seemed to be at her bedside, talking to her.

"Go away!" she snapped. "I can't hear what they're singing about."

The figure retreated from the bed, and she returned to the song again. It was a song of autumn, even though she knew that it was midsummer. It was a song of things dying and of rebirth and it brought back memories that were too bitter and too frightening. She would stop listening. As if knowing that they were about to lose her to their song, the trees changed the content and the tempo. Now it was more reassuring, more comforting but still with a sense of urgency. That sense of urgency was now forming into a clear urging summons.

Time to get up, said the song. *Time to get out of your bed.*

"Why? What for?"

Because it's time to make sense of everything you've been through, Veronica. Time truly to forget all the fear and the sorrow and the regret that has made you hide from the world. Wouldn't you truly like to be purged of all those feelings, purged of the guilt and the shame and the fear?

"Oh yes, yes. I'd like that more than anything."

Wouldn't you like everything to be the way it was before?

"Yes, oh yes. Can you do that? Will you do that for me?"

Then rise from your bed, Veronica. Come outside to us, and listen to our song.

Veronica opened her eyes to make sure that the nurse

had really gone away. There were still visitors in the ward, with enough people walking around and talking to prevent her from being seen.

She slid from underneath the bedcovers, smoothing down her hair. She felt very weak, but the song of the trees gave her the extra strength she needed. She believed their promise, and she must go outside to join them. Holding herself erect, Veronica walked towards the French windows which were open at the other side of the ward. The sunlight shining through in golden shafts reminded her of the light from a cathedral window, and she walked into the golden glow with her heart bursting in joyful expectation.

Come join us. Come listen to our song.

Expecting to be stopped at any moment by one of those interfering nurses or orderlies, Veronica was suddenly outside on the flagged patio, looking out across the gardens to where the trees sang in the wind. There was a light breeze; the coolness of it on her skin seemed somehow cleansing.

"I'm coming . . ."

She descended the stone stairs from the patio which led out into the gardens. The grass felt warm and soft underfoot. The trees beckoned, branches swaying.

The truth, Veronica. Time for the truth . . . and the end to all fear.

A figure stepped out of the cover of the trees ahead of her. It was too far away for her to see any details, but she knew that this figure was the subject of the trees' song; that the figure would resolve all of her lost years, all of her fear and pain. As she drew nearer, she could see that it was a young man.

"Paul?"

No, this young man was a stranger. He was about Paul's age, and he was smiling as she drew closer to him. He was standing at his ease, holding something in both hands; something that looked like a stick, or a branch or . . .

The lament of the trees filled her mind, crying out for her to join them quickly. She began to run, crying now in joy as she held out her arms to the young man for the embrace that would resolve everything.

Smiling, the young man lifted the double-barrelled shotgun to his hip and fired both barrels.

Chapter Four
Yvonne Remembers

"I can't go back feeling like this, can't go back feeling like this, can't go back . . ."

The words were repeating endlessly inside Yvonne's head as she pushed on down the main street and through the crowds. Now that she had left the other two women—Bernice and Jacqueline—she felt disorientated and strange as she moved on down the street. After everything that had happened, she was feeling somehow detached from herself; as if she were floating somewhere above, looking down at the pathetic woman battling her way through the crowds. The terror inside, the terror of him, was gone now that he was dead. He had deserved to die and she could go back to her life again. But now she felt sick and disorientated, and knew that she couldn't go back to Satch unless her head was together again.

Satch was clever, could see things; could see the way she was feeling. And if he knew that something was wrong he would bully it out of her. If that happened, God knew what he would do to her. Things had been bad before, but if Satch ever found out . . .

Oh, Christ, please let him never find out.

Gideon was gone. Everything would be all right again.

An image of her baby son, Jason, flashed before her eyes. She convulsed, pushing that image from her mind, refusing to let the anxiety overwhelm her. The baby was safe at home with her mother. Satch would be out at the Working Men's Club as usual (*working* men . . . she permitted herself a desperate and strangled laugh . . . Satch hadn't worked in fifteen years). All she had to do was pull herself together.

It was over.

Gideon was dead.

An elderly woman with two large carrier bags nearly collided with her.

"You stupid . . . !" Yvonne raised both hands, almost lashing out at the startled old woman, then checked herself. Trying to ignore the hostile stares of other shoppers, she hurried on ahead.

"Can't go back feeling like this, can't go back . . ."

She suddenly realised where she was. This was Grainger Street and Mark Toney's coffee house was just ahead of her, somewhere beside the chemist and the bookshop. She almost stopped, flinching, but then it somehow seemed appropriate that she should be back here again.

Because this was *the* coffee shop.

It was the place where she had first met Gideon.

And maybe a coffee would steady her nerves.

Yvonne hurried purposefully ahead, shrugging off the sick feeling inside as she pushed open the glass doors and entered. For a second, she couldn't bring herself to look across the café to the table in the far corner. What would she do if Gideon was sitting there the way he'd been on that first

day? What would she do if he looked slowly up from his coffee and smiled at her? What would happen to her mind?
Yvonne steeled herself to look.

The table was empty.

(Ridiculous, of course, you silly cow. What did you expect?)

"Yes?" The voice of the girl serving behind the counter was
like a smack across the face. Her heart leaped.

"Coffee, please."

The coffee house was half-full of shoppers and children,
but Yvonne saw none of them. Her focus was centred on
that particular table . . . and now, as she moved towards it
with her coffee on a tray, she found that she could never,
ever sit at that table, as she'd originally intended. The table
next to it was vacant, so she sat at that. Her fingers were
trembling as she tore open the small packet of sugar . . . it
spilled over the table top. She gripped the cup with both
hands and drank. The coffee was hot and good, filling her
with warmth and melting the icy chill that had settled deep
in her stomach.

She drank, and looked at the table. In her mind's eye, she
could see herself sitting there, as if she were watching a
video. It was like travelling back in time. She watched her
doppelgänger sit there with a coffee, three large carrier bags
of shopping at her feet, Jason in her lap, eleven months old.
She watched herself, remembered how she'd felt. Her back
was aching badly, and she was worn out. She had almost
burst into tears on the street outside. Shopping to do, a crying baby to handle, a crowded bus, and a husband who was
lying at home in a drunken stupor; unwilling and unable to
assist. She watched herself tenderly touching her own
cheek, hoping that her carefully applied make-up was still
hiding the bruise that Satch had given her for daring to suggest that he help her with the shopping today. Jason smiled.
Wind . . . or a real smile? And she remembered the ache in

her throat, and now that ache was there again as she re-membered that voice saying . . .

"Is anybody sitting there?"

Her first reaction was to yell, "Yes! Can't you see I need the space?"

Then she saw him.

And she realised now, for the very first time as she watched herself on video, that it was his smile that had done it. Able now to work out her instantaneous feelings at the time, she saw a vision of herself sitting at home in front of the television watching commercials while Satch snored on the settee. She remembered (was this the way a person saw their life flash before them when they were drowning?) watching the false promises and the false smiles of beautiful men in shampoo or beefburger commercials. The way they moved, the way they looked at their girlfriends. The way they all laughed, the way they all smiled. And God, oh God, why couldn't someone ever have smiled at her like that? Was it real? Did people actually smile like that? Sexy and . . . and . . . *honest* with the people they were smiling at? Satch had snorted and turned over.

And the man with a smile that seemed to reaffirm the truth of those stupid commercials sat down next to her before she could answer.

Instantly, it seemed, she recognised him. He had a bronzed complexion, as if he had just come back from holi-day—somewhere exotic. And he had the face of a male model. Was that where she had seen him after all? On televi-sion? In one of those soap commercials? His eyes were a dark and liquid brown. He had a designer stubble, just like the one she loved on George Michael. His hair was dark and slightly long, wet-long, and beautifully styled. His teeth were perfect when he smiled at her. The dark, ankle-length coat was draped around him like some kind of Byronic cloak.

"What's your name?" he asked. And those eyes seemed to strip away her flesh and bones to find her soul.

"Yvonne?" he said. And she realised that she had answered without hearing herself. "Nice name."

Nice. The word was more than a word. It had more meaning than the word, and somehow touched her heart. In one word, he was telling Yvonne that life didn't have to be like this for her. He had told her that she was beautiful . . . and in that knowledge, she could feel a crippling dam of emotion beginning to shudder inside her. She tried to speak, but could not. Somewhere, a baby was crying.

"It's time to go, Yvonne," the man was saying.

And instead of saying, *Who are you? Where do you want me to go?* she said, "Yes . . ."

He stood up from his seat, and she could see that he was very tall. She began to rise . . . and then Jason almost slipped from her lap on to the floor. The air seemed to swell and ripple before her eyes, and she caught him before he could fall.

"Leave the baby," said the man. There was a coldness in his voice that had not been there before. When she looked up at him again, the dream was acquiring hard edges that she didn't like.

"I can't . . ." she began. The man's warm brown eyes were now somehow a cold and icy grey, reflecting the light from the strip lighting overhead. Her vision rippled again when she looked at those eyes. Now, she almost whimpered when she looked at him. Because something in those eyes terrified the hell out of her. How could she have been so wrong? Those eyes had no warmth at all, only the certain knowledge that if she dared to defy him he would tear her to pieces right here in this restaurant. Satch had suddenly become only the second man she was most afraid of in the world.

"Please . . ."

Two women at a table not far away were watching now, and whispering. The man gave them both a half look, then turned back to Yvonne. When he spoke again, the words were clipped, carved from ice.

"Then bring it."

He turned and walked away towards the exit. The long black coat flowed behind him, and it seemed to Yvonne that he was gliding away from her. Grasping Jason to her breast, she hurried after him.

"Miss! Miss!" called one of the whispering women. "You've left your shopping." But Yvonne did not hear her as she followed the man out on to the main street and into the crowds.

He was creating a wake of people before him as he strode ahead, the crowd on the pavement moving out of his way as if on a silent instruction. Yvonne made use of that wake to catch him up.

"Don't . . ." She struggled to call out to him. "Don't go so fast . . ."

The man forged ahead, either unaware of her now or simply ignoring her pleas. Jason whimpered against her breast as she hurried onwards. Up ahead, there was a crossroads and traffic lights. Yvonne could see that they were just changing to red. The man must stop there. She would be able to talk to him, try to attract his attention, try to ask him . . .

The man stepped straight out into the traffic.

A van screamed to a halt right next to him, tyres screeching. Yvonne cried out in shock, and Jason began to squall. The man just kept on walking.

"You stupid bastard!" yelled the van driver, beginning to open his door. A woollen cap and ragged beard framed a face that was white with shock and rage. The stranger turned back to look at the driver.

Glass, thought Yvonne, and felt sick inside. *His eyes are made of glass.*

Yvonne watched as the driver scrambled back into the van and slammed the door. Now, all she wanted to do was call out to the driver; beg him to drag her into the van and just drive away from there. But she could not . . . and even from where she stood on the pavement, Yvonne could see that the man was also terrified of the stranger and his eyes. He looked as sick as Yvonne felt inside. The van screeched on down the High Street and the stranger turned nonchalantly and headed for the other pavement. The lights changed again, and Yvonne stumbled across the road, hurrying to catch the man up.

He was heading down one of the many side-streets now, away from the crowd. Yvonne had never been down there before, but she knew that at least two Chinese restaurants had their back kitchens leading out into it. She could see steam gushing through the gratings in the ground. There was a cheap bar down there somewhere, too. A seedy, back-alley place that Satch sometimes frequented to pick up so-called "certain" betting tips.

Oh God, what if some of his friends are down there? What if they see me . . . ?

She hesitated at the side-street entrance. Jason was giving full vent to his hunger and tiredness and outrage now. His cries echoed and carried down the side-street, bouncing sharply off the soot-engrimed walls on either side and the encrusted verandas and fire escapes.

The man turned and looked back at her. His eyes were still reflecting the light, and she was so filled with the terror of that gleaming in his eyes that the fear cramped her stomach. Her stomach was reacting, she would throw up. And then she would collapse, and then . . .

Come, said the man, in a voice that was so quiet that there was no way she could possibly hear him from there. And that word was just like the *nice* word in the restaurant. The ice and the cold and the fear were dissipating before the power of this new word. The crippling nausea in her stomach subsided, the fear dissolved from her throat, and escaped like invisible vapour up into that darkened concrete canyon. The feeling that overwhelmed her now was just like the Valium when it took hold properly. There was nothing to be afraid of now.

The steam from the pavement gratings was rising all around her as she walked down the side-street towards the dark figure. It *was* a video commercial, after all . . . just like the ones on television. And as she neared him, floating forwards just as he had appeared to glide out of the restaurant, she could see that she had been completely mistaken about the coldness and the terrifying eyes. He was just as she'd first seen him in the café. He was holding out a hand towards her as she came. So romantic, so warm. His smile was . . . was . . .

Angelic.

Yes . . . yes . . . that's perfect. He's like some kind of angel.

Jason was still crying when she finally reached him.

He looked down from her, at the baby.

Was that a hint, a shadow of . . . ?

No, of course not. Because now the baby had stopped crying.

The man took her by the arm. His hand was large and powerful. She looked down at it. The nails were long and perfectly manicured.

You are a male model. Aren't you?

Yes, I am what you want.

I thought so. I knew it.

Come . . .

Again, that word. But this time it brought with it something new as she allowed herself to be led into another alley

that led off from the side-street. There was only one grimy
blue light above a back door, leading God knew where. But
the light made it seem as if this really was some set from an
avant garde theatre. As she allowed herself to be led, she
could feel that new emotion overwhelming her.

She knew that this beautiful stranger wanted her body.

And now, she wanted him—wanted him desperately.
More than anything in the world. She could feel that excit-
ing warmth beginning to glow and spread. Her breath was
beginning to catch in her throat as her excitement began to
swell. In the blue-black darkness, the man pointed to the
child, still held against her breast by one arm.

"Get rid of it."

It was the most natural thing for him to ask.

She looked quickly around, feeling that glow between her
legs. Feeling that ache in her nipples.

There was a dustbin standing next to railings, filled with
trash and rotting vegetables. Swiftly, Yvonne hurried over to
the dustbin and placed Jason inside, on top of the garbage.
He had gone to sleep.

She turned and hurried back to the man in the shadows.
He was still waiting there in the darkness to embrace her.
Steam from the pavement gutters had shrouded his feet, the
long black coat hung at his side like a cloak.

She was swept into his embrace, and her orgasm began as
soon as their lips touched. His body was cold and hard, not
warm—but the cold did not deter her. It excited her. His
mouth smothered her own. She could no longer breathe,
but found somehow, dimly as the pleasure engulfed her, that
she did not need to breathe. His hands moved to her shoulders, now tearing the blouse away from her neck downwards. The fabric came away in those perfectly manicured
hands like tissue paper, the buttons popping. The bra strap
was cut as if by scissors. It fell away, and she crushed herself

deeper into that embrace. She fumbled at his crotch, feeling the hardness, realising that her orgasm was going on and on . . . and he still hadn't entered her. She was groaning into his mouth now as her skirt and panties fell around her legs.

He would not let her touch him there.

Instead, he seized her with both hands on her buttocks, raised her to his own height and whirled to the grimy side-street wall. Her voice still smothered, she could only groan and moan into his own mouth as he forced himself into her with her back against that wall. Heaving himself into her, the pleasure was so exquisite, so animalistic, that the rough pain of the brick wall on her back meant nothing by comparison. The orgasm was going on and on and on . . . and she must surely faint or die or go mad or . . .

Arms wrapped around his neck, legs wrapped around his waist, nothing else mattered now except that he fill her with himself; for ever and ever. His tongue was already filling her mouth, somehow giving her the air that she couldn't get through her nostrils. Her own tongue tried to meet his, but his tongue was literally filling her mouth and slowly . . . slowly . . . that tongue was sliding into her throat; literally— into her throat. And now faster, faster . . . Down her throat, filling the entire cavity and making Yvonne gag as it slid down into her gullet. But God, oh God, it didn't matter . . . nothing mattered as long as he kept doing it . . . and she was coming and coming and coming . . . and that tongue was in her belly, filling her completely, just as he had filled her completely from below and . . .

He's in me from above and below.

Both are met.

I'm his. He's feeding, God, he's feeding and I'm going to die if this never stops because it's never ever been like this ever in my life not ever and I just want him to keep on and on and on and . . .

The bliss was all. Yvonne fainted.

There were no dreams.

She wanted it to be bed.

But there was no comfort here, no reassurance. No soft and yielding pillows to meet her feebly outstretched hand. No warm quilt to pull up around her neck.

She was lying on something cruelly hard and bitterly cold. That cold had seeped into her body, into her bones, so that each slight movement was agonising. The hip on which she was lying seemed paralysed by that cold. The pain in her head was like a dozen hangovers. She could not open her eyes.

Is that what it is? Have I been to a party? Am I hung over? Maybe . . . just maybe, please God I'm not . . . (and now the bitter sorrow started to choke in her throat) *. . . not married to Satch. Because Satch doesn't exist and I've never met him and I'm still at home with Mam and Dad, still typing up building surveyors' reports in Gilroe and Sands and going to nightclubs with my friends and . . .*

Knowing with desperate sorrow that when she opened her eyes the wish would be a bad and cruel joke, Yvonne began to open painful eyes. She tried to rise and then, utterly instinctively and with fierce and passionate concern remembered . . .

"Jason!"

Yvonne scrabbled to her feet, instantly alert—despite the agonising pain—and assailed by stabbing images.

Side-street. Night. It was day before.

Naked. (Her arms tried to conceal that nakedness, but now she could see her clothes, dirty and discarded. She snatched them up to hide her body.)

Railings. Dustbin . . . dustbin . . . dustbin . . . and . . .

"Oh God, NO!"

Yvonne threw herself across the alley to the dustbin, colliding with it in her anguish. It was full of garbage. But there was no sign of . . .

"Please, please, please!"

Yvonne clawed at rotten, shredded cabbage, at coffee grounds, at crumpled newspaper and knew that he wouldn't be there. Clawed further, throwing aside polystyrene take-away trays, indeterminate wet matter, empty pop bottles and . . .

. . . Somewhere beneath, something gave an inarticulate, muffled cry.

"GOD, GOD, GOD, GOD!"

Yvonne tore away a crumpled mass of newspaper.

Jason was there, as she'd left him, face purple and crimson in the throes of a cry that might never come before he suffocated; arms and legs wavering, nostrils distended. Yvonne scooped him up from the bin and crushed him to her breast. Instantly, that cry came. Full-blooded and distressed. But at least it came. With those cries, something inside Yvonne was also released. She collapsed to her knees on the pavement, the pain there meaning nothing to her. She began to cry, too.

Somewhere above, someone threw open a rusted window and yelled, "Shut that bloody noise up!"

But Yvonne kept on crying, letting it all out, rationalising what had happened.

She had been drunk. *I must have been drunk. Just like sometimes when I get drunk 'cos Satch has been hitting me and I take some of his vodka and then go shopping. The vodka and the pills help me then*.

She had let some bastard pick her up. *It's never happened before but, maybe . . . maybe . . .* Her cries echoed and bounced back to her. *That's what I've always wanted.*

And she'd let that bastard screw her in some dirty back alley while she'd left her son in . . .

"Shut up, you stupid bitch, or I'll . . ."

"OR YOU'LL WHAT, YOU BASTARD! COME DOWN HERE AND I'LL . . . AND I'LL . . . AND I'LL . . ."

"Crazy cow!" And the rusted window was slammed with a rasping echo.

Yvonne's grief continued. Her hate and disgust of herself knew no bounds. Her cries paralleled her infant, gave him what he wanted. He stopped crying, let his mother's crying take over.

Yvonne knelt there for a long time.

Chapter Five
Paul

Paul had been standing at the kitchen window, looking down into the garden, when he heard the front door open and shut.

"Hi, I'm home. Anybody in?"

"I'm in the kitchen."

"Great. Got the kettle on?"

"Wouldn't suit me."

"Haw haw."

Paul turned from his contemplation of the garden as the kitchen door opened and his father entered.

"God, I'm tired."

"Is that a statement, a prayer or a blasphemy?"

Paul's father grinned as he began to unfasten the clerical collar around his neck. He was still wearing the black cassock.

"I don't know which is harder for who. A vicar with a son like you, or a son with a vicar for a father. Every unguarded statement has to be weighed up for theological content." He groaned in exasperation, unable to unfasten the collar. "Do you think it would be unseemly for priests to have Velcro collars instead of these clips? Would make life a lot easier . . ."

"Here, let me."

The Reverend Anthony Shapiro was a tall man. Even with his permanent stoop, he stood a head taller than Paul. And he blamed that stoop on his need to have a one-on-one with his parishioners. Although the faithful needed a priest to look up to, he felt uncomfortable with the literalness of it . . . and the Reverend Shapiro liked to be a man of the people. The stoop was a physical result of wanting to *know* his flock, and of having to bend down to everyone all the time. The wings of grey hair at his temples gave him the look of a soap opera actor, playing a priest . . . and that was *his* summation, not that of his parishioners.

Paul finished unbuttoning and the reverend sighed as if a burden had been lifted. He took off the collar, dropping it on the kitchen table.

"What about that tea, then?"

As Paul filled the kettle at the sink, his father watched him carefully. After a while, he said, "You've already been, haven't you?"

"Yes," said Paul without turning around.

"You could have waited, you know. We could have gone together this afternoon. You know I had mass this morning."

"I know that, Dad. I just wanted to . . . oh, I don't know."

"It's okay. Sorry. How is she?"

"How is she, ever?"

"You *are* handling this, aren't you? It's just that this past few weeks, you've been . . ."

"I'm handling it, Dad."

"Okay . . . okay . . . Well, look, I'm just going to take my frock off. Any plans today?"

Paul didn't answer the question. His gaze was directed back out into the garden.

"Paul, if there's anything . . ."

"Have you told me everything, Dad?"

"Everything? I don't understand what you mean."

"Everything about Mother."

For a moment, his father did not reply. Unaware that Paul could see his reflection in the kitchen window, he turned aside and ran a hand through one of the grey-white streaks at his temple.

"You know everything there is to know."

Paul did not reply as his father left the kitchen.

Now, for a long time, he looked at his own reflection in the window, asking himself the same questions.

And then Paul heard his father say, "There's someone in the garden," in a voice which seemed almost too matter-of-fact.

Paul turned and saw him standing in the living room and moved to join him, following his father's gaze through the French windows.

A young man was walking towards the house. He was well over a hundred and fifty yards away but he seemed to be looking directly at them as he marched onwards.

"Bloody nerve . . ."

"That's not a Christian thing to say," said Paul.

His father grunted. "Let's not start that all over again." He flicked the catch on the French windows and slid them open in one quick, fluid motion. Paul followed as he stepped out on to the porch.

The young man was still coming on. Now Paul could see that he was wearing a green anorak . . . and he was carrying something that looked at first like a folded fishing rod.

"Excuse me," called Paul's father, an unnecessary gambit to attract the young man's attention, bearing in mind that this stranger's gaze seemed to remain fixed on them as he came. "Can I help you?"

The young man was shifting the fishing rod so that he was holding it in both hands now, the rhythm of his approach unchanged. But he did not answer.

"This *is* private property, you know," rejoined Paul. His father gave him an impatient look. "Well, what the hell *does* he want, then?" said Paul, as his father turned back and began to descend the stairs towards the silent, approaching figure.

"Can I . . . ?" began Paul's father again, and then halted on the stone steps as the stranger lifted the folded fishing rod to hip-height . . . and cocked the trigger.

"Paul!" His father whirled on the stairs and lunged back, strong hands seizing both shoulders and pushing him forcefully back through the opened French windows. Paul blundered backwards, still uncomprehending. His foot twisted on a fold in the living room carpet and he fell heavily to the floor.

"Dad! What the hell are you . . . ?"

Angry and confused, Paul saw his father charge into the room after him; turn and swing the French windows closed with one fast, slithering motion; turn towards him, face white and shocked, begin to speak as he blundered forward . . .

And then the French windows exploded behind him with a detonating roar. A cloud of glass fragments slashed into the room, and Paul saw his father hurled through the air towards him, colliding with the table and flailing to the floor. The table collapsed. Paul's hands flew instinctively to his face to protect his eyes. He lay there frozen in sudden shock and sick fear, his mind unable to register what was going on as the roaring explosion muted to a crashing tinkle of glass.

Somewhere beside him, hidden by the overturned table, his father groaned and tried to crawl.

"Paul . . . get away . . . get away . . . he's . . ."

Paul scrabbled to his knees, uncaring of the glass-littered carpet as he shoved the table aside to get to his father. He was lying face down, and his back was a shredded, bleeding mass.

". . . get away . . ."

"You've been *shot!*"

A shadow appeared in the ragged aperture that had been the French windows, glass crunching underfoot.

Paul twisted back in shock as the green-anoraked figure stepped into the room, breaking open the breech of the shotgun so that the two spent shells ejected with a brittle clatter. In spite of his shock, some ridiculously calm part of Paul seemed to recognise the stranger's face, tried to make some sort of sense of what had happened, what *was* happening.

The stranger was about Paul's age. His face seemed marble white under the hood of the anorak, the eyes luminous black and unblinking.

He's mad, thought Paul.

And when the stranger saw Paul's face, he smiled. It was a malevolent rictus of the face, with no humour—only a horrifying malice. Reaching into his anorak pocket, the stranger fumbled and brought out two fresh redjacketed shells.

"Get away, Paul . . ." said Paul's father from the floor. "It's *you* he wants."

We're going to die! The realisation transformed the horror and shock in Paul into a raw and desperate action. His body was still quivering as he lunged to his feet, grabbed the cross-brace of the overturned table like some kind of round wooden shield . . . and charged roaring towards the French windows.

The stranger tried to level the shotgun, stepping back.

But Paul slammed the table into him, knocking the shotgun aside. They both slammed hard against the lounge wall. The shotgun clattered to the floor as Paul dropped the table . . . just as the stranger's hands fastened around his throat. They thrashed away from the wall, the stranger's face screaming obscenities only inches from Paul's own. Paul's effort seemed to have robbed him of all further strength in the grip of this thing which seemed more animal than human. He tried to aim a punch at his attacker's face but the blow was ineffectual. Their feet tangled on the littered floor and now they were falling back, the stranger on top of Paul, teeth champing, foul breath in Paul's face. Momentarily the grip on Paul was released as the stranger tried to scrabble with one hand for the fallen shotgun. Paul tangled a hand in the stranger's hair, yanking him back, yelling in horror.

The stranger seized the shotgun.

And now Paul had twisted so that he too had one hand on the shotgun, preventing the stranger from bringing it to bear. They were both holding it with both hands now as the stranger struggled to his feet, dragging Paul up with him as he clung to the shotgun like a brace. The stranger began to lash out with one foot. Paul twisted so that the blows avoided his crotch, glancing instead from his thighs as he struggled to get his feet. Paul clung on grimly, knowing that if he let go, death was only an instant away.

The stranger was screaming again, but this time not at Paul . . . but at something at his feet, something on which he seemed to be caught. He thrashed backwards, enabling Paul to get a better two-handed grip on the shotgun . . . and now Paul could see what it was that had tangled in the stranger's legs.

It was his father, back shredded and gleaming. Clinging grimly to the stranger's leg, Paul heard him hiss, "Get *away*, Paul! Get away!" The stranger lashed out at Shapiro, kicking him away . . . and in that moment, lost control of the shot-gun. Caught off balance, with all his weight given to tugging at the gun, Paul fell backwards to the floor, the shotgun in his hands. The stranger lashed out again and again at Paul's father, then turned back to Paul.

White face. Mad, staring smile.

Still lying on the floor, Paul levelled the shotgun at him.

"Stay where you are . . ."

Face still fixed in that rictus grin, the stranger reached into his anorak pocket again and stepped towards Paul.

"I'm telling you! Stay where you are!"

The stranger drew a hunting knife from his anorak pocket and unsheathed it. The sheath fell to the floor. Light glinted on the serrated edge of the knife as the stranger came on.

Oh Jesus, I can't . . . I've never . . . oh Jesus . . .

The stranger screamed and lunged downwards for Paul.

Screaming back, Paul pulled both triggers.

The detonating roar was a continuation of their joint screams.

The stranger flew backwards across the lounge in a ragged, liquid spray; slamming back against the wall where Paul had first pinned him. He bounced, whirling to the floor again, leaving a dark red and dripping patch on the wall. He didn't move again.

Paul lay there, breath hoarse and whining in his throat.

Oh God, I've killed him. Oh God, I've killed him. Oh God . . .

Paul's father was no longer moving. Paul discarded the shotgun with fierce disgust and scrabbled over broken glass, unheeding of the shards that slashed into his knees and palms. He reached him and gently tried to turn him over, tried to speak, but could not.

"Paul . . . is it . . . is he . . . ?"

"I killed him, Dad. I *killed* him . . ." And now the shock and the horror swelled within him as he covered his face with one hand and was racked with sobbing.

"I prayed, Paul," continued his father, grimacing in pain. "I prayed that it was all over . . . prayed and hoped . . ."

"Don't talk, Dad. I'll get an ambulance . . . just don't . . ."

"He's found us again, Paul. God help us."

"He's dead. I've killed him."

"Not him . . . not him . . . he was sent, that's all. God help us, it's beginning all over again . . ."

"What? What do you mean? Dad, what . . . ?"

The Reverend Shapiro fainted again, blood seeping from his lips.

"Oh Christ, no!"

Paul dragged himself painfully to his feet and stumbled to where he hoped the telephone receiver was lying, still connected. It was. He stabbed out the 999 code before looking back at his father and the young man he'd just killed. His father's words were still echoing in his mind when the emergency operator answered.

He's found us again, Paul. It's beginning all over again . . .

Chapter Six
Jacqueline Remembers

And Jacqueline remembered as she walked through the crowds that . . .

The bus was five minutes late that morning, but Jacqueline didn't mind. It was a beautiful morning, 8:40 a.m., the air was fresh and clear, and she was looking forward to work.

How many people can say that, I wonder?

She stood at the bus stop, waiting for Janis, and let her relaxed gaze sweep over the cemetery on the other side of the road. The lattice-iron front gate was open as usual, bushes crowding around it and framing it. It reminded her somehow of the magical childhood gateways that you might read about in tales of Narnia. When the bus eventually arrived, and Janis alighted (as she most always did at this time in the morning), they would walk across the road together and pass through that gate. The library where they worked was on the other side of the cemetery; only a quarter of a mile or so . . . but it was a walk that she always looked forward to. The cemetery was pretty well looked after by the Parks and Recreation Department (with one or two aesthetic hints and complaints throughout the year from Janis and herself—all good-humoured and not pushy in any way, of course), and Jacqueline loved to see the effect that the changing of the seasons had on its familiar topography. The golds and russets of autumn, the way that the trees and shrubberies thinned out, gradually revealing views hidden during the lush days of summer. The way that the snow covered the tombstones and memorial stones in winter—nothing ghastly or spooky or morbid, just a very cold beauty, when it seemed that everything had been ordered to sleep. Spring— when familiar flowers and bushes crept back from the earth. Day by day she gloried in these transformations. Such simple things—but they gave her so much pleasure.

Except that some bugger's dropped his take-away right in front of the gate, thrown up, and scattered last night's chips all over the place.

No respect for Narnian gateways, some people.

Jacqueline checked her watch again and then opened out the newspaper which had been rolled up and shoved in her anorak pocket. Doom and gloom. She refused to let the headlines about the latest sex murder spoil her day.

The bus rounded the street corner with a grinding of gears and lurched towards the stop. Even before it arrived, she could see Janis standing at the door, hanging on to a handle. As she watched the bus approach, it occurred to her that neither of them adhered to the clichéd description of a librarian. No spectacles, no hair tied tightly back in a bun, no bookish look. Janis was wearing a bright yellow raincoat. Her ginger hair looked, as she had described it herself, "like an explosion in a mattress factory." She played a great deal of tennis, kept very fit and once when threatened by some drunken man with violence for not being allowed to sleep it off on one of the library tables, had thrown said drunken gentleman bodily through the front doors. Her language on that occasion would not have been found in the collected works of the Brontë sisters.

Jacqueline herself had a tendency towards brightly coloured, if not bizarre, non-library-person clothes. It was a statement that said "I am not your idea of a library person." But the truth of the matter was that she loved books deeply. Married at seventeen—happily—Brian and she had decided to start their family early. Now, with two boys (one ten-year-old and another just about to have his eighth birthday), Jacqueline had returned to her first job at the age of twenty-seven, having passed her final exams as a "mature" student.

The bus juddered to a halt and Janis skipped from the platform to the pavement like a ten-year-old.

"I am the Green Cross Code Lady," said Jacqueline. "Good morning."

"It is that," replied Janis. "Very perceptive. What's my stars say?"

Jacqueline looked in the newspaper as Janis took her

arm and guided them both across the road towards the cemetery gate.

"Let's see. Libra . . . 'You will spend most of the day stamping books and sorting shelves. Drunken customers will provide the opportunity for strenuous exercise.' "

"Hah, hah. No, really."

" 'Money problems may come to a head today. Do not rely on the advice of associates in financial transactions. A recent romance may blossom and take on more substantial form.' "

"Well, that's lies for a start. We had another bloody row last night. Same thing. What's yours?" They had reached the cemetery gate. Janis gave a disgusted groan as they stepped over the discarded polystyrene tray and its soggy contents.

"Aries . . . 'Do not be taken in by the guile of a stranger. His or her smooth exterior may well conceal something altogether different.' That's it . . . bit stark, isn't it?"

"Can't say that either of those are going to make it a better day really."

"You say that every morning. Don't know why you bother to get me to read them."

"Got to keep your eyes on the stars, Jackie. You never know what's around the corner."

Somewhere behind them, on the main road, car tyres screeched and a horn blared—knifing through the morning air and making them wince.

Between 9:00 a.m. and 9:30 a.m. they prepared the library for the days work: changing date stamps to show three weeks hence on those books borrowed that day, took the cash "float" out of the huge old-fashioned cast-iron safe that would have put off Butch Cassidy and the Sundance Kid, unlocked the cassette and video drawers, unlocked the car park gate. They switched on the microfiche reader and photocopier, replaced the cash box in the public photocopier and prepared the issue sheet for the day's statistics.

At 9:30 a.m. on the dot, the doors were opened to the public.

And throughout the day, as Jacqueline issued and discharged readers' books, answered enquiries . . . her thoughts seemed constantly to be returning to home. And to Brian, who seemed to be having a bad time of it at his own work recently. He was works foreman at Bruissons, a haulage contractor. He organised the shifts and rotas of long-distance lorry drivers employed by the firm on an independent basis. He was also a bibliophile—which was probably how the two of them had got together in the first place. But in the last week or so, he seemed preoccupied after a day at work. It was unlike him. And he wouldn't be drawn, shrugging off his quiet moods as "just another one of those bloody days." As she worked, she found herself scanning the past few days and previous conversations, looking for any signs of an answer to his moods . . . but none seemed to present itself. And as she thought these things, a voice suddenly said, "Hello!"

The sound of that voice startled her. Jacqueline reached for the book which had been slid across the counter towards her.

"Hi," she replied. "Nice book."

"Certainly is. Means a lot to me."

"You've read it before?"

"Oh, yes. I've got the McGuiness paperback edition at home."

"Really? Well, if you like it, I suppose . . ."

A low and friendly laugh. A laugh that she found incredibly sexy.

"I know, I know," the man said. "It's stupid of me. But I

couldn't find another damned thing to read. And . . . well, I suppose you know . . . this is a first-edition hardback."

At last, Jacqueline looked up.

The man's head was bowed. And the way that it was bowed suggested to her that he was an intensely shy person. Even so, he was so tall on the other side of the counter that she could still see his face, even bowed. He was dark-haired, with a pale complexion . . . but even as she looked she could see that his pale complexion was flushing like a schoolboy, and he was trying unsuccessfully to conceal it.

"Not going to steal it, are you?" asked Jacqueline, and then regretted having said that when the young man cleared his throat nervously. "Just joking," she said quickly and stamped the book. The young man thanked her and looked up at her for the first time. His eyes were a striking brown, his face more than boyishly handsome. It was a smile that disarmed and unsettled her as she handed the book to him.

"Thank you." And now the young man was gone, striding towards the glass doors. She watched him go and suddenly realised that for reasons she couldn't make out, her heart was racing.

"Excuse me, miss!" Another customer, angrily waiting to be served. She could tell by the look on the elderly man's face that he disapproved of her reaction, as if he knew just what kind of effect a certain man could have on a certain woman. Guiltily, she took the man's books.

"You feeling okay?" said Janis while they were sipping mid-morning coffee. Customer trade had eased off, and there were now only half a dozen people in the library, lounging back in padded chairs with books, or leaning over a spread-out newspaper on one of the oak tables.

"Yeah, why?"

"Dunno. You just seem . . . well, preoccupied. Everything's okay at home, isn't it?"

"My home life is the height of stability compared to yours."

"Oh, him. Well, it'll be over by tonight. Can't keep a huff going for longer than forty-eight hours. Sort of an unspoken rule at our place. But you're sure you're . . ."

"Ever seen him before?" asked Jacqueline.

"Who?" And Janis followed her gaze out through the glass library walls into the cemetery. At first she couldn't see anyone; only the path outside which wound its way between gravestones before becoming lost altogether; the weeping willow swaying gently in the breeze. But then she saw the dark-coated figure who was sitting on the bench, almost obscured by the hydrangeas. She strained forward to get a closer look. "You mean him, on the bench?"

"Yeah. Do you know what his name is?"

"Never seen him before. He's reading a book or something, isn't he?"

"He borrowed it from here about two hours ago. He's been out there reading ever since."

"Why the interest, Jacqueline? Not straying from the narrow path, I hope."

Jacqueline laughed. "I'm a librarian, remember. A sexless establishment figure, just like you. No . . . he just seemed, well . . . a little strange, that's all."

"A pervert? Should I go out there and bounce him around a little?"

"You want to scare trade away and have the city librarian bawling us out? No, he didn't seem to be a pervert. Just . . . I don't know . . ."

"Don't give me that bull, Jackie. You just fancy him, and that's that."

Jacqueline made a disgusted sound at the back of her throat, and turned away, sipping her coffee. Something inside seemed to tell her that although the young man was holding a book before him, he was actually staring straight at the glass library walls . . . and directly *at* her as she stood talking to Janis.

She turned back again to look at the young man—and something peculiar seemed to happen then. As if for the first time, she seemed to be seeing his eyes *properly*, the same striking brown eyes in the slightly boyish face—but now those eyes seemed, in her mind's eye, to have been a swirl of colours, not just brown. And that face wasn't so boyish as she'd thought. Surely it had been more sallow and with a kind of . . . well, *feral* look to it. She turned quickly away again, and was suddenly cramped by nausea. Sweat had broken out on her brow, and now she felt unsteady on her feet. She moved awkwardly to the counter, tried to put down her coffee cup and missed. It fell with a sharp crack and splash to the library floor; steam curled around her legs.

"Jackie!" Janis rushed to her side, saw her distress and helped her carefully to a seat behind the counter. "Are you okay? What's wrong?"

His eyes . . . the dark, swirling colours of his eyes . . .

"I don't know. Just . . . feel funny."

. . . eyes that you could be lost in . . . eyes that could draw you in, until the irises swallowed you like a whirling pit and you emerged on to the other side where . . .

"You'd better go home. You look terrible."

"Yes . . . yes, maybe I better had. I'll just have a rest. Then I'll be okay."

"I'll get someone to take you home."

"No, that's all right. I'll be fine."

"Are you sure you're going to be okay?" asked Janis. "I can get someone to run you home if you . . . ?"

"No, really. It's all right. I'll just get home and have a lie down. I'll be all right."

"Well . . . okay. But give me a ring at home later on."

"You're just a born worrier, Janis."

"Got to look after my staff, you know."

"Bloody cheek. But thanks. See you later." And Jacqueline stood up again, feeling better than before, but somehow feeling very weak when she thought about . . .

The eyes. Innocent, at first glance. But now . . . looking like . . . well, like the eyes of an animal. Like the eyes of a wolf or some other night-time creature.

Janis helped her to the glass library doors after Jacqueline had retrieved her coat and handbag.

"Take care," said Janis, genuine concern on her face as Jacqueline pushed through the glass double doors, walked carefully around the front of the library and told herself that she would avoid walking through the cemetery. If she kept on this path, she could skirt right around it to the main road.

But that's ridiculous. It takes me right out of my way. And if I shortcut through the cemetery, the bus stop is just across the main road.

And now, as she walked down the path at the side of the library and pushed through the wrought-iron gate, she knew that she had always intended to go this way, had always intended to find this strange man and find out just what the hell was the matter with her no matter how she was feeling at the moment. Strangely, her heart was racing as she walked quickly down the paved pathway that wound between the graves. The nausea had suddenly gone and her energy had mysteriously returned as she walked. Her breath was tight, she could feel a flush rising to her face. She tried to sort out and control her mixed emotions. Now, incredibly—stupidly—part of her felt like the fifteen-year-old girl she used to be, out on a first date. That sense of excitement also shamed her. What the hell was she doing? And what if Janis should move down to the glass library walls and look out into the cemetery? What would she think if she saw her striding out to find the young man on the bench who had so fascinated her? First she had cried off work, feeling ill, now she was about to hunt out and flirt with a total stranger. What if she . . . ?

He was sitting just as she had seen him all day. Relaxed, legs crossed, one arm outstretched along the back of the bench, the other holding the book out in front of him in almost classical pose while he read.

Except that he was not reading at all.

He was looking directly over the top of the book at her, with the shadow of a smile on his face that seemed to confirm her previous thoughts and containing an almost certain assumption that she would eventually come to him.

Her flush had risen. Her heart was beating fast and now she could not swallow as she walked on nervously towards him.

What on earth am I doing?

Coming to me, a voice inside seemed to say, a voice that sounded just like the stranger's voice when he finally rose from the bench to meet her and said, "You had to come, didn't you?"

"Yes." *Is that my voice?*

"Do you know why you came?"

"No." *That can't be my voice!*

"Because I wanted you to. It's as simple as that."

The man stepped forward and put a caressing hand on her shoulder. She did not want him to do that, but she couldn't move. She dropped her gaze from his pale and boyishly handsome face. Behind him, coming down the cemetery path towards them both was an elderly man walking his dog, a terrier.

"Look at me," said the stranger.

Now there was fear in Jacqueline's heart. She did not want to look at that face. He was standing so close to her now, so intimately close. She did not want this. She tried to shout to the man behind them, tried to call for help. But she could neither move nor speak.

"Look at me!"

Helpless to resist, she looked up into his face. The irises of the man's eyes were completely black. They were deeply attractive and deeply terrifying.

The man and the dog were walking past them now. And part of Jacqueline wanted to scream, *For God's sake, help me!* and another part, *For God's sake, go away!*

"Are you all right, miss?" The old man had stopped. Jacqueline could hear his dog snarling, almost fearfully.

The stranger's face blurred as he twisted his head away from her to stare at the old man. The momentary disappearance of those eyes left Jacqueline's senses reeling. Nausea took a bitter grip deep in her throat. She staggered to regain her balance, then froze in terror as she felt the shocking and powerful vibration of the stranger's voice even in the hand which held her shoulder.

"GO AWAY!"

Jacqueline would have fallen but for that immensely powerful hand holding her shoulder, literally holding her on her feet. She heard the old man's dog squeal in utter terror, heard the leash jerk away from the old man's grip as the dog ran scrabbling away across the cemetery, heard the old man say, "Oh . . . my *God* . . ." in utter terror, heard him staggering away, following his dog.

And then she was lost in those bottomless eyes again.

"What's your name?" There was a scent on his breath, something which she seemed to recognise but could not place, something that smelled at once repellent and yet deeply attractive.

"Jacqueline . . ." *My voice. That surely can't be my voice.*

The stranger's smile filled her vision. The teeth were perfect. She shuddered when he ran his tongue along them lasciviously.

"Do you know what you want, Jacqueline?"

"Yes . . ."

She was moving backwards now, being pushed towards the hydrangeas and hawthorn bushes, where she knew that they would not be seen.

"And what do you want?" Again, that acrid but enveloping scent.

"You," she heard herself saying. "I want you."

The stranger was smiling again. They were behind the bushes, screened from the library.

"Take your clothes off, Jacqueline."

Shaking hands fumbled at the buttons of her blouse.

"I'm hungry," said the stranger, throwing the library book casually over his shoulder.

There was nothing else in the world but those eyes.

It was cold.

There was damp earth beneath her . . . and she was naked.

Confused, dazed, and now aware that her body was aching all over, Jacqueline pushed herself into a sitting position and tried to remember who she was, where she was . . . and what she was doing here. Through slitted eyes, she could see that she was surrounded by bushes. They were hissing and swaying in the wind, late afternoon sunlight dappling through the branches and the leaves. A crippling headache throbbed in her temples and at the base of her skull. Then the reality of her nakedness brought with it a feeling of panic.

"What's happened? Oh God, what's *happened*?"

Her clothes lay strewn around her. Jacqueline snatched at them and hurriedly pulled them on again, panic rising. And as she hurriedly dressed, the same panic-stricken phrase was on her lips.

"What's happened? What's happened?"

Groaning, she pulled herself upright by clutching at clumps of grass. Then she felt the pain between her legs, saw the cemetery bench and the cast-aside book . . . and remembered.

"Oh *God* . . ."

Nausea and dizziness threatened to overwhelm her. Jacqueline reeled towards the cemetery bench, clutched at the arm-rest and managed to stagger around it, collapsing on to the bench itself. She lay back, gasping in lungfuls of air, wiping the hair from her face.

"Oh God, oh God, oh God . . ."

I've been raped. Oh my God, I've been raped.

But had she been raped? The whole sequence of events began to spin inside her mind like some confused and terrifying nightmare. The young man in the library who had been so shy. Her confused fascination with him that had so occupied her mind while he sat out there on the cemetery bench reading his book. The way that she had felt *drawn* to him. Had she really made an excuse to Janis about feeling ill and needing to go home—just so that she could go out there into the cemetery and talk to him? Why? What had happened to her? And had she lost her mind then? Had he really become something so fearful, so inhuman? He had told her what to do, what he wanted . . . and she had done it. Yes, a part of her had been terrified, but hadn't a part of her been *made* to want him? And so she had submitted . . .

"No!" she said aloud. "I *didn't* submit! God, I was . . . was . . ."

The word "hypnotised" wanted to jump into her mind, but she wouldn't allow it there.

Jacqueline tried to calm herself. Still breathing deeply, feeling hurt and terribly, terribly *soiled*, she sat forward again. She looked at her watch. It was 4:50 p.m. She had been lying there for hours. Refusing to let that confusing swirl of memory deter her, Jacqueline struggled to her feet and walked back through the lengthening shadows of early evening towards the library. She would telephone the police, tell them what had happened to her, report the rape . . . report the . . . report . . .

And the terror descended upon her. Unreasoning, unqualified terror. Now, she remembered his voice; a voice that spoke to her after it was all over and she was lying on the grass behind the bushes.

You will tell no one what has happened. Do you understand? No one.

Jacqueline stopped, swaying from side to side as that voice echoed in her head.

"I will report this. I *will* . . ."

You will tell no one *what has happened.* No one!

Jacqueline reeled, the pain between her legs merging with the fear which gripped her stomach.

No one!

Reeling, Jacqueline turned and staggered in the opposite direction, towards the cemetery gates, the main road . . . and to the bus that would take her home.

Chapter Seven
Paul

The twenty-four-hour period after the madman had exploded into their home was a fragmented blur of images and experience. Even now, two weeks later, it seemed to Paul that he had dreamed it all.

Shock, the doctors had said. Delayed stress syndrome.

Paul's killing of the intruder was obviously self-defence, the police had informally assured him of their views of that, although the full inquest and investigation would still have to be endured. Paul remembered little of the actual police questioning and investigation, and there had been a complete memory loss for him of several hours when an uncomfortable detective sergeant had advised him that the same maniac who had tried to kill his father and himself had also killed his mother in the hospital grounds.

He remembered the policeman telling him these things, and then he could remember nothing else until the next day. He couldn't remember how he had reacted, what he had said, what he had done. But it was obvious that he had been sedated and had remained sedated for some time after that, which probably accounted more than anything else for the blurred and disjointed memories. He had been admitted to hospital for two days before discharging himself. The media news coverage of the event on the ward television set had been too much for him. He wanted to get away from that place and back to the vicarage where he could shut himself away and not speak to anyone.

His father was in intensive care. No longer on the critical list, his condition was, as they said, "stable"—but he had been comatose ever since the attack.

Paul had been pacing the living room for well over an hour, his attention constantly returning to the bare wooden boards that had been nailed up over the shattered French windows' aperture. Conversation from the previous two weeks had been playing and replaying in his head as he paced, trying to make some kind of sense of everything that had happened.

Who was he? Why the hell did he do it? I just don't understand.

We don't understand either, Paul. His name was William Trafford. Does that name mean anything to you?

Trafford? No . . . I don't think so . . . no, I'm definite. I've never known anyone called Trafford.

And you've never been to Low Haddon in Northumberland?

Never heard of the place. Why?

That's where he's from. He's a farmer's son. The shotgun he tried to kill you with belongs to his father.

But why did he do it? Why?

We just don't know. His mother and father have no idea either. Seems like an ordinary enough young man. Your age actually. Been working on the family farm ever since he was fourteen or so. Very placid kid by all accounts. No history of mental illness. No trouble with the law. Seems he suddenly just took his father's gun, wrapped it up, went to the nearest railway station and bought a connecting ticket to Doncaster. A taxi driver from there recognised Trafford as being the young fella he collected and drove to Beckham. Have a look at this photograph again. Are you sure you've never seen him before?

Never.

Well he obviously knows you and your family. He knew that your mother was in Craigfern, he knew just exactly where to go after he'd . . . he'd killed her.

Oh, Jesus . . .

Not much of a comfort for you, Paul. But you must know that she died instantly.

Life was just a living hell for her. But to die like that . . .

There has to be some kind of connecting thread here, Paul. This isn't just a random killing. When your father recovers, maybe he'll be able to throw some light on the matter.

Paul threw himself into an armchair, exhaling loudly. He was wearing himself out and he knew it.

Hello, Paul? It was Linda. *I've heard what happened, and I hope it's okay me telephoning you. But I didn't know what to do. Are you okay?* Paul and she had been "serious" for over a year. They had met at university, where they were both taking the same Humanities degree and he had thought that everything was going fine, until he found out that she had also been sleeping with a married British Telecom engineer. Now, during the holidays, Paul had returned from his shared, rented flat to spend some time at home with his father and to think things over. The emotional turmoil he had felt then seemed to have completely dissipated in the light of what had subsequently occurred. *Are you there, Paul?*

"Don't come over. I don't want to see you."

Paul stood up and began pacing again, thought about coffee, changed his mind and threw himself down on the settee.

Hi, Paul. It's Todd. Look, me and the boys wondered if you felt up to coming out for a few beers, know what I mean?

"No, thanks. Maybe later."

Paul rubbed his hands over his face. The flesh of his face felt alien, as if he was touching someone else's face. The feeling disturbed him. He wondered if he should go for a walk in the garden.

Mr. Shapiro? Paul Shapiro? I'm from the Echo. *Terrible thing to happen, I know. How do you feel?*

I feel like hitting you in the face for asking such a stupid fucking question. Let's see you print that one. Now get off my telephone line, you parasite.

He had gone ex-directory shortly thereafter, getting special service from British Telecom in view of his "circumstances." Even so, the press had still tried to get a personal interview. He had ignored their ringing on the front doorbell, and now kept away from the living room windows when he'd seen one of the bastards trying to take a photograph of him from the far field with a telephoto lens. Maybe having a walk in the garden was not such a good idea after all.

Paul stood up again, paced, sat down and considered whether he should have a drink. He was only a social drinker, but the whisky bottle on the cabinet looked inviting.

How is he, Doctor?

The internal injuries aren't nearly so bad as we feared. He's making a good recovery.

But how long will he stay like this, in this coma?

We've no way of knowing. There have been no brain injuries, so we're hoping that he'll make a full recovery. His left shoulder will need to be reconstructed over time, of course. But we'll begin considering that once he's emerged from trauma.

Funny.

Sorry? What's funny?

I used to visit my mother in this hospital. Now she's gone . . . and Dad's lying in this bed. Think something somewhere is trying to tell me something?

Maybe you should go home now, Paul. The stress . . .

Yeah, yeah. The stress.

Paul stood up again and moved to the drinks cabinet. He screwed the top off the bottle and stood looking at it for a long time. Then, angrily, he poured a large measure into a cut-crystal glass, swirled it and drank it. It burned all the way down.

"You killed him," he said aloud, looking at the empty glass. *Yeah, but he was going to kill me, he was going to kill us!*

Paul poured himself another and sipped at it.

"What did you mean, Dad? 'It's starting again.' "

He considered the other words his father had said: *It's not me he wants, it's you.* Obviously, his father either knew Trafford, or knew why he had come. He knew that he should have told the police about what his father had said. But he wanted to talk to him first.

The whisky was turning sour in his gut. The burning feeling was spreading to the rest of his body. He knew that he shouldn't have drunk it. He wasn't used to hard liquor. Strictly a one or two pints of beer man, and that was it. His vision was fogging, but he couldn't believe that two whiskies could do this to him.

"The drugs," he said, remembering the medication that the doctors had given him to cope with the potential after-effects of stress and shock.

That burning was turning to dizziness. He felt himself reeling, and clutched at the bureau, running the other hand over his face. He had broken out into a cold sweat. With startling clarity he could see Trafford's face before him, with that hideously evil grin. The placid boy who wouldn't hurt a fly but who had travelled over a hundred and thirty miles to kill three perfect strangers.

The burning feeling suddenly exploded in his stomach, coursing like liquid fire through his veins and arteries. Paul was suddenly possessed of a hate so fierce that it raged instantly and uncontrollably through him.

"You *bastard!*"

The cut-crystal glass suddenly shattered in his hand. The

pain of the broken glass slicing into his flesh further fuelled that uncontrollable anger. With the other hand he swept the whisky bottle and other glasses to the floor. Roaring, he whirled like some savage animal in the centre of the room, lashing out at the armchair with one foot, overturning it; flinging the broken, bloody shards of glass from his bleeding hand. He hurled himself across the room, seized the television set and heaved it over on its side. The screen shattered. Electrics fizzed and sputtered within.

And Paul knew that he was totally and completely out of control.

He destroyed the living room.

Curtains were torn from their pelmets. The living room windows were shattered by hurled plantpots. Cupboard doors were ripped from their hinges and thrown into the centre of the room. Vases and china ornaments exploded against the walls. Plants were mangled and shredded. Furniture overturned. The record and CD collection strewn over the wreckage of the room.

And then, exhausted and sobbing, Paul collapsed amidst that wreckage and slept.

There were no dreams—but there was a Voice. Urgent, insistent, angry. It disturbed him deeply and he struggled to escape from it. But the Voice held him in this unconscious limbo that was somehow not a dream and whispered its demands at him incessantly.

You've killed him, and that's good. But there is Another. You have to find him before he finds you. Because he'll come for you if you stay here, Paul. He'll hunt you down and find you and then he'll kill you.

"Leave me alone . . . let me rest . . . go away . . ."

You've got to find the Other. He's coming for you now. He wants to kill you. Paul, you have to find him and kill him first. He hates you. You must hate him. Don't you see?

". . . please . . . let me alone . . ."

When you wake up, Paul. When you wake. When you wake . . .

"The Other . . ."

Yes, the Other. He hates you. Just the way that Trafford hated you and wanted to kill you. Trafford is the same as the Other. Trafford killed your mother, Paul, and would have killed your father. The Other will find and kill your father now, then he'll kill you. You hate the Other, don't don't you, Paul? You hate the Other. You hate and you want to kill him, don't you, Paul?

". . . hate him . . ."

Yes, that's right. Hate the Other, hate the Other. Hate the Other!

"I hate the Other . . ."

Yes, yes, yes!

"I HATE HIM!"

Paul was suddenly awake and alert, lying in the wreckage of the living room. And somehow, that Voice was still there.

Find the Other, Paul! Find him and kill him!

Filled with a cold and lethal fury, Paul picked himself up and walked unsteadily to the front door of the vicarage. He stood for a while with his hand on the door-frame, sucking in deep breaths until he had fully recovered. Then, with a deep and purposeful hate gleaming in his eyes, he flung the door wide and walked out into the daylight.

Chapter Eight
Bernice Remembers

Bernice Adams kept walking down the street, taking comfort in the swell of passers-by; for the first time in many years not allowing herself to be worried about whether she was noticed by anyone in the crowd. She was less concerned about being recognised by a "fan," but kept her dark glasses on as she moved. What had happened in the hotel car park was part of a nightmare, a bad dream. As she walked, she remembered, and could not stop remembering.

No, I don't want to . . .

But there it was anyway, replaying in her mind like a film and no matter how hard she tried, she couldn't prevent herself from remembering that night when . . .

She was sitting in her Peugeot, in the car park of Radio Novacastria. It was 11:30 p.m. and she was worn out, too exhausted at present to start the drive home, trying to settle the anger which was gnawing inside her.

She had just finished her "slot" on a late night talk show, and the resident DJ was a man with whom she'd crossed swords before. The talk hadn't gone well. She knew that her interviewer was himself interviewed for the job she had obtained at the local TV station—newslink anchorwoman for the regional news—and that he had never forgiven her for getting the job before him. She knew that she shouldn't have accepted the invitation to talk about the play she was going to appear in at the Phoenix Theatre, feeling that perhaps his innate professionalism would overcome his bitchiness at being passed over all those years ago. But she was wrong—and the interview which should really have been a "plug" for the play had become a sneering attack on the outmoded appeal of such clap-trap and innuendoes that second-rate drama productions were simply havens for washed-up local media people who had aspirations to be stars.

But she'd also held her own very well. She'd kept calm and managed to neutralise his sarcasm. She'd managed to put him in his place with creative witticisms that she was quite pleased about, as she thought about them now, sitting in her car and letting the anger evaporate. And she'd also managed to "plug" the play quite nicely, too.

She lit a cigarette and looked back at the radio headquarters—at its dark cinder-block outline against the night sky, at its blue neon sign. The airport was not far away, and as she watched, the neon-lit outline of a returning holiday flight passed overhead.

Maybe she needed a holiday.

She certainly needed something.

She looked at herself in the rear-view mirror.

Forty-three and perhaps old in terms of the network's view. But the network was perhaps only too aware of the need to be seen not to be sexist or ageist. Is that why she still had her job? Academic, really. They were probably afraid of her popularity. Afraid of giving her job to a younger woman despite those behind-the-scenes activities of Traycee Manton. The face wasn't too bad. Dark complexion, but youthful for her age. No real crow's-feet to talk about, except when she smiled . . . and she'd been told that they looked sexy on her anyway. Not too much make-up, even the heavily layered stuff necessary in the studio. No need for dark eyeliner, or an over-the-top perm. She smoothed back dark curls from her face. Hair dyeing was

*another thing, of course. She did it regularly, and wondered
whether her hair really had turned grey. Perhaps she would
never know.*

She considered returning the favour by dropping this un-
professional newscaster very heavily in the shit with his superiors. There must be some kind of dirty business in his
past that she could use. But then she started thinking about
the "two wrongs never making a right" business—and decided to be professional about it.

And then an arm leaned through the window and a
leather-gloved hand took the keys from the ignition.

Bernice started in shock, saw only the shadow now at
the side of the car beside her. An involuntary cry escaped
from her lips, and she frantically locked the car door and
wound up the window; now quickly shrinking back in the
driving seat.

The shadow stayed where it was, and she watched with
fear mounting in her throat as the dark figure weighed the
keys in its gloved hand, began lazily throwing them and
catching them, throwing and catching them.

"Pervert!" she shouted at the shadow.

The shadow laughed. A man's voice.

Bernice cursed again and slammed her hand down hard
on the car horn. The noise blared in the car park. She'd keep
it there until someone heard and came to investigate.

She whirled to look at the shadow again, and this time
she froze in alarm . . . because the man was stooping to
look directly at her through the driver's window. And that
face terrified and hypnotised her.

The face was darkly shadowed, but the eyes had an intense luminosity. The face was sallow, but handsome, with
high cheekbones. He was clean-shaven, with dark—almost
manicured—eyebrows. The jawline was strong, the teeth
perfectly even and white. In a terrified instant she had taken

it all in, but she could not move, could not cry out. Because the eyes had caught her. She was lost in them. At first they seemed to be brown, then blue. At their centre was a swirling redness which could be madness, but was not, and there was something in them that by turns frightened her, and then thrilled her. She was lost and helpless . . . and her hand fell away from the car horn.

"Open the door," he said.

Bernice saw her hand moving to the catch, saw her fingers pull it up so that he could swing open the door. He threw the keys into her lap, but still she could not move.

"Open the passenger door," said the man, and she felt herself leaning across to the other door as the man slammed the driver's door shut. The car swayed on its suspension and he walked around the front of the car. At last she could see that he was wearing a long black overcoat and dark scarf, which whirled and flapped around his head in the cold night air. His hair was dark and slightly long. Dark wings of it furled and unfurled over his face as he finally reached the passenger door, swung it wide and slid gracefully into the car to sit beside her. The interior of the car was brightly lit for only an instant, and she wasn't able to see him properly as he slammed the door shut again and looked at her.

The eyes, she thought. And then something stupidly inappropriate which said: *The eyes have it*.

And the eyes were all she could see now as he swiftly fastened his safety belt.

"Do you live alone?" asked the man. Even his voice was hypnotic. Low, perfectly modulated, well-spoken.

"No . . ."

"Will you be alone tonight? Will anyone be there?"

"No . . . I mean, yes . . . someone will be there."

"Very well. Do you know the Manor Hotel on the North Road?"

"The Manor Hotel? Yes . . ."

"Does anyone know you at the hotel? Have you ever been there on television business?"

"I don't know anyone there. No one knows me. I was there four years ago for an interview, but that was just in the lounge. No one knows . . ."

"Then take me there."

The eyes, she thought again. *The eyes have it.*

"Now," said the man, and Bernice saw her hand lifting the keys from her lap, slotting them into the ignition. She reversed out of the car park and headed for the North Road. The Manor Hotel was about twelve minutes away.

She tried to speak as the car reached the slip road and turned on to the North Road, joining the stream of traffic. Somehow, the words refused to come as the stranger sat impassively beside her, staring straight ahead at the road. There was a perfume in the car now, something that she had never smelled before, but which seemed by turns fascinating and nauseating.

"What are you . . . ?" Bernice began to find her voice again.

"Be quiet," said the man calmly, and Bernice's voice dried up again.

Why am I doing this? What's wrong with me? Is it a dream? Is that it? Well for God's sake, wake up, Bernice! I don't like this . . . don't like . . .

Already, she could see the dark outline of the Manor Hotel up ahead. It was a modern, twelve-storey hotel. It had no real style, just an anonymous building that could pass for an office block from a distance, catering for businessmen attending conventions and, as such, with no real desire to look olde worlde or prestigious. Bernice did not want to go there. The sight of it filled her with a horror of anticipation.

She struggled to wrench the driving wheel over, preferring

to ram straight into oncoming traffic rather than continue on with the stranger. But her hands were fastened to the wheel.

There was a traffic roundabout ahead. Bernice turned into it, swerved around and the car swept into the main entrance. There were two fake Olympian bowls on either side of the drive connected to a gas pipe. Plumes of yellow flame illuminated the car as it entered.

"Park over there," said the stranger quietly, waving at the darkened ranks of parked cars. "Anywhere."

Bernice found a space, and the car slid into it. She turned off the ignition and the lights and the car was plunged into darkness. The sound of her breathing seemed to fill the interior of the car. She struggled to speak again, and only a cracked sob came from her throat. She could sense without looking that the stranger was smiling.

"You're Bernice Adams, aren't you?" the stranger asked at last.

The question was an allowance for her to speak. Suddenly, her voice returned.

"Yes."

The stranger touched her hand, and now Bernice was filled with strange and conflicting emotions.

"I've seen you on the television," said the stranger. "You're very attractive."

Bernice was terrified. Terrified and revolted. But there was a heat being transferred from this man's touch. A heat which was filling her with desire, even though what she wanted to do most was to fling open the car door and run screaming into the night.

"This is what you're going to do, Bernice. Are you listening?"

"Yes . . ."

"Look into my eyes when I'm talking to you." Those eyes

seemed feral, glittering in the darkness like the eyes of some night beast waiting to spring out on its prey. Wind-tossed hair framed the man's sallow face. "Good. You will go into the hotel and you will pay and register for a double room. You will register in your name. Do you understand, Bernice?"

"Yes . . ."

"When you have registered and paid you will go to the main elevators. You will wait for me there."

No. Oh God, no! I don't want to do this. Why can't I wake up? Why can't I . . . ?

"Do you understand, Bernice?"

"Yes . . ."

"Then do it."

Bernice saw her hand move to the door handle and willed it to stop. But suddenly, she was climbing out into the night, into the car park. The stranger remained impassive in the passenger seat, staring ahead. She saw the faintest of light reflecting in his marble eyes, and that desire arose within her. A part of her wanted him to take her now, in the car, on the wet tarmac of the car park, anywhere . . . and an-other part of her wanted to scream: *No, no, no, no!*

Bernice turned and walked towards the hotel.

It's a dream, a terrible dream. I can wake up if I want to!

She entered the main lobby of the hotel through the re-volving doors.

Then why can't I wake up? Why? What's happening to me?

The desk clerk smiled as she reached the reception desk. A woman about Bernice's age, dark-haired, attractive. Ready and willing to help.

"How can I help you?"

Help me, please help me!

"A double room, please. Just for the night."

"Certainly. Cash or credit card?"

I need the police. I need help. I need to get away. For the love of God . . .

"Credit card." And Bernice provided the credit card from her handbag, watched as the receptionist filled in the necessary details.

"Do you have any baggage?"

"No."

"Continental breakfast, or full English breakfast?"

"I don't know, he didn't say."

"Excuse me?"

"Nothing. I mean, no breakfast at all, thank you."

Get me out of here! Get me out!

"Very well, if you could sign here . . . and here . . . and this is the register . . ."

Bernice saw a movement from the corner of her eye. A shadow was moving across the glass frontage of the hotel reception area—she knew that it was the man. Hurriedly, she finished the paperwork.

"Room 212. On the second floor. Have a comfortable night," said the receptionist, and Bernice wanted to hurl herself at the receptionist, grab her by the neck and scream for help directly into her face. But instead, she thanked her and moved quickly to the elevators. The revolving doors were turning, the shadow was moving to meet her, but Bernice could not bring herself to look as she reached the elevators and stabbed the button.

The shadow joined her.

Her heart was racing, there was sweat on her brow.

The elevator began its descent from Floor 4.

Bernice tried to speak, but could not. There was a terrible war going on inside her. A war of fear and desire. She felt as if she must . . .

"You won't faint," said the stranger, calmly and matter-of-fact.

The elevator doors slid open, and Bernice walked straight inside, followed by the shadow.

Please God. Please help me . . .

She pressed the button for Floor 2.

The elevator doors slid shut.

Something happened then. Bernice faded out of consciousness, and when her mind focused again she was walking down the hotel corridor, her footsteps muffled by the carpet pile. The shadow of someone behind fell over her as she walked, and the fear was lodged deep inside, silently screaming.

Automatically, when they entered Room 212, Bernice switched on the light. There was nothing here to distinguish the room from all the other hotel rooms she'd ever stayed in over the years. Pastel blue walls, an anonymous print on one wall and a double bed with the quilt fiercely tucked under.

"Put the light out," said the stranger, closing the door behind him as he entered after her.

Bernice did so and stood in the darkness as he brushed past her. She heard him move through the darkness to the windows. He swept the curtains open in one swift motion and the utter darkness was transformed to a dark midnight blue. Now, she could see the shapes of the furniture and the bare outlines of the room.

He turned back to her; a stark silhouette against a backdrop of dark blue.

She waited.

"I've seen you on the television," said the man quietly, but in a voice which seemed to fill the room. "You tell the world of its sorrows and its shames, all with the same impassiveness. All with the same distance in your voice. Don't you know sorrow or shame, Bernice?"

"I . . . don't . . ."

"I know your secrets, Bernice. You can't hide them from me."

She wanted to scream, wanted to run away. Her fear made her feel physically sick.

"When I saw you on television, I wanted you."

She wanted to run screaming from the room, but could not move. She could not see the stranger's face in the darkness, but knew that he was smiling. She groaned in fear.

"You want me," said the stranger, holding his arms wide.

And she wanted him. More than anything else, she wanted him.

"Remove your clothes."

Bernice began to do so.

"Faster, Bernice. You can't wait. You have to have me now."

Hands trembling, Bernice removed her blouse and bra. Shivering, she removed her skirt and panties. When her hands were fumbling at her stockings, the stranger said, "Enough. Come here."

Fear and nausea, dizziness and desire. Bernice moved towards the shadow.

"Kneel . . ."

"Please . . ."

"Kneel!"

The stranger fumbled with his clothing. He placed a hand on her head.

The night enfolded her.

It was 3:30 a.m. when Bernice and the stranger left the hotel. They said nothing to each other as they descended in the elevator, nothing as they crossed the lobby to the revolving door. There was no one behind the reception desk to see them leave.

They walked in darkness to her car. Bernice unlocked her

door, climbed in, and popped the lock catch on the passenger door. The stranger climbed in beside her. She sat in the darkness, waiting for the next instruction.

"Do you know the Hendon Road?"

"I think so, yes. That's the road at the top of the North Road, leading on to the Coast Road."

"Take me there."

Bernice turned the ignition key. Seconds later, the car slid out of the Hotel Entrance Road and on to the North Road. There was no traffic at this time in the morning. She drove in silence until they had reached the turn for Hendon Road. Something had happened to the streetlamps here. There had been a power cut or something, and the only light on the road now was from the car headlights.

They had travelled half a mile down the Hendon Road, when the stranger said, "Stop."

"But it's not possible to stop here. If anyone comes up behind . . ."

"Stop!"

Bernice stopped the car . . . and waited.

"Do you have a pen and paper?"

Bernice fumbled in her handbag, found a pen and an old supermarket voucher.

"Write down your address and telephone number."

Bernice did as instructed and handed the voucher to the stranger. He took it, pushed it into his pocket and opened the car door. Cold air invaded the car as he stood on the verge looking back at her. His face seemed white, spectral.

"What do I do now?" asked Bernice.

"Drive home. Carry on with your business. Tell no one of what has happened. Do you understand?"

"Yes . . ."

"Then do it."

The stranger slammed the door shut, rocking the car on

its suspension. Instantly, it seemed, he was swallowed by the darkness.

Drive on.

Bernice drove into the darkness. There was no sign of the stranger in the rear-view mirror.

Before the Coast Road turn-off, Bernice swung the car into a layby. Flinging the car door open, she staggered to the embankment and retched. She stayed there for a long time, trying to retch out the disgust and the fear and the horror.

Somewhere, in the darkness, she knew he was still out there.

Bernice staggered back to the car again, bracing her hands on the roof, praying that there would be no passing car, no concerned bypasser to pull over, come across and find out if they could offer help. The moon finally came out from behind ragged clouds, painting the embankment and motorway in stark black and white. The face on the moon was leering at her.

Bernice slammed her clenched hands down hard on the car roof and vented her fear and terror and fury at the sky. Somewhere over on the other side of the embankment a dog began to bark. Bernice directed her fury at it.

"Shut up! Shut up! Shut up!"

An orange light appeared in the darkness; someone's bedroom. Bernice gave vent to one last wordless yell at their wretched animal and then flung herself back into the car. Ramming the car into first gear, Bernice missed the bite-point between the clutch and the accelerator, stalling the engine. She had never done that since she'd learned to drive as a teenager. Sobbing, she engaged ignition and moved off into the darkness. Tears were flowing down her face now.

And driving home on automatic pilot, she tried to rationalise what had happened to her—but could not.

She had done *everything* the man had told her.

Everything! Without question. He had never threatened her, cajoled her, blackmailed her or even attempted to seduce her. He had simply told her what to do.

A breakdown? Is that what I've had? she thought in the darkness, as she turned off from the Coast Road and headed for home. The memory of what had happened in that hotel room was too gross and too immediate; too real to be a fantasy. It *had* happened. *But how had she let it happen? What the hell had* happened *to her?*

In the garage forecourt outside the luxury apartment block where she lived, Bernice stopped the car and switched on the light. Looking in the rear-view mirror, she could see that her face was streaked with mascara.

Oh God, I can't be seen like this.

Bernice fumbled in her handbag, found a Clean-Wipe, and rubbed away the smears.

It was 4:00 a.m. in the morning by the time she had parked the car and passed through the security door into the main block. Feeling on the verge of collapse, she waited for the elevator cab—remembering as the overhead light panel descended how she had stood in the hotel with the stranger, waiting for that elevator to descend. When the light *pinged!* and the door opened, Bernice had to hold the frame of the opened door to support herself when she stepped inside. Stabbing the Floor 8 button, she slumped back against the cab wall as the doors slid shut and she began the ascent.

Why did you do it, Bernice? What on earth happened?

She hugged herself, trying to still the trembling. A deep and debilitating chill enveloped her and her legs felt weak, ready to give way beneath her at any moment.

On Floor 8, moving down the corridor towards her apartment, Bernice prayed that Sam would be asleep and would stay asleep as she entered. How could she explain where she'd been? Their relationship was special, she had never known a person to be so attuned to the way she was feeling. If Sam saw her looking the way she did, then concerned questions would be asked and Bernice had no real answers. She needed to sleep, needed to think.

Her trembling fingers could barely put the key into the lock.

The apartment was in darkness.

Praying, Bernice let herself in, carefully closing the door behind her.

I mustn't bump into anything. Mustn't knock anything over.

Bernice undressed quickly, leaving her clothes on the sofa. As quietly as she could she found the bathroom, fought down the impulse to throw up in the toilet bowl. She gripped the sides of the sink and stared hard at herself in the bathroom mirror.

Bernice! Don't do it! Come on!

Grimly, she halted the nausea, reached for mouthwash and took it straight from the bottle. Rinsed, spat. Took deep, quiet breaths. When she had finished, Bernice moved like a naked ghost back through the living room to the bedroom. In the darkness, the strange silhouettes of furniture made the place seem not only unfamiliar, but alien.

Why, Bernice? Why?

The bedroom door opened noiselessly as she entered. In the darkness, she could see Sam's beautiful body beneath the sheets.

For God's sake, what happened? Why did I do it?

Sam stirred as Bernice pulled back the duvet and slipped into bed.

Oh Christ help me. What's happening to me?

"Berny . . ." Sam turned over into Bernice's embrace.

"Shhh . . . go back to sleep." *Stay asleep, please stay asleep. I don't want you to see my face.*

And Bernice, stroking Sam's long, red hair as she faded back to sleep, lay in the darkness watching the rise and fall of Samantha's breasts as she slept, watched the oncoming dawn and could only ask of herself, *Why, oh God why? What's happened to me?*

Chapter Nine
Paul

Paul lurched to one side as the car passed, misjudged his step down the side of the gully, and slipped. His shoe skidded on the grass and suddenly he was falling. Instinctively, he leaned into the fall, knowing that an awkward landing would be dangerous. He rolled, the impetus of his running hurling him downwards, over and over. The world spun crazily before his eyes, his vision suddenly filled with a bone-jarring explosion of cold, dirty water as he plunged heavily into the stream at the bottom of the ditch.

Gasping for breath, he lay half in, half out of the stream, watching as the water flowed over his mud-spattered jeans. He tried to raise himself on one elbow—but the fall had winded him. He collapsed back on to the bank, dragging himself clear of the stream and looked back up to the road. A Tizer pop can floated sedately past him.

Get up! Get up now!

"Look . . . look . . ." he said out loud. "I've got to rest. Got to eat . . ."

Get up and find him! Find him!

"I'll . . . burn out. It's impossible . . . impossible to keep this up. I'll just collapse, have a . . . heart attack or something, and then what will . . ."

Hissing, impatient sounds of anger in his head. And then, *All right, all right! Eat then. But hurry. He's coming.*

Paul scrabbled in his jerkin pocket and pulled out the sandwich-in-a-packet. It was crumpled and dog-eared, but he feverishly ripped the cellophane away and bit into it like an animal. Cheese and ham, but it could be anything. His taste buds seemed just as screwed up as the rest of him. The cellophane fluttered into the stream and sailed away as Paul slumped on to his back again, stuffing the sandwich into his mouth.

Hurry, hurry. He's coming to find you.

Paul chewed in a frenzy, groaning.

Find him first. Find him!

". . . got to . . . got to . . ." Paul mumbled through a mouthful of food. "Drink . . . got to drink . . ."

No time! No time! No time! screamed the Voice in his head.

"Drink!" shouted Paul in a spray of half-chewed food. He clawed to the stream and angrily shoved his face into the brackish water, knowing that the water could be polluted, knowing that he could be poisoning himself, but desperately needing to drink. It was cool and soothing. He gulped mouthfuls of the brackish water and then dragged himself back to the bank, coughing and spluttering.

There, you've had drink. Now hurry, hurry! Find him!

Paul crammed the rest of the sandwich into his mouth, feeling the revolt in his stomach at the brackish water he'd swallowed, steeling himself not to vomit, not knowing when the Voice would allow him to eat and drink again. He clambered up the bank towards the road again.

Find him!

A blue Volvo blurred past him as he reached the top of the bank.

"I can't . . . can't . . ."

You must!

"I CAN'T!"

Then flag down a car. Kill the driver and take it.

"No, no, no!" Paul tried physically to shrug off the intent of the Voice. "All right . . . I'm moving. I'll find him . . ."

Hurry, hurry, hurry!

Paul began to jog down the road again.

Something was happening to him. As if in answer to his pleas about collapsing with fatigue or hunger, the "something" inside seemed to be giving him a surge of power. His breathing was smooth and regular, his arms pistoning like a professional event runner. His legs hammered out a rhythm on the tarmac as he ran. And with that burst of controlled energy, he could feel the single-minded bloodlust focusing on the horizon ahead. Now he knew, without doubt, that the Other was coming. Somewhere beyond that horizon, somewhere down that road . . . the Other was hurrying to meet him.

Up ahead, on his right, Paul could see a petrol station set back from the road. There were petrol pumps in its forecourt, but no cars. "Running on empty," breathed Paul. "And I don't need topping up." The forecourt itself seemed littered with debris and dead grass, but Paul had no time to speculate on it as he jogged onwards. The stream continued to whisper from the gulley at his left.

And then a car curved into view over the crest of the hill ahead.

The bottom of the car's chassis and wheels was blurred by the heat haze on the road, giving the impression that it was floating above the tarmac. It was travelling at speed and for a moment wandered into the wrong lane.

The car corrected—and sped on towards Paul.

It's him! said the Voice. *He's here!*

The bloodlust surged in Paul, taking him over completely. He broke from a jog into a mad and savage run towards the car, a roar of rage breaking from his throat as he moved.

The car was kicking up a dust trail behind it, the driver only a blur behind the wheel.

The bloodlust surged in Paul. At first, nausea. Then horror. And finally the urge to kill was all . . . as he ran directly towards the car that was bearing down on him.

He wants you dead! Kill him first!

In the split-second that it took for him to see the half-brick lying in the middle of the road, Paul stooped, seized it and carried on running at the car.

The car was almost upon him, hurtling onwards in a blur, ready to smash him over the bonnet and into the air, breaking every bone in his body.

They were fifty feet apart, a second away from deadly impact.

Roaring, Paul hurled the half-brick directly at the blurred figure which crouched behind the driving wheel. The windscreen crumped into a crazed mass of spiderweb, the car swerved and screeched . . . and Paul had somehow twisted aside, whirling to the grass verge as the car continued on past him in a screeching cloud of dust as the unseen driver slammed on the brakes. The grass on the verge had cushioned Paul's fall, but he had still fallen heavily and there was a sharp pain under his ribcage now as he pulled himself to his feet, choking in the dustcloud kicked up by the car.

The bloodlust was all.

Paul ran screaming at the car like an animal as the driver rammed the gears into reverse. The car slewed backwards across the road to meet him.

Paul hurled himself at the car, landing with both feet

firmly on the boot and launching himself over the top of the roof. The car hit the grass verge from which he'd come and juddered to a halt again as he slid and clambered forward, now upside down and peering over the rim of the roof, down into the cobwebbed windscreen. He began to hammer at the glass with the flat of his hand, screaming obscene words of hate as he tried to widen the hole which the half-brick had made. Another blurred and bloodied hand snatched and clawed through the ragged gap at his own—a man's hand.

And now the car was screaming forward again.

Towards the rusting pumps of the abandoned petrol station on the other side of the road.

Even in the frenzy of the bloodlust, Paul could see what the Other was trying to do. He slithered backwards over the roof, still trying to retain his grip on the rim.

Inside the car, the driver was screaming in rage.

The car rammed into one of the petrol pumps with a rending screech of metal. Paul was catapulted forward across the roof of the car and flung on to the weed-infested forecourt of the garage. The elbows of his jacket and the knees of his trousers were shorn away, together with the skin beneath, leaving a sliding smear of blood on the stained concrete. He flipped, bounded and rolled; pain exploding inside his gut and his head and his lungs.

Sobbing in pain and rage, he looked back to see that the car had knocked the pump out of its base and that it was mounted on the wreckage of it, front wheels raised in the air, engine roaring. The driver tried to drive on over it towards him, but the entanglement was too great.

In a blur of frenzied motion, the still unseen driver rammed the gears into reverse again and began to slide back, the engine roaring and coughing, the shattered wreckage of the petrol pump screeching and squealing on the concrete. Part of the petrol pump hose had somehow embedded into the radiator grille of the car and would not come free. The car jerked and reversed, jerked and reversed, dragging the wreckage of the pump with it.

Paul clambered in agony to his feet.

The car was free of the hose, steam gushing from the bonnet . . . and the driver was swinging it around now, clear of the pumps—and with a straight run ahead at Paul.

The frontage of the garage was behind Paul, with a bitumen canopy overhanging it, supported by two iron stanchions. The car was already roaring after him as Paul ran towards the garage.

This time, it must surely run him down.

But the something inside him was still burning with rage and violence.

Paul flung himself high at the nearest iron stanchion, grabbing it with both hands and whirling bodily around the iron pole like some athletic matador as the bull roared on past him . . . straight into the glass frontage of the abandoned garage. The car ploughed through in a whirling explosion of broken glass, shattered masonry and a cloud of plaster dust.

Paul completed his swing around the stanchion, tottering to his feet again and watching as the car hurtled into the depths of the abandoned petrol station. He scrambled through the ragged gap in the front of the petrol station, pushing shattered spars of wood to one side. Then he plunged on after it, straight into the gushing cloud of plaster dust. Somewhere inside, he heard the car crashing to a halt.

Coughing and gagging, pain searing his arms and legs and punching a hole in his gut, Paul blundered on ahead. The dust was already clearing, and he could see that the car had rammed through a dilapidated serving counter and the empty shelves behind, swerving to one side before hitting the far wall sideways-on. There was no movement from within the car.

He reached the passenger door and grabbed at the handle, twisting savagely. It was locked. And the billowing dust was still too dense to see inside the car. Paul seized a broken piece of shelving and jabbed it hard at the window. The glass shattered. Discarding the shelving, he lunged through the ragged gap, popped the lock . . . and yanked the door open.

There was no one in the driving seat.

No one in the back seat.

Paul stood back out of the car.

And then a shape came roaring over the top of the car at him, hands outflung towards his face like claws. Those claw-hands seized his hair. Paul gripped at the wrists as the shape thrashed and squirmed over the roof of the car to get at him. The Other pulled him hard towards the car, banging his head on the frame of the door. Lights exploded behind Paul's eyes. Almost gratefully, he grasped at this chance to collapse and disengage himself from what was happening, but then the Voice screamed . . .

No! Don't give in! Fight! Fight!

Paul gripped hard at the wrists again; reared back, dragging the man—for he could see through blurred vision now that it *was* a man—across the car roof completely. The man fell on top of Paul, and now they were clawing and gouging for each other's eyes, thrashing over and over on the littered floor of the ruined petrol station. The man jerked one hand free from Paul's grip and punched him on the side of the head. Paul grabbed the wrist and sank his teeth into the flailing hand. The man screamed and a billowing cloud of plaster dust enshrouded them as they thrashed backwards and forwards over the floor.

Kill! Kill! Kill!

The Other was stronger, had not received the injuries or

suffered the exertion that Paul had endured. He dragged himself free, lashing out with a foot as he rose. The blow caught Paul in the ribs, flipping him over. The Other pressed on with his advantage, aiming kick after kick at him on the floor. A kick in the stomach completely winded Paul. Bent double, hugging his midriff, the bloodlust still consumed him, his hate still radiated at the shape above . . . but he was too hurt and winded to move. The Other stood back, breath catching in his throat in dry sobs. Now, at last, Paul could see him properly.

He was about Paul's age, wearing a checked black and white jacket. He did not have the face of a killer. The face was too gentle, too effete, too pale. He wore an open-neck shirt, torn down the front and bloody. His hair was long and black, now matted with the blood that streamed from the bridge of his nose—where the thrown half-brick had come through the windscreen. His eyes were wild . . . and even from where he lay, Paul could see that the familiar bloodlust was in him. This Other was consumed by the same hatred, and the same need to kill. Paul tried to lunge at him, clawing the air. But the pain was too great, making him retch. The Other laughed. A cracked and brittle sound.

Paul hated him.

The Other stood back, a mad kind of triumph in his eyes, nodding his head as if this was just exactly the way that things should be. Still keeping an eye on Paul, he was looking around him for something. He continued to look, backing away towards the car. Paul could only rise to his knees, but heard the hollow laughter and looked back as the Other flung open the dented boot of his car, watched as he quickly stooped inside and emerged with the tyre iron in his hand.

The coup de grâce.

The final kill.

The Voice inside Paul's head was now strangely quiet as

the Other walked purposefully back towards him, weighing the tyre iron in his hand.

"No . . ." Paul struggled to rise.

The Other moved in quickly, aiming another savage blow at his stomach. The impact hurled Paul over flat on to his back, the wheezing breath whooshing out of his lungs. He retched and vomited out the little brackish water and food that he had recently eaten.

The Other was laughing again as he stooped down, took a fistful of Paul's hair in one hand, and raised the tyre iron high above his head to cave in his skull.

And then Paul stabbed upwards with the triangle of broken glass he'd found on the floor, stabbed hard with his last remaining strength into the Other's crotch. The glass embedded between the Other's legs, juddered and snapped. Paul felt the glass embedding in his own palm as he fell back.

A spurt of crimson rain showered him.

The Other screamed and whooped, clutching at his groin, scrabbling at the embedded glass. The tyre iron clattered to the floor. Sobbing and gibbering, the Other staggered to the car and collapsed on his knees beside it, hugging his castrated manhood to himself as a scarlet pool spread around him.

Paul crawled towards him, grabbed for the tyre iron and pulled himself to his feet. He tottered back to the car and to where the Other knelt spasming in his hideous agony. The Other had forgotten for ever that he was there.

Paul raised the tyre iron . . .

When it was over, he staggered back and collapsed to his own knees, the pain of his shorn flesh somehow numbed.

He knelt there for a long time, looking back at the stranger he had just murdered.

The Voice had gone away. The bloodlust faded from red madness to the cold blue horror of what had happened.

Paul became aware of a movement on his left. He looked slowly over to see that it was his reflection, caught in the one remaining pane of a glass door leading out the back of the petrol station. At first, he could not recognise the dishevelled, dust-smeared, bloody figure which knelt there. And when he did recognise it, he also somehow recalled walking down that hospital corridor to visit his mother. He recalled seeing his reflection walking towards him, recalled how strange that figure looked.

"Who am I?" Paul said out loud to his reflection. "WHO AM I?"

In answer, that reflection hurled the tyre iron at him—shattering itself.

He began to weep then.

Chapter Ten
Yvonne Remembers

Yvonne blundered through the front door and into the passageway. Still cradling Jason under one arm, she hurried down the passage to the living room door.

I'll tell him that the bus was late, or there was an accident or . . .

"You're late!" shouted Satch, as soon as she opened the door. "Where the hell have you been?" He was lying on the settee, watching television. Still in his vest, and with empty beer cans lying on the carpet. He hadn't shaved again.

"Sorry . . ."

It was the only word she could manage as Satch struggled from the sofa and rose groggily to his feet. "Sorry . . ."

Satch moved awkwardly towards her, rubbing his bleary face with one hand.

"Have you eaten?" asked Yvonne, trying to calm the quavering of her voice. "It won't take me long to make . . ."

"You're LATE!" Satch lashed out with the back of his hand, the knuckles rapping hard across her face. From the kitchen, the two Dobermans began to bark furiously. "So you can keep your fucking dinner, right? I have been waiting here for two hours while you were gallivanting around town. Had to lock those two fucking dogs up in the kitchen. Getting on me nerves."

Yvonne tried to speak, but nothing would come. Her face was stinging and the words died, trembling in her mouth. *Don't fall apart. Don't do that, or he'll make it worse. He always does. He likes to see you upset.*

Jason began to cry now and Yvonne held him close. The dogs continued to bark and scratch at the kitchen door.

"Stay!" yelled Satch, the bitter smell of booze wafting into her face. At the command word, the dogs became silent.

Satch was weaving back and forth in front of her. Beyond him, she could see that there was also an empty half-bottle of Scotch on the sofa. On the video, the *Neighbours* theme song began, telling her how good neighbours could be good friends.

He was looking at her now, waiting for a response. Waiting for her to scream at him, waiting for her to break down into sobbing. Then he could start into her again. His eyes were dulled, filled with a stupid brutality.

When she didn't react, he made a sound of disgust and reeled away from her again.

"I'm going to the club. Get something to eat there."

Yvonne nodded, still unable to speak.

"And when I get back, I want that kid fed, bedded and asleep. Understand?"

Yvonne nodded again, biting her lip.

Satch staggered off to the bedroom to find a clean shirt, kicking and scattering the pile of beer cans by the sofa.

When he'd gone, Yvonne at last gave in to the grief.

"Out again, is he?" said her mother—and Yvonne wished that she would just go away again and leave her alone. "Well . . . men will be men, I suppose."

"I suppose," said Yvonne without inflection, the effort of those words seeming enormous.

"Well?"

"Well, what?"

"Are you going to ask me inside, or do I have to stand on the doorstep like a stranger for the rest of the morning?"

"Come in."

Her mother pushed past, down the small hallway and into the living room.

"Those dogs aren't around, are they?"

"He's taken them with him," said Yvonne, closing the door and following her mother.

"Good. Can't stand the bloody things. Don't know why you put up with it. Having a baby, and all."

"They're gentle, Mother. They wouldn't hurt Jason."

"That's what they all say. Then next thing you know you're reading about it in the newspaper. Now, where is he . . . ahhhhhhhh."

"Please, Mother! Don't disturb him, I've just . . ."

Yvonne entered the living room to see that her mother had swept Jason up from the carrycot, and was cradling him. He began to squall.

". . . fed him . . ." *And it's taken me bloody hours to get him off to sleep. Don't you know that, you stupid woman? Hours and bloody hours!*

"Look at him. No wonder he's crying, you've got him

wrapped up too tightly. He's too hot. Here . . . I'll just undo him and let the air get to him."

Jason hiccuped, and threw up over the front of her mother's coat. "Oh my *God!*" Her mother thrust the child back into Yvonne's hands. "This is brand new. Brand *new!*"

Good for you, son.

Her mother vanished into the kitchen, hunting for a cloth.

"Don't know what you're feeding him on, Yvonne. He shouldn't be throwing up like that. Are you sure you're giving him the right feed?"

"Shut up, Mother."

"What did you say, love?"

"I said, 'I think so.' "

"Well, I wonder. Doesn't seem natural to me."

"All babies throw up."

"Yes, well . . . I suppose you know what you're doing. He just doesn't seem to be putting on as much weight as he should. What a mess this kitchen is . . . where are the *cloths*, love?"

"Oh, here! I'll find something."

Her mother returned, taking off her coat and handing it to Yvonne as she exchanged it for the baby. Her mother began cradling again, shushing excessively. Yvonne strode angrily into the kitchen, opened the cupboard beneath the sink unit and found a J-cloth. She moved back to the sink, rinsed it and twisted it dry and . . .

And recoiled in terror from the shape that was standing on the other side of the window, staring at her.

Water sprayed into the sink as she stood, her hand on the tap, eyes wide and staring.

It was him again.

He was standing so close to the glass that she could see the breath on the pane. He was smiling . . . and those terrifying, beautiful eyes were staring right into her soul again, stripping away all her raw secrets.

"I don't want to tell you what to do all the time, Yvonne," continued her mother. "But I have done all of this before, you know. You were a baby yourself once. And the way I brought you up didn't do you any harm, did it?"

It's time to come with me again, Yvonne, said the stranger. Except that he wasn't speaking to her again. She knew somehow what he was saying, even though no words came from his lips. His eyes told her everything.

"Yvonne?"

"Yes, Mother . . ." *Is that me speaking? Is that my voice?* "I can hear you."

"Hurry up with that cloth before the sick dries."

"All right . . ." Yvonne held the cloth under the stream of water, squeezed it out and then turned off the tap . . . never once taking her gaze from the stranger's eyes.

Now, Yvonne. You must come with me now. Do you understand?

"Yes . . ."

"What was that? I can't hear you."

"I said, 'Yes, I'm coming.' "

The stranger moved away from the window, turned and began to walk towards the back yard door which led out into the back alley beyond. Yvonne left the kitchen window, returned to the living room. Her mother continued to give advice as she picked up the coat again and began to sponge at the lapel. But Yvonne could hear none of it now. The only thing that mattered to her was that she must do as she'd been told.

". . . So I would tell him if I was you. Not that I'm one to come between a husband and wife, but you know how I feel about him getting . . ."

"I've got to go out for a while, Mother."

"Oh . . . Out? Where to? If it's the shop, I can go and get something for you if you like."

"No, it's all right. I need to get a few things, but would you be able to look after Jason for me until I get back? I won't be long."

Yvonne's mother smiled.

"You don't ask enough of me. What would you have done if I hadn't called around, eh? Well, all right. But you mustn't be too long, because I've got to . . ."

"Thanks." Yvonne dropped the coat on to the sofa and moved quickly to the cupboard, retrieving her own coat.

"I won't be long, I promise. I'll go the back way . . ." Yvonne headed for the kitchen again.

"Yvonne?"

"Yes, Mother . . ."

"Your handbag, dear. Your purse. Hardly worth going to the shops if you haven't got any money, is it?"

"Oh . . . no. Thanks. I won't be long."

"Too scatterbrained by half, that's your trouble."

Her mother kissed her on the cheek, but somehow she couldn't feel a thing as she hurried through the kitchen and out into the back yard. From behind, she heard her mother call "Bye!" and Jason begin to squall again. But she did not answer as she hurried across the yard to the latch door. She flung it open, heart hammering, head swimming.

He was striding away from her down the back alley.

She wanted to call out, wanted to scream her fear and terror. But she could not; she could only hurry after him.

Come, said the stranger's voice in her head.

Sobbing, Yvonne ran to catch up with the tall, striding figure and the long black coat that swirled around him as he moved.

Come . . .

Chapter Eleven
Jacqueline Remembers

And Jacqueline remembered how . . .

She had been watching her sons—Martin and James—messing around in the kitchen for over five minutes, when Jacqueline's husband touched her arm and startled her. Her nervous overreaction to that touch seemed to justify his inner concerns.

"Easy, Jackie," said Brian. "Easy."

Jacqueline tried to give a smile, but it was fractured around the edges.

"Sorry, just got a fright, that's all."

In the kitchen, one of the boys dropped a fork on the tiled floor. The sound made her wince.

"Now be careful!" admonished Brian, fastening the kitchen apron tighter around his waist before turning back to her.

"Are you *sure* you're all right?"

"Yeah. Really. I suppose I'm just overworked or something. Regular bookworm, that's me."

Brian looked at her hard and long again. There were so many things he wanted to say to her. He'd been watching her for as long as she'd been watching Martin and James messing about in the kitchen, preparing the utensils for "Dad's Day": the one day of the week where he tried out his cordon bleu on the family, usually with decidedly mixed results. He wanted to say: *Maybe you should see the doctor. You've been looking really run-down just recently, and I'm worried about you.* He wanted to say: *I think it's time for that holiday we keep talking about and never get around to booking.* Most of all, he wanted to say: *There's something really heavy on your mind, Jackie. It hurts me that you're keeping it from me, because I want to help. But I know what you're like. I know that I can't force it, and that you'll tell me when you're ready. But I'm worried, and I want you to be your normal self again.* But instead, all he could say was . . .

"Okay."

. . . as he finished tightening the apron strings with a vengeance and ran his hand over his beard, then smoothed down his hair.

Martin and James were arguing when he entered the kitchen and pulled them apart. "Right! Martin, you're cutting the carrots. The way Mum showed you. James, you're my Potato Man."

Martin began to guffaw, ruffling his brother's blond hair. James pulled away, obviously deeply offended by the Potato Man tag which would probably stick for the rest of the meal.

"Chicken fillets," mumbled Brian as he swung open the refrigerator door, and Jacqueline watched him as she leaned against the kitchen door jamb, telling the kids that fooling-around time was over and done now that the pans were going on the hob to boil. She watched Brian stooping into the fridge, and felt a wave of love blossoming by just watching him do these ordinary, everyday things. He was a big man—six foot two inches—and her love for him was still strong after all these years.

But you let that man take you, Jacqueline. You let him take you into the bushes like some cheap whore. You did everything that he wanted.

She turned away from the door jamb lest one of them should see the change of expression on her face. Her throat was constricted, her pulse was racing and a deep flush of shame had risen to her cheeks.

"Can I use the Sabatier knife, Dad? It's much sharper."

"No you bloody can't."

"Oh, *Dad*. But it's easier."

"Like you said, it's much sharper. I don't fancy taking you on a trip to the hospital tonight, thank you. The safety knife's just as good."

I didn't let him take me. I was raped. RAPED for God's sake!

"Pass the safety then, Potato Man."

"If he calls me that again, Dad, I'll stick his head in the bowl."

"That's enough, Martin. Behave yourself."

"Suck on that, Carrot Man."

"James?"

"Dad?"

"Do you *want* a glass of grown-up wine with the meal?"

"Yeah . . ."

"Do I need to say any more?"

"No."

"Good."

So what happened? He hypnotised you. Is that what happened? You must *have wanted it, Jackie. People just don't let themselves be taken like that. You* must *have wanted it.* No, no, no! I DIDN'T.

The front doorbell rang. Now anxious that she didn't want a close friend or relative to be at the door to see what must surely be the tell-tale signs of guilt, and equally not ready for one of the boys or Brian to see her in a clearly distressed state, Jacqueline hovered for an instant. The doorbell rang again.

"Are you getting that, Jackie?" called Brian from the kitchen.

"Yes . . . yes . . . I'm going."

Jacqueline took a crumpled paper handkerchief from her sleeve and pushed it to her lips as she hurried to the front door. Hopefully, she could conceal the upset.

She opened the door.

And almost collapsed.

He was standing casually in the door-frame, just as she'd remembered him from that day outside the library.

The same face, the same long dark coat. The same hint of cruel amusement on his face.

The same eyes.

She pressed the crumpled paper tissue into her mouth, trying to stifle the scream that surely must burst from her. She felt sick and now terribly dizzy as she looked into those eyes again, drawn to them just as she'd been drawn on that terrible day. His smile widened, revealing those perfectly white sharp teeth.

The room began to tilt. She reeled and steadied herself against the door.

You won't faint, said the man. *Stand still.*

Jacqueline righted herself, now wanting to scream.

And you won't scream, either. Who's in the house?

"My husband." She heard her voice again, just as she'd heard it on that day. "My two sons."

The stranger's smile widened again.

"Who is it?" came Brian's voice from the kitchen. Another utensil clattered to the kitchen floor. "James, I've told you not to do that."

Make an excuse. You're leaving with me. Get your coat. Now.

"It's . . . it's the library, Brian."

"Christ, not work again!"

"I'm sorry. There's been . . . a break-in. Kids, the police think. I'll have to get over there. I'm the key holder."

Jacqueline snatched her handbag from the sofa and her raincoat from the stand in the hall.

"But Jackie . . . our *meal*, for crying out loud."

"I'm sorry, love. Really. But I've got to go."

The stranger stepped smiling back into the shadows beyond the door, just as Brian, pan in hand, came awkwardly around the kitchen door and caught sight of her pulling on her raincoat.

"Who is it? Who's . . . ?"

"It's Janis. I've got to go, Brian. I'll be back . . ." *Oh God in heaven, help me.* ". . . I'll be back as quickly as I can."

"Jacqueline . . ."

She closed the door on him, turning to see that the stranger was already striding down the communal staircase of their block of flats into the darkness.

God oh God, what is happening *to me?*

She followed.

Chapter Twelve
Bernice Remembers

"You wouldn't lie to me, would you, Bernice?" Samantha had asked—and the remembrance of the look on her face made Bernice's throat tight as she thought back to that conversation.

"Lie to you? About what?"

"Last week, when you were interviewed on radio about the play."

"Samantha, what on earth are you talking about?"

"Nothing . . . it doesn't matter."

"Obviously, it *does* matter. What's wrong?"

"I listened to you on the radio, while I was in bed."

"Well?"

"Bernice . . . you said you drove straight home after that broadcast. But you couldn't have." And now the tears were starting to flow, but she tried to stem them, tried to keep control. "I waited for you to come home after that interview was finished. You didn't get home until hours later."

"Really, Sam." *Oh my God, what do I say?* "What's got into you?" *What do I say?* "So you think I've been kerb-crawling at 2:00 a.m. in the morning, looking for other women? Is that what you think?"

Again, struggling to control the tears: "Then where *were* you, Bernice? What took you so long to get home?"

I let a man take me, Samantha. God help me I don't know how or why. But he took me, and used me and abused me to the point where I can't bear to think about it any more. It's the worst thing that's ever happened to me in my life . . . and just thinking about it makes me want to retch, or cut my throat or run screaming out of this room or . . .

"Who were you with?"

"Mike—the interviewer—and I got talking after the interview. I suppose I lost touch of the time."

"But you can't stand him."

"I know, sweetheart. But sometimes you have to do things you don't want to do if you want to get the right 'plug' at the right time."

"There isn't someone else, is there, Bernice?"

And Bernice laughed then, hoping that it sounded genuine, and felt only sickness and fear and outrage and anger inside. "Only you, Sam. Only you."

The telephone rang in the living room.

"Now you stay here and get some rest. That flu's just running you down, making you too sensitive."

"Maybe you're right. But Bernice . . . ?"

"Yes?"

"You wouldn't leave me, would you?"

"Never. Now get some sleep if you can."

Bernice left the bedroom, hurting inside, wanting to scream out her distress. She crossed the living room and reached for the telephone.

"Hello?"

You won't scream, said the voice. *You won't hang up . . . and you'll do everything I say. Do you understand?*

". . . yes . . ."

You will make an excuse to leave. You will come to the Metropole Hotel, Gateshead. Room 59.

". . . room 59 . . ."

Now.

". . . now . . ."

The line died in her hands.

Bernice replaced the telephone receiver. She could not scream, could not swallow. She wanted to be sick, but that was not possible either. She looked down at the telephone again, tears welling in her eyes . . . and then back to the bedroom.

Oh my God in heaven, please stop me. I don't want to go. I DON'T WANT TO GO!

Ten minutes later, Bernice was heading west in the car.

To Gateshead.

To the Metropole Hotel.

To him.

Chapter Thirteen
Paul

Paul dreamed that he had been buried alive.

The farmer's son—Trafford—had first killed his mother in the hospital grounds, then his father . . . and had raised that shotgun again before Paul could raise the overturned table to protect himself. The exploding twin barrels had erupted in his vision as he stood there, and Paul could see—could actually *see*—the deadly spray of lead shot slicing directly through the air towards him—just before it blew him apart.

Now, somehow, he was in his coffin.

It was utterly black and his arms were pinned to his sides.

Screaming, Paul lashed out and even though his hands came into contact with something that was soft and somehow shredded (and most certainly not the wooden sides of a casket), he continued to lunge and scream.

A tunnel! That's what it is! I'm buried in a tunnel—not a coffin!

In an utter terror of panic and claustrophobia, Paul clawed his way through the darkness, saw light at the end of his tunnel and sobbed in relief. Clawing through the aperture, he fell headlong on to muddy ground.

As panic abated, Paul could see at last where he was and where he had been. He was lying at the foot of a haystack in a field off the main road. It was the haystack he had crawled into for shelter for the night, having trudged for hours down the highway with his mind in some kind of abstract limbo—

protection against what he had done and what he thought had happened to him.

Insane, he thought, the deep icy chill wrapping itself around him like a cloak. *I've lost my mind.* Paul pulled his muddied jerkin tight around his neck and looked around. His watch had stopped in that nightmare fight to the death, but he guessed that it must be about eight or nine in the morning. Sleep had not refreshed him. His ribs were inflamed, probably cracked, and his kidneys ached. He had not eaten since that sandwich yesterday but the thought of food made him retch. He leaned against the haystack for a full minute, breathing deeply. Then he turned and looked out across the mist-enshrouded field. There was only one thing he could do now.

Give himself up to the police, and tell them what he'd done.

And what have you done?

I've killed a man.

But he was trying to kill you.

But I must have gone mad. I began hearing voices. They told me what to do. I killed that man for the Voice.

Then he must have been mad, too. He must have been hearing the same Voice. Because he wanted to kill you just as badly as you wanted to kill him.

I must be mad!

You've never met the man before. He was hunting you just as you were hunting him. He drove over that hill, knowing you'd be there. Just as you knew that he was coming to find you . . .

"Shut up, shut up!"

. . . just as you were destined to seek each other out. Only one can survive, Paul. You've killed him, you've won. But there is Another.

"Shut up! Shut up! SHUT UP!" Paul collapsed to his knees,

his hands clasped tightly over his ears. But the returning Voice was already inside his head.

And you must kill this Other, before he kills you. Even now he is hunting for you. He can smell you, Paul. He knows your scent and can follow it . . .

"Oh, Christ . . ."

. . . just as I can show you where to find him. So arise now, Paul. Arise and follow. Find the Other and destroy him. He is as guilty as the first.

"No, no, no, no . . ."

Find the Other, Paul. Find the Other and kill.

". . . no . . ."

I can make you strong again.

And somehow those words brought with them a sudden burst of strength, as if he had been injected instantaneously with adrenalin. The strength flooded his veins, his arteries, his muscles. Now, each breath he drew of the crisp morning air was also imbued with that super-drug, each gasp of oxygen containing so much more than mere oxygen. With the strength came something else; something that made Paul leap to his feet again, legs firmly braced on the crumbling soil, fists clenched. Something that made him want to scream his defiance across the field at anyone or anything that might hear.

It was anger. A pure and undiluted anger.

Find the Other, Paul. Before he finds you.

". . . yes . . ."

Find him and kill him.

"Yes!"

Renewed, and with the anger upon him, Paul strode back across the field.

Towards the road.

Towards the Other.

Chapter Fourteen
Gregory Leonard

Gregory Leonard insisted on being called "Greg" and had been carefully grooming his bushy eyebrows ever since his teenage days, chiefly because he thought they were very similar to Gregory Peck's eyebrows. And what the hell . . . they shared the same first name, so why not? He had always felt that Peck had such charisma—a person in whom a client could have such confidence. Quite why Gregory Peck had never played the part of a private eye in any of his films was quite beyond Leonard. He seemed tailor-made for the part. So Leonard had been playing that part on behalf of Peck for over fifteen years since retiring from the security firm which had in turn employed him for twenty-five years.

Leonard's secret fantasy fuelled the grim, down-at-heel reality of the real job. Deep down, he still believed that the big murder case would come along. Until it did, he was spending his time serving writs and collecting debts. His forte was beneficiaries. In love with Hammett and Chandler, and with posters of Dick Powell and Bogart plastered on the toilet wall, Leonard had allowed his office to develop the seediness of cliché. Access to that tenth-floor office, situated in a fairly dilapidated office block in the west of the city, was only possible through an estate agent's office.

A few years earlier, the biggest firm of American private investigators had come over to Britain to snap up the more expansive and progressive British companies. Gregory Leonard had not been on their list for acquisition. In an age of computer surveillance and recording briefcases, Leonard's only concession to modern technology was a battered pair of binoculars—which he now hardly ever used at all, except for his infrequent trips to the racecourse. Time spent snooping through bedroom windows with a flash camera was a thing of the past: The Divorce Reform Act meant that adultery didn't have to be proved any more.

When the knock came on his fluted-glass office door, Leonard tried to swing nonchalantly in his swivel chair the way that Bogart might have done in *The Big Sleep*. The swivel joint squealed rustily, his foot flipped a pile of *The New Investigator* magazines from his desk on to the floor and his coffee tipped over on to the carpet.

Angrily, he snapped, "Come!"

Mopping at the spilled coffee with a bunched-up newspaper, Leonard first thought that the woman who came through the door must be very ill. Her face seemed unnaturally white, with dark hollows beneath her eyes. She was well dressed, with a long tan raincoat over a trouser-suit and rings on both hands that shouted well-to-do. And then he seemed to recognise her, but couldn't place the face.

"Mr. Leonard?"

"Uh-hmmm." Leonard finished mopping up, screwed the newspaper into a ball and threw it at the waste-basket. It missed, hit the wall and rebounded to the floor, where it began to uncurl like some huge papier-mâché flower. "Would you like to take a seat?"

"Where?" asked the woman, looking around, and Leonard realised that both of the battered garage-sale chairs were piled high with newspapers and *The New Investigator*. Bogart-pretence now dissipated, Leonard hopped to his feet, overturned a pile from one of the chairs to the floor and hopped back to his seat. The woman wrinkled her nose in distaste at the cloud of dust that he had stirred. "If you don't mind, I'd rather stand."

Snotty cow. "Okay. How can I help you?"

"I'm not sure about these things. But you're an . . . investigator, is that the right word?"

"It'll do." *Good one, Greg. Just like Powell.*

"Good. I want you to . . ."

"I charge twenty-five pounds an hour, and you'll also have to take care of any expenses I might incur along the way."

"The money doesn't matter. I want you to find out all you can about someone."

"Who?"

"I don't know. That's why I'm here, damn it."

"I'm sorry, can we start again?" And then he recognised the face: *Bernice Adams, the television newsreader. Bloody hell, she looks rougher in real life than she does on the box.*

Bernice took a deep breath, and Leonard saw an angst in that expression which he had never seen before on any of the faces of his clients.

"There's a man I need to know about. I don't know who he is, or what his name is. I want you to follow him, find out about him. And I want the utmost discretion."

"Ms. Adams," said Leonard slowly, disappointed that she didn't react to the fact that he recognised her. "Discretion is what you're paying me for. But I have to tell you, if you're in serious trouble because of this man, whoever he may be, I would recommend that you get in touch with the police. I don't want to take your money if this is something that the police could sort out for you."

Bernice laughed: a sound without humour. "You have a code of ethics in your line of work?"

"I believe in happy endings. I've had two people kill themselves after I turned up information on them. I'm not a monster, Ms. Adams. I can care as well. One of them drove off a cliff, the other one took pills. I'd rather that didn't happen, if it's possible."

"I don't want the police involved. I just want you to find out who this person is."

"So you don't know his name. Where can I find him?"

"I don't know."

"What does he do for a living?"

"I don't know that either."

"So you know nothing at all about him?"

"Nothing."

"I've had some tough jobs in my time, Ms. Adams. But this one may take the prize. How the hell do you expect me to follow up on this one?"

"I want you to be on . . . how do I put it? . . . on *stand-by*. Day or night. I'll pay you five hundred pounds as a retainer. I want to be able to ring you at any time of the night or day. And when I telephone you, I'll tell you where I'm going."

"You'll be going somewhere to meet this person?"

"Yes. Probably a . . . hotel or a motel. I want you to be there, to watch and wait. Then . . . afterwards . . . I want you to follow him. That's the only way you'll be able to find out what I need to know."

"You're sure about the police, Ms. Adams?"

"I'm sure," said Bernice, reaching for her handbag. "Will a cheque suffice for the five hundred?"

"Is my fee reclaimable against the five hundred, or is the retainer on top of what I earn?"

"Don't push your luck, Mr. Leonard. If you can do the job for less than the five hundred, I won't be asking for any change back."

"I'm your man, Ms. Adams. Consider the job done."

Bernice began to scribble out a cheque.

Chapter Fifteen
Paul

Too many people, thought Paul at first, as he pushed through the swivel doors of the shopping mall. *Too much colour*. It hurt his eyes; the sharp blues, reds and yellows of the walls, ceiling and tiled floor looking more like a colour-negative photograph. The inane Muzak playing over the Tannoy system seemed to be filtering through to his ears in a discordant jangle and when two shopping trolleys clashed in front of him, the sound cut into his brain like a knife.

He's here, said the Voice in Paul's head. *Here in the shopping mall somewhere.*

The hate swelled in him again; surging through his veins like some powerful drug. It cleared his head, dissipated the pain in his broken rib. Paul straightened and forged on ahead, shoving a trolley out of the way in front of him and drawing a disgusted response from the young woman who was pushing it.

Find him, Paul. Find the Other.

Ahead of him was a flight of stairs leading to the first floor of the Plaza. On his left, a supermarket entrance—on his right, a bookshop. He hesitated for a second, waiting for the Voice to direct him. But instead of the Voice came an impulse which compelled him towards the stairs. The Other was on a higher level somewhere. He knew it.

Find him.

Fuelled by this further surge of strength, Paul strode quickly up the staircase, taking the steps two at a time. He did not notice the newspaper seller at the bottom of those stairs, or the headline written in felt-tip pen on his bulletin board: "Man murdered in abandoned petrol station." Nor would it have concerned him.

He reached the first floor and stood looking at the crowd as it swirled around him. He searched the faces of those who passed; alarming the men, women, children and the couples who swirled around him on their shopping destinations. But none of those faces belonged to the Other.

"Where?" he asked aloud.

"Pardon me?" said an elderly man with two brightly coloured shopping bags.

"WHERE?" snapped Paul, and the startled man quickly hurried on.

He's coming, Paul. Coming to find you. Coming to kill you. Find him first. Find him and kill him.

"BUT WHERE?"

People in front of Paul scattered as he charged on ahead past an HMV Record store.

Chapter Sixteen
Van Buren

Van Buren knew that he was coming to the shopping mall.

For an hour and fifteen minutes he had been sitting in his car, outside in the car park; looking at the red brick walls, at the plate-glass frontage, at the crowds ascending and descending staircases. His legs were aching again. At sixty-eight years of age, he was a fit man—but not immune from the creeping agony of rheumatics. He had punched his legs angrily as he sat, as if that act of violence could kill the pain and make him young again.

So many years wasted.

He had arrived at 9:00 a.m., parked his car facing the mall, and had watched the early morning shoppers come and go—knowing that his quarry would not arrive until 10:30 a.m. at the earliest. That knowledge nevertheless did not prevent him from checking his watch impatiently every ten minutes. He had tried the car radio to distract him, but some of the old dance tunes had begun to depress him, reminding him of younger and happier days.

Happier days? When exactly were they? He had laughed bitterly as he switched off the radio.

He adjusted the rear-view mirror of the BMW, so that he could see his face. Iron-grey hair that was a little too long for his age and which became a bleached white at his temples and in the curls around his neck. His face was weathered and lined, but the eyes were an unsettling deep and icy blue—which still made him very attractive to women. But his wife had been the only woman in his life . . . and she had died fifty years ago. Looking at his face always reminded him of that one photograph, taken at their wedding all that time ago. Just the two of them together, and the smile on her face which matched the smile on his own. He had been so very young then, and when he looked at himself in the rear-view mirror—in *any* mirror—he always saw his eighteen-year-old face beneath the old, weathered and bitter mask which the following fifty years had overlaid. And as the years passed, the hate and the bitterness had consolidated that mask.

He checked his watch again. Ten thirty a.m. Looking

back at the shopping mall frontage, he knew that the one he wanted would be arriving somewhere. He had never seen his face, did not know who he was looking for. But he knew that the man in question would be young—and looking to kill.

Van Buren climbed stiffly out of the car and slammed the door shut with unnecessary force. Moving to the boot, he looked around to see whether he was being observed. He was not. Opening the boot, he leaned in and opened out an oilskin wrapper big enough to contain a fishing rod.

Sliding the sawn-off double-barrelled shotgun into the specially sewn pocket of his long greatcoat, he hastily buttoned the coat, adjusting the stock of the shotgun so that it was under his right armpit. There was no bottom in his right-hand pocket, so that the barrel pointed unimpeded towards the ground, and when he put his hand into that pocket, it found the grip and trigger guard straight away.

Slamming the boot shut, he began to walk towards the shopping mall.

Chapter Seventeen
Satch

It had not been a good day for Satch.

Most days, it seemed lately, were not good days. Mistaking varying degrees of hangover as latent ill-health which destroyed his employment opportunities, Satch seemed filled with a brutal rage at the world. That rage could only be dampened at certain times; usually at nine thirty in the pub.

Funny how the feeling he strove to maintain all day via his alcohol input could only be achieved at that time. Between nine thirty and ten every night in the pub. Funny. Just a pity that the bitch couldn't make him as happy as that.

Tonight, the nine thirty "buzz" had not been achievable. He had waited for it impatiently until ten thirty, downing cheap whisky instead of the pints of beer. The "buzz" refused to come. And then Porter McFadden had come into the pub with two mates. Porter McFadden specialised in "loans": cash dispensed with a smile at staggeringly high interest rates. Failure to meet payment dates was met with something less than a smile and the possibility of a long-term hospital stay.

They caught Satch in the men's toilets, trying to escape through the ventilation window.

Fortunately, he had just enough cash on him to pay the outstanding interest payment and avoid a hiding. They took it, and one of McFadden's hard lads had shoved Satch's head down an unflushed toilet bowl while the other pulled the chain. All in all, he had got off lightly.

Now, on his way home, Satch staggered down a dimly lit back alley with a half-bottle of Mackinlay's in his pocket. Rage ebbed and flowed as he played over and over in his mind what he would do to McFadden one day.

Wait for him one night with a fucking crowbar . . .

Somewhere, two cats were perched on a wall, face to face and howling banshee threats at each other.

Drop a fucking dustbin on him . . .

A young man and woman recoiled in a back doorway as he passed, straightening their clothes.

Fucking petrol bomb through his fucking window . . .

Ahead of Satch, a dustbin had spilled its contents on to the cracked pavement.

"Bastard!" Satch hurled himself at it, kicking it over with a ringing clatter. Each kick of the scattered rubbish was a kick in his mind's eye that scattered McFadden's innards all over the back alley. Behind him, the young couple hurried away into the darkness.

Eventually, Satch blundered against his own back door. Somebody seemed to have moved the catch. As he scrabbled to find it, the dogs in the back yard began to bark furiously at the potential intruder.

"S'only me, s'only me . . ."

The door flew open under his weight and he fell to his hands and knees in the yard, the pain of his skinned knees and hands anaesthetised by the alcohol. Grinning stupidly, he crawled towards the two mesh-covered kennels that he had constructed himself. Inside, the two Doberman Pinschers were throwing themselves at the mesh, their barked threat now a frenzied welcome when they recognised their pack-leader's scent—despite how much it had been covered by other assorted scents. Satch crawled to the mesh like a dog himself, pressing his fingers through, pushing his face up close so that the animals could lick him in turn.

"The only ones . . . the *only* ones who give a shit . . ." He began to blubber like a child as he crawled from kennel to kennel.

Slabs of orange light spilled down into the yard from neighbours' windows. Satch pulled himself to his feet, tears streaming down his face as one of those windows was yanked angrily open. The blurred silhouette of a woman snapped, "What on *earth* is going on?"

"Tell you what's going on," growled Satch, unzipping his flies. "*This* is what's going on . . ." He began to urinate in her direction, trying to get it as high up the wall as possible towards her. A cry of disgust. A window slamming. Now laughing, and with the dogs still barking furiously behind him, Satch finished urinating and staggered to the back door of the house. If she'd locked it, when he told her to leave it open . . . ?

The door was open.

Satch blundered through the kitchen, leaving the door wide open to the night. Pausing only long enough to retch into the sink, he fell into the living room and crawled to the sofa in the darkness. Three deep draughts of the Mackinlay's later, he was sleeping like a dead man.

His dreams were troubled.

He dreamed that he was in the living room, lying on the sofa, in the darkness. He dreamed that he was drinking from a half-bottle of Mackinlay's. Somewhere out there in the night, those same two bloody cats were howling; but now they seemed to be right underneath the window. There was a full bright moon; shafts of moonlight were beaming into the living room. In his dream, Satch clambered to his feet and walked slowly over to the window. As he reached it, the mournful howling stopped. There was no sign of the cats down there; just the back yard and the back alley beyond.

But someone was standing out there in the back alley, looking up at him.

The figure was standing in a doorway, just visible as a man-sized shape in the darkness. Harsh angular shadows were cast all around that doorway by a crooked streetlamp a little further down the alley. At first, Satch thought that it must be a combination of those stark shadows, contriving to make it seem as if someone was there. But something inside, something purely instinctive, told him that there was someone there; that it was a man. And in that knowledge came a deep and unreasoning fear. But this was not the same kind of fear engendered by, say, McFadden and his boys . . . this was something entirely new, born of nightmare. Just the sight of that motionless figure, standing in the doorway looking up at him, was enough to make his stomach knot. He felt physically ill with fear; thrills of horror spasmed from his stomach, making his skin crawl. He broke out into an instant sweat. More than anything in the world, Satch wanted to be away from the gaze of that invisible face. He tried to step backwards and the movement became impossibly slow . . . this was, after all, a dream. It was a nightmare where escape from the dream horror was impossible; where limbs moved with lead-heavy dullness as the horror approached.

The figure stepped out of the darkness.

Just as Satch managed to pull himself backwards away from the window, before he could see the details of whoever or whatever it was down there. The logic of nightmare demanded that should he see its face, then he would die insane. Satch threw himself backwards across the room to the sofa—a child retreating to the sanctuary of the bedsheet. He pulled a sofa cushion over his head.

And then remembered that he had left the kitchen door wide open.

Somewhere, out there in the night, he heard the back alley door into the yard creaking open.

The dogs! They'll hear! They'll bark and scare it away! It won't come past the dogs! It won't . . .

Footsteps in the yard, heading towards the door. Slow, steady footsteps.

No dogs barking.

Satch pulled the cushion tighter over his head, too terrified to flee from the sofa.

The sofa's a raft. I'm safe here. Just like bed. Just like the dreams I had when I was a kid . . .

The sound of the kitchen door swinging open. A sound like something *breathing.*

Oh God, let me wake up! Please let me wake up. I don't want to see! I don't want . . .

Footsteps in the kitchen now, on the linoleum. Slow and deliberate. Heading towards the living room with a horrifying intent.

"Don't want to see!"

Slowly . . . slowly . . . the living room door began to open.

"OH MY GOD, I DON'T WANT TO SEE!"

Satch was awake now, flinging the cushion from him across the room and thrashing to his feet. Blind in the darkness, he threw himself to the light switch and flicked it on. Stark, unshaded light scourged the room of nightmare. Now he could see that the kitchen door was still closed and that the living room curtains were drawn. He could not have seen that figure down below in the back alley. But the horror was still inside him, its nearness propelling him across the living room to the kitchen door. He flung it wide, as if challenging the nightmare.

There was no one there.

Flicking on the kitchen light, he stumbled back across the kitchen and shut the door, throwing the heavy bolt and latch into place before returning to the sofa. The whisky bottle had fallen to the floor, but the cap was still on tight. He retrieved it and took another swallow.

Bad pint, he thought. *Never trusted that bloody landlord's booze.*

Satch drained the bottle and dropped it with a clatter into the cheap waste-bin beside the electric bar-fire. Nightmare safely banished, he switched off the light and headed for the bedroom, pulling off his shirt as he went. He dropped it in the passageway, tried to remove his trousers as he walked and fell heavily against the wall. Cursing, he pulled them all the way off. The stinging in his knees reminded him of his fall. They were crusted with blood, but they could wait until tomorrow for bathing. He'd get the bitch to do it. Pushing open the bedroom door, he stood naked for a long while looking at the sleeping form of his wife. Although she had her back to him in the darkness, he could see the steady rise and fall of her rhythmic breathing.

Pretending. That's what she's doing. Pretending to sleep. Hoping I won't bother her. Ungrateful little cow.

Satch blundered to the bed in the darkness and pulled back the covers. Yvonne did not move, continued to sleep. Now he *knew* that she was pretending.

"Wake up . . ."

Yvonne did not move.

"Come on, wake up!"

Nothing.

Angrily, Satch pulled back the covers further and fell heavily into bed beside her. Her body bounced on the mattress beside him, but still she didn't wake.

"Playing dead, eh?" said Satch again, as he pulled the covers back. "Well, that won't do no good, Yvonne."

No answer.

The brutal rage was returning to Satch. She was his wife. He had rights.

"Yvonne, I'm giving you just one last chance. Turn over."

Still nothing.

"I'm *warning* you, bitch!"

Roughly, Satch grabbed her shoulder and pulled her over hard to face him.

Screaming, he frantically thrashed back out of the bed away from her.

The nightmare had not ended.

"Please . . ." moaned Yvonne. "Please . . . help me . . ." And Satch looked on in horror at her face, which had somehow aged horrifically. The face of a one-hundred-and-thirty-year-old woman pleaded with Satch from the bed as he backed off on his rump until he was stopped by the bedroom wall. "Don't let him do it, Satch. Please . . . help me . . ." The hair was white, the eye sockets sunken. The thin, ragged lips were drawn back from Yvonne's teeth, giving her the appearance of a death's head. Her sunken eyes had cataracts, and her face was a mask of wrinkled grey skin. When she raised a hand towards him, it was like a claw.

Satch was in a nightmare within a nightmare within a nightmare. His mind retreated to the only safe place it knew.

The thing on the bed said ". . . help me . . ." one last time before he slid down the bedroom wall to the floor, unconscious.

Chapter Eighteen
Jacqueline Remembers

Janis had been speaking for over five minutes, but Jacqueline had not heard a word.

"Jackie?"

She continued to leaf through the file index. The book for which she had been searching was long since forgotten.

"Jackie?"

"Hmmm . . ."

"What's wrong?"

"Hmmm . . ."

"Jackie!"

Jacqueline started, and the file index drawer fell to the library floor with a clatter, spilling its contents. From somewhere in the library came a sibilant, echoing "shush!" As Jacqueline stooped to pick up the cards, she said, "Sorry, Janis. I'm just . . . not myself today."

Janis knelt down beside her to help. "Haven't been your-self for ages now, if you ask me. What's wrong, Jackie?"

"Nothing. Really."

"Bullshit! Listen, we've been good enough friends these last few years. You really helped me out when I was having that bad time. Set me straight. Made me believe in myself again. I owe you a hell of a lot. So let me try to begin repaying the favour. You know you can trust me."

"I don't know. I can't . . . I'm just run-down, under the weather all the time. I think I'll make an appointment with the doctor, get myself some iron tablets or something."

"Are you having trouble at home? Is that what this is all about?"

"No trouble at home. Honest."

"Jackie . . . you're starting to bloody annoy me now. All right, maybe it's nothing to do with me, maybe I should mind my own business. But I don't like to see you like this . . . and I think it's got something to do with that young chap who came into the library a fortnight ago. The one who sat on the cemetery bench all day looking at you."

"You *saw* that?!"

"Course I saw it. Not blind, am I?"

"You didn't say anything . . ." *Oh God, did she see anything else?*

"So it *is* something to do with him."

"Janis . . . I'm in a mess. A terrible, terrible mess. I just don't know what to do. I don't understand what's happening. Don't know what . . ."

And then a terrible nausea gripped Jacqueline. She dropped the cards she had been collecting and clutched at her stomach.

"Jackie?" Concerned, Janis grabbed her arm. "What's wrong?"

"Sick . . ."

"Right, that's it. You're going home again." Janis began to help her to stand. Customers were beginning to look over at them now as Janis lifted her to a seat. Jacqueline lifted a shaking hand to her pallid face. "I'm going to ring for an ambulance," said Janis.

"No . . . no . . . I'll be all right. I just need a little bit of time."

Again, a sibilant "shush" from a disturbed customer.

"Oh 'shush' yourself!" snapped Janis angrily, and then turned back to Jacqueline: "All right, then. Have a lie down in the day room, on the couch. I'll bring you a cup of tea . . ."

"Just water would be nice."

"Okay, love. Water then."

Janis helped Jacqueline across the library, holding on to one arm. Everyone in the library was watching now as they reached the day room. Once inside, Janis helped her to lie down on one of the couches. She stroked one hand across Jacqueline's white brow. It felt clay cold.

"Are you sure you don't want me to get a doctor . . . ?"

"Sure, thanks. Just some water. And maybe a few minutes alone."

Janis brought a glass of water back from the communal sink and watched her drink it. "More?"

"No thanks."

"Okay, I'll leave you for a bit. But anything you want . . . just shout."

"No shouting in a library, remember?"

"Screw them for a change."

"Thanks, Janis."

"Take care."

And when Janis had left, Jacqueline pushed herself from the couch and hurried to the door. Locking it, she leaned back against the wood and bit her lip, trying to control herself, trying not to scream out her fear and misery.

It was happening again.

Jacqueline staggered across the day room to the sink. There was a mirror above. Bracing her hands on the sink, she stared at her face . . . and waited.

She thanked God that Janis had left when she did.

Because it was happening even now as she looked at her face in the mirror.

The hollows under her eyes were darkening, as if someone were holding a light directly above her head. Her skin seemed stretched. The eyes were glazing to a dull sheen. She retched, and was repelled by the sound that came from her mouth. It was the sound of something ancient and dying.

"Nooooo . . ."

And now her voice was the voice of something ancient, not a woman of twenty-eight.

Jacqueline watched the skin of her face draw tight and taut around her skull. She clung to the rim of the sink and willed herself not to faint. Looking down, she saw that the skin of her hands had also shrunk and compressed. They were practically skeletal now, with a network tracery of blue veins.

Don't faint. Keep control. It'll pass . . . it'll pass like last time . . . and the time before.

But another voice inside seemed to be saying to her, *No, it won't pass. Remember what he said: "I want you to feed me." That's what he's doing, Jacqueline. He's feeding from you . . . feeding . . . feeding . . .*

No! It'll pass! I'll be all right, I'll be . . .

You're dying, Jacqueline. He's draining you . . . and you're dying!

No, no, no!!

* * *

Janis returned to the day room and tried to open the door. It was locked. Puzzled, she rattled the handle and called out, "Jackie?"

There was no sound from within.

Anxiety began to develop into outright fear.

"Jacqueline, are you all right?"

No answer.

Janis looked around, as if someone or something could help. She turned back to the door and rattled the handle again. "Jacqueline!" If someone shushed her again, bones would be broken. "If you don't answer me, I'm going to break the door down." Heads began to turn again in the library. "I mean it."

No answer.

"All right! One, two . . ."

And then Jacqueline opened the door.

Her face was pale, but she seemed better than before, with a fragile smile that reassured Janis.

"Sorry," said Jacqueline. "I must have fallen asleep."

"How do you feel now?"

"A lot better, thanks. The rest was just what I needed."

"Want to go home?"

"No, I'm okay. Best if I just get on with the job. Maybe have an early night tonight."

"Well, all right. But only if you're sure."

"Sure."

They began to walk back to the main library counter. Three impatient customers were waiting to hand back books, or have books checked out.

"We need to have a talk, Jackie," said Janis, just before they resumed work again.

Jacqueline didn't answer.

Chapter Nineteen
Bernice Remembers

"Good evening, this is Bernice Adams. And the headlines on the nine o'clock news tonight . . . The Stradner child snatch case finally reaches court: 'I only did it for the money,' says Piers Jakin. 'I never meant the child to die.' The government's statistics on economic recovery are challenged in the House of Commons by the London School of Economics. And the enquiry on the Tottenham Court Road tube crash finds 'Driver error' to be the main cause of the accident . . ."

The sweating began.

Oh God, no. Not now. Not now!

"First, the Stradner child kidnapping. Reporting restrictions having been lifted, the jury for the case today heard how Piers Jakin, unemployed fitter from Sunderland, meticulously planned the abduction of eight-year-old Janine Stradner from her private school in Kilnhope . . ."

Bernice felt the skin tightening around her face as she spoke. Felt the tightness at the nape of her neck, and her lips drawing apart.

". . . Using chloroform stolen from a medical supplier in Sunderland, Jakin abducted Janine as she walked to meet her mother at the end of the street. Pathologists' evidence revealed that Jakin had used too much chloroform and that the child had subsequently smothered in the boot of his car.

There were distraught scenes in court today when Mrs. Stradner collapsed during evidence . . ."

The skin on her hands began to crawl. Bernice felt the shuddering begin deep within her chest cavity, felt her vocal chords begin to constrict.

". . . the case continues. And in the House of Commons today, MP Jack Burnett challenged the government's statistics on economic recovery by quoting from a recently published document of the London School of Economics. For a report, over to our political correspondent, Peter Harris . . ."

"Okay," said a voice in Bernice's earpiece. "Cue tape."

And Bernice pulled out the earpiece and lunged back from her seat.

"What the hell are you doing, Bernice?" shouted the floor manager.

Got to get out, got to get out before they see. Got to . . . got to . . .

"Bernice! For fuck's sake!"

She lunged past a bewildered camera crew. There was confusion in the control room as she shouted, "Get Andrew to cover my slot. I'm . . . I'm ILL!"

She felt the skin tightening all over her body. Felt the muscles constricting. Felt the pain begin again.

The studio "Exit" door was before her. She hit the safety bar with both hands and the door crashed open. The staircase loomed before her and she plunged down the steps, careering from the walls and almost losing her balance. She knew that if she fell in that condition, her bones would shatter. The sounds of her descent crashed and echoed up the staircase. Two landings down, she heard the floor manager calling to her from the Exit door, angry and concerned.

On the third level below, she saw the staff toilets and

blundered into the Ladies. Fortunately, there was no one there. She staggered to the sinks and mirrors. A terrified, wizened and hunched figure stared back at her in horror.

"Oh my GOD!!!"

Weeping, Bernice raised skeletal hands to cover her face. She staggered back away from the mirror, found a cubicle and entered. With frail arms, she pushed the door shut, slid home the latch. Still weeping, she carefully lowered herself until she was sitting on the toilet seat.

Kelly or Joan would probably come down in a moment from the studio to find out what had happened to her. She struggled to regain control, lowering her hands and staring at them, trying to suppress the tears. She knew that she would have to make an excuse about illness, about not wanting three-quarters of a million viewers see her throw up on screen. She knew that she would have to stay in that cubicle, no matter how much Kelly or Joan implored her to come out. She knew that she must stay that way and pray that the effect would wear off the way it had done these past three times.

Deep in her heart, she knew that he would be calling for her that night.

And that horror threatened to overwhelm her.

Bernice gritted her teeth, clenched her fists and waited.

And waited.

The external toilet door opened and Kelly called, "Bernice?"

"In here," she replied, trying to control her voice.

His face swam before her eyes and the nausea rose. She struggled to rise and vomited into the toilet bowl.

"Oh my poor love," said Kelly in sympathy.

You won't have me! screamed Bernice in her mind. *You bastard . . . YOU WON'T HAVE ME!*

Chapter Twenty
Paul

Paul leaned back against one of the tiled walls between Greggs the Baker and Top Man Tailoring. He loosened a grimy shirt collar and struggled to regain his breath as the crowds of shoppers streamed past him.

The Other is here. Hunting for you. Paul, you must find him first.

"But where is he? Where?!"

Paul staggered away from the wall again, passing shoppers giving this strange young wild man a wide berth. He searched the frightened faces that passed him, knowing only one thing: that the Other was male, not female. That was the only thing that the hate instinct would allow him. But he did not know whether the Other was young or old, or from which direction he would be coming.

Paul ran to a balustrade and looked down to the other levels. He was on the third level, and could see the series of escalators leading both up and down. There were furniture showrooms on the floor below, and on the ground floor was an indoor fruit and vegetable market. He could see the tops of the stalls, and scanned the milling crowd to see if anything registered.

Nothing.

But the Other was close and getting closer.

"Where? WHERE?!"

Instinctively now, he knew that his quarry was not on the third level. Shoving aside a protesting elderly couple, Paul blundered to a down escalator. Moving clumsily but quickly downwards he pushed people aside as he moved. One man grabbed at his sleeve, outraged. Paul whirled on him. Was this the one? The man was clearly startled and afraid of what he might have started. But this was not the Other, so Paul blundered ahead; reaching the second level and whirling around to search the mall.

The colour was too much for him. The brightly lit displays, the multicoloured garments in shop windows, the sparkling reflections of water from the indoor fountains. The sound of the crowd all around him. The sound of Muzak playing on overhead speaker systems. Paul reeled, the input too much for him. His heightened awareness and heightened sensitivity were too much to handle. Groaning, he clutched at his head and reeled into a shop window.

Something or someone was near at hand. Crouching. Waiting to spring on him. He opened screwed-up eyes to see a shadowed shape not three inches from him, on the other side of the plate-glass shop window. Paul reared backwards, ready to fight.

It was a shop dummy.

Breathing heavily, he blundered ahead down the mall.

Closer, said the Voice. *You're getting closer.*

"But where? Where . . . ?"

Paul reached another escalator leading down to the ground floor.

Below. He's down there. Hunting for you. Find and kill, Paul. Find and kill!

Paul lunged forward on to the next escalator. There was no one before him. From the top, he had a clear view of the entire ground floor. He scanned the stalls and the crowd, shading his eyes against the glare of colour. Almost skidding on the plate steel at the bottom of the staircase, where the escalator slid underground, Paul lunged forward again and then stood at the foot of that staircase.

Every nerve ending seemed to shriek the nearness of the Other.

Drenched in sweat, eyes wild, hair flying, Paul stood crouched—like an animal—knowing that his quarry was so close he might even be able to reach out and touch him.

Now, Paul! Now! The Other is here! THE OTHER IS Here!

"Where? For God's sake, where?!"

And then something hit Paul hard from behind. Something that seemed to crack and splinter his skull. The pain overwhelmed and blinded him, the force of the impact slamming him heavily to the cold, tiled floor at the foot of the escalator. Lights sparked. The pain knifed hot and cold. Shards of broken pottery splintered and tinkled around his face. Somehow, his head was covered in soil. He struggled to rise, but the pain in his head made him gasp. When he touched his face, there was blood on his hands.

Get up, Paul! screamed the Voice in his head. *Get up and fight!*

"Can't . . . can't see . . ."

Paul pulled himself to a kneeling position and looked up. The shopping mall corridor ahead of him swung back and forth from crazy angles. Someone, somewhere, was screaming.

Concussed vision focused . . . and Paul saw the man striding swiftly towards him down that corridor.

He was a man in his late sixties, early seventies. His shoulder-length hair was grey and flowing back from his face as he strode purposefully towards him, face set and grim.

Paul groped at the tiled floor, seized a piece of jagged pottery, realising that the Other had almost brained him with a potted flower arrangement from one of the shopping mall aisles. He struggled to rise as the man reached inside his long raincoat.

"Drop it!" shouted the man as he came. His coat swirled and suddenly, he had pulled a sawn-off shotgun from that coat and was pointing it in Paul's direction.

Kill, Paul! Kill, Kill, KILL!

And now, from somewhere behind Paul there was a sound of screaming. Confused, now knowing that there was no way he could prevent the Other from blowing him apart, Paul looked back.

A young man in a parka was bounding down the moving escalator towards him. He was screaming—and holding another potted floral display high above his head in both hands as he came.

"Drop it!" shouted the white-haired man again.

The young man leaped screeching towards Paul, his eyes filled with mad hate which he recognised, even from where he lay, as belonging to the Other. This was the one. This was the person who had almost brained him from the top of the escalator. This was the Other who—even now—was about to kill him.

A stabbing, detonating roar filled the shopping mall corridor.

Paul saw the young man explode on the escalator; saw him fly backwards and sideways over the escalator rail in a whirling arc of arms and legs; saw him plunge into the ornamental pool behind in a spray of water and blood.

Bewildered, shocked and dazed, Paul turned back to the white-haired man just as he chambered another round into the shotgun.

"Who . . . ?" he began.

Still grim-faced, the grey-haired man looked down at him.

Then lashed out savagely, hitting Paul on the side of the head with the butt of the shotgun.

Van Buren leaned down and grabbed Paul by the collar of his jerkin. Dragging him to a sitting position, he knelt down and swung one of the unconscious man's arms around his shoulder. He stood again, dragging Paul to his feet by holding on to that wrist; still keeping the shotgun levelled.

People were milling and screaming now as the horror of what had happened finally began to register. Casting one brief glance back to the ornamental pond to check on the other young man in the parka—he was floating face down in an ever-widening dark crimson stain—Van Buren strode back the way he had come, dragging Paul with him.

Two uniformed security men moved forward from a department store entrance on Van Buren's right. Without hesitating in his stride, he levelled the shotgun at them as he moved. They backed off.

Someone yelled above the confusion, "For God's sake, somebody! Telephone for the police!"

Van Buren reached the main Exit/Entrance at the front of the shopping mall. Pausing only to shove the shotgun into the interior pocket of his raincoat, he dragged Paul through the swing doors, ignoring the staring, puzzled faces of shoppers just arriving at the mall.

In less than a minute, Van Buren had reached his car.

He flung Paul across the back seat and climbed in.

In less than two minutes, his car screeched out of the shopping mall car park and on to the highway.

No one had taken his car registration number.

Chapter Twenty-One
Gregory Leonard

Leonard sat in his Nissan Sunny saloon car, watching the strange patterns that the motel's neon sign was making on the windscreen as rain troughed and funnelled across it. His windscreen wipers were switched off, since he didn't want anyone inside the motel noticing his presence. Visibility was poor, but he could see the entrance well enough . . . as well as the window of Room 22 on the second floor.

King's Road Motel was a fair- to medium-sized building, built in the same manner as the Holiday Inn—no doubt to suggest a connection (which did not, of course, exist) and which would draw salesmen and travellers on the nearby Coast Road. Leonard had stayed at one of the King's Motels in Southampton once, while working on a "case." Basic facilities, basic food, basic cost. Although he had never stayed in the Coast Road facility, he supposed that the layout and the provision would be pretty much the same.

He wound down the window a fraction and lit a cigarette, not sure how long he would be waiting here. But his meter was ticking away, just like your average taxi driver—and as long as she was prepared to pay, he was prepared to stay.

It had been eight o'clock that evening when she had telephoned. Leonard had been busy fabricating expenses for his last "case." Similar to the one he was on now, really. Tracking down a vagrant husband for a wife who was owed considerable amounts of maintenance money. Officially, it had taken him a fortnight to track him down. In actuality, he had walked into one of the husband's pub haunts on the first day of his enquiries, had asked the publican, "Do you know where he is?" And the publican had said, "Yeah, he's sitting over there by the juke box." Still, as long as the customer was satisfied . . .

Leonard played over the telephone conversation of that evening in his mind:

Leonard?

Yeah?

This . . . this is . . . Bernice Adams . . .

She sounded ill, desperately ill. It seemed as if she were having trouble with her breathing; with her ability just to get the words out. As if she didn't want to speak to him at all, but was fighting some kind of inner battle to push those words out.

Yes, Ms. Adams?

Tonight . . . I want you to . . . tonight . . .

All right. Just tell me when and where.

King's . . .

Ms. Adams? Are you all right?

King's Road Motel.

Okay, the one on the Coast Road. I know it.

Nine o'clock tonight . . . Room 22.

Got it. Listen, are you sure you're . . . ?

Just be there, Leonard! He's already registered. Be there . . . and follow him . . . after . . . after . . .

Listen, Ms. Adams. Why don't you just stay home? Leave the rest to me, I'll go down there, make a few enquiries and take it from there.

Just . . . just do what I tell you, Mr. Leonard.

Are you sure you're . . .

Listen to me . . . it's always a different place . . . he never stays overnight . . . at the place we go to . . . so . . . when

*we're . . . finished . . . he'll leave. He always leaves . . . so
just follow him afterwards . . .*

I'm not really sure that you're . . .

JUST FOLLOW HIM AFTERWARDS . . .

All right, all right, for God's sake!

She had slammed the telephone down then, and
Leonard had a strong feeling that something had *made* her
slam it down. Shrugging, he had pulled on his coat and left
the office.

He had arrived at the motel almost an hour early and had
found a good parking spot out front in between a whole
bunch of other cars so as not to be conspicuous. With an
empty briefcase and a pork-pie hat, he had fussily pretended to lock his car and used his "salesman" walk into the
lobby. It was a walk that he called his "I-don't-want-to-be-
here-doing-this-lousy-job-but-as-long-as-I-am-I-may-as-well-
get-on-with-it" walk.

The young man behind the reception desk seemed to
have much the same attitude.

Good, thought Leonard. *A soul mate.*

He had been right about the interior of the motel. He
might just as well have been in Southampton.

"Good evening, sir. Can I help?" asked the young, dark-
haired man in a voice that failed to disguise his boredom.

"Yes, please. My name's Thornton. I'm here to meet up
with Mr. Barry. He's in Room 22."

The young man checked the register. Leonard resisted the
impulse to smile when puzzlement registered on his face.

"Mr. Barry, did you say?"

"Yes, that's right. Mr. Arthur Barry. Of Drews Mechanical
Engineering."

"We have someone registered in Room 22. But not Mr.
Barry."

"Oh no, there must be some mistake. I've definitely

arranged to meet him here. He telephoned me, said he's registered, gave me the room number and everything."

"Sorry, sir. But I . . ."

"Wait a moment. I wonder if he's using the alias again?"

"Alias?"

"Well the company likes us to do that sometimes, know what I mean? Firms in our line of work get very sensitive when it comes to poaching on established sales territories. I wonder . . . I mean, I wonder if you could tell me"—and Leonard now utilised his rehearsed buddy-buddy laugh—"just who is registered in Room 22?"

The young man checked the register again.

"Mr. B. Adams."

The crafty bastard's using her name. "And the firm?"

"Well, we don't usually give details of . . ."

"Oh go on, I promise you it's okay." Again the buddy-buddy laugh.

"Well . . . he hasn't given one."

"How about the address?"

The young man looked up at him, thought about professionalism and then discarded it. What the hell. He'd had a fight with the duty manager that night anyway.

"Ashleigh House, Glanton."

"That's my man, all right. Thanks a lot."

"Shall I tell him you're on your way up?"

"Yes, please," said Leonard, feigning enthusiasm and bonhomie. Then, quickly, "Oh . . . no, wait a moment." Leonard swung his empty briefcase up on to the reception desk, opened it slightly in a way that kept its lack of contents hidden from the young man, and then said, "Bugger it, I thought I'd left it behind . . . On second thought . . ." Leonard checked his watch. It was 8:30 p.m. "Don't bother him. I'll just pop back to the office and get my reports. I wasn't expected until nine, anyway."

The reception telephone rang and the young man answered, clearly ready to forget all about him.

"Thanks, anyway," smiled Leonard . . . and left the hotel lobby for his car again.

It had started to rain.

Twenty minutes later, when the downpour was at its strongest, another car had pulled into the car park. Leonard had watched quietly as Bernice Adams had emerged and hurried through the rain and into the lobby without attempting to look around for him. He had seen women in trouble before—but Bernice Adams was surely the sorriest sight he'd seen in a long while. He couldn't believe that this was the self-assured woman he had watched on the evening news only two nights ago.

Ashleigh House, Glanton.

Leonard couldn't be sure, of course. But it seemed a strong possibility to him that it was a false address.

"The woman said wait and follow. So I'll wait and follow."

He was fairly sure that he had identified Room 22 from where he was sitting. Five minutes after the TV woman had entered the lobby, the light in that window had gone out.

Leonard sat looking up at the window, wondering.

What kind of man could do this to a woman? She was clearly terrified of him, whoever he was; but she still went ahead with their rendezvous anyway. Was her fear of him so great? He began to feel uncomfortable as he sat there, wondering whether this shouldn't be a job for the police after all. But maybe . . . maybe . . . he was reading this thing all wrong? Maybe it wasn't fear of the man at all. Maybe it was simply a fear of discovery. Was Bernice Adams married? He made a mental note to check it out later. Maybe she was so attracted to this man and their secret liaisons, she was simply terrified that her husband would ever find out. That would explain her strange behaviour on the telephone.

What if that fella up there, giving her a good time at this very moment, was some kind of gigolo? That would explain a lot. She didn't know his name, was paying a private investigator to follow the man and find out who he was. Didn't it make better sense to assume that she was paying some anonymous hired stud for a series of one-night stands and she had simply become infatuated with him?

Feeling less guilty about Bernice Adams's fears (*private investigators can have feelings too, you know,* he reminded himself again), Leonard turned on the radio low and sat back, eyes fixed on the darkened rain-blurred pane of Room 22.

Wonder how studs like that advertise their services? Contact magazines? Word of mouth? Recommendations from friends?

Leonard was mulling these and associated issues over in his head when movement in the lobby caught his attention. He sat forward, peering through the windscreen.

Bernice Adams was pushing through the swivel door, pulling her coat collar tight around her neck.

Leonard looked quickly back at Room 22.

"Never even put the light on again . . ."

Bernice seemed to cast a quick glance around the car park, as if expecting to see Leonard standing out there in the rain like something from a Humphrey Bogart picture. Didn't she realise by now that he was a professional, not a Hollywood cliché? Pulling a headscarf tight around her head, she hurried out into the rain and over to her car. Leonard watched her, still keeping a close eye on the window and on the motel reception. There was no back exit to King's Road Motel. The man he was after would eventually have to come out through the front reception area. The only other way would be down the fire escape at the side of the building, of which he also had a clear view. He didn't suppose that he would use that fire escape.

Bernice climbed into her car. She sat there for a long time. And Leonard could see the slight rise and fall of her shoulders as she sat facing front. Was she weeping? After a while, she started the engine. The car swung out of the car park into the rain and down the slip road which would eventually lead her to the Coast Road. Leonard watched the car vanish in a hissing spray.

He turned to face the hotel reception area again, his gaze shifting from the lobby, to the window of Room 22, to the fire escape . . . and back again. He lit another cigarette, reached over to turn up the radio . . . and then started back in alarm when he saw the figure standing on the hotel reception steps, apparently looking straight at him.

The man was tall, perhaps six foot three, and wearing a long black raincoat which fell around him like some kind of cloak.

Male model, was the first thought that flashed through Leonard's mind. *Gigolo.*

Leonard knew, without doubt, that this was the man he was after. Had he really seen him sitting out here in the car? For a long while, the man just stood at the top of these stairs, shielded from the rain by the overhanging parapet of the motel reception area. Leonard waited.

And a feeling of unease began to creep over him.

Leonard could see no real details of the man's face, could not tell whether he was staring directly at him or not. The runnels of rainwater on the windscreen were obscuring a direct view. But something about the man's stance was creating this feeling of unease which was mounting now with each second.

The man began to walk down the steps into the rain, and as he moved with a kind of lithe grace, Leonard sensed an aura of what he could only describe as *power*. This man was extremely dangerous, and that instinctive feeling served to put into context Bernice Adams's own deep fear.

Leonard steeled himself as the man reached the bottom of the stairs and began walking towards him through the rain. As the man came, Leonard realised that he was gritting his teeth; that he was clenching the steering wheel, and that sweat was trickling down the small of his back.

Christ, who in hell *are you?*

And then the man swerved to the right, and strode towards the parked black Mercedes. With one swift motion, he unlocked the car door and slid inside. Almost before Leonard could react, the car was streaking through the rain, turning sharply on to the slip road and away.

"Shit!"

Leonard's fingers were somehow trembling when he switched on the ignition. Angry with himself and with this unease from nowhere, he gunned the engine into life and followed.

"Okay, Mr. Mystery Man," he said through gritted teeth. "Let's find out just *who* you are."

Part Two
Rage

Chapter One
Gregory Leonard

When she knocked on the fluted-glass door, Leonard knew instinctively that it was Bernice Adams.

She entered without waiting to be invited, and his first thought on seeing her was: *Bloody hell, you're going to have to use a little more make-up on the telly tonight, Bernice.* She looked even more pale, even more haggard than the previous time he'd seen her in his office.

Leonard slid his desk drawer shut. There was a full glass of whisky in there. Normally, he never drank at all in the office—even though most of his fictional detective heroes did. In the past, he'd known where to draw the line. But of late, he seemed to be acutely more twitchy than he'd ever been in the past. Maybe he was getting too old for the job. Maybe he should start thinking about retirement . . .

"Well?" asked Bernice, sitting down.

Leonard thought about offering her a drink, saw the tight, rigid line of her mouth—and decided against it.

"His name is Gideon."

Bernice shifted uncomfortably. "Gideon. Is that a first name or a second name?"

"I don't know. Just Gideon."

"And?"

"He . . . lives, if that's the right word . . . in a hotel in the centre of town. The Grand. He's been there for about two months now. One of the night porters—and there's a bribe to add to my expenses, by the way—tells me that he booked into the most expensive suite they've got. Paid cash. And he's been there ever since. Comes and goes pretty much as he pleases."

"Where is he from? What's his address? What does he do for a living?"

"Well, I checked the register at the King's Road Motel first, Ms. Adams. Not only did he register in your name, but he used a false address. I checked it out afterwards. I haven't had a chance to look at the register at the Grand—but I'm willing to bet that he's used a false address there, too. Anyway, I'll find out soon enough."

"So apart from his name, you don't know anything else?"

"One thing I can tell you—he has other girlfriends. Lots of them. I've seen him with them. Don't know what the attraction is, apart from the obvious physical one—he seems to treat them like dirt." Leonard watched Bernice stiffen as he spoke. "Picks 'em up. Takes them to motels or hotels. Sometimes he just . . . stays in the car. I followed two of them home, afterwards. Not happy people, Ms. Adams."

"Who are they?"

"If I were you I would just keep away from him. There's nothing but trouble for you there. Like I said before, if there's more to this than you're letting me know, then the police should . . ."

"What are their names?"

Leonard shook his head and leaned back to the desk, flipping open a notepad.

"Jacqueline Brennan. Yvonne Gillis. The addresses are . . ."

"Write them down for me."

"Am I still on the case? Do you want me to follow through, interview these two women?"

"I don't want you to do anything else until you hear from me. Just let me have the addresses for the time being."

"I hope you know what you're doing," said Leonard, copying down the addresses on a scrap of paper. He handed it to her. Bernice folded it and put it in her handbag.

"So now what?" asked Leonard, leaning back in his seat again.

"Don't do anything else until you hear from me."

Turning briskly, Bernice left the office.

Leonard shrugged and watched her leave. After a while, he slid open the desk drawer and took out the whisky glass. His hand was shaking again.

"Damn," he muttered, taking a mouthful. "Time I retired."

Chapter Two
Paul

Paul emerged from unconsciousness feeling violently nauseous. That spasm of nausea brought him out of the dark pit into which he had fallen. He struggled to bring his hands up to his face, but his arms would not move. He struggled to stand, but could not. And when the nausea boiled from the pit of his stomach and into his throat, Paul tried to bend over double to let it out—but again he could not move.

There was nothing inside him, nothing in his stomach. When that nausea caused him to retch, it was a dry retch. His eyes bulged, his head throbbed. Sweat streamed down his face, dripping from his chin. When the retching stopped at last, Paul was able to focus his vision. Gasping for breath, he could see that he was in a sparely furnished room. Too sparely furnished to be a motel or hotel room. There was a single bed and a couple of chairs. A washstand sink and unit. Faded blue wallpaper that seemed to have seen too much sun. The wall opposite him was taken up by a large window. A venetian blind covered that window, undrawn, but he could see bright sunshine trying to get through the slats. The hissing murmur that he at first took to be traffic passing was now plainly the sound of the sea. Somewhere, gulls cried in the sky.

Now Paul could see why he was unable to move.

He had been tied to a chair.

His hands were bound behind him, his legs tied to the front legs of that chair. Paul twisted, but the hessian rope bit deeply into the flesh of his wrists and shins. Another length of rope had been fastened around his neck, binding him to the chair headrest. The pain of his effort made the pain in his head and neck almost unbearable. He groaned, the sound unnaturally loud in the close confines of this small room.

"So you're awake," said a voice from behind.

Paul tried to turn. Again, the effort caused him great pain. Again from behind, he heard the sound of someone rising from a chair. Fear began to uncurl in his gut now.

The Other!

But now the figure was walking slowly around to face him, and when Paul saw the old man with the long grey hair, memories came back to him. This was not the Other.

This was the man who had suddenly turned up out of nowhere and saved him from the Other. Paul's fear must have registered on his face. The old man laughed when he spoke.

"No, you needn't have any fear of me. I'm not going to harm you . . . unless I have to."

"Who the hell are you?" Paul's voice was cracked. There was a foul taste in his mouth.

"Your name is Paul Shapiro," continued the old man.

"How do you know me?"

"I went through your pockets while you were unconscious."

"You . . . you hit me in the *head*, you bastard! With a shotgun butt."

"Yes, that's right. The Rage was upon you, so I couldn't risk anything. I also saved your life, in case you hadn't noticed."

The Rage . . . Those words perfectly summed up the psychotic anger, the need to kill, that had possessed Paul. The old man pulled up a chair and turned it around, sitting down to face Paul with his arms over the backrest. Even in the faint light of this room, Paul could see the eerie and youthful blue of the man's eyes, so incongruous in that lined and battered face.

"Where am I?"

"You're in a beach hut. Near a place called Swarwell."

"What in Christ's name is *happening* to me?" groaned Paul, more to himself than to the man sitting opposite.

"Nothing in Christ's name, son. That's for sure. But tell me—how many young men have you killed?"

Paul groaned again, the knowledge of what he had done filling him with the deepest anguish. "I'm insane. Are you the police? No, of course you're not. Look, you'd better dial 999, get someone out here . . ."

"This doesn't involve the police at all. Now tell me, how many have you killed?"

"Who *are* you? How the hell do you know . . . ?"

"Tell me!"

"Two people! I've killed two people, God damn you! But if you don't turn me in, God knows when that . . . that . . . *Rage* . . . will be on me again. Oh Christ, he couldn't have been any older than me . . ."

"He wasn't any older or younger than you. He was exactly the same age as you. Born on the same day, the same month, the same year. Just like the boy I killed back there in the shopping mall. Same day, same month, same year."

"What the hell are you talking about? Who *are* you, anyway?"

The old man smiled. "My name is Van Buren. You've never heard of me. But I know all about you . . . and your brothers."

"Brothers?"

"That's what I said. Or should I say, half-brothers."

Paul tried to protest again, but his voice cracked and he began to choke. Van Buren moved quickly to the washbasin, drew off a half-pint of water into a plastic beaker and moved back to him. Paul drank down the water greedily from Van Buren's hand and asked for more. Van Buren made a return to the basin. Finally, breath recovered, Paul shook his head and looked the old man directly in the eye.

"If you know what's happening to me, if you know what's going on . . . then I wish to God you would just tell me."

The old man looked at him, long and hard, as if deliberating. He stood up and moved to the venetian blind, opening one of the slats with a finger to look outside, as if searching for someone. A single spear of sunlight invaded the room. Slowly, head down, Van Buren returned to his seat. He sighed.

"All right, Paul. I don't see why not. Time for explanations . . ."

Chapter Three
The Women

As soon as Bernice opened the door, Jacqueline said, "I know you. You're the woman on television."

The woman's fragile smile perfectly reflected the way that Jacqueline felt inside: "Bernice Adams. The newsreader, yes. Please come in."

Still with the fear gnawing at her insides, Jacqueline stepped into the woman's apartment. The extravagance of its furnishings seemed to be well in accord with someone working in the media, but to Jacqueline the place seemed to shriek *"Showbiz"* just a little too loudly for her taste. Impressions of decor were fleeting. Anxiety gnawed at her as Bernice closed the door and waved her into the living room.

"Please have a seat. Drink?"

"Yes, that would be nice," replied Jacqueline, now desperately needing a drink to quench the way she was feeling inside. "Vodka."

"Mixer?"

"Tonic, if you've got it."

"Fine."

Still too nervous to sit, Jacqueline walked over to the wall-to-ceiling windows which looked out over the city. Standing so close to the glass with that immense drop also served to fuel her unease. She moved back to one of the sofas and sat as Bernice arrived with her drink. When Bernice sat opposite to her, Jacqueline could see her own unease and anxiety perfectly reflected.

At last, Jacqueline said, "He's your husband, isn't he?"

Bernice sipped anxiously at her own drink. "What makes you say that?"

"The note that you slipped under my door." Jacqueline reached into her handbag and took it out. " 'Is there a man in your life that you'd rather be without? B.A.' And then this address, and a time to meet."

"The man in question isn't my husband . . . or my lover. I'm not married."

"Then I'm not sure what . . ."

"Someone else should be coming tonight. Another woman. Maybe we should wait until she's here."

"I don't like mysteries, Ms. Adams. Things are happening to me that I can't explain. My life is falling apart. I just want to put an end to what's happening, and if you know what's going on, then . . ."

"The same thing is happening to me. And to the other girl I've asked to come here . . . and perhaps to dozens of others."

"And what's happening exactly, Ms. Adams?"

Bernice paused to sip at her own drink, and to light a cigarette. Then she said, "The bastard's been using me, just taking me whenever he wants. And I think he'll probably kill me if he doesn't stop."

"For how long?" asked Jacqueline, surprised at her willingness to open up so easily.

"Seven weeks. And you?"

"I don't know." Jacqueline felt panic rising inside, cursed herself and swallowed the feeling. "Six weeks, I think. Something like that."

"He comes. He takes me. And he makes me do everything he wants."

"It's got to be . . ." began Jacqueline. Things were moving too fast, her whole life was at stake and she didn't know whether she could trust or believe this woman or not. But here she was, anxious to talk, desperate to relate if this woman was also somehow sharing her nightmare. "I don't know . . . but it must be . . . *hypnotism*, or something. Isn't it?"

"Something like that. It must be. But I don't know how in God's name he has the power to do what he does."

"And then, afterwards . . ."

"Afterwards, you feel drained. As if the life is being sucked out of your body by him."

"My face." And the words were spilling out of Jacqueline now. "Sometimes, sometimes it happens after I've . . . been with him. My face, my hands, my body . . ."

"You age," said Bernice, still somehow so calm as Jacqueline spilled out the words. "In an instant, like some cheap and horrible effect from a horror movie. You wither and age. It stays that way for a while . . . then it wears off, and you return to the way you were before."

"But each time it lasts longer. Longer than the time before."

"I think . . ." said Bernice, taking a long sip from her drink. "I think that . . . eventually . . . he'll kill us. Drain us completely."

Suddenly, Jacqueline could not control her trembling. "Who is he?" she asked in a cracked and wavering voice.

"His name is Gideon. That's all I know about him personally. But I also know where he's living."

"Have you tried . . . going to the police?"

"Have you?"

"I thought about it. Even tried to telephone them once . . ."

"And what happened?"

"I couldn't do it."

"Why?"

"I don't know why. A *fear* came over me, a feeling like nothing I've ever . . ."

"The reason that you haven't been able to do anything about it is because he *told* you not to do it. The same way that he told me. And when you try to resist, or fight back, he's able to fill you with a terror so dreadful that you're helpless." The tension had enveloped Bernice now as she drained her glass. "Or almost helpless," she said as she put the glass down. Her voice carried a bitter tone of defiance.

"How can he *do* what he does? I don't understand . . ."

"Post-hypnotic suggestion or something. I don't know. But that's the way it is, isn't it?"

"Yes. And I can't tell my husband either. Jesus, what can I say? 'I'm letting this man fuck me whenever he wants to, Brian. I can't help myself. Can't say 'No.' And then afterwards, I'm turning into something from a horror movie . . .' "

"He'll kill us. You know that, don't you?"

Someone knocked on the front door.

Jacqueline felt a deep chill of fear inside as Bernice stubbed out her cigarette and headed for the door. Jacqueline finished off her vodka and began to fidget with her empty glass.

"This will be our other guest," said Bernice. "Yvonne Gillis. Just another girl who can't say no." There was a bitter grimness in her voice as she opened the door.

And recoiled backwards, crying out in shock. Jacqueline leaped from her seat in alarm.

Something was standing in the door-frame, weaving back and forth on unsteady legs.

Something in a blue floral dress, but with a face that was hideously withered. Something that raised an almost skeletal hand to its face, and cried, "*For God's sake, do something to help me!*" as it staggered into the room.

Bernice recoiled further as it tottered forward, then collapsed sobbing to its knees.

But Bernice's horror was turning into something else now.

"Yvonne . . . ?" she heard herself ask. "Yvonne Gillis?"

The withered thing kneeling on the carpet turned its ravaged face to look at her. Tears were coursing from rheumy eyes.

"Yes . . . yes . . ." sobbed Yvonne. "Please . . . please . . . *help me!*"

Bernice slammed the door as Yvonne's withered husk began to topple forward. There were tears in her own eyes now as she rushed forward and took one of Yvonne's frail arms. It felt as if she could snap it off with no effort at all. She held her back from falling forward . . . and now Jacqueline had rushed forward and taken another arm. Together, they carried the fragile, withered body to one of the sofas and laid her down.

"It's . . . never . . . *never* . . . been as bad as that for me," said Jacqueline, and when Bernice looked up at her, she could see tears there, too.

"He's probably been seeing her longer than you and me," said Bernice, her throat hurting. "But we'll end up this way . . . and worse."

"What are we going to do?"

Bernice looked long and hard at Jacqueline, as she stroked Yvonne's wrinkled and furrowed brow. Yvonne's sobbing was slowing, she seemed now on the verge of sleep.

"We have to look after her. Until she . . . gets better, comes around."

"And then what, for God's sake—and *then* what?"

When Bernice spoke again, there was a grim resolution in her voice.

"There's only one thing we can do. And you know it."

Chapter Four
Gregory Leonard

"Why the hell doesn't she telephone?" Leonard said out loud to the phone, as if it could answer him back.

Cursing when it didn't, he stood up and moved to the window. The sun was going down and flocks of starlings were circling the office blocks in their usual frenzied massing before heading into town. Leonard often watched them: massive spiralling clouds of birds swooping and diving in the last rays of daylight, looking from a distance like clouds of locusts about to descend on the city. They roosted on the ledges and cornices of the Central Station and the huge Victorian buildings downtown, their massed feathered ranks jostling for position, filling the city with a vast and echoing chittering until the early hours of the morning. On his various "errands" in the city centre, his "private investigator" persona had often wondered why, given that most of the Central Station and surrounding buildings were covered in thousands of these roosting birds, there was never a dead one lying in the gutter. How many birds must there be up there? Fifty thousand, sixty thousand . . . a hundred thousand? And not one dead 'un in the gutter on the following morning? Surely the law of averages should dictate that *one* starling would die in its sleep and fall down into the street?

Maybe the street-cleaning operatives were supereffective? Maybe a special team of them went out in the early hours, scouring the streets for dead birds? Maybe they

got their pay docked if a member of the public ever saw
them slipping one into the garbage can? Maybe a horde of
hungry cats padded silently over the pavements when
everyone was in bed, searching for titbits?

Leonard watched the birds swooping and diving. A great
cloud of starlings swept around the very block in which he
was standing, passing just below him on the tenth floor.

He tried to think of starlings, and the two "cases" he'd recently been contracted for: another missing person, and a
debt collection. But somehow, he could not concentrate on
them. Only one thing occupied his mind. The same thing
that had been bugging him for days now. Bernice Adams
and her mystery man—Gideon, or Mr. Gideon, or whatever.

She had told him that he was "still on the case" and that
she would telephone him in due course; but that telephone
call was still unforthcoming, and Leonard felt that it would
be a betrayal of his professionalism if he telephoned her
himself. It was driving him mad. There was something about
the whole business which he found deeply fascinating. He
needed to find out more, if not for the Adams woman, then
for himself. He had never felt like this before about any as-
pect of his work. In the past, a job had been a job—and
nothing more. But something . . . *something* about this
whole business was really getting to him. More than anything else, while he had been "tailing" that tall, dark stranger
with all the girlfriends he remembered that instinctive gut
feeling. The feeling which had come over him when Gideon
had walked out of the hotel reception, stood at the top of
the steps in the rain and seemed to have been looking directly at him (although that was impossible, of course).

That feeling had been fear. A cold, unreasoning fear.

And somehow, far from making Leonard want to drop this
case like a hot brick, far from making him telephone Bernice
Adams and tell her that he couldn't help her any more—it

only served to make him want to know more. He didn't like
this feeling inside. It gnawed at his stomach, eroded his confidence, had put him back on the booze again. In knowledge was control. He had to know more, whether the
newsreader lady was going to pay him for it or not.

When a familiar black Mercedes slid from the shadows of
the Grand Hotel's underground car park and on to the main
street, Leonard was not far behind in his Nissan Sunny. He
knew the city streets well, had done this kind of job so often
that he could almost second-guess which way his quarry
would go, which junction the car would probably turn at,
which exit the car would take. Even so, his gut feeling made
him hang back just that little bit further than he would have
done with anyone else. That same gut feeling had prevented
him from trying out the same trick at the Grand that he had
tried at the King's Road Motel. Something about making that
kind of approach made him feel deeply uneasy, for reasons
that he could not fathom. Instead, he had opted for a little
surveillance in the first instance.

  The windows of the Mercedes were tinted. There was no
way he could tell whether the man called Gideon was
alone, or whether he had one of his girlfriends with him.

  The car was heading for the Quayside.

  Leonard followed the Mercedes, as it turned down Dean
Street, a steeply sloping street leading directly down to the
Guildhall building and the redeveloped bars and hotels
which fronted the new Quayside. Once, this had been a
thriving port area, but the recession in the English ship-
building industry had hit hard. There were no working ships
at berth here now. Derelict and decrepit buildings had been
reclaimed and redeveloped. Luxury flats now replaced
shipping offices, wine bars replaced grain stores. On the
other side of the River Tyne a luxury liner was at permanent

berth under the shadow of the Tyne Bridge, now a floating nightclub and restaurant. Even from Dean Street, Leonard could see the blue and red neon of the deck lights reflected in the dark, oily water of the Tyne River. Was this where he was going tonight? Was this where he would make his latest pick-up?

No . . . the Mercedes was turning left halfway down Dean Street into the multi-storey car park. Leonard did not follow. He continued on down past the car park, looking to his left as the car vanished past the barriers and into the concrete depths. He would have to be quick. Driving in straight after his quarry would be too risky, might cause suspicion. He had a better idea. At the bottom of Dean Street, looking out over the River Tyne, was the Guildhall. There was a private car park behind there, directly on the concrete river frontage. The local government staff working there would all have gone home by now. By lifting one of the bollards from its setting, he could park safely behind there.

Swooping into the car park, Leonard had replaced the bollard within a minute and was hurrying back up Dean Street through the growing crowd of early evening revellers swarming down to the Quayside from the city centre. In two minutes, he was standing in a doorway opposite the multi-storey car park. There was only one way that his man could come. Straight through the front entrance. In the darkness, Leonard reviewed his strategy. Would following this guy around town really bring him any nearer to the truth? Why not just lean a little bit on one of the women whom he had seen with Gideon? He knew their addresses now. What on earth could he expect to find out tonight?

Better than sitting in the office, wondering . . .

The tall man in the long dark coat swept out of the entrance and strode away up Dean Street so quickly, it almost took Leonard by surprise. Carefully, hugging the doorways

and the shadowed recesses on the other side of the street,
Leonard kept well back. The street was steep, and Leonard
was soon out of breath, but the man ahead was undaunted
as he strode onwards and upwards.

God, you're bloody fit.

Leonard knew where Gideon was heading now. There
could be only one place.

The Bigg Market.

It was the one area in Newcastle town centre where bus-
loads of revellers from both sides of the Border would head
on a Friday and Saturday night. A quarter-square mile of
pubs and clubs and restaurants, replacing the former
market-place in the centre of the city.

There were more crowds of youngsters on the street now,
already getting tanked up on Happy Hour booze. *Three
shots for a quid and ready to party,* thought Leonard as he
passed the towering stone pillars which fronted the Theatre
Royal. The Royal Shakespeare Company was producing
Julius Caesar, and Leonard could not suppress a grim laugh,
wondering which lucky Juliet was going to score with the
Romeo he was following.

Gideon turned sharp left down another street, and
Leonard knew that he had been right. The street led directly
to the heart of the Bigg Market. He hurried to catch up, not
wanting his quarry to duck into a pub and be lost. Turning
the corner, he had a clear view of the man striding down
that street towards the milling crowd at the far end.

As usual for Friday night, there were queues of people for
the various pubs around the perimeter of the Bigg Market
"square." Neon flashed. Party revellers whooped. Leonard
watched a brace of policemen making themselves "visible,"
calmly walking down the pavement on the far side of the
square.

Gideon walked straight across the cobbled square, past a taxi rank and turned down towards Thomson House: location of the local newspaper.

Don't want to queue, eh?

Leonard hung back slightly, letting his quarry move on ahead down the far pavement. He was at least a head taller than anyone in the crowd through which he moved, and it was easy to keep track of him from here. Now, Leonard knew just which pub he was heading for: The Blackie Boy. When the man entered, Leonard hurried across the square to the far pavement, breaking into a brief trot as he pushed through the crowd towards the pub. There was no queue here, but there were two bouncers on the door. They barely glanced at him as he pushed through the doors and into the pub.

The bar occupied most of the left-hand side of the pub, but it was almost impossible to see it for heaving bodies. The pub was packed, and with Happy Hour due to end in ten minutes' time at 8:00 p.m. everyone wanted to be served at once. Leonard strained to see through the closely packed crowd, winced at the heavy rock music coming from the overhead speakers. There was some serious "partying" going on here.

The man he was following had pushed through to the far side of the pub, and was moving to the bar. Leonard pushed on through the crowd after him, realising that this was the perfect place for getting close to him and listening in to any conversation he might be having if he was meeting someone here. *If? Big if.* No, Leonard's gut instinct told him that this man called Gideon was here to meet someone. There was a purpose in the way he moved.

Gideon had shouldered through to the bar now, and Leonard was less than twenty feet from him, pushing through a hen party. The bride-to-be was wearing a huge paper hat and streamers. Mild obscenities cut from newspapers had been sellotaped or stapled to her dress. Full of Happy Hour vodka, she suddenly seized Leonard by the shoulders. Her friends whooped in delight at this sudden lunge at a total stranger. The whooping laughter was drawing attention to Leonard.

Gideon looked up from the bar, straight at him.

Quickly feigning drunkenness himself, Leonard pulled the girl close and pretended to waltz; a physical impossibility in such a cramped crowd of partygoers. He began to sing a tuneless, drunken accompaniment. The bride-to-be's friends howled with drunken laughter again. From the corner of his eye, Leonard saw that Gideon's attention was no longer on him. Leonard pushed past the hen party, fixing that big drunken grin on his face.

There were dozens of people at the bar waiting to be served, but Leonard watched in incredulity when Gideon snapped his fingers and one of the young men serving came quickly over. Was that *fear* on the young man's face, too?

"Can I take your order?"

"Whisky. Large one."

What the hell *was* there about this man? A gangster, or something? Someone known and feared by all? No, instinctively again, Leonard felt in his gut that Gideon was new to this city, new to this bar, even. Leonard watched the young man in the bow tie move off to get the whisky and as he passed him at the bar, Leonard got a closer look at the unease in the young man's eyes. That unease matched his own. Angry at himself, he shoved up close to the bar, pretending to be a customer, moving inch by inch closer to where Gideon stood. Keeping up the drunk act, he was able to get a closer look at him now.

Thirty years old. Maybe thirty-five.

The young man returned with Gideon's drink.

Yeah, he could be a male model or something, couldn't he? Expensive clothes. Well groomed. Dark hair swept back. Is that gel he's got on?

Somehow, Leonard could not bring himself to look into those eyes.

Gideon was turning now, to the two young women on his right at the bar. They were in their early twenties. Both with blonde, cropped hair and leather jackets. Dark red lipstick like cruel slashes across white faces.

Gideon spoke to the first woman.

"What's your name?"

She turned to level a frozen and withering look at him. Leonard pushed closer.

"Fuck off," said the woman.

And then Leonard saw that hostile look turn into something else. He watched as that hostility dissolved, watched as a creeping unease began to register in her eyes. She slowly began to pull away from him as he held her eyes with a cold and level stare.

"Go away," said Gideon.

"What?"

"I said, 'Go away.' And I mean, go away now."

Incredibly, the woman had quickly risen from her seat, taking her bag from the bar. Without a word to her friend, she pushed away through the crowd and was gone. Leonard watched as she passed him at the bar. That look of unease on her face had turned to outright terror. Reaching the doors, she fled from the pub into the night. Mesmerised, Leonard looked back to Gideon and the remaining girl.

Now, he could see that there was an even greater look of terror on her face.

Gideon smiled. It was a horribly glacial expression.

"You haven't been answering the telephone, Angela."

She's going to scream, thought Leonard. *She's going to fly into hysterics, cause a crushing panic in the pub.*

"You won't scream," said Gideon. "Change the expression on your face. You're happy."

Incredibly again, the young woman changed her expression, trying to smile. It looked wretched.

Gideon finished his drink. "We're leaving. Come with me."

The woman called Angela groped at the bar for her bag, without taking her eyes from him. Gideon helped her to stand.

Another voice from behind the bar startled Leonard into reeling away from the bar.

"Well, what *do* you want then?"

A girl in bobbed hair and with the trademark bow tie was waiting to take his order. Leonard quickly returned to his drunk act. "Three whiskies and soda. Two vodkas with lime and a pint of lager." The girl moved away to get his drinks. When Leonard turned around, Gideon and Angela were already pushing through the pub doors and on to the pavement. Quickly, he pushed away from the bar and followed.

It wasn't hard to follow them.

They did not walk together as lovers. He did not have his arm around her. She did not attempt to hang on his own arm. There was no laughter, no exchanged glances. Just as before, Gideon strode on ahead through the crowd, long dark coat flapping. Angela had difficulty in keeping pace because of her high heels. Eventually, she pulled them off and ran after him in bare stockinged feet.

Who the hell are you? What the hell are you? asked Leonard as he hurried after them.

Gideon did not return to the multi-storey car park on Dean Street. He kept on walking through the centre of town, heading west up Northumberland Street to the Haymarket.

And as he walked, the drunken teenagers who staggered into his path seemed to stagger quickly out of the way again.

Again, Leonard's gut instinct told him where they were headed.

Godley's Hotel. Last main building on the fringe of the Haymarket, overlooking the Great North Road.

Within ten minutes, Gideon had reached the main ground-floor entrance. There was good cover here for Leonard. The hotel was right next to a nightclub, and queues of punters obscured the entrance. Leonard pushed into the crowd, watched as Gideon waited for Angela to catch up. When she did, he bent down and whispered into her ear. Angela nodded vigorously, and Leonard felt a twinge of anger when he saw the pathetic look on her face; a pathetic eagerness to please. She hurried ahead through the hotel reception entrance. Gideon hung back, turning to look out over the crowd. Leonard melted back into a doorway. When he looked back again, Gideon was walking through the entrance doors.

From the shelter of a concrete cornice at the side of the reception area, Leonard watched the girl finish paying and signing for a room, while Gideon stood back in the lobby area. The girl moved to the elevators and Gideon joined her there. When the elevator arrived, they both entered together.

Leonard strode into the reception area.

There were two receptionists behind the desk. Both female, one black, one white—but both wearing the same smart red uniform. And it was plain that they were not seeing eye to eye about something. They had been maintaining a polite and professional pretence while Angela signed for the room, but now that she had gone they were returning to the argument that had been in progress before she had entered. Leonard had been sharpening up the patter that he would use, but now saw that there might be no need for it. Both women were hissing angrily at each other, now moving out of sight into an ante-room behind the reception area to sort out whatever difficulties they might have. Leonard had not yet been seen. This was his chance.

He hurried quickly over to the reception desk, swivelled the register around and looked at the last entry.

Angela Robertson. An address in Byker. Signed in for Room 432. Floor 4.

Same trick, eh, Gideon? Still no give-away information.

Quickly again, able to hear the hissing argument that was taking place in the ante-room, Leonard swivelled the register back around to its previous position and then twinkle-toed silently back across the carpeted lobby area to the entrance doors. Once safely outside again, Leonard joined the queue for the nightclub. As the queue shuffled forward, Leonard let the punters past him, maintaining his position, with a clear view of the reception area.

So now what, Greg? What the hell do you expect to find out just standing here? Did you really expect anything else to-night? Maybe you should have followed up on those other two women, just like you thought in the first place?

The same thoughts were still whirling around in his mind an hour later. The queue had dwindled, depriving him of his cover. The night air was chill now, and he wished that he'd brought some of that whisky from his top right-hand drawer. A light drizzle had begun, and Leonard was just about to give it all up when a movement in the reception area caught his eye.

A stab of fear in his gut.

Why the hell does that happen? How the hell does he do that to me?

Gideon strode straight through the reception doors. Leonard turned his back, lighting a cigarette in the protective shelter of his coat lapel. Gideon continued straight on by. Leonard watched him vanish into the night.

Another one chalked up, eh, you bastard?

He turned to look back into the reception. There was no sign of Angela.

Right! I'm going to do what I should have done in the first place.

Discarding his cigarette in the rain, he marched straight through the reception area and up to the desk. Only the black girl remained, and by the look on her face it seemed as if she had won that argument an hour ago. The white girl was nowhere to be seen.

"Can I help you, sir?"

"You have an Angela Robertson staying here. Room 432."

The receptionist checked the computerised register below desk level.

"That's right."

"She's expecting me."

"Fine."

Yeah, thought Leonard. *And if I said that I was an axe-murderer and that I was just going up there for a bit of practice, you'd probably say "Fine" again, wouldn't you?*

Leonard returned the smile and headed for the elevator.

Room 432 was on the fourth floor, last room at the end of the carpeted corridor. At this time of night, there was no one about. When he found it, he cleared his throat, straightened his tie . . . and knocked.

There was no answer.

He knocked again, with visions of Gideon's latest conquest lying there in bed; probably smoking a cigarette, probably dreaming of Mr. Hunk. Still no answer. He knocked once more, this time loud enough to echo down the corridor. Had she left? Had he somehow missed her?

"Ms. Robertson?" Another knock. "Angela?"

Leonard took his wallet-of-tricks out of his inside pocket; inserted the nail file and credit card into the computerised lock. In seconds, the door was open. Quickly he slipped inside, closing the door behind him. Now, he was in utter darkness. The curtains must be fully drawn. There was no bedside lamp to give illumination.

"Ms. Robertson?" said Leonard again. He tried to modulate his voice. The last thing he wanted was a woman awaking to find a complete stranger in her hotel room and screaming bloody murder. "Angela?" His words sounded hollow and muffled in the room. Convinced that there was no one in the room after all, Leonard groped for the light switch.

The light came on.

And when he saw what was lying on the bed, he reeled back against the door in shock.

She was naked and lying on top of the double bed. And at first, he thought that she had been burned; her body somehow reduced to a blackened, carboned, shrivelled skeleton. But the bed itself was unmarked where the thing lay. There were no burn marks on the mattress or on the floor, no scorch marks on the wall or ceiling. Fighting to keep down his bile, Leonard walked on none too steady legs towards the centre of the room, keeping one hand on the wall to steady himself. He fumbled in his pocket for a handkerchief and brought it up to his face. He gagged when he saw the face properly for the first time. He had seen some bad things in his time, but he had never, ever seen anything like *this* . . .

Now he could see the body had not been burned.

In fact, this could surely not be Angela Robertson at all. This was some kind of sick joke. Some kind of dummy placed there to play a hideous joke on the hotel staff when they came to clean the room on the following morning. A dummy made up to look like a decomposed body; a corpse that had been lying in a shallow grave for months, the skin blackened and shrivelled and barely covering the clearly defined ribs and pelvis. Skeletal hands raised like claws as if trying to ward off death. The blackened shrivelled skull screaming silently at the ceiling; eye sockets black and hollow.

Then Leonard saw the clothes lying on the floor at the foot of the bed. He saw the black leather jacket, and the familiar handbag. He stooped, keeping the handkerchief over his face and scooped up the handbag. Rummaging inside, he found a social security form: *Angela Robertson.* And an address in Byker.

Leonard dropped the handbag to the floor again and backed off to the door.

I don't believe this. I don't believe any of it. It doesn't make any sense. It's just a joke, some kind of horrible, stupid joke.

But another voice inside Leonard was saying at the same time: *That's not a dummy, Greg. And you know it. You've seen dead bodies before. Remember that girl who was buried in the woods? The one you watched the coppers dig out? It was just like that, wasn't it? And the smell . . . can you remember the* smell?

Leonard gagged and reeled to the door, flinging it open.

The door slammed behind him, but there was no one in the corridor to see as he headed for the staircase. Even if it was a joke . . .

It is a joke! It is a joke! IT IS A JOKE!

. . . he didn't want to be seen by anyone in the elevator. Hurrying down the main staircase, he opened the Exit/Entrance door at the bottom, nervously wiping his face with his handkerchief and looked out into the reception area.

There was no one behind the reception desk.

The cold night air made him feel better. The rain on his face felt cleansing. Trembling, telling himself that it was the cold air, Leonard hurried on through the night, somehow glad of the crowds of "good-timers" on the streets; feeling comfort in these crowds.

No sense. None of this makes any sense at all.

Should he go to the police? To report what? That a man and a woman had gone into Room 432. That the man had come out and the woman had stayed in the room? That he'd forced an illegal entry into that room and found . . . what? A burned and shrivelled body? Or a mutilated tailor's dummy? Or . . . ? He desperately needed to get home and think.

Even though he knew that Gideon must be long since gone from the multi-storey car park, Leonard took a different route down to the Quayside. His hands were trembling when he removed the bollard from the car park behind the Guildhall. His was the only car there. Just beyond the car park, he could see the glass frontage of a restaurant, could see the people in there sitting at their tables, talking, looking out over the river at the neon reflections in the water. All doing normal things as part of their normal lives. Suddenly, it seemed to Leonard that he'd taken a wrong turn in his own life by becoming interested in Gideon and his women. It seemed as if he'd stepped through some kind of hole in reality, stepped through to the other side. He wanted to be like those people in the restaurant now, safe in the real world . . . and not in a place of nightmares. Still trembling, he opened the car door and climbed inside. For a while, he just sat, looking out at the swirling night river, clutching the steering wheel, trying to control his shaking hands.

No sense. None of it makes sense.

Drawing in deep breaths he switched on the ignition, and checked the rear-view mirror.

"Good evening," said the figure in the back seat.

The eyes in the rear-view mirror seemed somehow luminous and despite the lurching terror that gripped him, despite the fact that he had lost control of his bowels at the sight of that familiar face, he could not look away from those eyes.

"Now tell me everything," said Gideon. "Tell me who you are and why you've been following me."

The night held more terrors than Leonard could ever have dreamed.

Chapter Five
Van Buren and Paul

"You really have no idea what this is all about, do you?" said Van Buren, leaning over the back of his chair.

Paul shifted uncomfortably against his bonds. The hessian rope had rubbed a raw patch across his neck, adding to the numerous aches and pains that he had accumulated over the last few days. The pain in his side throbbed continually. He was convinced that a rib had been broken.

"Answers, you said. Explanations."

"Very well. First of all, my name is Van Buren. That won't mean anything to you, of course. But I suppose knowing something about me—about what happened to me—might prove . . . well, illuminating."

"Can you untie me first?"

"And wait for the Rage to descend on you again? I don't think so. I want you here." Van Buren sat back, running both hands through his long grey hair.

"I was young but already rich before I married," he continued. "And I married Anna when I was very young. We were both eighteen, which will give you some idea as to how long ago that was, both second-generation Dutch, living in England. My father had developed a large heavy machinery business. Industrial plant, that sort of thing. By the time I entered the business at sixteen, we were already expanding into Europe. Anna also came from a wealthy family. She inherited a substantial legacy when we were married.

"And then, six months after we were married she met someone else.

"I never knew anything about it until it was too late."

Van Buren paused. He was staring into the middle distance, now completely lost in his thoughts.

"Too late?" asked Paul.

"She was murdered. By her lover. And I've spent the last fifty years hunting him down."

"Wait a minute," groaned Paul. "What has this to do with me?"

"Your mother died shortly after she gave birth to you, am I right?"

"What? No, of course she didn't . . ."

"She *didn't?*" Van Buren was leaning forward, towards him now, eyes gleaming. "But that's not the way it happens. That's not the way . . ."

"She was killed, God damn it! Four days ago. She was shot by some bloody maniac."

"Ah." Van Buren sat back again. "And you killed the boy who killed her?"

Paul glared at Van Buren, struggling against the ropes despite the pain.

"That part at least makes sense . . . fits the pattern."

"Pattern? What fucking *pattern*?!"

"Your father is still alive?"

"Yes, he's a vicar."

"A vicar? Interesting. I wonder if he . . . yes, I wonder . . ."

"Are these supposed to be explanations? Why don't you talk some sense?"

"It transpired that my wife had been seeing this other man for months," continued Van Buren, ignoring Paul. "And during that time she . . . sickened. I could see the change in her, never suspecting what was happening. She began to lose weight. She seemed preoccupied, fearful even. Towards the end, I had to seek specialist medical advice. All they could tell me was that she was . . . she was dying. But they didn't know how or why. It was her lover, do you see? He was killing her."

"You're not making any sense."

"He was loving her to death."

Paul groaned in frustration.

"I had been away on business. Abroad. I didn't want to go. Hell, we had only been married a short time. But my father was a very domineering man. He was expecting me to take over the business from him eventually, so I suppose that it was a sort of test, sending me over there, keeping us apart—to see how I would handle it. When I returned . . . I found her in our bed. She was dead—and what had happened to Anna didn't seem possible . . ."

The Other is coming, Paul.

"Oh my God . . ."

"What's wrong?"

"I feel . . . Oh God, I feel . . ."

You must get free. The Other is on his way to find you, Paul.

"The Voice. It's back. It's telling me . . . Oh God . . ."

"So it begins again," said Van Buren, rising from his chair.

"Good. That's exactly what I want. Exactly what I've planned."

"Let me loose, you bastard! Cut me free!"

Kill the Other, Paul. Find and kill the Other!

Van Buren moved away from him, smiling.

"God damn you! Damn you! *Damn you! Let me free!*" Paul thrashed and squirmed in a frenzy against his bonds, trying to twist around to see where Van Buren was going.

The Other is coming! Find and kill, Paul! Find and kill!

"Van Buren, you bastard! LET ME FREEEEEE!"

Paul thrashed and squirmed at his bonds in a frenzy, but Van Buren had known exactly what he was doing when he'd tied those knots. And the more that Paul struggled and screamed to be free, the more angry and frustrated the Voice became. Paul could not look behind him to see where Van Buren had gone; could only twist his head impotently from right to left in his frenzy. The rope had worn away the top level of skin around his neck and around his wrists. Blood flowed like lubricant down from his neck and began to spot his already stained shirt. Dark globules dripped from the end of his straining outstretched fingers to the floor. The agony caused by his bindings accelerated Paul's rage and the fury of the Voice.

Tears filled his eyes.

Sweat soaked his body and his blood-flecked shirt.

The Voice filled his skull: *Kill, kill, kill!*

And Paul screamed and howled like a trapped, demented beast.

Thrashing backwards, the chair on which he was sitting flipped over to the floor; now giving him only a blurred view of a wooden ceiling. The impact sent fresh waves of agony through his wrists and arms. Now, on his back, Paul was even more limited in his movements, further fuelling the fury.

The bloodlust became all.

. . . The stranger hopping down the escalator, plant holder upraised, ready to bring it down heavily on his head, smashing his skull. The man with the grey hair raising the sawn-off shotgun. The stranger whirling backwards from the escalator like some exploding, liquid sack; cartwheeling into the mall's ornamental fountain . . .

Paul shrieked out that bloodlust like a wild and wounded animal.

A car plunging into the collapsing wreck of an abandoned petrol station. A man leaping across the car roof at him, shrieking. The pain, the agony of the man's attack. The urging, the frantic driving-force of the Voice. The man with his wild face, the raised tyre iron.

Kill, kill, kill, kill.

"Van Buren, you, you, you . . . !"

The jagged sliver of glass in his hands. The man's wild whoops of pain as he doubles over, clutching his groin.

Kill, kill, kill, kill.

Tears streamed from Paul's eyes. His voice hoarse and ululating.

The tyre iron in his own hand now, raised to strike.

Kill, kill, kill, kill.

"VAN BURENNNN!!"

The stranger in the parka, stepping through the shattered gap in the French windows. Smoke curling from the barrel of his shotgun. The same wild look on that white face as . . .

Kill, kill, kill, kill.

. . . he looks around, looking for another victim. Looking for the Other. And Paul sees his father, the Reverend Shapiro, lying on the carpet covered in broken glass, his back shredded . . .

Kill, kill, kill, kill.

And the sight of his father lying there—the sight of his father's blood—did something to Paul's rage. Still screaming like a wild animal, heart pounding, sweat soaking his body, blood clotting around the bindings which held him—Paul's hate inverted. And that inverted rage momentarily became his own and not allied to the Voice within. In a moment of pure and razor-sharp hate for what the Voice had made him become, Paul shrieked and reached out from within; reached out towards that vision of his father on the littered bloody carpet, reached out and screamed for . . .

Chapter Six
Shapiro

"Paul!" The Reverend Shapiro sat bolt upright in his hospital bed, clutching at the air. The nurse who had been smoothing down the sheets at the bottom of the bed shrieked in fright, recoiling from the bed.

Shapiro's face was a white mask, sweat beading above his eyebrows. His wild, uncomprehending eyes scanned the room, trying to make sense of where he was. Now, the horrific pain in his back was registering. His eyes glazed and he lay back down on his side as the nurse hurried to him.

"Easy, easy now, Mr. . . . I mean . . . Reverend Shapiro." Her heart was hammering. She'd never seen *anyone* come out of a semi-comatose state like that before.

"My son," said Shapiro. "He needs me . . ."

"Everything's all right, Father," said the nurse, feeling uncomfortable with that word *father.* "Just relax. I'm going for Dr. Pallister. Now you take it easy, easy . . ."

Shapiro screwed his eyes shut.

My God, what's happened to me?

He opened his eyes again, staring straight ahead at the blue pastel of the hospital wall. Somewhere behind him, the ward door slapped shut as the nurse hurried from the room. The pain in his back felt like a living cancer. He raised a hand to look at it. There were black and blue bruises around the veins which he'd seen before on hospital visits to parishioners. He'd been injected there, several times. He rubbed his face, the sheer physical touch a confirmation that he was not in some kind of dream world.

Hospital.

Pain.

Shapiro struggled to rise on an elbow again, gritting his teeth to counteract the savage pain in his back. There was a faded print on the wall: two kittens playing with a ball of wool while an old Labrador looked on. Cupboards. Window. No other beds—he was in a single room. A wall clock with a date.

How long?

He struggled to remember what had happened to him. "Paul . . ."

And then he remembered the boy in the garden, the boy with the shotgun. He remembered running back to warn Paul, pushing him on ahead as the world had suddenly exploded around him.

"Dad! For God's sake help me! I need you, I neeeeeeed . . ."

"Paul!" Shapiro tried to lunge from his bed, the pain beating him back, making him gasp for air. It was Paul's voice, and it was so near that he must somehow be right here in the room with him. But that was impossible. He was the only one here.

"BeachbeachbeachbeachBEACH HUT!"

"For God's sake, son where are you?"

"SwarwellSwarwellSwarwellSWARWELL! Help me, Dad! HELP ME!"

Shapiro clasped his hands over his ears. The sound of his son's voice had stabbed into his eardrums. Now that voice was fading in a flurry of diminishing echoes. Shapiro looked frantically around the room. There was no one but him there. Had he gone mad? He slumped back again, trying to remember, trying to make some sense.

Hospital.

Pain.

Veronica!

Still unable to rationalise what was happening to him, Shapiro was suddenly flooded with cold horror. Instinctively, he knew that something had happened to his wife. Nausea began to creep from his gut as the door slapped open again, admitting a blur of white-coated personnel.

"My wife . . ."

"Just lie back, Reverend," said a man's voice. "Everything's all right." There were hands on him now, gently but firmly pushing him back down on to the bed.

"But everything's *not* all right!" he shouted gutturally. "Please! Tell me! My wife, where is my . . ."

"We're just going to give you something to relax you, Father. Don't struggle now."

"No! You can't . . . I won't . . . They need me! Paul . . ." Shapiro felt the sting of the hypodermic in his upper arm. He tried to lash out at them, but was held fast. "For God's sake, no! I've got to go to them, got to help . . . got to . . ."

"You're in good hands, Father. Just relax."

"Good hands . . . I've been so weak . . . Christ forgive me, I couldn't do anything then . . . couldn't . . ."

"All right, Nurse. What happened?"

"He just came awake with a shout. Couldn't believe it. He nearly . . ."

"Oh hell, he's bleeding again. Quick, get the covers back."

". . . I was so frightened then, you see . . . I tried my best . . . but I was so frightened . . . now, they . . . they need . . . need me . . . need . . ."

"He's out."

"Better let the police know about this."

"When do we tell him about his wife?"

"We don't. We'll let the police handle that dirty job, I think."

Chapter Seven
Gideon

They strained to listen, but there was no sound in these cata-combs. Just the faraway hiss of traffic somewhere above in a world that should care, but didn't. Water dripping, like water in a cave. The sounds of their own frightened breathing.

And then the footsteps.

Bernice shrank further back into the recess, next to the other two, merging with the shadows. Jacqueline twisted to see where the footsteps were coming from. They seemed close, impossibly close, and drawing nearer.

Yvonne began to whimper again. Bernice clamped a hand across her mouth and as Yvonne struggled to be free, to run away, the other two women held her back.

A figure moved into view. Walking slowly, head down and deep in thought. He stopped beside the Mercedes. Slowly, his head turned in their direction.

Yvonne could contain the fear no longer; her screams echoed and bounced in the underground car park like panic-stricken, terrified birds. In her panic, she had dragged the other two out into the open and into full view.

The tall silhouette remained unmoved.

"I'm sorry!" shouted Yvonne. "I'm sorry! I'm sorry! I didn't want to do it. Honest! They made me . . ." Jacqueline shook her hard, and she was silent.

Bernice stared at the silhouette, and said, "You bastard."

"Was this all your idea, Bernice?" said the shadow.

"No!" snapped Jacqueline. "It was all of us."

"Even little Yvonne?"

"Even her," said Bernice.

"I told you never to follow me. How could you disobey me after I've been so nice to you?"

"Don't turn on the charm," said Jacqueline. "Not now."

"The charm? Is that what you call it? Yes—it's a good word."

And then he stepped forward so that the faint overhead light spilled down over his face.

"Oh Jesus . . ." said Bernice.

"Don't look," said Jacqueline. "For Christ's sake, don't look."

"I told you what would happen," said the silhouette. He began to walk towards them.

"Do it, do it!" Jacqueline screamed at Bernice. "For God's sake, just do it."

And the Webley service revolver—her father's gun—was in Bernice's hands.

"Do it!"

The shadow came on.

The gunshot was agonisingly loud: stabbing their eardrums, lighting the car park in a split-second thunderbolt of blue-white. The man staggered, his raincoat flying . . . and

then froze. Dark drops pattered at the ground around his feet.
He came on.

Another detonating roar—and the shadow dropped to his
knees, hugging his midriff. He looked up, directly at Bernice,
and the gun began to lower.

"You can't have me!"Yvonne seized the gun from Bernice
as the shadow began to rise. "You can't!" The third shot
slammed the shadow backwards across the bonnet of the
Mercedes. His arms flip-flopped as he rolled from the bonnet
and slapped on to the cold concrete floor.

And as he crawled, Yvonne fired into his back, at point-
blank range.

The figure still crawled.

"He won't die," said Yvonne. "He won't die . . ."The revolver
clattered from her nerveless fingers. And then Yvonne swayed
and collapsed to the ground.

The shape continued to crawl.

Bernice tried to retrieve the gun. Jacqueline took it from
her, and Bernice did not resist.

And when the man braced his gnarled white hands on the
concrete and raised his blood-masked face to look at her, she
stepped forward and shot him in the face.

Any further shot was unnecessary, because now the man
was dead at last.

But she shot him again anyway, and kept pulling the trigger as the hammer fell on empty chambers.

Chapter Eight
Gregory Leonard and Bernice

Bernice stood at the estate agent's property display, as if examining details of the various houses for sale. She turned her face away as two customers walked past her, grumbling about high interest rates. She was wearing a tight headscarf, sunglasses, and the hem of her overcoat was dragging slightly due to the weight in her pocket.

She stood there for a long time in the reception area of Norris Estates looking at the board, staring at the promises of semi-detached suburbia, but not taking any of it in. Her careful self-control was more than frayed and she struggled to control her trembling.

She did not know what to do.

It was almost five-thirty and she was aware of the fact that the estate agent would be "shutting up shop" soon; that the few staff remaining might notice, might be able to remember what she looked like when questions were asked; might recognise that face from the television screens; might remember . . .

Damn!

Bernice turned sharply from the board and strode across the carpeted landing to a familiar fluted-glass door.

Maybe he's not here. Maybe I should . . .

She hesitated for a while, hand raised to knock on the door, heart racing.

But I don't know what I'm going to say. Don't know what I'm going to do!

Part of her wanted to turn and flee, to hurl herself down those ten flights of stairs and back into the streets again. But another part of her—a part which was filled with even greater fear—knew that she had to go on, had to do *something* about this last loose thread; this only incriminating contact.

She steeled herself to knock.

"Come in, Ms. Adams," said Leonard from beyond the door, before she could do it. His familiar voice was quiet, but the sound of it still made her flinch. Swallowing hard, Bernice grabbed the handle and swung the door wide.

The office was in darkness.

Leonard had closed the window blinds but had not switched on the light.

He was sitting at his desk, surrounded by the detritus of magazines, coffee cups and paperwork that Bernice remembered from her previous visits. Strangely, he was sitting with his back to her, away from the desk and facing those closed window blinds.

"How did . . . ?" began Bernice, and found that her voice had dried out in her throat.

"Reflection in the glass door," said Leonard, still not turning around, still with that relaxed—almost languid—tone in his voice. "Remembered your profile."

"Very professional," said Bernice, clearing her throat and stepping into the room. The weight in her raincoat pocket seemed twice as heavy now as she stood waiting for a further response. When it seemed that none would be forthcoming, she said, "Can we have some light?"

Leonard turned slowly in his swivel chair until he was facing her at last. She could see no details of the expression on his face in the darkness. But there was something about the slow deliberateness of that movement which filled her with sick horror.

Oh God, he knows . . .

Leonard leaned forward and flicked the switch on his table lamp. Instantly, he was bathed in an orange-yellow spotlight and the office was filled with sharp and angular shadows. The light from the table lamp also underlit his face, making for a melodramatic effect that reminded Bernice with great discomfort, despite the corniness of that image, of an old Bela Lugosi film she had seen as a child.

"That better?" asked Leonard and waved casually at one of the time-ravaged seats on the other side of his desk. Bernice closed the door and forced herself to march confidently to one of those seats.

"I had a feeling you would be coming."

"Yes, it's about . . ."

"About Gideon. I know."

Does he know? God, does he know? "I don't . . . don't want you to make any more enquiries."

Leonard looked directly at her. His face was somehow horribly white and when he smiled it was a grotesque caricature of the face she remembered.

"I'm sure you don't. Particularly not since you killed him."

Bernice's throat felt constricted, her chest cavity seeming to pulse with the surge of blood from her pounding heart.

"All right, Mr. Leonard. How much?"

"How much what?"

"Money, damn it! How much money do you want?"

"Nothing."

Bernice's hand tightened on the weight in her pocket.

What? "I'll give you ten thousand."

"I said I don't want anything. As I can't take your case any longer—owing to the subject's demise—there won't be a charge. Can't follow a dead man, can I?"

This is crazy! "But . . . but I contracted you. I owe you expenses. Isn't there an arrangement we can . . . ?"

"You're a nice lady. Have you heard the starlings? They always flock and mass at this time of day."

He's either playing with me, or he's gone mad.

"What's your game, Leonard?"

"Game?"

"Are you going to the police?"

Again, Leonard's face slowly twisted into that grotesque smile before he spoke.

"Perhaps he deserved to die."

"So you don't want anything? No money. And you won't even take the money that I already owe you."

"That's right."

"So I'm supposed to say 'Thanks very much' and just walk out of here and everything will be all right."

"Walk away, Ms. Adams. That's all you have to do."

"None of this makes sense."

Leonard sat back in his chair again, out of the circular pool of orange light on his desk and into the shadows. His face was a silhouette again.

"It's been three days," continued Bernice. "Three days and nothing's happened. No police report in the media. Nothing in the newspapers."

"Maybe there's nothing to report. Maybe nobody's found the body."

"In the underground car park of a hotel?"

"You'd never make a professional murderess, Bernice. How do you know that this office isn't bugged? How do you know there isn't a team of detectives in the next office, sitting there and taking notes?"

Bernice felt nausea rising from her stomach. Her skin felt cold and clammy, but a bead of perspiration trickled down her back.

"But there isn't," continued Leonard. "So you don't have to worry about that. And you don't have to worry about blackmail, either."

"No police. No blackmail. Nothing to fear?"

"Oh, I never said there might be nothing to fear."

"So what have I to fear?"

Leonard laughed in the darkness. The sound of it deeply chilled her, and now Bernice had the most uncanny feeling that Leonard was somehow *not* Leonard; the sound of that laugh seemed so different from the normal timbre of his voice.

"Fear itself," said the shadow.

Now Bernice did not know what to do. The heavy weight in her pocket felt icy cold. Her fingers let it slide to the hem of her coat pocket. Leonard's strange demeanour, the peculiar sound of his voice and his obtuse, lethargic attitude had all deeply unnerved her. She had come to his office without any real clear plan, despite the ultimate answer in her pocket, hoping that her action would result in some kind of resolution for this last, loose thread. But instead she felt hopelessly afraid, disorientated and—even as she sat there, looking at Leonard's shadowed face—deeply afraid. She tried to pull away from that fear, tried to use the anger that was also somehow inside her to solve the situation.

"Stop talking in riddles, Leonard. Tell me straight what you want."

"Like I said—nothing."

Bernice jumped up from the chair angrily. It flipped backwards to the floor with a sharp slap. Leonard remained unmoved by the sudden outburst as Bernice slammed her handbag down on to the table, pulled it open and took out her cheque book and a pen. Her fingers were trembling very badly as she scribbled out a cheque.

"All right, you bastard. Just keep speaking in riddles if you like. But you're not fooling me! This is a cheque made payable to you. Are you listening?"

Leonard did not move behind his desk.

"It's for ten thousand pounds. To buy your silence and for you to forget any other little plans that you might have had in mind. You don't know me, I never contracted you to follow anybody. And that's an end to the matter. Right?"

Bernice slammed the cheque down hard on the table. The lamp quivered, sending shadows chasing around the office wall. Still Leonard did not move or speak. Bernice grabbed up her handbag again and strode to the office door. She whirled back to him before opening it.

"That's all you'll get, Leonard. Better take it and just forget."

"There's always a price to pay for everything," said Leonard in a voice that was just too calm. "And some pay more than others."

Bernice strode back to the centre of the office, glaring at him. Trembling with rage, she reached into her coat pocket.

The Webley pointed straight at Leonard's shadowed face. Somehow, it was not heavy any more.

"I could kill you now. Do you understand? Kill you, and take back that cheque."

Leonard did not reply.

"So take it . . . and forget. Because believe me, Leonard, if you try anything I will blow your fucking head off before the police get to me."

Bernice rammed the pistol back into her pocket and backed off to the door.

The door crashed against the wall . . . and then Bernice was gone.

After a while, Leonard turned slowly in his swivel chair to face the drawn blinds. He reached for the draw-cord and opened them.

Evening was beginning to shade the city. Burning

canyons of clouds hung over the office blocks and factories. Below, the street was filled with workers on their way home or last-minute shoppers queueing for buses. Leonard stood for a long time, waiting and watching. The first flocks of starlings swirled and drifted over the city in ragged threads, but soon those threads had become thick black ribbons against the beckoning sunset. Leonard watched them come, watched them swirl and eddy around his own office block, just as he'd watched them so many times before. Tonight, it seemed, they were putting on a special and beautiful show just for him. Black chittering clouds of them were buffeting against the very window at which he was standing, rather than the windows below. Ordinarily he would have found the spectacle amazing and delightful.

The shadows of their buffeting wings filled his office as they chittered and flapped against the glass. Their sounds filled the office.

Someone had told him to despair. And so he did.

Leonard stood watching the starlings . . . and began to weep hysterically.

Chapter Nine
Yvonne

When will it change? thought Yvonne. *When will it change? Change, change, change.* The word kept repeating in her head; over and over—like some kind of mantra. And with each repetition of the word, she savagely swept the iron over

Satch's shirt; so savagely that she'd create a crease where none was before, and have to re-iron every time.

She had been working on the same shirt for half an hour now.

The television set played to itself over in the far corner of the living room next to the window—an *I Love Lucy* re-run. Lucy was having trouble with the household bills this week, but the humour was lost on Yvonne. On the small side-table next to her, Radio 1 was playing golden oldies; none of them had any sentimental attractions for her. One of the legs of that table had been smashed by Satch in one of his drunken rages. It was a table that had been bought by her mother and every time Yvonne looked at her rough sellotape-patching of that leg it made her want to cry. So she didn't look at it any more. Jason squirmed and wriggled in the carrycot beside her. Automatically, as she ironed, she would lean into the cot and mop milky gloop from his mouth with a tissue, check his Babygro for tell-tale signs, or replace his comforter.

When the front door slammed, she could hear the anger in that sound. She winced, squeezed the steam iron over a freshly made crease and patted Jason back to sleep when he spasmed at the sharp noise; small delicate fingers clutching at the air. The sound also brought a spasm of fear to her stomach.

No, Yvonne. You won't be afraid. Not now. Not tonight. Not after everything you've been through. Not after Gideon.

Satch cursed in the passageway as his foot caught in a fold in the carpet and he reeled against the wall. The curse spoke of more than faulty balance. It was the essence of a lifetime of self-frustration. Self-defeat born of self-indulgence, looking for someone to blame.

Yvonne's face was set, lips a firm tight line as she stabbed the steam iron over the shirt, creating a triangular furrow in the cotton. The living room door banged open. Yvonne reacted with anger to the knot of apprehension in her stomach. That anger swamped the fear. A lost and forgotten studio audience from the 1950s howled in enthusiastic laughter from the TV screen as Satch staggered into the room.

". . . fuckin' carpet . . ."

He leaned against the door jamb and awkwardly kicked off his shoes.

Yvonne concentrated on ironing out the new triangular furrow she had created, as those shoes landed on the sofa and somewhere out of vision. She was aware now that Satch was standing against the door jamb, just looking. In her mind's eye she saw herself putting the steam iron down, picking up his discarded shoes and saying, "Hello, sweetheart. Are you all right?"

Not today, Yvonne, she thought; biting her lip as Satch kicked the door shut and reeled to the sofa.

"Typical," slurred Satch, still watching her from the sofa.

Yvonne kept on ironing, face set.

"So what's the matter with you, then?" continued Satch.

Yvonne leaned heavily down on another freshly created crease.

"Better change that expression on your face, Yvonne. Before I change it for you."

"You're not laying another hand on me."

Yvonne was looking down at the shirt she was ironing as she spoke, but she could still see the expression on Satch's face from the corner of her eye. He was goggling at her. Then he laughed; a snort of derision.

"Oh *yeahhh*. You been watching one of those afternoon talk shows again?"

"I don't want a fight, Satch. I don't want anything to start, cos I've had enough of it."

"It's your bloody mother again, isn't it?"

"I've not been talking to anyone. I've been thinking, that's all."

"Thinking?" Satch laughed again. "*Thinking?* What with, you stupid cow? I'm the one who does the thinking in this house. If it wasn't for me . . ."

"If it wasn't for *you!*" And now when Yvonne finally looked at him, her face was white, her eyes sparkling with rage. "If it wasn't for you, I might have a decent life. If it wasn't for you, Jason might stand a better chance of growing up properly."

Satch's laughter had choked away. He was goggling at her again. Never in their married life had Yvonne spoken to him this way. And as she continued, his face began to colour as that sarcastic amusement began to turn into something else.

"Never had a job. Never *tried* to get a job, even. Social security handouts and bloody useless racing tips. Well, it's not *on* any more, do you hear me? Things have to change. These past few weeks, I've . . . I've seen things differently. My life's almost falling apart and I want things to change. You can't keep on treating me like dirt, Satch."

"Oh yeah," said Satch, face now turning a blotched purple-red. "Anything else?"

"Yes, I want you to stop drinking. I know it'll be hard for you, but I don't expect you to give it all up straight away. I've read up on alcoholism and I know that you can have really bad withdrawal symptoms if you stop altogether. So, you need to cut down—and keep cutting down until you don't need it at all. Maybe the doctor could help . . ."

"Shut the fuck up, Yvonne!"

The knot of fear began to twist in Yvonne's stomach again. She knew that she'd gone too far by the look in his eyes; the dull glazed look of brutal stupidity which she'd seen before and learned to fear. But damn it, she was *right!* Everything she had said, she'd meant—so she swallowed hard and tried to force the fear to disappear. She gripped the ironing board hard with one hand to control her trembling.

"I know what's happening," Satch continued, nodding his head in a drunken, exaggerated fashion. "There is somebody else, isn't there? Some other fella. I was right, wasn't I? Some clever fucker who's come along and put fancy ideas in your head. Has he turned you into a Women's Libber then, Yvonne? You in love with him, then? He been giving you a good shagging and promising to take you away from all that?"

Satch began slowly and clumsily to rise from the sofa.

"I'm warning you, Satch." Yvonne struggled to keep her voice from quivering. "You touch me once more and I'll leave you."

"Leave me," nodded Satch again. "Leave me for lover boy. I should have seen this coming, should have put you in hospital."

Jason began to squirm and cry in his carrycot. Satch had risen to his feet now. She could smell his beer breath, and now that knot of fear in her stomach had been replaced by terror.

"Satch . . . I'll call the police. They'll put you away."

"Not before I've sorted you out, darling," said Satch—and then he lunged towards her.

Yvonne screamed and jumped back. Satch collided with the ironing board and fell heavily to the floor, tangled in the metal struts. In the kitchen, the dogs began to bark in a frenzy. Jason was squalling now too, and the TV audience howled in laughter as Satch clumsily knocked the ironing board away and began to scramble to his feet.

His eyes were starting from his head; they seemed to bulge in and out as he sucked in lungfuls of air. His face was purple-crimson. Consumed with rage, he balled his meaty fists as he stood up again. Yvonne could hear the knuckles cracking.

"Please, Satch."

A thin gossamer thread of spittle dropped from his lower lip.

"Don't . . ."

Satch stepped towards her.

And the steam iron was still in her hand as she swung it around in an arc, catching him hard on the side of the head with a rattling *slap*. The impact sent a shiver down her arm. Satch grunted and keeled over sideways like the proverbial felled ox, his body collapsing to the sofa with the lumpen thud of a sack full of coal.

"Oh God . . ."

Yvonne stood back in horror as Satch rolled groggily on the sofa. There was a red vee-shaped mark on his temple where the iron had connected, the hair beside his ear was frizzled and burned.

"Oh no . . ."

She put the iron down safely on the coffee table, yanked the flex and plug out of the wall socket.

Satch was beginning to rise again.

The dogs howled and scratched and threw themselves at the kitchen door.

Jason was crying hard and shrill in distress. Yvonne moved towards the carrycot.

"You *bitch!*"

Satch flung himself at her, eyes glittering and insane, a wisp of smoke curling from the singed hair at his temple. Yvonne shrieked and dodged, wincing away from his grasp. His finger caught in her blouse collar, ripping it—and as Satch blundered, trying to regain his balance, Yvonne fled. Flinging open the passage door, she threw herself towards the front door. Behind her, something shattered (the vase on the TV set?) and the TV audience howled with laughter again. He was coming after her—she could hear his coarse, wordless grunt of anger. When the passage door slammed hard against the wall, she had thrown open the front door and was out on the street.

"You . . . you . . . bitch . . ."

Sobbing, Yvonne ran on into the rain.

Chapter Ten
Bernice

"Good afternoon, this is Bernice Adams with the one o'clock news. And today's headlines . . .

"Novocastria's Chief Constable, Sir Paul McManus, has appealed for help in the fight against the highest crime rates in England and Wales. In an annual report to the Joint Police Committee, he admits that the thin blue line needs more officers as well as greater public support. The Joint Consultative Committee is to organise a joint approach to central government for increased funding to tackle the problem, together with a series of campaigns to heighten public awareness . . .

"Cancer sufferers, victims of blindness and animals are to benefit from a £1.2 million windfall after Helen Goldsmith, of Brinkley Hall, Croft-on-Tyne, left the bulk of her fortune to help others. Now, twelve charities will each receive an equal share in one of the largest donations to fund-raising bodies in the North-East . . .

"Vandals have wreaked havoc at a wildlife haven over the weekend, damaging a bird-watching hide and killing several protected species. A spokesman for the Tregarthen Reserve said today, 'Local people will be as appalled as we are by this mindless vandalism, because we are trying to provide something for the local community. We will not be put off by thugs.'

"And police are this morning investigating the bizarre death of a . . ."

Oh my God. Oh no . . . oh no . . .

". . . the death of a local private investigator, based in the city centre. Mr. Gregory . . . Gregory Leonard . . . fell from the window of his tenth storey office on Grainger Street and . . ."

oh no no no no no no . . .

"Bernice, what the hell is the matter? George, what's wrong with the autocue? Bernice love, can you . . ."

"Eye-witness reports indicate that a flock of starlings in the city centre, attempting to perch en masse, appeared to be blinded by the setting sun and exploded through the windows of Mr. Leonard's detective agency . . ."

Oh God, no. This isn't happening. This can't be happening . . .

"Of course there's nothing wrong with the bloody autocue. It's her again, isn't it? Just like the last time . . ."

"Bernice, just take it easy now. Take it easy and don't . . ."

". . . in the resulting confusion, Mr. Leonard is believed to have fallen from the broken window to his . . . to his . . ."

"Are you *sure* it's not the autocue?"

"Of course I'm fucking sure! Bernice, darling. Come on. Pull yourself together."

". . . police investigations are continuing, with the advice of local wildlife and aviary experts . . .

"Returning to the recent crime statistics and the reaction of Novocastria's Chief Constable, we have in the studio tonight a spokesman on behalf of . . ."

And Bernice conducted the rest of the news without hearing anything of what she said.

Chapter Eleven
Satch

It was only when Satch had paced around the living room for fifteen minutes that he was able to think of something that would take the raw burning rage that was eating up his guts like engine fuel. Still dabbing with a wet towel at the burned vee-mark on his temple and still with the stink of burned hair in the air, he pushed the dogs away from him and moved to the china cabinet. The dogs had ceased their wild barking when he'd opened the kitchen door to let them in; they'd followed him restlessly as he paced the room, angrily kicking them out of the way. Jason, too, had ceased squalling—which was just as well for him.

Smiling, Satch opened the cabinet door and took out the "best china" that Yvonne's mother had bought for their wedding. Carefully, he placed each piece on the fake silver tray, pushed the door shut with his knee and moved towards the kitchen. The dogs brushed close against his legs, threatening to trip him.

"Get off out of it."

The dogs cringed and Jason made a small sound of distress in his cot.

Still smiling, Satch pushed the kitchen door closed behind him to prevent the dogs getting out. The smile twisted when he smelt the excrement. The dogs had been locked in the kitchen for too long. With the utmost care, Satch reached the outside door and fumbled with the latch. The tray tipped, but he quickly compensated in balance to prevent any of the delicate crockery falling to the linoleum floor.

It was raining outside. Black cataracts of water gushed in the drains, or ran silver across the cracked concrete of the back yard. A blue shimmering mist of rain haloed the bent streetlamp in the alley beyond, casting eerie light and shadow across every ragged stone wall, every darkened window. The outermost back door hadn't been locked properly; it swung slowly back and forth in the rain so that Satch could see straight out into the alley.

Smiling again, Satch steadied himself in the door-frame . . . and then threw the contents of the tray into the back yard. The crockery cracked, shattered and splintered on the concrete in a cloud of shards which fell back to that concrete again like some kind of exotic, solidified rain. Then he threw the tray like an expensive frisbee. It clattered against the outermost door. Inside, the dogs began barking again, making Jason howl

"There you go, Yvonne," said Satch to the rain. "Front door is going to be double-locked. So you can't get in there. Means you'll have to come round the back, bitch. And there'll be a nice surprise there for you when you do."

Satch moved back to close the door against the night.

But then he saw the shadow standing in the alley looking at him.

The door swung shut again, blocking his vision. But Satch was certain that he had seen the figure of a man standing in one of the doorways on the other side of the alley; just standing and looking at him. Fear traced a finger down his spine. The shadow reminded him instantly of the shadow from his dream on the night he'd had too much booze; the night that shadow had come into the house, the night that he dreamed Yvonne had turned into an ancient crone before his eyes.

The door creaked open again in the wind and rain.

But the shadow had not disappeared. It was still there, still watching. And as Satch watched, it shifted slightly to one side as the door swung shut again, obscuring Satch's view.

The unreasoning fear began to turn into anger.

"Hi you! Fuck off out of it!"

His raised voice excited the dogs in the living room. They began to jump up at the living room window; he could see their leaping shadows from the window off to his right. Their excitement made him bolder. He stepped forward and down one of the kitchen steps into the rain.

A dream. That's all. Nothing to do with this.

The door swung open again. The man had stepped out of the doorway into the middle of the alley. Satch could only see his backlit silhouette; could see the rain glinting on his black hair and his long, black coat, but could see no details of the man's face. But God, that figure looked so much like the shadow from his dream.

Satch stepped back up into the kitchen again, out of the rain and away from the figure in the alley.

"What the hell do you want then?" Satch shouted again as the door began to close once more. "Bloody Peeping Tom, is that it? Bloody pervert?"

Satch didn't like this man's confidence, didn't like the way that he just stood and looked, didn't like the way he emanated such aggression and power.

And when the man started walking towards him, Satch backed off into the kitchen and began to shout at the top of his voice.

"I'm fucking warning you, pal! Clear out of it or you'll be fucking sorry."

The dogs recognised the note of fear in their master's voice. Their excited barking grew louder, filled with aggression and menace, obliterating Jason's cries.

When the outermost door began to open again, Satch could see that it was because the stranger was pushing it open slowly with one hand. And all the time, even though Satch could see no details of the stranger's face, he knew that he was fixing him with a steady gaze.

"Another step and you're fucking dead!"

The stranger stepped into the back yard.

"I got dogs in here. Dobermans! I give the command word and they'll tear your fucking arm off, I'm warning you."

The man began to walk slowly across the yard towards him.

"Right . . . if that's the way you want it, you bastard!"

Satch turned and ran through the kitchen, his foot skidding once on dog shit. He blundered against the living room door, made a sound that could have been a laugh but was not, as the dogs began to throw themselves angrily at the other side of that door. He looked back once, to see that the shadow was stepping through the door into the kitchen— and then Satch threw open the living room door with a face-splitting grin without humour.

He yelled the command-attack word as the Dobermans burst through the door.

"Skinhead, boys! Skinhead! *Kill the bastard!*"

Chapter Twelve
Jacqueline

Jacqueline snatched up the newspaper from the doormat, just as she'd done these past six evenings. She moved back into the living room, scanning the headlines.

Rising unemployment figures. A stabbing in the west end of the city. An illegal immigrants' ring. Newcastle United Football Club beaten at home again.

Still nothing!

"Watch out, Mum!" snapped James, hastily snatching away the Nintendo game from the floor before she could stand on it.

"Sorry . . . well don't be stupid playing on the floor. Take it to the table."

"Can't. He's there," said James, meaning his brother.

"And he's not sharing," said Martin, busily gluing the tail-piece to an Action Galaxy Starfighter model.

"Tongue's hanging out," replied James in a sing-song voice.

Martin blurted in response.

Brian swung around from where he lay on the sofa, and shoved James out of the way now that he was blocking his view of the television.

New measures to combat crime. More police on the beat.

Jacqueline took the newspaper to her chair, still scanning.

Soap star visits region to open new supermarket chain.

"Stars again?" said Brian.

"What?"

"Star signs?"

"What do you mean?"

"This past week you've been grabbing that paper before anyone else has a chance. Janis got you hooked on astrology at last?"

"Oh . . . oh that. Yeah, I suppose so."

"So what does it say?"

Hastily, Jacqueline scanned the page before her. Fortune was providing no comforts today—there it was: Aries. " 'Problems you believed solved may have a habit of multiplying. Share your confidences with a stranger.' Want yours?"

"Nah," said Brian, returning to the television. "All rubbish, really."

"Like game shows?"

Brian laughed. "You're right. I don't know what I'm watching this rubbish for either. Right . . ." He pushed himself up from the sofa and started telling the boys that it was homework time; a regular hour-long ritual in the Brennan household. The usual protestations were beginning as Jacqueline returned to the newspaper and began to re-scan the headlines again.

There must be something. It's been nearly a week, and there's been nothing. How can that happen? My God, how can that happen? Someone must have discovered the . . . body (careful, Jacqueline. It's a word. Just a word) . . . by now.

Brian shoved the protesting kids out of the living room with a warning that he would be up to check on them in twenty minutes to make sure that work was under way. After that, they could watch whatever video they felt like. It was going to be hard work tonight persuading them. He closed the door behind him and Jacqueline heard him herding them up the stairs.

He wasn't hidden or anything. He must have been in plain sight, just lying there in . . . in . . . the mess. Just the way we left him.

Jacqueline shuddered and closed her eyes, not wanting to remember anything about the incident. So far, she had succeeded in banishing the worst memories of it to the back of her mind until it was like a barely remembered nightmare; but if she concentrated for too long on the whole event, it would creep back into the forefront of her consciousness in all its horrifying detail. The way she had reacted to him, the way that she had done everything that he wanted, no matter what. The way she had been *made* to want him. The way she had been made to sacrifice everything. The way her body had twisted and shrunk and grown old. It all made no sense; belonging solely to the worst, most hideous nightmare possible—where a person simply lost control of their will and their mind.

But still no news.

Jacqueline dropped the newspaper to the floor and sat for a long time, listening to the arguments upstairs and looking at her hands. She turned those hands over and over as she looked at them. They were the hands of a twenty-eight-year-old woman. No more, no less. Not shrivelled, not arthritic, not drained of their youth. She touched her face, feeling the flesh. It was smooth and unblemished, just as it had always been.

A nightmare, that's what it was. Things like that don't happen in real life.

But there was still no report in the newspaper.

The door opened again and Brian quickly re-entered, heading for the sofa. He paused. "You want a coffee or a drink or something?"

"No, I'm fine."

"Okay." Brian slumped on the sofa, groaning.

After a while, Jacqueline became aware that he was watching her. She smiled.

"What are you looking at?" she asked.

"Something special."

Jacqueline pushed herself out of the chair and crossed to the sofa, sliding quickly down beside him. He held her tightly where they lay, keeping them both snug on the sofa.

"You okay, Jackie?"

"Yeah. Fine."

"No, I mean *okay.*"

"Really, I'm fine. I've just been, you know . . . run-down or something."

"Remember that old movie you like so much?"

"Which one? There's lots."

"You know, the Noël Coward one."

"Brief Encounter?"

"That's it. Well . . . there's a scene at the end of that film. It's where that actress . . ."

"Celia Johnson."

"Yeah, Celia Johnson. It's where she comes home after she's seen Trevor Howard for the last time. And she's sitting there, thinking. And her husband looks up and says something about her having been away for a long time, but he's glad now that she's back."

Jacqueline felt a terrible cold inside. But Brian must be feeling how rigid she had become, how cold she was inside, because he was holding her even closer than before.

"Are you okay, Jackie?"

At first, she felt as if she couldn't speak. Something that was love and hurt and grief had risen from her heart. Her throat was constricted. She swallowed hard, feeling Brian holding tight.

Finally, she said; "Yes, Brian, I'm back for good."

He buried his face into her shoulder.

They lay like that for a long time, and maybe something special was smiling on them tonight because the kids stayed upstairs until they'd finished their homework.

Chapter Thirteen
Yvonne

She was prepared for the worst, prepared for the pain, when she pushed the key into the front door lock. She was soaked to the skin, her hair hanging like damp string in front of her face. She had fallen on her way home, a final indignity that had brought the tears to mingle with the rain on her cold and frozen face. Her stockings were laddered, her leg cut and bleeding.

When the key would not turn in the lock, she knew immediately what he had done. He had turned on the double-lock. A statement of intent for her benefit as well as an inconvenience. She began to cry, her hand still on the key, and wished that she was stronger, wished that she could go to someone, wished she could go to the police in spite of the trouble it would inevitably lead to . . . wished, in fact, that she was someone else.

Jason was inside . . . and he needed her, no matter how Satch would make her suffer. She pulled away from the front door, stood back in the street and looked up at the windows. They were dark. For a moment, she thought about simply knocking on the door. But . . . maybe Satch had got drunk and fallen asleep. Maybe he would awake with little knowledge of what had happened that night if he was undisturbed. And maybe if she knocked on the door and woke him up, he might still be in a surly, vengeful mood. Far better that she should take no chances.

And maybe he was just sitting in the front room with a bottle of whisky, watching television and waiting for her to show her face again?

Yvonne skipped nervously on the pavement, wiped her face, and strained to listen for the sounds of Jason crying. There was nothing. She was deeply ashamed that she had left her son alone with Satch like that, deeply ashamed that her terror of him was so great that she had simply fled. Sobbing, she began to walk towards the end of the street.

Rain whispered and hissed on the black glistening pavements.

A soughing wind swirled sprays of water against casements and dripping concrete walls.

Water made monotonous musical sounds in the drains.

It all seemed somehow stage-managed for Yvonne. All just there to deepen her loneliness and to mock her.

Reaching the end of the street, Yvonne turned down a side alley. This would lead to the back door, and she would be able to let herself in that way without any problem.

Someone was leaning against the back alley wall as she turned the corner. A man, leaning against the brick with one hand while he pissed on to the pavement with the other. She kept to the other side of the alley, but now he had heard her footsteps and turned drunkenly as she passed. He was also soaked to the skin.

"Here, sweetheart." He fiddled with his fly, making an exaggerated and obscene gesture. "Get hold of this."

Something sparked inside Yvonne. The fear and the indignity and the wet and the pain, all somehow inverted into a spark of rage at this new development.

"You bloody *pervert!*"

Stooping quickly in the rain, Yvonne took off one of her high-heeled shoes and flung it at the man. The shoe whirled end-over-end, a perfect but accidental shot. It smacked into the man's forehead, the high heel stabbing a mark above his eyebrow that he would find difficult to explain to his wife on the following morning. He grunted and slid down the back alley wall. Yvonne stormed on ahead, not pausing to retrieve the shoe.

Jason. He needs me.

Yvonne swung her back door open and stepped through into the yard.

At the creaking sound of the door, the dogs inside the house began to snarl and throw themselves at the living room window. The lamp on the top of the television set was switched on, giving that low-angle light to the room that she found so soothing. But now the two dogs were leaping and bounding up at the window, their shadows fierce and gigantic against that low orange light. Normally, they only reacted like that when Satch returned home. Although she fed them, they had little time for her. Satch's regular beatings and training had ensured in their minds that he was the pack-leader, and that she was a mere adjunct, a basic food provider. Thanks to Satch, she was living with two of the world's most sexist dogs. And if they were reacting like that, then they must think that it was Satch returning home. He was out, thank God. Out ... but what about Jason? He would never take Jason out with him to the pub (the only place that Satch ever went to), so he must have left the child alone with the dogs.

The bastard!

The dogs might belong to Satch, might have given their
ever-loving canine hearts to him, but she knew from experience that her own raised voice could have them cowering
in the corner. Brimming with anger, Yvonne strode across
the back yard to the interior back door.

And saw the milk bottle on the step.

There was a scrap of paper stuffed into the bottle-top,
sheltered from the rain by an overhanging eave of the roof.

*But we put the milk bottles on the step outside the front
door. Not here.*

Cursing silently at the dogs as they jumped snarling at the
window, casting rearing and leaping shadows over the yard,
Yvonne snatched the note from the milk bottle, anxious to
get inside and make sure that Jason was all right. The handwriting was familiar—Satch.

*You bitch. I've gone out. Jason is up-stairs. Here him
cryin bitch. And gess what. The dogs got the cimand.
Read it again. They got the CIMAND. They bin clawin at
the bedroom door. Gess how long for they get in and
then theyll get yor BASTID by that BASTID you bin seeing. You think Im fucken stupid or what? Think I dont no?
Well now yor going to PAY!!!*

The note fluttered from Yvonne's hand and was immediately whisked away on a gobbling trough of water towards
the drains. She sobbed, steadying her hand against a
running-wet wall, listening to the dogs leaping and snarling
at the window. For a moment, she considered running to
the neighbours and asking for help, then remembered all
the times that Satch and she had fought and screamed and
broken crockery. Not once had neighbours tried to inter-
vene. And on the times that neighbouring lights in windows
had gone on, and voices of concern had been raised, Satch

had made it plain that he would simply set the dogs on anyone who tried to interfere in their personal lives.

The police?

Oh God, no! I can't! Not the police. 'Cause once they're involved, there's no turning back. There's always the chance I can make things okay again, but if the police get involved, it'll be like Mum and Dad all over again. I can't . . . I just can't.

He was bluffing. He *must* be bluffing. Yvonne began to nod vigorously. This was Satch's lesson for her. He was just trying to scare her for what had happened tonight. He couldn't possibly have given the dogs the command word, because if he had, and then gone out—there was no turning back there, either. They had been trained to attack on that word. And they would stay in what Satch liked to call "killer-mode" until he gave them the counter-command. And only Satch's voice would "de-killerise" them, in another of his favourite phrases. He couldn't possibly have given that command and left the dogs in the house with Jason.

The bastard!

Gathering her courage, Yvonne pushed the back door open and stepped into the darkness.

The kitchen was pitch black, which meant that the interior door to the living room was closed. Beyond, Yvonne heard the dogs scrabbling away from the window and across the room to the interior door; alerted no doubt by the sounds of the kitchen door opening. Squinting in the darkness, Yvonne could see a faint orange line of light at the bottom of that door, could see the dogs' shadows blurring that line as they began to jump up at it. Gritting her teeth, Yvonne fumbled for the light switch.

As it came on, she strode across the kitchen to the door. *Don't let them see that you're scared. That's the way to do it.*

"All right! Pack that noise in *now*!"

The dogs were still barking furiously.

"Do you hear me? I said NOW!"

Grunting and snuffling on the other side of the door.

"Right! Back off, away from the door! NOW!"

At last, the dogs were silent.

That's the way, Yvonne.

Keeping her anger alive, not wanting the dogs to get any scent of fear, Yvonne shoved the door wide open and stepped into the living room.

At first, all she could hear now that the dogs were quiet was the distant sounds of a baby crying. It was Jason. And that part of the note had at least been true; her son was upstairs in the bedroom, locked away from the dogs, which now stood side by side in the middle of the room, quietly watching her with tongues lolling, chests heaving with the exertion of their barking and leaping. But the sight of what had happened in that room momentarily stunned and shocked Yvonne into silence and inaction.

Satch had wrecked the room before he had gone out.

The sofa was ripped and torn. Stuffing from the seats lay all over the floor. The clothes she had been ironing had been given to the dogs. They had ripped everything to tattered shreds. Even the fabric of the upturned ironing board had been ripped open. Potted plants had been thrown to the floor, the soil scattered. But perhaps worst of all, Satch had taken some of the paint tins from the cupboard under the sink and splashed them all over the living room walls; huge livid brown-red splashes. It was the paint they'd bought over two years ago so that he could do the front and back doors, but (surprise, surprise) he'd never got around to it. Now at last, he'd found a use for it.

A familiar desperate sorrow began to crush her chest. But Yvonne steadied herself, refusing to allow it to debilitate her. She cleared her throat, brought the sternness back to her voice; the only way to deal with the dogs.

"All right! Over there—both of you, in your baskets."

The dogs shifted only slightly, grumbling in their throats.

"Move it!"

The dogs stood their ground, looking at her.

And then she saw Satch.

"You drunken bastard . . ."

He was lying behind the sofa, pissed out of his mind again. She could see his arm and hand. He'd written the note to scare her out of her wits, drunk the last of the whisky (she could see the empty half-bottle lying in a pile of stuffing from the sofa) and then passed out. Cursing, Yvonne crossed the room and shoved the sofa away from the wall. Somehow, Satch had managed to get himself wedged behind it.

"Satch, wake up! Come on, see to these bloody dogs and . . ."

Now she could see that he'd managed to get that paint all over himself as he'd splashed it over the wall and furniture. It was all over his face and shirt front and . . .

. . . that was when she realised that everything she'd assumed had been wrong. And with that realisation came no shrieking panic, no hopeless sorrow. Only a numbness as she looked and looked and saw that . . .

Satch was dead.

The dogs had gone wild, attacked him and ripped his throat out.

He had tried to get away from them, and the room had been wrecked in the process. Finally, he had tried to hide himself like a child behind the sofa as they'd torn and worried at him. Now, she could see that his trouser legs were shredded. And how could she have thought that the stuff on the walls was paint? It wasn't like the colour band on the paint tin at all, now that she saw it up close. And she remembered that she hadn't wanted that colour at all, really;

had meant to return it for something else, something brighter and cheerier and . . .

The dogs inched forward, growling in threat.

The command word.

Yvonne turned away from the glistening black-red ruin of Satch's throat and the insane rictus grin on his face. She faced the dogs.

Only me, Yvonne. She seemed to hear Satch's voice from the past. *They'll only obey the "de-killeriser" when I give it. They're a man's dogs, Yvonne. Never forget that.*

"Damn you, Satch. Damn you for what you've done to Jason and me."

The dogs inched forward again, shoulder muscles taut; lips drawn back from salivating jaws.

"Nice!" shouted Yvonne, straining to keep the sound of panic from her voice. "Nice! You hear me? Nice!"

One of the dogs—Quinn—seemed to back off slightly, to pull away . . . and Yvonne breathed a sigh of relief.

But the dog had been gathering to leap. And now it flew straight at her throat with a guttural growl of rage. The other dog raced in low, aiming for her legs. There was only one other sound as the dogs moved in—the faint sound of Jason's cries. And that was the only thing that mattered now as, still wondering why she wasn't shrieking in terror or collapsing with fear, Yvonne caught Quinn by the neck and side-stepped, flinging him past her. His jaws fastened on her left hand, the teeth tearing a long gouge down the heel of her hand and forearm as the velocity of his charge carried him on. Yvonne staggered as Gus fastened on to her leg and began to worry it. Somehow feeling no pain, she watched as Quinn hit the wall hard with a yelp and fell down the back of the sofa on to Satch. The dog scrabbled to right itself, the sofa bumping against Yvonne as the other dog tore a strip of flesh from the inside of her calf. Blood spouted like spilled

Campbell's soup on the carpet. The steam iron that Yvonne had hit Satch with earlier that evening was still lying next to the overturned ironing board. Calmly, as the dog snarled and ripped at her leg, Yvonne leaned down none too steadily and picked it up.

This can't be me. I'm too calm.

Quinn was almost out from behind the sofa.

Yvonne brought the iron down hard across the flat base of Gus's skull. The dog made a *grumping* noise. She swung it hard again, and again . . . the dog hunched and bounded backwards out of reach. Quinn was struggling and writhing to get to her. Upstairs, it seemed as if Jason's cries were louder. Could he hear what was going on down here?

One at a time, Yvonne. One at a time. Together they'll kill you like they killed Satch.

There was still no pain, but Yvonne's savaged leg had become stiff and unable to support her weight. She lunged for the kitchen door, still holding the steam iron and its dangling flex. Gus rallied again, shaking his head, unsteady on his own legs and with blood smearing his muzzle. He flew at Yvonne as Quinn finally managed to get around the sofa.

Yvonne fell against the kitchen door as Gus leaped and hit her squarely between the shoulder blades. Winded, Yvonne clung to the door handle as the door swung inward. The steam iron fell from her grasp with a clatter, and Gus flew on past her into the kitchen, paws skittering on the tiled floor.

One at a time!

Quinn was bounding straight at her as she slammed the kitchen door directly into the animal's face. She felt him hit the door hard on the other side, heard him snarling furiously as he fell to the floor and began to hurl himself repeatedly back at it, trying to get through. Paws still skittering on the tiles, like a novice skater, Gus charged at her again.

Yvonne seized the only thing that she could use as a weapon: a tin of Heinz macaroni from the kitchen shelf. She threw it hard, but missed . . . and Gus seized her other leg, shaking his head savagely; teeth shearing through her flesh. She could *feel* his growling right through her body as she dragged herself across the kitchen, with Gus still hanging on. The tiled floor was sticky with blood, and Yvonne was starting to hurt, as she reached the cutlery drawer.

A wedding present.

Mum and Dad bought me a set of these as a wedding present.

This is the one we used to cut the cake.

The drawer fell to the floor, scattering knives and forks. The noise sent Quinn into a renewed frenzy on the other side of the door.

Yvonne slashed the knife downwards, back and forth across Gus's head. She couldn't help herself now; she began screaming as she stabbed; angry, frightened, wordless yells. She could feel the blade, sharpest in the house, parting the thin skin over the dog's head and muzzle—and didn't want to do this to him; some secret part of her realising that despite everything, she still had love for this animal, even if Satch had corrupted him.

Gus pulled away from her leg, shaking his head. Droplets of blood spattered the kitchen. It was as if he'd been on the beach, plunging in the sea, and was now shaking himself dry. But this sea was red. Blinded by blood, snapping and snarling at the pain, Gus began to hurl himself around the kitchen in a frenzy. Yvonne was forgotten now.

And now the calmness in Yvonne had become something else. Five years of brutality and pain at the hands of the man who had promised in church to love her. The man called Gideon who had used and abused her, who had made her want him no matter what he had done. The man who had sapped the very life out of her and almost killed her. The man who had fucked her in some dirty back alley while her child cried out in distress from a garbage bin. The man she had helped to murder. And now, Satch had set their dogs on to her, had given them the command to kill while their son cried out from the bedroom upstairs, his own safety at risk. All of these things seemed to come together inside Yvonne. Holding the carving knife like a dagger, her face white and set, Yvonne hobbled to the interior living room door where Quinn was still hurling himself against the panelling. Behind her, Gus was skittering around on the tiled floor, like some overgrown puppy chasing his tail, except that this overgrown puppy was tearing chunks out of its own flank as it span, trying to kill the pain, trying to attack the source of that pain in a blind fury.

Yvonne rested her hand on the doorknob for a moment, breathing in deeply, feeling the pain beginning to creep up her legs, willing herself not to look at the horrifying gashes in her legs or the glistening pools of red on the kitchen floor—the same floor that she had washed so scrupulously on hands and knees with Flash, a bucket and an old dishcloth not two days ago.

And what bleach do you use on the floors, Mrs. Gillis? Can't be too careful with a small child in the house, you know. Why don't you change to our brand? It's biodissoluble. That means it takes care of every stain. Mud, soup, coffee.

Blood?

"Jason . . ."

Yvonne dragged the door open.

Quinn hurtled into the kitchen, and something that Yvonne hadn't planned upon happened. The smell of blood, the sound of fury—and now Gus pounced on Quinn in his agony, finding what he thought was the source of his pain, and attacking it instantly. Instinctively also, ready to attack Yvonne, Quinn responded to Gus in his savagery. And as both dogs hurled themselves at each other, Yvonne threw herself sobbing through the door and fell on to the littered carpet. Right before her eyes: a Tommie-Tippie cup, splashed with something that could only be Satch's blood. Eyes glued to that cup, and full of rage, Yvonne kicked backwards with both ravaged legs. The kitchen door slapped shut. She squirmed to rise; controlling pain worse than Satch could ever have given her in one of their "domestics."

From where she was lying, she could see Satch's hand protruding from around the sofa. Jason was still crying upstairs.

"I'm coming, baby."

Yvonne scrabbled to her feet, and now the pain had really begun; liquid fire was coursing through her legs, like acid in her veins, as she staggered across the room to the passage door beyond the sofa. Beyond that door was the passageway leading to the front door—and immediately on her left, the small staircase leading up to the two bedrooms. Jason was in the smaller room.

Yvonne fell against the door, her head spinning. The pain in her legs was like fire now, as if she was being burned at the stake.

No, Yvonne! Don't faint! For God's sake, not now!

With the sounds of the dogfight behind her, Yvonne looked down to see that she was standing on Satch's outstretched hand. Something made her want to lean down and take that hand; take it and tuck it in neatly beside him. She didn't want it to be sticking out like that—like some tailor's dummy hand.

". . . sorry . . ."

Yvonne stepped back, sucked in a lungful of air and flung the door open. But the same fate that had thrown the two dogs at each other in the kitchen was working against her now. Yvonne heard a guttural grunting from behind her and half turned to see that the kitchen door had not been completely shut when she'd kicked it—and now the two dogs had stopped tearing into each other. Even now, Gus was nosing and clawing around the edge of the door as it began to swing open.

Yvonne stifled a scream and threw herself into the passageway, seeing the savage blur of the dogs streaking across the littered living room floor towards her as she swung the door shut. Both animals hit the door heavily as she fell backwards to the carpet. Now, they were throwing themselves at the wood panelling and Yvonne elbowed herself backwards away from it. It quivered and rattled in its frame.

"Nice! Nice!"

Upstairs, Jason's cries reached a new pitch.

This door was much flimsier than the kitchen door, and Yvonne knew it. Satch had come home in a drunken rage and kicked the panelling out over a year ago. He had attempted to patch it over, but hadn't done a good job and *God, please, God, don't let them get through, don't let them . . .*

A splinter of wood was torn away from the door in gnashing jaws, admitting a sliver of light into the hallway. The dogs were in a state of utter frenzy. Yvonne lunged forward as another splinter was worried loose and the gap was suddenly filled with a salivating muzzle. The knife was still in her hand, and she hacked at the dog's snout. Blood sprayed on the wood panelling, and now the dogs were insane in their frenzy.

Yvonne clambered to her feet and looked towards the front door at the end of the hallway.

Get help! Get the police! Now!

Upstairs, Jason's wailing was still shrill and plaintive over the savage growling and rending of the interior door.

But Jason . . .

The wood panelling *cracked*! and Quinn shoved his bloodied head through the gap. He shook it furiously, spraying blood and saliva. In seconds, the dogs would be through the door. There was no time.

Shouting one wordless yell of rage, Yvonne jerked past the lunging dog's head like a puppet with several strings cut and began to clamber up the stairs. Tears were streaming down her face now as she climbed on all fours.

"I'm coming, baby! I'm coming."

Above her, the stairs seemed to stretch endlessly; like the staircase from some terrible child's nightmare. The staircase walls tilted at her crazily as she scrabbled upwards. The entire lower half of her body seemed to be on fire now. She was climbing out of a hell pit, with the flames of hell licking at her feet. And demons were even now scrabbling up after her, wanting to seize her and drag her back in their jaws.

Climb! Climb! Climb!

The dogs were through the door. She could hear them ravening as they finally tore the wood panelling inwards and hurled themselves up the stairs after her. Somehow, she had lost the knife on the stairs as she climbed.

"No!"

Still on all fours, Yvonne reached the landing. Jason's crying and sobbing from the other side of the pink, painted door gave her the extra spurt of energy that she needed. Yvonne scrabbled at the door handle and dragged herself through, still on all fours. Breath catching in her throat in sobbing rasps, Yvonne rolled back against the door—just as the first dog reached the landing. A bloodied muzzle jammed itself in the crack as Yvonne swung it shut. The dog began to howl its insane anger and Yvonne howled right back as she threw herself repeatedly at the door. The other dog had joined in the attack—and the door began to nudge open again.

"No, you bloody DON'T!" Yvonne hurled herself back at the wood. The muzzle on the other side was suddenly withdrawn, and the door slammed shut with a solid chunking sound. Yvonne lay against the wood panelling, feeling the animals tearing at the other side. Her tears were tears of relief now, because this door to the baby's room was probably the most solid in the house. They would never get through.

"All right, you bastards," she said at last. "Don't be nice, then."

Still not wanting to look down at her legs, or at the slippery stuff that was still pooling around her on the floor, Yvonne dragged herself across the room to the cot at the far side of the room, pulling the overhead cord which flicked on the baby-light. She could see Jason now, standing on the mattress, his face red with the effort of crying, cheeks glistening with tears and mucus. He was clinging on to the cot bars, like some mini-prisoner in this jail designed by grownups. He'd begun to crawl early and had already taken his first few steps. A recent fall from the cot had necessitated the bars.

Yvonne staggered to the cot, reached in and lifted Jason out, burying his face against her breast as she turned to face the door again. Already, his cries of distress were subsiding as she murmured words of comfort. Beyond, the dogs still ravened at the door like wild animals. But they would never get through. And if none of the neighbours finally relented and telephoned for the police (and surely the noise coming from the house today *must* seem to someone to be more than just another one of their "domestics"), then she'd open the bedroom window and yell for help from a passer-by.

But for now, as Jason finally began to fall quiet, she felt so desperately tired. Shock and loss of blood were taking their toll now that she was with Jason and the dogs were safely locked outside. Her legs would not support her; the fire in her veins was crippling. Still crooning, Yvonne moved the chair beside the bedroom window. If necessary, she could open it from here and God, she did need to sit down. Still holding Jason close as she sat, she could see the main street below through the window. Although there was no one around at this time in the morning, there would be someone out there soon making their way to an early morning shift somewhere. Maybe even a policeman on the beat. They were all right. They could get help if they needed it; the police would send in someone to take care of the dogs, to take care of Jason while someone stitched up the gashes in her legs and . . .

Instantly, she slept.

And almost as instantly, it seemed, she was awake.

The fire in her legs had muted to a red, ember-hot slow burn. Her head ached terribly, and her shoulders and arms were stiff and aching. The baby-light still cast deep and irregular shadows in the corners of the room, so she knew that she could not have been asleep for long. Outside, the dogs still snarled and nuzzled at the door, now apparently aware that they could not get through the solid oak but still waiting for her to come out with a savage and chilling patience.

Jason was no longer on her lap.

Starting in alarm, Yvonne pulled herself back into an erect sitting position, heart hammering. Her panic subsided when she saw him in his blue romper suit, crawling on all fours in the middle of the room, just as she'd crawled earlier. But there was blood on the floor—her blood—and she didn't want him to be getting messed up in it as he reached the cot and began to pull himself shakily to his feet. Yvonne moved forward, ready to rise and pick him up again. Pain stabbed through her legs; much, much worse than before. The agony made her cry out, and the dogs began a renewed attack on the door at the sound of her voice. Her legs were stiff and numb. No matter how much she pinched them and massaged them, she could not move from the chair. Groaning through clenched teeth, Yvonne kneaded the cold flesh and watched as Jason steadied himself by holding on to one of the cot bars. Then he pushed himself off and began to totter across the room.

Towards the door.

"Jason!"

The impetus of his "walk" brought the child up against the wood panelling with a hollow bump. The dogs began to throw themselves at the door now, working themselves up into a renewed frenzy.

"Jason, sweetheart! Come away from the door . . ."

The child moved across the door, bracing small pink hands on the woodwork to keep himself steady.

He was heading for the doorknob.

"Oh my GOD! Jason, keep away from that!"

Yvonne braced her hands on the arm-rests of the chair and heaved herself bodily up into a standing position. She lunged forward—but her legs were like artificial limbs. They would not obey her, and Yvonne fell heavily to the floor.

The dogs on the other side of the door sounded like a hunting pack of wolves, as the small figure padded across the door and reached for the handle.

"No, Jason! No! Naughty!"

Yvonne began to drag herself across the room towards him, hand over hand, her legs a dead weight behind her.

Jason grabbed the door handle with both chubby hands and swayed there for a moment.

He's too small. He's not heavy enough. He can't open it. He doesn't know . . .

And then her eleven-month-old son turned back to look at her, still holding the door handle in both hands—and smiled.

Yvonne froze in mid-crawl, right in the middle of the

room. Now she knew that she must still be asleep in the chair with her child cradled in her arms, and that she would awake at any moment and begin to call for help from the bedroom window. Because what she was seeing now could only take place in a nightmare.

It was Jason who was standing at the bedroom door, all two feet three inches of him in his blue baby-romper suit. She could see his baby-blond curls, his plump pink face.

But those were not Jason's eyes.

They were the eyes of an adult, not a child. They were *knowing* eyes. Dark and glinting in the baby-light. She had seen those eyes before. And that recognition filled her with a terror which prevented her from crying out, prevented her from moving.

They were Gideon's eyes.

And—still smiling—the baby began to turn the door handle.

Chapter Fourteen
Van Buren

Van Buren stood at the beach chalet window, looking out through the slats of the venetian blind on to a deserted stretch of sand leading down to the sea—and then looked back over his shoulder as Paul screamed and thrashed to be free from his bonds.

Since the onset of the Rage, Van Buren had circled the chalet and climbed the surrounding dunes. From that vantage point, he could see far along the beach in both directions. No one could approach without being seen well in advance.

After the first half-hour, the boy had exhausted himself and fallen unconscious; occasionally murmuring or crying out. When he had been sure that he was unconscious, Van Buren had crossed the chalet room again, taken a length of cloth torn from old sacking and had securely gagged him, making sure that he would still be able to breathe through clenched teeth. The last thing he wanted was the boy biting through his tongue and choking on his own blood. It was important that he stay alive.

After another half-hour or so, the madness had begun again. Sitting on the bare frame mattress at the other side of the room, Van Buren had watched Paul lying on the floor where he had fallen, still securely bound to the chair. He watched as the Rage began again, watched as Paul thrashed his head from side to side, watched as he tried to scream his hate and bloodlust through the gag. And when he faded into unconsciousness again, Van Buren resumed his vigilance on the dunes overlooking the beach.

Very soon now, the Other would come.

Chapter Fifteen
Shapiro

"I'm afraid that there's no easy way to tell you this, Father Shapiro."

The man standing at the foot of the bed was dressed in a powder blue suit. His hair was white and well groomed, his

Join the Leisure Horror Book Club and
GET 2 FREE BOOKS NOW—
An $11.98 value!

— Yes! I want to subscribe to — the Leisure Horror Book Club.

Please send me my **2 FREE BOOKS**. I have enclosed $2.00 for shipping/handling. Each month I'll receive the two newest Leisure Horror selections to preview for 10 days. If I decide to keep them, I will pay the Special Members Only discounted price of just $4.25 each, a total of $8.50, plus $2.00 shipping/handling. This is a **SAVINGS OF AT LEAST $3.48** off the bookstore price. There is no minimum number of books I must buy and I may cancel the program at any time. In any case, the **2 FREE BOOKS** are mine to keep.

Not available in Canada.

NAME: _____

ADDRESS: _____

CITY: _____ STATE: _____

COUNTRY: _____ ZIP: _____

TELEPHONE: _____

E-MAIL: _____

SIGNATURE: _____

If under 18, Parent or Guardian must sign. Terms, prices, and conditions subject to change. Subscription subject to acceptance. Dorchester Publishing reserves the right to reject any order or cancel any subscription.

The Best in Horror!
Get Two Books Totally FREE!

An $11.98 Value! FREE!

✂

PLEASE RUSH MY TWO FREE BOOKS TO ME RIGHT AWAY!

Enclose this card with $2.00 in an envelope and send to:

Leisure Horror Book Club
20 Academy Street
Norwalk, CT 06850-4032

✂

face somehow curiously blank. He had introduced himself
as "Greaves, CID" and from his bed, Shapiro wondered
whether this detective inspector watched his fictional coun-
terparts on television and had taken his dress, stance and
bed-manner from one of them. Behind him, a uniformed
constable stood guard at the door. He gave a wan smile to
one of the two nurses who were also in the room. She
looked away, obviously offended. The doctor who had advised that he was "all right to talk" stood by the bed.

"Paul?" Shapiro barely recognised the cracked voice that
came from his lips.

"He's fine, as far as we know. Look, Mr. . . . I mean . . . Father Shapiro, I'm sorry there's no easy way I can tell you
this—but you have to prepare yourself for a shock. I'm sorry
to say that the young man who shot you . . . also killed your
wife in the grounds of Craigfern Hospital."

There was a silence, then, as if the CID man were waiting
for a response. When there was none, he looked at the doctor—who nodded almost imperceptibly.

"It seems that he made his way directly to the hospital
first," continued Greaves. "Your wife was out in the grounds
for some reason. It was . . . very quick. She couldn't have felt
anything."

Shapiro said nothing. He only expelled a long, quiet
breath. Greaves looked at the doctor again.

"He then came straight to your house."

Shapiro closed his eyes.

"He *knew* where to go, Father. He knew that your wife was
in that hospital, and he knew where you lived. This . . ."
Greaves moved closer to the bed and slid a glossy black and
white four-by-eight photograph from the envelope he was
carrying. "This is the young man. William Trafford. Nineteen
years old, from Northumberland. Do you know this person,
Father Shapiro?"

Shapiro looked blankly at the picture.

"No . . ."

"Look again, Father. Look closer. Are you sure you don't know him?"

"I've never seen this boy before in my life."

Greaves made an impatient sound, hissing through his teeth.

"I'm afraid I can't believe that, Father. Your son Paul killed this boy—in self-defence of course—I don't think there's any doubt about that, even though the incident will still have to be subject to the normal course of law. But your son has gone missing. Now, why would he do that?"

"I have no idea," said Shapiro in the same blank and un-emotional voice.

Greaves turned to the doctor. "Look, am I getting through to him? Is he still drugged up?"

"I'm afraid I can't give you much more time, Inspector," replied the doctor. Greaves made his impatient sound again.

"Father, the way we look at it, there must be a reason for what this boy did. He knew where to find your wife and killed her; knew where to find Paul and yourself and also tried to kill you both. Now Paul has gone missing. Are you absolutely sure that you've never seen this boy before? Have another look at the . . ."

Shapiro's eyes were closed again, his breathing deep and regular.

"That's it for the time being, I'm afraid," said the doctor.

Greaves bit down on his impatience, and then snatched the photograph back before turning from the bed.

"Maybe later this evening," continued the doctor, checking Shapiro's pulse. "But I can't guarantee anything."

The police constable opened the door as Greaves pushed

past, earnestly leaning forward as the detective inspector prepared to leave. "I'm due for a spell shortly, sir. I wonder if . . ."

"Keep wondering, Constable," snapped Greaves. "I want a twenty-four-hour watch on this man, and you stay here until someone else turns up. Understand?"

"Sir."

Later, when the doctor and nurses had left his room for the evening, Shapiro slid out of bed; stifling a groan at the pain in his back and shoulder.

They had been feeding him with solids for two days now, but he was still nevertheless very weak. He steadied himself against the head of the bed for a while, hunched over in his bed-smock against the pain, breathing carefully and listening for any tell-tale sound from the hospital corridor that someone might be on their way in. At last, he found the strength to cross the room.

Opening the door by only the slightest crack, Shapiro could see the young constable further down the corridor. He looked tired and bored, and was getting himself a cup of coffee from a vending machine. He looked as if he'd rather be anywhere than here tonight. Shapiro closed the door again carefully, and then moved to the cabinet opposite to his bed. Again carefully, he opened it. His clothes were in there—not the ones he had been wearing, which must now surely be shredded and blood-soaked, but his sober dark suit and tie. Paul had obviously brought them from home. Shapiro's face cracked into a fractured smile. He could almost hear Paul's voice. *This one's your Civilian Sunday Best, is it, Dad?*

The memory of Paul quickly erased the smile as Shapiro reached into the cabinet for his clothes. *Paul's gone missing,* the policeman had said. The sight of the empty buttonhole in the jacket made him think of Veronica. He paused, his head bowed.

No time for grief, Shapiro. Only time to do what you have to do.

Quickly and quietly, Shapiro took off the bed-smock and changed into his suit. The window on the far side of the room had a standard household window lock on it and he prayed that his room wasn't twelve storeys high. And all the time that he changed, Shapiro forced himself to think of only two things above all others.

He thought of his son's anguished cry.

And of a beach hut in Swarwell.

Chapter Sixteen
Paul

Paul awoke with a strangled scream. He was still strapped to the chair, still lying on his back and staring at the mottled chalet ceiling. He twisted his head furiously, clamping down hard on the cloth which gagged him. That cloth was soaked now, tasting harsh and bitter.

Kill! Kill! Kill!

The internal voice, that Voice of Rage, had long since given up cajoling and abusing him. Now, only one word was repeated over and over in his head as the Other drew closer by the minute. But the intensity of the Rage had exhausted Paul, despite the brief interludes of sleep. It was a sleep without refreshment; filled with nightmare shapes of the past; of violence and bloodlust and death.

Paul spasmed again, trying to arch his back and kick his legs—all to no avail. He groaned . . . and now, somehow, the Voice was beginning to fade. The same word was repeated, over and over, but it was as if that Voice was retreating from him, down a long and echoing corridor in his mind. Still insistent, but definitely going away.

Away? Paul thought, his first really lucid thought in what seemed years. *Is it really going away?*

The Voice faded into nothingness.

Paul began to sob in relief. The tension in his muscles began to slacken. The fire in his arms and wrists, and around his neck, still burned. But the rigidity in his body, the rabid reaction to that damned Voice, was dissipating. Paul strained to look over to his right and left. Movement was still limited, so he could not tell whether the man called Van Buren was still in the room.

"Wa . . ." Paul tried to shout through the gag, desperate for water. He tried again, and again. His cries sounded flat and hollow in the room. There was no answer. Either Van Buren was not in the room, or had chosen simply not to answer. Paul groaned again and tried to twist his legs. The fabric of his trouser legs had been frayed, where Van Buren had tied him. The rope still bit into his flesh, but was there really a little more give down there than before? Paul gritted his teeth. The frenzy of his bloodlust had been unfocused and undirected, but maybe he could now work on the little slack that had been created with a cool and clearer head. His bleeding flesh had acted as a lubricant. Slowly, he began to pull his right leg back and forwards against the rope, feeling that small amount of "give." And as he worked, he realised with sick horror why the Voice had finally abandoned him.

The Other must be very near.

And now, whatever it was inside that had driven Paul to seek out his enemies and destroy them, the same thing no doubt which also drove the Others to find him and each other, had realised that he would not be able to get free from his bindings. It *knew* that he was trapped and that he would be unable to free himself before the Other finally arrived and found him. He could not fight back. He was easy meat for the Other, and that was why the Voice had left him.

He was as good as dead.

Paul struggled to look around him again, but could still barely move his head. Only the ceiling and part of the wall off to his left were in view. Above all, he must not panic. But panic was very real and alive inside his gut as Paul tried to resist the temptation to fly into a frenzied writhing rage against these ropes, this time unbidden by the Voice. He closed his eyes, concentrating hard on the rope around his feet ... and yes, God yes ... there was a little give now. There was agony in his flesh where the rope bit, and Paul knew that the sliding and burning he could feel as his right leg moved back and forth was only now possible because the flesh there had been well and truly skinned. The top layer of skin had been rubbed off, and the blood was continuing to act as a lubricant as he pulled up his right leg, pulled harder, harder ... and felt the rope slip away from his shin.

Gasping with pain into the gag clenched between his teeth, Paul knew that the bottom part of his right leg was almost free. The knotted rope had slipped down to his ankle now. With a little more twisting, that foot and leg would be completely free. But he knew that he could not rest for long. When the Voice had departed, so had the instinct about the Other and the feeling of its drawing close. The Other could almost be here, and now he just wouldn't know. Paul strained again, dragging his foot up hard, groaning into the gag. With three sharp and savage kicks, his foot was free.

Paul waited for some kind of reaction. When there was none, he knew that Van Buren could not be in the room. Bracing his freed leg on the floor, Paul paused for a moment longer to gather his strength, still breathing heavily into the gag because of his exertions. The tension in the rope was gone now. It would soon be an easy matter for him to work his other leg free. Paul braced his leg and began to twist the other, causing the chair to tilt precariously. He quickly compensated for the balance, ceasing momentarily to struggle. If he was not careful, he would tilt the chair over completely, slamming his face down on the floor, with the chair on top of him. Carefully again, Paul began to ease his left leg free of the loosened ropes. This time, it was easy.

But what now?

Both legs were free, but his arms and neck were still tied to the chair. He tried to tug at the bindings around his wrists, but even though the flesh was skinned and he could feel blood on his hands from the deep abrasions, there was no "give" there. There was only one thing that he could do. He would have to brace his legs on the floor and try to flip himself over on to his front, the very thing he had just been trying to avoid. He would just have to hope that the action didn't flatten his face on the floor, the force of the manoeuvre and the weight of the chair smashing his nose and filling his mouth with blood. But maybe from that position, he could get his knees up under him, and manage to struggle to his feet from there. Quite what he could do after that, he didn't know. But at least he would be awkwardly mobile. Maybe there was something here in the chalet he'd be able to use. Some old cutlery—anything sharp. Even so, it would be difficult getting his hands on anything, but this was his only chance.

Taking a deep breath, Paul braced both feet hard on the floor and shoved.

The chair tilted and swayed, but the force was not enough. He was back where he was before: on his side, looking at the ceiling and the wall. He kicked harder again, and this time when the chair swayed over, he tried to twist his bodyweight with it, to give the swing impetus. The chair joints squeaked in protest, Paul managed to give an extra push with his right foot—and the chair flipped over.

The impact knocked the breath from his body as he was slammed face down on to the floor. He gasped for air through the gag, the restriction in his breathing almost bringing on another panic. He fought against the feeling of suffocation, screwing his eyes tightly shut and trying to control his tortured breathing. There was a strong smell of disinfectant from the floor in his nostrils.

Okay, so far so good. Now, get your knees under you and stand . . .

And now Paul realised that he was well and truly trapped. Without the necessary leverage of his arms and upper body, he could not bring up his legs the way he had intended. Just as a turtle would be helpless if upended on the beach, held down by the weight of its shell, he was now just as helpless with the weight of the chair on his back and the inability to move the upper half of his body. He strained to rise, calling out through the gag in pain, anger and frustration. But this only exacerbated his breathing problem. He beat his forehead on the linoleum floor, fighting to regain control again. At last, he strained to look up. At the far side of the room, he could see the window and the drawn venetian blind. The draw-cord clattered against the plastic tines in the breeze.

A shadow passed across the blind.

There was someone outside. Van Buren?

Or the Other?

Paul began trying to rock himself from side to side. Maybe he could simply roll himself back over, and at least get back to the position he was in before. But no matter how much he struggled, he could not move the chair. All he could do now was wait for Van Buren to come back and hope that the shadow that had passed by the window outside was not the Other. If it was, then . . .

Paul jerked his head up again as the window shattered.

The venetian blinds flapped and clattered inwards in a fractured cloud of broken glass—a fractured cloud of sparkling fragments that were somehow too bright to be just glass; fragments that suddenly blossomed like glittering flowers, erupting into a gobbling cloud of orange-black flame.

The Other!

A pool of blazing petrol sprayed the floor and wall next to the window; a hail of burning glass fragments showered the room. The venetian blinds melted and flared, spreading flame to the ceiling. Paul watched in an agony of fear and horror as the burning pool of petrol began to creep across the floor towards him. The impact of the petrol bomb on the window, and its ensnarlment by the venetian blind had prevented the hurled soda bottle from coming straight through into the room and exploding in the centre. But in seconds that flame would be on him, and all Paul could do was thrash and yell into his gag as it crept closer. Above him a tongue of flame lapped across the ceiling.

Somewhere behind him, the chalet door burst open.

Oh, Jesus . . .

Paul dropped his head to the linoleum floor once again. So this was the way it was to end. Without any real answers. Without knowing what this madness was all about. But far better to be killed outright by the Other than be eaten alive in a slow-burning, petrol hell.

Footsteps behind him. Slow and measured. And now the fierce heat on his forehead . . . and the sickening, horrifying knowledge that the Other wasn't going to put him out of his misery at all. That his enemy was just going to stand and watch and smile as the fire reached him; would stand and watch him writhe and scream in his death throes as the lake of burning petrol covered him, stripping and melting the flesh from his bones.

No!

Paul twisted his head again, eyes blinded by smoke and the fierce heat.

And now something exploded behind Paul: a roaring, detonating blast and a sound like shattering furniture.

Please God, let me be shot!

But there was no pain, and somehow Paul was still alive.

Rough hands seized one of his arms and the back of the chair. Fire swirled and tilted before his eyes as someone heaved him up from the floor into a sitting position again. Confused, with vision blurred, Paul felt someone tearing at the ropes binding him to the chair, but could not believe that someone was actually trying to save him. Now his arms were free, but he had no feeling in them, could barely move them, as the same rough hands grabbed the gag at the back of his head and cut it free. He spat it out, and now Paul was being dragged upright.

"Come on, then! Move it!"

Van Buren swam before his eyes in a blur as the man propelled him towards the open doorway. Smoke belched and roiled in the room as Paul staggered towards it. Behind him, the window wall and half of the floor area were ablaze. Paul almost tripped on something that was lying on the floor, but Van Buren still had hold of his arm and gave another almighty shove in the direction of that door. As Paul blundered out on to the sand, he realised that the "something" was a dead body: a ragged, bloody mass that—by the shape of it—was another young man. A young man about Paul's age. Another young man who had been blasted by Van Buren's sawn-off shotgun.

The Other.

And as he staggered to his knees on the sand, propelled by Van Buren's shove, Paul knew just exactly what had happened.

He had been used as bait.

Paul tried to turn, tried to see what was happening in the chalet behind him, but all of his energy had gone. More than anything, he knew that he should just get up now and run; knew that he must get as far as possible away from Van Buren.

Instead, the sand and the sea and the sky tilted in front of Paul, and he collapsed face down on to the sand.

Chapter Seventeen
Bernice

"Hello, this is Bernice Adams and here are the headlines for the nine o'clock news. Police are this morning investigating . . ."

And she was suddenly unable to read more.

"For God's sake, Bernice, not again?"

But as long as she remained silent, then the autocue would not move. She had to keep talking, to see what each of the next sickening, terrifying words were going to be.

". . . investigating the death of three people in the

Grangeover area of the town. Phillip Gillis, his wife Yvonne and their eleven-month-old baby son, Jason, were this morning found dead at their home in Hastings Street. It is believed that all three were savaged to death by their two Doberman Pinscher dogs some time last night. In a scene which has horrified and sickened investigating officers, questions are now being asked as to how such a horrifying incident could happen. The two dogs have been destroyed and . . . and a full investigation is taking place. Over now to Andrew Lane for an outside location report . . ."

"Cue outside location and, 'Go!' George, we'll need . . . for fuck's sake, someone do something! Bernice, are you all right, love? Jimmy! Get someone on the floor now before she keels over completely and . . . oh Christ!"

Chapter Eighteen
Paul

Paul awoke to a bitter and acrid smell that made him gag. It was dark, and he was aware that he was lying down. Still very weak, and with a body that ached and burned, Paul moved a hand to his face, trying to wipe away a foul taste from his mouth. Still disorientated, he could not understand how he was untied. The movement made his body sway, and something beneath him gave a faint, rusty scratching sound. He groaned, trying to focus his eyes, and then became aware that there was a shadow at his side. Unable to react now after everything that he had been through, unable to squirm away or fight back as that shadow bent down over him, Paul felt his head being lifted. He choked as water was poured into his mouth, and then he greedily fumbled for the flask. Water spilled down over his chin and on to his chest. Glorious, gorgeous water. Finally sated, and gasping for air, Paul felt the same hands pushing something soft behind his head, propping him up. At last his eyes focused.

He was back in the chalet.

Somehow, Van Buren had managed to put out the blaze.

A sheet of oily tarpaulin had been hung across the shattered window-frame. The skeletal, melted remnants of the venetian blind lay on the charred floor like the thin bones of some long-dead animal. The walls and ceiling were blackened by soot, and in the far corner Paul could see the charred legs of the overturned chair to which he had been bound. The chalet floor had a new carpet of broken and fused glass from the shattered window. The smoke had long since cleared, but the smell of burning was still thick and acrid in the air. It was the smell which had awoken him. He remembered the body lying by the door—but when he looked, it had been removed. Only a dark stain remained amidst the debris.

Paul tried to rise, realising at last that he had been placed, untied, on the bed. He did not have the strength, and sank back against the propped-up pillow as the shadow became Van Buren. Expressionless, he pulled up another of the chalet's undamaged chairs and placed it at the foot of the bed. Calmly seating himself there, he cradled the sawn-off shotgun in his hands and looked at Paul for a long time.

"There are two Others," he said at last.

The words didn't seem to make sense to Paul. His senses were still confused.

"There are always seven," continued Van Buren. "Only you and two Others are left. Can you feel the Rage?"

" . . . Voice . . ."

"Yes, the Voice. Is it with you now?"

"No . . . it's gone." Paul shook his head. At last, his senses were unfogging.

"For now, yes. But it'll come back."

"You killed someone else."

"If you move, even an inch, I'll kill you as well. Do you understand?"

"What the fucking hell is going on?"

"The man who seduced and killed my wife fifty years ago is your father."

"You're crazed. My father is a vicar, Reverend Shapiro. Parish of Beckham."

"And the four boys who have been killed so far are his sons. There are three other sons remaining. You—and two other strangers, somewhere in this country, hunting for each other or for you."

Paul tried to protest against this bizarre madman's warped stories, but didn't have the strength. Why should he protest? He too was insane, he too was a murderer. Was this some kind of communicable illness that they were both sharing?

"It doesn't surprise me that you know nothing of your parentage. Very few of his offspring do. I am only surprised that you were adopted by a man of the cloth. In the normal course of events"—Van Buren laughed softly at the word "normal"—"the child is driven to kill the adopted parents, when the Rage descends and the time is upon them. Thereafter, they will hunt each other down using that infernal instinct. And they will kill each other until only one is left. That is why you are here."

"Nothing . . ." groaned Paul. "None of this makes any sense."

"Your father's name is Gideon," said Van Buren quietly. "He is a vampire."

Paul began to laugh then. The laughter seemed to rise in a

choking fit from his stomach to his lungs, uncontrollable, despite the pain in his ribs and the searing gouges in his arms and legs. Tears began to stream down his face as he laughed, uncaring whether this madman's mind finally snapped and he finished him off, at last, with the shotgun. Finally, his laughter began to subside. Paul saw mental images of himself wielding a tyre iron, pulling the triggers on a shotgun. He saw blood and agony. And knew that he was just as insane as the man at the bottom of the bed. The laughter died in his teeth.

Van Buren had been waiting for him to finish laughing.

"Just like you," continued the man, "I've seen the films, read the books. And they're all wrong, all fairytales. Vampires are real."

Van Buren paused again, as if waiting for another outburst. Paul wondered whether he did have the strength to throw himself across the bed at him and wrestle the shotgun from his grasp. Van Buren's finger was not in the trigger-guard.

"Even the oldest Central European myths about the vampire were elaborations on the fact of their existence. Since then, popular fiction—like Mr. Stoker's famous book—and films have continued to invent and elaborate upon the nature of these . . . things. And by so doing, they've served to provide a perfect protection for them. You laugh at my mention of the word vampire, and so does everyone else. Creatures that sleep in their graves by day, and come out only at night. Creatures of the 'undead' that fear the cross, and garlic, and running water, and the rays of the sun. Creatures that suck the blood of the living, and create more of their kind when their victims die. Creatures that can only be killed by a stake through the heart. Creatures that can transform themselves into bats or wolves." Van Buren laughed quietly, shifting the balance of the shotgun on his lap. "All wrong."

Paul tried to see whether the shifting of the shotgun would make it easier for him to make a move.

"All fictional elaboration on the reality. And all welcomed by the vampire itself, because each of these elaborations shifts it even further into the realms of fantasy fiction. And with that perfect protection—the knowledge that its prey has come to regard it as a thing of the imagination—it is free to feed on us in secrecy.

"I have spent fifty years hunting for your father. When he . . . took . . . my wife, nothing else mattered to me. I used the family fortune—a considerable sum—for the sole purpose of finding him. So far, he's always kept ahead of me. In fact, I'm not even sure whether he knows I've been hunting him. But in those fifty years, I've come to know how he hunts . . . and how he procreates.

"Blood is *not* the life . . . for a vampire. In fact, it detests the taste of it. It detests the taste of all food. There is only one thing upon which it feeds. And that 'thing' is sexual intercourse. There has been a blending of myth about this creature. The myth of the vampire has been confused with the myth of the incubus. You've heard of an incubus? A creature of darkness, an evil demon which was supposed to have sexual intercourse with women while they slept. Both myths—the vampire and the incubus—were early attempts to describe this one creature which, via the sex act, is able to feed upon and drain the very life force of its female victims. The creature has been with man since the beginning of history. Always there, always secretly feeding. Where they originally came from, only they can say. There aren't many left now. They're solitary feeders, not pack animals. Each regards the other as a potential competitor, so they leave each other well alone. Somehow, the very act of sex is . . . a predation."

Keep him talking, thought Paul. *Challenge his logic. Try to calm him down enough to have a go for the gun.* "So if I'm one of seven sons of this—Gideon, why the hell are we hunting and killing each other this way?"

"Because he's dead."

"That doesn't make sense. I don't understand."

"Very well. Here is one myth about the vampire which is actually true, albeit elaborated upon, like everything else. He is immortal—or, rather, he *can* be immortal. He (and there are *only* male vampires, there are no females) has the normal lifespan of a human, but has the power to *embody*, the power to transfer his very essence, his very individuality into an offspring. Do you understand? Most of the women who are his prey will not survive his attentions. Just as the spider will devour its mate. But in the case of the vampire, the roles are reversed. In the case of the vampire, it is the male who is the devourer, the Praying Mantis. And his attack is tantamount to supernatural, hypnotic rape. But he needs to regenerate—so every twenty years or so he will impregnate seven women. Always seven, for reasons I haven't been able to work out. The number seven has always had a supernatural significance, so maybe there is a reason. Whatever—he can control his own seed, and will only impregnate when the time is right, usually when he is approaching what in human terms we would call middle age. All of the seven women he impregnates will be left to survive their ordeal. For many, the experience will prove too much. They may lose their minds as a result . . ."

Van Buren noted the way that Paul reacted to his last statement, but continued in his monologue.

". . . but in each case a baby *will* be born. And each of the seven will give birth to a son, never a daughter. The sons may grow up in the family unit to which the mother belongs. If there is a husband, maybe she will convince him that the son is his own. In other cases the child will grow up in local authority or private care. There has never, to my knowledge, been an abortion. Maybe the vampire's influence still extends to the mother throughout pregnancy. Eventually, its sons will grow and mature, unaware of their heritage. Then, when the vampire has reached the age at which it needs to embody . . . it will initiate the Rage."

Paul shifted on the bed.

Instantly, Van Buren had brought the shotgun to bear, resting the barrel on the iron frame of the bedstead with a hollow *clunk*! "Talking of which, my friend, remember what I said. I can tell that the Rage has momentarily left you, but I'll know when it begins to return. You're young and you're strong, even if you have been knocked around a bit. I'm an old man, so I'm bound to be slower. But if you make another move like that, I'll let you have both barrels."

Paul sank back against the pillow.

"The Rage," continued Van Buren, "will consume each of the vampire's seven sons. Still human, and without his powers, they will nevertheless be driven by a purely supernatural instinct to hunt each other out, and to kill each other. When only one is left, the vampire father will draw that last survivor to him. Even in his world, the survival of the fittest holds sway. He will then transfer himself to the son, embodying within his youthful shell. The son will die, will be squeezed out of existence, and the vampire will continue onwards . . . in a renewed, youthful body; discarding the shell of the old. And so the process will continue every twenty years or so. In this way, the vampire can, in theory, live forever."

"In theory?"

"The unforeseen is still a hazard, even for the vampire. Each of the seven sons may die. My own researches seem to bear out the fact that a vampire's sons are usually prodigiously healthy. Take yourself—you will not have had a day's illness in your life. Am I correct? Of course I am. But accidents can happen. And if, by some chance within that twenty-year span, all of a vampire's seven sons are killed in accidents—then the vampire himself will perish. It's taken many thousands of years, but as I've told you, there are very few vampires left. So they must be careful, and cunning. However, in the case of your own father, it seems that Gideon was not cunning enough—because something has happened to hasten the process. How old are you, boy? Eighteen?"

"Nineteen . . ."

"As I thought. The process does not begin until the sons are at least in their twenties. The Rage has begun earlier. And that can be for only one reason. Gideon has been killed."

"So you're hunting a dead man?"

Van Buren smiled. There was no humour in that smile. "Yes, he's dead . . . and infinitely more dangerous than when he was alive. Only an act of violence will kill him. And we can rule out muggings or other criminal activity, since the vampire's strength could tear any assailant apart. No, if I had to guess, I would say that he's been murdered by a particularly lucky jealous lover or victim. Careless, Gideon. Careless. This has happened to him once before, in Bucharest in the early 1950s. He let his arrogance cloud him then, and a young army officer was able to put a bayonet through him while he fed on his fiancée."

"How can he be more dangerous now that he's dead?"

"While alive, the vampire has enormous strength: both physical strength and strength of will. Another myth I've learned that was incorporated into the myth of the vampire—the Gorgon: the mythical creature that could turn a man into stone if he looked into its eyes. That relates to the hypnotic power of the vampire. Once eye contact is established, the vampire can exert its phenomenal power of hypnotism. It can will a human to do anything that it wants. All of these things it can do when alive. It will die instantly if all its sons die. It will die instantly if it is unable for any reason to embody in its last son. But if it is killed prematurely—a rare event, but it can happen—then somehow, again for reasons I can't explain, its supernatural powers become enormously enhanced. I saw it happen in Bucharest. The army officer, his family and his friends, were all wiped out in the most hideous manner imaginable. It's as if the vampire was seeking vengeance for having been denied its flesh, for being denied its ability to have sex, to feed. The very state of death enhances its power, until such time as it is able to live again, in one of its sons. It's probably in this state that some of the original superstitions developed. Only in death does it have these powers."

"Powers?"

"Let's say . . . power over the lower orders."

"So he was alive, now he's dead. Then he'll be alive again."

"You could say that."

"You're full of shit, Van Buren."

Van Buren tapped the barrel of the shotgun on the bed-frame again. "I'm indulging you, boy. For once, it's nice to be able to share what I know. Whether you believe any of it or not is matterless to me. Because in the long run, you're here to serve a purpose."

"So indulge me. What purpose?"

"I've spent fifty years hunting Gideon. In that time, I know that he's been through three cycles. One full-term, the other two—including this one—premature. I've very little money left now, so I won't be able to track him as I once was able. But now, I have the biggest opportunity that I've ever had. You see, I knew that two of the sons would be at Fernleigh

Shopping Centre on that day. I knew that they would be hunting each other down."

"So you're a clairvoyant as well as a madman?"

"I admire your flippancy, boy. I may well be mad, but I can't read minds or see into the future. But there are people who can. Believe me, I know. I spent two hundred and thirteen thousand pounds on the best. But it's a dangerous business tapping into the psychic wavelength of the vampire. That one piece of information was given to me by Karl Neuhauser. You've heard of him? No, perhaps not. What's left of him as a result of that 'tap' sits in the secure unit of a Stockholm institution, eating his own excrement. No doubt the fee he got for the job will keep him in diapers for the remainder of his days. I digress—I needed to capture one of Gideon's sons. In the event, it turned out to be you."

"Why?"

"Mohammed and the Mountain. If I can't get to Gideon, then Gideon will come to me. You're the bait. The Rage draws the sons together for the killing. I've already killed two, and you've told me that you've killed two yourself. That leaves two others out there somewhere—and you. On the premise that this Rage seems to operate on a geographical basis—the nearest are drawn to each other—then the boy who came to the chalet to kill you must have lived close. As to the other two, perhaps they're busy hunting each other at this very moment because I've taken you out of the game. The survivor—provided that they don't kill each other—will have to come for you."

"And then you'll kill him, just like the other one?"

"Precisely. Like I said, you're the bait. And you're a perfect barometer, too. The Rage in you will tell me how close he's getting. And I'll be ready for him when he does come."

"And then?"

"And then there'll be one—you. And you'll be unable to go to Gideon. So he will have to find you. And when he comes, I'll be here, waiting for him."

"So how do you kill a dead man, Van Buren?"

Van Buren laughed. This time there was a grim humour in his eyes. "Not with crucifixes, or holy water, or a stake through the heart. But there is a way."

"Which way?"

Van Buren waved the shotgun back and forth at Paul, as if he was wagging a reproachful finger. "I think you've been indulged too much. Some things I'll keep to myself."

"You really want to have the coup de grâce . . ."

"It's all I've wanted for fifty years. Believe me, it's the only thing I've been living for."

"Then in that case," said Paul, sliding his feet from the bed, "I think I'll just get up and stretch my legs."

"Get back on the bed, boy!"

"You won't kill me, Van Buren. Not if you want Gideon."

Van Buren stood up, eyes glowering. He cocked both hammers on the shotgun. "Lie *down!*"

"Because if you shoot me, then that really *does* take me out of the game, doesn't it? I'll be dead, and the other two will be out there somewhere, and you'll never find them. Gideon will have escaped from you again, won't he?"

"All right, boy. That's a good bluff. And you're right—I won't kill you. But the first thing I'll do if you don't put your legs back on the bed is to blow one of your feet off. I'm pretty good with a tourniquet, believe me. Then I'll blow off the other one so that you can't run away. Then maybe a hand . . . ?"

"Okay," said Paul, sliding his legs back on to the bed. "I get the picture."

"Put your hands back against the bedframe. I'm going to tie you again. You've been indulged enough."

"I've got to pee, Van Buren."

"Then use the pisspot on the floor beside you there."

"I've also got to eat."

"I'll feed you once you're tied. We've enough to last for some time."

"And how long will that be?"

"As long as it takes, boy. As long as it takes."

Chapter Nineteen
Shapiro

He hated the colour of the clouds—so he indicated left and began to pull over into the hard shoulder.

The driver of the car behind him jammed his hand down hard on the horn as he blared past. He had braked too soon.

Braked too soon . . . braked too soon . . .

"If only I'd had the strength to press on," he said, as the car slewed into the hard shoulder. The distance was badly judged; the car mounted the grass verge, putting the vehicle at an uncomfortable angle. He sat for a long time, looking through the splashed fly-grease on the windscreen—and felt ineffably sad about the creatures that ended their lives smeared across that glass.

Dominion over the beasts and creatures of the field.

The Biblical thought did not comfort him—and as a result, his despair and confusion began to overwhelm him. Cars flashed by him on the right. He wanted to run out into the road, flag them down and ask them if they were all right, if they were happy. The fact that he was missing cars with people who might need him, filled him with greater despair.

Crying aloud, and aware of how ridiculous he was, he threw the car door open and clambered out. More cars flashed past, more people he could help.

But not on your own.

He braced his hands on the roof and watched the cars pass.

And then, for the first time, he began to weep. That grief was not only for the events of the last few weeks: the death of his wife, the attempt on their lives, the disappearance of his son. It was also the fact that somehow, his kidnapped son had communicated to him such anguish in a "dream." That anguish was so real, so unimagined, that it brought back the horrific past.

I'd planned for this. I'd waited and planned . . .

He had not planned, and he knew it. Now, hands braced on the car roof and watching the traffic scream past, he realised that the passage of nineteen years had dimmed the horror of the past. He could see how it had happened. For a year he had been terrified, for another two years anxious. And thereafter, as Paul had grown and matured, he had rationalised what had happened. He had . . .

"Stuck my head in the sand!" he yelled at the sky, and at those horrendously tinged clouds.

Instantly, he was ashamed of himself, ashamed of losing control—and ashamed that this grief which had descended upon him had also brought with it a kind of desperate naïveté. Did he really expect an answer from the sky? After a lifetime in the ministry, was he really throwing himself open to the childhood expectations that God or his angels would give him an answer from storybook heaven? Shapiro slammed his hand down hard on the car roof, and bowed his head. Through gritted teeth he tried to steady his breathing, tried to get himself under control again.

No, by God, I won't give in to the fear.

Grief and fear had taken possession of him when he'd left the hospital. Fortunately, his room was on the ground floor, so there had been no need to shin down drainpipes, or hurl himself from a window ledge. With a few twists and turns down what appeared to be a side entrance for laundry deliveries, he had quickly made his way to the car park. He had paused only to lean against a stone eave, regaining his breath and trying to quell the pain in his side. So this was what it felt like to be shot. A bit like gallstones, really, he thought. Thereafter, it had been a relatively short, brisk walk to the hospital service bus parked outside the gates. And with every step towards those gates, he had expected the constable left on duty outside his door to come bounding down the road after him, yelling "Stop, priest!" Praising the twelve-minute service, he had stepped aboard the bus just before it pulled out of the hospital grounds.

The pain had swelled again, and with the pain came more grief. It swept over him in grey waves. Pain feeding grief feeding pain in a never-ending cycle. He could not think about Veronica if he was going to press ahead with his plan. Because if he thought too much about her, thought too much about the past and what had happened to her—what had happened to them both—then the grief and the sickening fear would rob him of any spirit to see this thing through. There seemed to be no colour in the office blocks, shops and buildings that passed by the bus window; everything seemed a terribly drab grey. And the skies overhead were also grey; the same grey clouds that he remembered on the night when . . . but he refused to think about it, pressed hard against the pain in his side and prayed that he could carry on.

Within another ten minutes the bus had dropped him off at the corner of his street. He could see the vicarage from there, expecting the front drive to be cordoned off and with officers on guard. But there was no evidence of a police presence; no panda cars parked outside, no beat policemen strolling past the trees in the front garden, looking meaningfully over the fence.

Shapiro had steeled himself, and had walked past the vicarage on the other side of the street, keeping an eye on the windows; expecting somehow to see some sign of movement. There was none. No sign that a crazed young man had attacked the local vicar and his son. Just a quiet, semi-suburban vicarage.

Shapiro had walked straight on past the vicarage. Even if everything did look quiet, he was not tempted to check the place over at any closer range, just in case. His car was parked in the drive at the side of the house: a blue Austin Maestro. He jangled the keys in his pocket as he passed. He would need the car, that was all. But that would be later—after he'd got what he really wanted.

Shapiro kept on walking until he could see the spire of his church. What he really needed was there.

No squad cars came screeching up the drive after him. No ambulance screamed around the corner, burning rubber on the road and disgorging medics waving sedative-loaded hypodermics. He could not believe his luck. Still believing at any moment that he would be stopped, Shapiro had pressed on to the church.

Procuring the car later had not been a problem. The engine had turned over immediately, and no one had leaped from the bushes to confront him as he turned the car out of the drive, on to the main road and away.

Now, two hours later, he wondered how long he would have before the police finally put out an alert on his car. So far, so good. Perhaps the bored police constable had fallen asleep outside his room, or was too busy trying to score with the nurses? In any event, he prayed that he could get to Swarwell before they caught up with him.

The pain in his side burned raw again. He groaned, resting his forehead on the cool metal of the car roof. What would he tell the police if they caught up with him, as they surely must? How could he explain flitting away like that, just as Paul had done?

Well, it's like this, Inspector. My son called out to me in a dream. Except that it wasn't a dream. His voice was as real as yours is now. No, it wasn't the drugs making me hallucinate. It was a desperate plea. And, no, I don't know what's happening to him. I just know that he's in the most terrible spiritual and physical torment, and it's the very fact that his spiritual torment is so great, I'm sure, that he was able to reach out and call to me like that. Because, you see, the way I felt when I heard his voice was exactly the way I felt myself over twenty years ago. It happened in a church—my former church before Beckham. Because I had to confront someone or something there that nearly drove me mad with fear. And the same spiritual anguish that the . . . thing . . . visited on me was there again, in Paul's voice. I thought I'd managed to forget that terrible, devouring feeling after all this time. But I haven't. And Paul was suffering it, too, when he called to me. So you see I have to go to him, have to get to him there at Swarwell before you do. Why before you do? Because I think I have one chance to save him. A chance that I could never explain to you without you thinking that I had gone insane, too. Something that even the Church authorities would not allow me to do if I went through normal channels. I have no doubt that you'll find me eventually—whether I'm dead or alive is another matter. But at least I can try, for Paul's sake, to deliver him from this suffering. Explanations can come later. There is too much at stake.

Breathing restored to normal again, Shapiro climbed carefully back into the car, holding his side. He sat with his hands on the wheel for a long time, staring at the road ahead. Swarwell could not be far away now, he knew. Just exactly how he was going to find his son when he got there was another matter altogether.

Because of the pain he could not turn around to look at what lay on the back seat. Instead, he adjusted the overhead mirror, twisting it until he could see the battered Gladstone bag.

Murmuring another prayer, he gunned the engine into life again.

The car slid out into the traffic and was gone.

Greater nightmares lay ahead.

Chapter Twenty
Jacqueline

"Oh my God," said Janis. She had been putting the day's newspapers out in their racks in the central area of the library. At last, one of the headlines had caught her eye.

"What is it?" said Jacqueline, sorting out the petty cash behind the counter for the day's fines and video rentals.

"The headlines. Some poor family torn apart by their own dogs. Oh God . . . you want to read it."

"No I don't," replied Jacqueline.

"No, really. It seems they were trained as attack dogs and . . ."

"I don't want to *know*, Janis. I don't want to know who, how or where."

Janis shoved the last newspaper into its bracket. "Can't hide from life, you know."

"I don't intend to. But I'm sick of bad news."

After a week, Jacqueline had stopped scouring every newspaper for a headline on the discovery of a certain body. Each day had been an agony of apprehension. Morning, afternoon and evening editions—but still no report. What could have happened? Surely somebody must have found the body by now? Her sleep had been fitful, broken by nightmares of what had happened to her over the last few weeks, and in particular what had happened in the hotel's underground car park. Whenever possible she had tuned in to the local news headlines, but one afternoon had caught Bernice Adams on screen. The sight of her had been a sudden and sickening shock. Jacqueline had quickly switched off, and avoided that channel ever since. On the hour, every hour she was able, she had tuned into the radio news.

Nothing.

At last, Jacqueline had refused to listen to any more radio news, had refused to look at a newspaper. She had to believe that at last her nightmare was over, and that she was free to take up the reins of her life again; free to rebuild. Both Bernice Adams and Yvonne Gillis must surely be doing the same thing. It was a difficult, anxious struggle. And the horror inside, the knowledge that she had killed—had murdered—surfaced at vulnerable times to haunt her, along with the fear of discovery and reckoning. But she had to learn to reconcile what had happened. It was vital. (*But where is the* body? *Be quiet, Jacqueline. Be quiet.*)

As Janis returned to the desk-counter to help her, Jacqueline thought back to the night when Brian had made his *Brief Encounter* reference, and of the way things had been since then. He *knew*, she was sure of that. But he had not pressed her, and was satisfied that now everything was back to normal again. She wondered if she could have done the same had the positions been reversed, and then knew that she probably would not have been able. There had been a lucky escape for her. It was time to forget and go on. But for the time being—no newspapers.

"You don't read the newspapers any more, do you?" asked Janis suddenly.

Jacqueline was startled. It was as if she had been reading her mind.

" 'Course I do," she said defensively, concentrating on the petty cash.

"No you don't. You don't even ask me what your stars are any more."

Jacqueline kept her head down. She could feel a flush beginning, and hated herself for it. Janis's hand on her shoulder startled Jacqueline again, and then she said, "We never did talk about it, you know."

"I know," said Jacqueline, still counting.

"Are you over it yet?"

"Yes . . . it's all finished."

"And Brian . . . ?"

"Everything's okay, Janis. For a while it was bad, but now I've sorted everything out. Talking about it isn't going to help me. But thanks."

Janis squeezed her arm, seemed about to say something else, then uttered a sound of exasperation. "Oh no . . ."

"What?"

"They're early."

Jacqueline followed Janis's eyes, and saw what seemed to be a small army of children being led in unruly double-file towards the main reception area. Through the glass reception doors, she could see Mrs. Pooley marshalling, directing and cajoling her class through the library gates towards the main building.

"They're not supposed to be here until nine thirty," said Jacqueline.

"You know Mrs. Pooley. She'll keep them out there standing to attention until it's time."

"The heck with it. I'll just go and let them in."

Mrs. Pooley, deputy headmistress of the local primary school, and fighting off retirement age as hard as she could, marched ahead of the children to meet Jacqueline at the main reception. This was to be the latest in several "field" trips from the school to the library, and both women were aware of Mrs. Pooley's enormous energy potential. An hour and a half with thirty seven-year-old kids would have had Janis and Jacqueline on their backs gasping for air. Not so with Mrs. Pooley. Clichéd words like "matronly" always seemed to spring to mind when she was around. Jacqueline watched as she strode ahead to meet her, hand outstretched. She was wearing a huge floral dress which, spread out on the ground, would have surely held a picnic for five. Grey curled hair and with cheeks the colour of polished apples, Mrs. Pooley exuded clean living and robust good humour. Jacqueline felt her energy wilt when the deputy headmistress seized her hand in a firm handshake.

"Well, here they are!" The announcement was almost a shout. "And keep in double-file!" The last announcement to the children behind her without turning her head and all in the same breath. "We'll stay out here until you're ready, if that's all right."

"Oh no, bring them in. We're ready."

"Champion!" stated Mrs. Pooley, her favourite remark when things were going well.

Jacqueline held the door wide and was instantly engulfed in a wave of excited seven-year-olds.

"Back!" Mrs. Pooley lunged to the reception door and Jacqueline skipped aside to prevent herself from being flattened against the glass by Mrs. Pooley's not inconsiderable bulk. Instantly, it seemed, the wave of children had retreated before her. "And QUIET!" Instantly again, the chattering ceased. "What . . . I say *what* . . . does the sign above this door read?"

"Creswell Library, Mrs. Pooley," said several uncoordinated voices in response.

"Exactly. And what do we expect in libraries?"

"Books," said a ginger-haired boy below her. Mrs. Pooley glowered and he was silent.

"Apart from books, what do we expect in a library?"

"Quiet, miss," said a small female voice from the crowd.

"Quiet. That's right. Quiet. Now, there'll be other people inside expecting us to be quiet and that's what we'll be. Won't we?"

"Yes, Mrs. Pooley," said the crowd in falsetto.

"*Now*, we can go in . . ." said Mrs. Pooley, sweeping the door wide. Jacqueline barely escaped being pinned again and headed back to Janis at the main reception area. Another familiar customer had come in through the side entrance and was returning his book to Janis when the commotion drew his attention.

"Good morning, Mr. Gough."

"Well it has been so far," replied the tall, stooped man in the raincoat and cap. His brown face was creased like old leather; wire-rimmed spectacles made his eyes look twice their size. "They're not coming in here, are they?"

"'Fraid so," said Janis as Jacqueline joined her behind the desk-counter.

"Oh, bloody hell."

"Today's pension day, Mr. Gough. We try to pick a day for the school that's going to disrupt as few of our customers as possible. You know we don't get many people in today."

"Not the point, is it?" said Mr. Gough. "*I'm* here, aren't I? Hope they're going to be . . ."

"Yes they are going to be quiet," announced Mrs. Pooley as her troupe scuffled into the reception area. "Aren't we, children?"

"YES, MRS. POOLEY!" rejoined thirty kids, making Mr. Gough wince.

"Another bloody school project, I expect." Mr. Gough watched with resentment as Mrs. Pooley shepherded the children towards the large tables in the library's central area.

"Dinosaurs," replied Jacqueline.

Mr. Gough looked at her as if she'd just sworn at him. Shaking his head, he headed for Fiction M to R. And when Janis looked up at Jacqueline to show the mirth she was trying to suppress, Jacqueline began to laugh, too. And something about that laughter seemed good and healthy and cleansing. In that moment, it seemed to her that life could continue as normal and the nightmare of the past could be banished, given time.

Mr. Gough chose an 87th Precinct novel and settled miserably in one of the battered armchairs, glowering over the top of his book as the children began raiding the natural history section for books on prehistoric life; returning to the central tables to work on what seemed to be a classroom frieze. Mrs. Pooley settled on one of the high-backed chairs; organising and instructing like some beneficent matronly general.

And everything seemed to be going fine, until Janis went to help retrieve some books that had fallen from one of the tables, returned to the desk-counter again and said, "Your friend's back."

"Which friend?" asked Jacqueline, without looking up from her work behind the counter.

"You know the one I mean, Jackie." Something about Janis's tone seemed odd.

"What are you talking about?"

"The guy that you're not supposed to be seeing any more."

Something deep inside Jacqueline turned cold. When she spoke again, her voice seemed strangled and alien.

"Where?"

"His usual place. Sitting out there on the cemetery bench, pretending to read and looking straight at you."

"He can't be . . ."

"Well he bloody *is*!" said Janis with disapproval.

Quickly, not wanting to give in to the fear which had begun to cramp her stomach, Jacqueline left the desk-counter and hurried over to the glass windows which gave a view out into the cemetery. Two children carrying books almost collided with her. She steered them back to their table, turned and looked out towards the cemetery bench.

Please God, please God, please . . .

It was empty.

Jacqueline braced both hands on the window and breathed out heavily in relief, misting the glass. Suddenly, Janis was at her side.

"There's no one there," said Jacqueline.

"Of course there is. I've just seen him . . . oh." Janis moved around her to get a better look. "But, I don't understand. I *saw* him—but he couldn't possibly have vanished so . . ." She twisted her head around to scan the cemetery. But there was no one in sight. Only the willows swaying in the breeze and a rippling curtain of grass around the gravestones and the monuments.

Jacqueline remembered what had happened in the

bushes behind that cemetery bench and moved quickly away again.

"I could have sworn I saw him out there," continued Janis. "Can't understand how he could have left so quickly. Look, Jackie, I'm not going to interfere but . . ."

But Jacqueline had moved off again back to the counter-desk, preoccupied in her thoughts . . . and now another pile of books had fallen to the floor. Mr. Gough was glaring again, so Janis went to assist.

Keep cool, Jacqueline told herself.

Two other customers had come through the main reception: a woman in her mid-thirties and an older woman with a shopping bag who might have been the younger woman's mother. They were standing at the counter waiting to hand over books. *Janis was mistaken, that's all. Gideon is dead, you know that.* Jacqueline took the books, managing only a fragile smile.

"Can't you do something about those dogs outside?" said the younger woman as Jacqueline took the books. She had an attractive face, but had managed to disguise it well with hair that was tied savagely back and out of sight, and what seemed to be a perpetual frown. Her mother shuffled in a circle behind her, examining her shopping trolley for unknown reasons.

"Dogs?"

"Outside. Milling around. Look half wild to me. Thought they were going to bite Mother."

Why just your mother? thought Jacqueline uncharitably. *Why not you as well?* Ashamed of her pettiness, she said, "I'm sorry to hear that. Where are the dogs?"

"Outside the main entrance. Milling around. Half wild they look to me. Should ring the council or somebody."

Jacqueline managed a tight smile. "I'll have a look outside."

"Should do, too. Kids about. Never know."

As the two women moved off into the library, Jacqueline skirted around the reception-counter, back to the glass reception area.

Steady, Jacqueline. Don't allow yourself to get worked up. Janis was mistaken. Cool it down, keep calm . . .

Jacqueline was still telling herself these things, giving only a perfunctory glance out of the main doors on to the flagged area comprising the walk-up entrance and the small patch of open parkland beyond. But what she saw there was enough to make her double-take.

There *were* dogs out there. About half a dozen of them . . . and something about them made her stand and watch for a long time.

The dogs were large. At least two German Shepherds, but the rest were mongrels, with mixed breeds that she couldn't place. All told, there were about seven or eight of them. In itself nothing new to see dogs wandering around housing estates during the day. There had even been an item in the local newspapers recently (during the time when she *had* been reading newspapers) expressing concern about dogs being left to their devices during the day while their owners went out to work. One child had been attacked and bitten by two dogs, leading to public outrage, which now seemed to have died down again.

But something about these dogs seemed strange.

And for a while, Jacqueline couldn't work out why. When she did, she shrank back from the glass frontage, feeling uneasy.

The dogs were spaced evenly across the park and the walkway. About twelve or thirteen feet between them; and they were all moving slowly towards the main reception, heads down but looking towards the library intently. There was something methodical about the way they were approaching, never once looking to one side or being distracted by anything else, be it the sounds of distant traffic from the main road, birds in the trees or each other. There were no people in the park. And as they moved slowly towards the library, slowly but gradually narrowing the gap between them, Jacqueline suddenly realised what they looked like. She had seen something like it on a television documentary only recently.

The documentary had been about Timber Wolves.

And the dogs out there looked like a hunting pack.

Slow, methodical, moving closer . . . until it was time to make a run.

Don't be so stupid, Jackie. Janis has managed to get you spooked.

Refusing to pay any more attention to what was patently her stupid imagination becoming overactive again, Jacqueline moved back into the library. Janis was working behind the reception-desk again. But as Jacqueline looked at her, she could see movement out in the cemetery, through the windows behind her where the kids and Mrs. Pooley were working.

And as Janis looked up again to say something, Jacqueline walked quickly on past her without saying a word. Janis's face clouded.

A blonde girl with her blouse completely unhitched from her skirt tugged at Jacqueline's arm as she passed.

"Are there any more books on . . . ?"

"They're all out on the shelves, sweetheart," said Jacqueline, without looking at the girl and moving straight on ahead to the floor-to-ceiling windows which she had just been looking through earlier. Something about those shapes was making her give in to stupid, nervous fears. She just had to see and then she could rationalise it and forget about . . .

There were more dogs out there in the cemetery.

They were moving slowly through the gravestones and monuments, heads down but looking up at the library as they came. Creeping through the swaying long grass. She could see that, just like the "pack" at the front, these were all large dogs. And there could be no doubt about the slow, methodical and stealthy way they were approaching the library through the cemetery, all equally spaced again like those at the front.

They were stalking.

This is ridiculous, thought Jacqueline. *It doesn't make any sense.*

Beyond the dogs, she could see the cemetery bench. Still empty.

Janis's words came back to her: *Your friend's . . .*

A coldness seemed to grip her then. A sick feeling inside began to spread to her limbs; her hands began to tremble.

Moving quickly away from the windows, Jacqueline hurried to the emergency fire exit. Above the side bar was a narrow window, giving a restricted view of the concrete ramp and walkway at the side of the building and the path that led down to the cemetery gates. There were no dogs there. And Jacqueline used that fact to quell her mounting fear and to try and bring some kind of rationality back. Yes, there were dogs out there but no, they couldn't possibly be moving in on the library like some wild hunting pack. Mongrel dogs on council housing estates simply didn't behave like that. All right, there had been instances where children had been bitten, but never an instance of dogs banding together and hunting down people. The thought was too ridiculous to contemplate. She was tired, had been through a lot and if those dogs out there were going to cause a nuisance, why then she would simply pick up a telephone and . . .

Two dogs padded slowly and stealthily into sight around the corner of the library and on to the path.

Heads down, ears back. They could see her now as she stared at them through this side window. And as Jacqueline watched, their lips drew back. Even through the glass pane, she could hear them snarling as they moved slowly and methodically down the concrete path towards the window.

Jacqueline suppressed an involuntary cry, turning it into a nervous cough which was unnoticed by the children at the table behind her. She stepped back quickly from the window, hand at her throat, pulse racing. Jacqueline turned to look at the children, still drawing their frieze pictures of dinosaurs, now engrossed. She watched Mrs. Pooley guiding one little boy's drawing hand as he tried to fill in the teeth on a Tyrannosaurus Rex. Mr. Gough was deep into the 87th Precinct now, paying no heed to the kids. Janis was back at the reception desk, concentrating on her work. The intense woman and her mother were browsing through "Historical Romance" . . . and the normality of everything she saw there somehow convinced Jacqueline now, without the shadow of a doubt, that the nightmare had returned—and that something very, very terrible was about to happen.

She could not move.

Could not speak.

And as Jacqueline looked, she saw that the same blonde girl with the unhitched shirt who had stopped her moments ago was standing apart from the others at the floor-to-ceiling windows overlooking the cemetery. She was standing silently and still, staring out through the windows with an engrossed expression. She looked back at the other children as if to say something, then changed her mind, her fascination returning to the windows again.

Jacqueline knew that she had seen the dogs.

But still she could not move, even when the little girl began to walk slowly towards the windows, again throwing back a glance to the others. Jacqueline saw her mouth the words: *"Mrs. Pooley"* . . . deliberating whether she should bring this strange sight to the attention of the teacher. But Mrs. Pooley was too busy to notice, and the little girl's attention returned to the windows again. Her mouth was open now as she reached the glass, entranced.

And Jacqueline wanted to shout, *"Get away from the window, little girl!"* But her voice was frozen in her throat. Now, in her mind's eye she could see the child suddenly panicking, suddenly screaming . . . and sending the others into a mad, screaming, disorganised panic. *Move, Jackie! For God's sake, move!*

The little girl pressed her face and hands close up against the window, her breath fogging the glass.

Overwhelmed by horror at the inevitability of what must happen, Jacqueline was somehow able to move now. But her legs were leaden, her every movement in slow motion, as she pushed herself on across the library floor.

She reached for the little girl, a movement that seemed to take an agonisingly long time.

The girl looked up as Jacqueline's shadow fell over her.

"Have you seen . . . ?" began the girl, and Jacqueline looked out past her to the cemetery.

Just as the encircling dogs, no more than twenty feet from the library, burst into a frenzied race directly at the window.

Jacqueline seized the child and swept her away from the glass.

The first dog hit the window head-on in a snarling blur. The window cobwebbed where the child's face had been pressed only a moment before, the sharp and jarring sound of the impact shocking the other children into an instant silence.

Jacqueline backed off from the window as it was suddenly filled with a frenzy of snarling animals, hurling themselves repeatedly at the glass. She whirled as the animals at the fire exit and the main entrance began to hurl themselves wildly at the windows. Wild, leaping shadows filled the library in an instant. The savage sounds of the snarling filled the building. The girl in Jacqueline's arms suddenly burst into wailing tears.

And then the children panicked and began to scream.

At the main reception area, Jacqueline heard the crashing splinter of glass and looked up to see that the dogs at the front of the building had somehow broken through the main reception door in a headlong rush. Glass was still flying in a glittering spray as a struggling blur of shadows streaked into the reception area. But Janis was moving now, uncomprehending, with her face white and set as she swept a pile of pamphlets and other printed literature from the table at the side of the interior library door leading out into the reception. With one quick motion and an astonishing display of desperate strength, she upended the table and rammed the laminated top surface against the glass door—just as the mad, scrabbling mass of dogs hit that door hard from the other side. Janis's reflection juddered and danced in the glass as the dogs hurled themselves at the door, leaping high and uttering the furious howling rage of a wolfpack. Janis put her weight grimly to the table, forcing it to keep the interior door closed as she turned her head back and yelled . . .

"Jacqueline! For fuck's sake, DO something to help!"

. . . as the windows overlooking the cemetery cracked and splintered, and the first dog—a Labrador mongrel—struggled through the gap, barking madly, blood streaming from its flanks where the glass had sliced its skin . . .

. . . and the children ran screaming and howling in all directions as . . .

. . . Mr. Gough stood up, still holding his 87th Precinct book and with his magnified eyes now wider than ever, as . . .

. . . the dog charged across the library floor, snapping and hurling two children to the floor as it came straight on, suddenly leaping straight through the air in a frenzy at Mr. Gough. The dog hit him squarely on the chest, and both man and dog catapulted backwards over the library armchair in a tangle of limbs. Mr. Gough began to shout wildly as the dog worried at his throat, fastening on the forearm which he threw up to protect himself and . . .

. . . a sheet of window-glass slid from the frame where other dogs were struggling to push through, exploding on the polished floor in a spraying ice-cloud.

"JACQUELINE!" yelled Janis again from the juddering reception door.

"CHILDREN STAND STILL!" commanded Mrs. Pooley, now recovering from the shock. Already, some of the children were running to her, sobbing.

And two more dogs were through the shattering windows and loping across the floor.

Unaware that she had broken from her frozen panic, unaware that she had made any kind of decision, unaware of what she was going to do . . . Jacqueline was suddenly running around the central library tables, pushing children behind her; now leaping over the struggling forms of Mr. Gough and the attacking dog, seizing a pile of dinosaur books from the tables and hurling them at the first dog streaking across the library floor. The books connected, knocking the dog—a German Shepherd—to one side on its haunches. But it quickly regained its footing and flew at the severe-looking woman and her mother crouched by the Romance section. The other dog kept on coming, but Jacqueline had no time to block it, no time to try and prevent it from attacking a little girl as she headed directly towards the shattering windows where the pack still leapt and twisted and tried to push in past the jagged glass framing the opening.

There was a mobile shelving unit to the side of the window. Only four shelves high, on coasters, and containing the recently returned fiction which was ready for putting back on the shelves. She hurled herself at it, putting all her weight behind a two-handed shove. The momentum made her stumble and she fell against the unit, but the fall provided the extra-needed impetus. The coasters on the unit pivoted and squealed—and the miniature bookcase flipped over backwards against the windows overlooking the cemetery. The remaining glass shards in the jagged window-frame aperture shattered. A dog with its front leg trapped between the unit and the wall began to howl frenziedly. But the other dogs were slammed back outside on to the library walkway in a scrabbling, barking mass.

Jacqueline regained her footing, the sounds of snarling and screaming now even more intense behind her. Knowing that the other two dogs had found victims, she jammed her body hard against the shelving. It wedged awkwardly in the shattered window-frame. Flecked, foaming muzzles tore and snapped around the gaps between the shelving and the window-frame aperture. Jacqueline kicked at them, screaming back angrily—turning to see Mr. Gough rolling over and over on the floor, now with his own arms around the attacking dog in a crazy embrace as it thrashed and scrabbled with him on the polished floor.

The German Shepherd had taken down the severe woman and was worrying at the back of her head as she screamed, her arms and legs thrashing on the library floor, while her elderly mother flapped ineffectively at it with both hands. The Labrador had seized a little girl, knocking her down, and was dragging her past one of the shelving units by the leg, shaking its head and worrying into the flesh. The girl was in shock, she was making no noise—and Mrs. Pooley was suddenly bearing down on the dog with an expression of high, blushing rage.

Jacqueline ran towards the German Shepherd, shouting. But it would not be scared off and began to drag the woman across the floor while the older woman continued to flap at it. She just had time to see Mrs. Pooley swooping down on the Labrador to grab it around the middle, hauling it bodily from the child on the floor. In a massive bear-hug, Mrs. Pooley charged into the library wall like some floral-bedecked sumo wrestler, slamming the animal hard against the brickwork . . .

. . . and Jacqueline was right on top of the German Shepherd now, seizing it by the scruff of its neck with both hands to haul it away from the woman. But the dog still clung tight, shaking its head, jaws still clamped shut so that Jacqueline was now hauling the dog and the screaming woman across the library floor while the other children screamed and ran and milled in confusion around her. The older woman collapsed to the floor, her face ashen, breath ragged. Still shouting wordless yells of anger at the animal, Jacqueline shifted one hand and gouged her fingers into the animal's right eye. The dog howled, whipped away from the woman on the floor and sank its teeth directly into Jacqueline's forearm. There was no pain—only a great fear and a great rage, as the German Shepherd twisted, ripping her flesh. Jacqueline clung on to the dog's ruff as it twisted and scrabbled on the polished floor. She clung on grimly, trying to keep her balance, but it was no good. The weight of the struggling animal threw her off balance and Jacqueline fell awkwardly to the floor. The dog twisted again, her grip on its ruff was lost . . . and now the animal darted again, diving directly on to Jacqueline's chest and worrying in close to bite at her throat. Jacqueline cried out again, jamming her hand into its mouth. The dog bit down and Jacqueline grabbed its lower jaw, as blood flowed.

From somewhere behind her, there was a heavy grunt and slap as Mrs. Pooley charged the struggling Labrador against the brickwork again. This time, the dog began to utter a ululating howl of pain. At the emergency exit, the main windows were holding fast even though dogs were leaping and jumping at the glass, howling to get in. Somewhere in the snarling, furious, mad zoo that had once been a library, Mr. Gough was cursing and swearing in pain. Chairs toppled. Books scattered.

At the main entrance, Janis tried to jam the table further into the door-frame. But when she moved away from it again, the glass doors began to judder open under the onslaught from the other side. Crying out in anguish and frustration, looking back at the horror that was taking place in the library, she was forced to throw herself back at the table, pinning the door shut. She could see the telephone on the reception desk, not fifteen feet from where she crouched, but she could not leave the door. She prayed furiously that another customer would come and see what was happening as . . .

Jacqueline rolled on top of the squirming, snarling German Shepherd. Her arms and face were covered in her own blood. Sobbing, she pinned it with her weight, gouging for an eye and seeing a knot of children cowering back from her beneath one of the bookcases, fists jammed into mouths, faces white as . . .

. . . Mrs. Pooley rammed the Labrador hard against the wall again. Held lengthwise, the animal was almost as tall as she was. This time, something *snapped!* and the dog was instantly silent. She staggered back, blood spotting her torn frock, face still crimson with rage and exertion. The dog fell awkwardly to the library floor in a tangle of furred limbs. It was dead.

"The day room, Mrs. Pooley!" shouted Jacqueline. Beneath her the German Shepherd screamed and struggled to be free of her body, snapping upwards at her neck. "Get the children into the day room!" The woman and her mother lay still on the library floor.

And Mrs. Pooley moved forward to help them, then saw the children milling around or cowering in shocked confusion.

"QUICKLY!" yelled Jacqueline again, and from the main entrance, Janis began to shout, "Come on, come on, come *on*!"

Mrs. Pooley began to gather the children. Still terrified, they had been waiting for an adult to tell them what to do and ran sobbing eagerly to the one they thought could rationalise this terrible nightmare and make things all right again. The German Shepherd squirmed and made savage sounds beneath Jacqueline as Mrs. Pooley swept the children on ahead towards the main reception where Janis still held the table against the door. Mrs. Pooley turned back again, ready to help her but Jacqueline snapped "No! Go on!" and the teacher turned and began to push the kids on ahead. Somewhere behind the fiction bookcases, Mr. Gough still cursed and cried out, his attacker snarling and growling furiously. Mrs. Pooley swept the children on past the shaking bookcases, and Jacqueline tried desperately to slam the dog's head on the floor to knock it out. It was a mistake. Her grip on its lower jaw slipped and the dog's head was free again in a spray of her own blood. The dog twisted from her and Jacqueline just had the chance to see with horror that the dogs outside were managing to push the bookcase unit away from the shattered window-frame. Already, it was juddering aside as furiously barking, foam-flecked muzzles were pushing in around the gaps.

And then the German Shepherd dog was on her again.

Its teeth ripped the blouse away from her throat and the jaws sank deep into her shoulder.

"Oh *Christ!*"

Jacqueline struggled to get hold of the dog's mane again, but now it seemed as if the strength was sapping from her as the dog ripped and worried and blood ran in her eyes and . . .

"In there! IN THERE!" yelled Janis, pointing furiously to the day room door. Mrs. Pooley threw it open and began to usher the children quickly inside. Janis looked back to where Jacqueline struggled and thrashed with the dog. It was standing astride her now, snarling and ripping, and Janis yelled, "For God's sake, Mrs. Pooley, get the kids inside and help me over here!" She had to have help at the reception door, she had to have Mrs. Pooley's weight to keep it closed so that she could help Jacqueline and . . .

"No, no, no, no . . ." she began to moan, as Mrs. Pooley swept the kids inside and Janis looked back to see that Jacqueline's hands were flapping down helplessly to her sides, as the dog worried at her and began to drag her body across the floor like downed prey towards the mobile bookcase, which even now was juddering further aside as dogs struggled to get through into the library and . . .

My sweet Brian, thought Jacqueline. *Martin and James*.

She was not in the library any more. She could still hear the screaming and the animals growling and snarling. But she had been somehow taken away from that insane animal house now. She was dimly aware that something was shaking her, but all she could think was . . .

I never realised how much I love them. Will they be able to look after each other if I'm not there? I'm stronger than Brian. Will he be able to manage if . . . ?

There was new screaming in the library now.

And that screaming seemed to be bringing Jacqueline back again. The thing that was shaking her was somehow being pulled away. Her vision focused, and with that focusing came the feeling that she was being dragged back down a long tunnel to where the library existed. There was pain here, great pain.

Real time stabbed into furious activity again.

Something alive, something with flashing jaws and teeth, something savage with fur, was being dragged from her. Pain ate like acid into her shoulder and neck, and she was back in the library again as she rolled over and retched on to the polished floor and then . . .

Oh no, what's Geraldine going to think when she comes to clean and finds that I've . . .

. . . Jacqueline twisted again as the air was filled with the savage growling of the beast that had been attacking her, mingled with the foulmouthed curses of Mr. Gough.

She rolled again, her neck and shoulder shrivelling in pain as she righted herself and looked back to see . . .

. . . that Mr. Gough was somehow there, and had dragged the German Shepherd from her. He was astride it now, holding it pinned to the floor by the neck and wielding something high above his head, ready to bring it down.

It was a book.

A thick, brown text-book, seized from one of the shelves as he'd staggered to her rescue. And Mr. Gough smashed that book down time and time again on the dog's skull, each blow accompanied by a foul epithet. Amazed, Jacqueline could see that Mr. Gough was still wearing his magnifying spectacles, but that one of the lenses had been smashed. His face was streaked with blood, his coat and sleeves in tatters. And that book kept rising and falling, rising and falling as she tried to get to her feet.

The German Shepherd uttered an un-doglike *squawk!* Mr. Gough called it an effing-cee.

And it was still at last. Its tongue protruded from its jaw, its eyes glazed doll-like and lifeless as it rolled away from him in a spreading pool.

"All right, miss. All right . . . all right . . ." said Mr. Gough, and tried to rise to help her. But his strength was gone, and all he could do was slide back on to his backside in the dog's blood, still holding the thick, battered book. Now, Jacqueline could see that the severe woman and her mother were helping each other up, staggering away towards the day room.

The wedged bookcase banged, rattled and juddered. One of the dogs was wedged into the gap now, snarling furiously. It was nearly through into the library and very soon the others would follow.

Jacqueline was suddenly flying backwards through the air. She watched as Mr. Gough receded from her, still sitting in the dog's blood and gaping in amazement at her. And as she watched, flying backwards, she saw Janis suddenly running past, rushing to Mr. Gough, seizing him by the shoulders like a sack and dragging him unprotesting after her over the polished floor.

"You're all right, all right . . ."

But this time, it was not Mr. Gough's voice, but Mrs. Pooley's voice, coming from above and behind her. The teacher had rushed back, seized her and was dragging her towards the day room, now overtaking the badly bitten woman and her mother. Jacqueline felt like a child in Mrs. Pooley's embrace. She did not have the strength to resist or assist, but might as well have been the weight of a child in Mrs. Pooley's grasp.

In a whirl, Jacqueline saw the day room ceiling tilt before

her, heard the sounds of children sobbing and crying . . .
and then Janis was right before her, dragging Mr. Gough into
the day room after them as the old woman tottered through
the doorway, helping her daughter.

"Quick, quick, quick!" yelled Janis. "They're into the library again!"

And Jacqueline leaned weakly against a wall, watching
from a sitting position as Mrs. Pooley threw herself against
the day room door, slamming it shut.

Instantly, the door began to judder and rattle.

Dogs howled and threw themselves at the door from the
other side.

"They can't get through," said Janis grimly, "we're safe."

Quickly, she hurried to Jacqueline, wincing at the wound
in her shoulder and around her neck. Dazed, Jacqueline
could see that she was struggling to keep back tears as she
dabbed at her shoulder with a handkerchief. Finally, she
balled it up and wadded it tight against the wound. "Hold it
there, Jackie. It's okay, we're safe now. Will you be all right?"

Jacqueline nodded. Her hands were trembling uncontrollably as she propped herself against the wall, now looking at
Mr. Gough beside her. He was breathing heavily, his face
smeared in blood, and still clutching the thick library book
which he had used to save her.

". . . kids all right . . . ?" he breathed.

The dogs still threw themselves at the day room door in
a rage.

"Everyone's fine," commanded Mrs. Pooley. "We're all al-
right, aren't we, children? Yes, we are." The teacher moved to
the little girl who had been savaged, holding her tight and
examining her wounds. The child was silent and white-
faced, obviously in shock. Unwrapping her scarf, Mrs. Pooley wrapped it around the girl's scalp; now moving quickly
to the boy who had been attacked by the Labrador. "Olivia's

fine and Barry's fine. We're all fine . . ." The severe woman sat against the far wall, her face as white and expressionless as a Victorian porcelain doll. Her mother waved her hands over her face, fanning her.

The dogs continued their onslaught as Janis dialled 999 and asked for the police.

"And we're all going to sing a song that we learned in school. Shall we do that? Sing a song for Mr. Gough and the ladies? Yes, we'll sing . . ." And Mrs. Pooley burst into full song: "Row, row, row your boat, gently down the stream . . . come on, Gillian, Tommy . . . merrily, merrily, merrily, merrily, life is but a dream . . ." And gradually the sobbing began to stop as the children joined in the song, drowning out the sounds of the pack on the other side of the door.

Janis was at Jacqueline's side now, checking the wound, and saying, "The police are coming. An ambulance is on its way."

"What made them *do* that . . . ?" muttered Mr. Gough, and Janis moved over to him, checking his own ravaged and bloody shirt front.

I know, thought Jacqueline, *God help me, I think I know*.

Mrs. Pooley waved her arms enthusiastically, occasionally dabbing at the blood which smeared her face in a bizarrely dainty manner. The song filled the room, drowning out the dogs.

"They'll have to shoot them or something," said Janis . . . and then Mr. Gough began to laugh; slowly at first and then louder.

"I don't believe it . . ." he managed to splutter at last.

"What?" asked Janis, afraid that the shock of what had happened might have turned his mind.

Mr. Gough held up the bloodied and battered book in his hand.

"Do you know what this is? Of all the books I could grab?"

Janis took it from him and read the lettering on the spine. *"Dog Obedience for Beginners."*

And now Janis began to laugh too, laughing until the tears streamed down her face. Mr. Gough grimaced at the pain the laughter was giving him, but continued anyway, unable to stop. And although the children did not appreciate why the adults were laughing, some of them began to laugh too as they continued to sing.

But even when the sounds of a police siren reached their ears, Jacqueline could neither laugh nor cry.

Chapter Twenty-One
Bernice

Bernice paced the floor for a full twenty minutes and was on to her third vodka before she finally decided to switch on the television. The local current affairs programme only ran for half an hour—there were still ten minutes left.

She knew that it was a mistake—but she had to see.

And, of course, the first thing she saw was Traycee Manton reading the latest local news. Traycee, with her extravagant perm that looked like candy floss under the studio lights. Traycee, with the lip gloss. The woman who had been one step behind her all the way, just waiting to slide into her place, no matter who she had to sleep with to get there.

Bernice finished her drink and banged another rattling handful of ice into the glass, pouring in another house-measure of vodka. She pulled her dressing-gown cord tight around her waist as if she was knotting a noose and sat heavily on the sofa in front of the television.

"I am *not* being bitchy, Traycee. But you have no style. No presentation, and you shouldn't be flashing your capped teeth in a beaming smile when you're telling the audience about child-abuse in an orphanage."

The vodka burned inside, but it was providing no comfort.

"And your real name is Mary McNaughton, born in Doncaster. Nothing wrong with that name is there, Traycee?"

Bernice listened to the summary of the news headlines and then to the usual "What's On In Town Tonight" slot. As the production crew credits began to roll over the signature tune which she had come to regard as *her* signature tune, Bernice watched without hearing anything that was said. When the advertisement "flash" brought in the first soap powder flag-waver, she reached for the remote-control and switched the television off.

She watched the blank screen for a long time.

And the little voice inside began to speak to her again. The voice that was her voice, and was saying things that she'd rather push out of her mind altogether. But still the voice persisted.

I could feel it while I was sitting there in front of the cameras. I could feel it while the autocue ran. And I couldn't look at the screen any more.

"Stop it, Bernice," she told herself, hugging herself tight as a profound chill gripped her. She felt as if she had been submerged in deep, ice-cold water. Her teeth began to chatter. A knot of fear curdled in her stomach.

Because I knew . . . knew . . . that he was out there.

Watching me.

Listening to me.

Knew that he was waiting for me to read those news items . . .

The fear gripped tight. She wanted to retch, wanted to scream out her fear. But she refused to give in, swirled the ice in the glass and took another deep swallow.

"He's dead, Bernice," she told herself sternly. "And dead people don't come back."

She wished that she hadn't spoken those words now. They hung in the air, flat and heavy and unconvincing. After everything that had happened to her, to the others . . . she knew that, somehow, Gideon was out there. And that he would be unforgiving for what they'd done.

Something scratched on the apartment door.

Bernice suppressed a moan of fear, freezing where she sat, one hand clutching her glass and the other taking a fistful of the sofa cushion. Somehow, she could not turn her head, could not cry out.

And then the door was open, and Samantha bustled through with two carrier bags of shopping.

"Hi, it's me. Can you believe those elevators? Broken down again. What was it the supervisor was saying about 'Quality Service?' Reckon we should try and negotiate the lease down, like you said . . ."

Bernice let out a deep breath, sinking back on to the sofa again.

Samantha pushed the door closed with her foot and took the shopping bags into the kitchenette, hauling them up and putting them on one of the benches.

"Not funny carrying this lot up the stairs."

"You . . ." Bernice's voice felt cracked. She took another sip of vodka. "You should have buzzed me from downstairs. I would have come down and given you a hand."

"What?" said Samantha, looking through the serving hatch. "In your dressing-gown? I don't think so. Much too bohemian. Wouldn't do to let the fans see you like that. Fancy pizza or salad?" Samantha flicked one of her red braids from her face as she threw off her jacket on to a nearby chair.

"How about a job?"

"Didn't have the pizzas you like, but I got the next best thing. You know, the McCain things . . . what?"

"They've fired me."

Bernice didn't turn to look at Samantha as she spoke; she just sat staring at the blank television screen. It seemed appropriate somehow that the screen should be blank. After all, once upon a time she had been centre-stage on that screen between six and six-thirty every evening. Now that screen was blank, just like her career. She heard Samantha walking slowly out of the kitchen, felt her presence at the side of the sofa.

"What?" she asked again, in a quieter voice, filled with disbelief.

"Like I said," replied Bernice, drinking again. Why the hell wasn't the alcohol working? It seemed that she just couldn't get drunk tonight. "They fired me."

"But they can't just do that. I mean . . . why? How?"

"Well, they haven't said it in as many words. But I've been sent home to recuperate. They seem to think I'm under some kind of nervous strain. That I haven't been myself. But what they really mean is that they're not renewing my contract."

"But they *can't* do that, can they?"

"My contract's up for renewal. Of course they can. I screwed up one too many times. You should have seen me."

"You know I don't like to watch you on television."

"Never were besotted by my showbiz image, were you?"

Samantha slid down on to the sofa next to her and put an arm around her shoulder.

"And Todd wants to see me about the play at the Phoenix Theatre," continued Bernice. "He's been contacted by their agents. They want to rediscuss the terms of the contract. So you know what that means . . ." Bernice couldn't find further words. She could feel the anguish building up inside to a danger point. Samantha cradled her head in her arms.

"They can't do that! It'll be all right, you'll see. Todd's the best agent you've ever had, you've always told me that the best thing you ever did was to split from those other bloodsuckers. Look what he's been able to do for you since then. You've got nothing to worry about. I can feel it."

"Maybe you could get me a job next to your desk in the building society," said Bernice. The joke was unconvincing and broke the floodgate inside.

They stayed on the sofa for a very long time.

The blank television screen stared back at Bernice throughout.

Later . . . much later still . . . Bernice awoke in bed, and prayed that it had all been a dream from which she was now awaking. But the reality was a crushing truth, making her turn face down into her pillow, groaning in anguish.

Love had not soothed or taken away the pain.

At first, she had felt herself incapable of sleeping, but the vodka had done its work, tipping her over into a dream-place. But this dream-place seemed far from safe, filled with vague and threatening shadows. In her dreams, she was running from someone . . . running down a dirty side-street, strewn with rubbish and lit by the neon of seedy club entrances. She turned to look back over her shoulder as she ran, and saw a tall shadow step out into the centre of that alley. It was a tall and horrifyingly familiar silhouette. And it strode after her, through the clouds of steam rising from pavement grilles, long coat flapping.

Bernice had screamed then, unable to move as the impossibly tall shadow swept towards her.

And the shock of that dream scream had propelled her from sleep.

Bernice reached out in the bed.

Samantha was not there.

The taste in her mouth was foul as she pulled back the quilt and slid her legs out on to the floor. There was sharp pain behind both eyes; her hangover had already started to gather momentum, and needed to be stopped before it could get a real hold.

"Solpadeine," muttered Bernice, and rose groggily from the bed, crossing the darkened room carefully to the door. The drugs were in the bathroom; obviously where Samantha had gone.

Bernice checked her watch as she moved yawning into the living room . . . halting abruptly when she saw Samantha sitting on the upholstered chair next to the window. The small reading light on the side-table cast its orange glow over her as she sat perched on the edge of the seat, reading something.

And something about the way that Samantha was sitting seemed wrong.

All wrong.

She looked tense, sitting on edge, and in the light of the reading lamp, Bernice could see her face as she moved further into the living room. That face was white and set. Samantha never looked up at her as she moved closer, even though she must have heard Bernice coming out of the bedroom.

"What's the matter, Sam?"

Samantha still didn't look up. She seemed to be reading a loose-leaf paper, or a letter. When she turned it over, something about the trembling of Samantha's fingers, something about the dry crackling of the paper which seemed somehow much too loud, filled Bernice with an anxious nausea.

Something bad had happened . . . something bad *was* happening, as Samantha continued to read.

"What is it? What are you reading?"

Samantha looked up again, and even from the other side of the room, Bernice could see that she had been weeping.

"What is it, love?" Bernice began to hurry across the room to her.

"Don't!" snapped Samantha, and the sharpness of her voice stopped Bernice in mid-stride. Quietly, this time, she said, "Just don't . . ."

"But what is it? What have you got?"

"It's a letter," said Samantha with difficulty. Her voice was dry and strained. "A letter addressed to me."

"Who's it from?"

"Can't you guess?"

"No, of course I can't. Just tell me, for God's sake."

"You've been lying to me all along."

"Samantha! What on earth are you talking about and who . . . ?"

"Don't LIE to me! It's from *him*. Your lover!"

"What are you talking about? I don't . . ."

"It's from Gideon!"

The name was like an electric shock to Bernice's nervous system. She could feel the scalp at the base of her neck tightening, could feel the prickling chill on her arms and legs as the blood sucked away and adrenalin swirled. The taste of terror was in her mouth, metallic and coppery.

And she could only stand and watch as Samantha pulled herself out of the upholstered chair, the savagery of her movement bumping the chair against the table lamp, so that wild angular slabs of orange light and deep shadow swung around the room. She crumpled up the letter and threw it at Bernice's feet, now giving in to tears and turning her back on her, stumbling to the floor-to-ceiling windows overlooking the night-glittering expanse of the city. She stood there, trying to control her tears as Bernice was finally able to move, stooping down unsteadily to pick up the letter.

Her hands could barely straighten out the paper.

Heart pounding, she first saw the unfamiliar crabbed handwriting and prayed that this was some kind of dream, or joke.

"It was pushed under the door," said Samantha. "I saw it on my way to the bathroom. It was addressed to me."

Leonard? thought Bernice. *Blackmailing me?*

But Leonard was dead.

Bernice began to read the letter then.

Dear Samantha: 'Splendide mendax e in omne virgo. Nobilis aevum.' Gloriously deceitful and a virgin renowned for ever. (xi 35 of the Danaid Hypermestra) 'Quis fallere posit amantem?' Who could deceive a lover? (iv 296) Quotations to consider while you read the following . . .

And each of the listed obscenities which followed also contained times, dates and locations. Sometimes a hotel, on other occasions a motel. And on each date, there was a graphic, obscene and humiliating description of all that had occurred. The handwriting was angular and crabbed; as if the person writing it had been having trouble controlling the pen; as if the fingers doing the writing were stiff.

As if those fingers might be dead.

The letter finished: *You think you have something special, but she's the Queen of Deceivers. Because what you can't give her, she begs of me.*

And then the signature. The name signed without flourish—a gash of angular letters: *Gideon.* Bernice stood looking at the letter for a long time, unable to react. Samantha spoke again, the sound of her voice jarred Bernice's already fractured nerves.

"I remember all those times. I remember all the excuses about working late, and business meetings."

"Samantha, I don't . . ."

"Are you going to deny it all?"

Bernice's hands fell to her side. "I love you, Samantha."

"Then who is HE!" screamed Samantha, whirling from the window and running at Bernice. She caught the blow before it could land across her face . . . and Samantha was hysterical now, trying to hit her across the face, crying out loud. And, in her anguish, Bernice tried to restrain her; tried to find words that would comfort and calm her down. No words would come as she manoeuvred Samantha back to the sofa, pushing her down there and holding her arms while she sobbed and cried uncontrollably.

The doorbell rang.

Bernice looked up at the door. "Samantha, please . . ."

The bell rang again, and this time there was a knock and a voice calling from the other side, "Is everything all right in there?" Bernice recognised the voice immediately: Mr. Fenner, the security manager of the apartment block, an interference at the best of times.

Samantha was quietened now, had ceased her struggling, but buried her face in her hands and continued weeping. Samantha stroked her hair and stood back. Fenner rang the doorbell once more, knocking again.

"Ms. Adams? Everything all right?"

"Yes . . . yes, Mr. Fenner. Everything's fine."

"Because if it isn't, I can always . . ."

"For God's sake, just go *away!*"

Bernice heard a grunt of disgust, and a noise that could have been Fenner kicking the bottom of the door before he moved off. The bastard seemed to spend most of his time on the apartment floor landings, listening in. Bernice knew that

he disapproved of her "lifestyle," as she had heard him eu-
phemistically refer to it in the past. Well he could go to hell.

"I thought . . ." Samantha could barely speak. "I thought
we had something good."

"We do, Sam. We *do*!"

"Then what is *that*!" cried Samantha, pointing to the letter
in Bernice's hand.

And Bernice knew now that she had to do something; she
had to break free of this petrifying fear, no matter what the
letter meant. The possibility that Gideon was not dead
seemed incredible. They had shot him six times with her father's revolver—Jacqueline, the last time, had shot him in
the face. Surely no one could survive that, no matter how
difficult it had seemed to kill him at the time. But in that moment, Bernice knew that her love for Samantha overrode
even the fear and that she could not allow what was happening to her to destroy what they had. The fear could wait.
Samantha could not. She had to say something to heal—
and right now, it didn't matter how big the lie.

"It's a pack of evil, filthy lies. And I know who sent it." Bernice packed as much venom into her words as possible; so
much so that Samantha looked up at her; eyes red, face
white—but waiting.

"Who?"

"Well, no one called Gideon. Because I don't know anyone by that name." Bernice's brain was racing, her mind on
two parallel tracks of thought: *He made me sign my own
name in the hotel registers. If Sam checks, she'll be able to
confirm those dates*. "No . . . this has been sent by Traycee.
Look at the handwriting—all crabbed and scrawled. She's
obviously trying to disguise it."

"But why?"

"To follow up on what she's already done. They've car-

278 Stephen Laws

peted me, Sam. They've fired me—helped along by Traycee's behind-the-scenes activities. She's always wanted my job, you know that. Now that she's got me fired, she wants to ruin my private life as well by sending these . . . these . . . sick, obscene letters." *I'll tell Sam I'm going to investigate those hotels myself. I'll come back indignant, saying someone's forged my name, tried to set me up. I'll manage. I'll do something.*

"But why would she do that, Bernice?"

"She's so straight, she's paranoid. She'd do anything to me. Like Mr. Fenner there, Sam—Traycee 'disapproves.'" *You've got to keep on the boil, Bernice. You've got to make it look as if you're the one suffering the greatest distress as a result of this letter. You're only lying to keep her. Keep telling yourself that!*

It seemed to be working. Samantha was sitting back now, breathing deeply. Bernice stroked the red hair out of her eyes. Something hissed against the window and Bernice looked over, expecting rain. But there was none.

"You wouldn't lie . . ." said Samantha.

"I'm taking this letter to the police," lied Bernice. "I'm not going to have that bitch upsetting you like this. We'll sue for defamation or libel or something." Bernice screwed the letter up and threw it across the room. It bounced from the window back on to the carpet.

"I need a drink," said Samantha at last, in a voice that seemed to indicate that Bernice's ploy had worked.

"So do I."

Bernice moved quickly to the drinks cabinet set into the far wall, letting down the loose shelf and bringing out two glasses.

"I don't want you getting upset about this, Samantha. The woman isn't worth it. What do you want, vodka?" She looked back to see Samantha nod her head, and by the way she was straightening her nightdress and smoothing down her hair, it looked as if Samantha was coming out of it now. Bernice's mind was whirling in confusion as she reached for the ice-bucket, but all that mattered was making things all right between them. The letter and all it implied could be faced later. The ice-bucket was empty.

"I'm sorry . . ." began Samantha as Bernice poured out two measures and headed back across the living room towards the kitchenette.

"Don't be. It was a sick, vicious letter. And we're not going to let her get away with it."

And as Bernice bumped her hip against the kitchenette door, holding the glasses of vodka high, another thought came to her. A thought that made definite sense.

Jacqueline.

Who else could have sent that letter? Yvonne Gillis was dead, killed in a bizarre accident. Gregory Leonard, too; in an utterly bizarre fashion. But things like that *did* happen, without there being any underlying connecting thread or motive force. She had been a newsreader long enough to know that. And the feelings about a dead man being out there somewhere watching Bernice on television? Well, perhaps she had been overworking, overachieving; perhaps burning the candle at both ends had resulted in her becoming hypersensitive. After all, she *had* been through an inexplicable hell; enough to make anyone crack up. Horrifying things that even now she couldn't bring herself to recall, since they challenged everything she'd ever known about the world and her place in it. Things that had happened to her body that defied nature but acknowledged her worst nightmare. But now all that had passed, just like the bad dream it had been.

Gideon was dead, after all.

And the only person alive who knew what she—what

they—had done, was Jacqueline Brennan. And even though they'd had a pact, didn't it make more sense that she had given the situation a little thought, knew that Bernice was in the public eye, and therefore susceptible to a little blackmail?

Yes, of course! That *had* to be it.

With each hand holding a glass, Bernice could not flick the light switch in the kitchenette. Instead, she judged her distance in the dark until she bumped against the fridge.

Jacqueline. Of course.

Well, she was playing a dangerous game now. Because she was just as implicated in the murder of Gideon. And Bernice still had the revolver, safely hidden. Jacqueline's fingerprints were bound to be on the gun. Bernice permitted herself a small, bitter laugh as she fumbled to put a drink down on one of the shelves and opened the fridge door. Cold yellow light flooded the kitchenette. She had been wearing gloves that day. Jacqueline had not.

Bernice had just reached into the ice-cabinet—when the kitchenette door slammed shut. The sharp noise startled her.

"You all right, Sam?"

Bernice grabbed a handful of ice—and then the serving hatch between the kitchenette and the living room slammed down.

"Sam?"

Bernice dropped the ice into the glasses and placed them on the bench, nudging the refrigerator door shut and moving quickly to the door. Flicking on the light switch, Bernice tried to open the door.

It was wedged tightly shut.

She pushed her weight against the door handle. This was silly. There was no lock on the kitchenette door and even if a draught of air had slammed it shut, it shouldn't be stuck so fast this way. Bernice rattled the door handle, pushing with the flat of her other hand. The door was immovable.

"Samantha, can you help? The door's stuck."

And then Bernice heard the same sound she had earlier. A sound like rain on the windows, when there was no rain. She cocked her head to listen. Yes, it was rain: a swishing, pattering, rustling sound—growing slowly but steadily louder.

"Samantha?"

Bernice pushed with her shoulder, but the door would not budge. She moved to the serving hatch, becoming angry now. But the flap would not lift no matter how hard she tugged at it. It was as if the flap had been nailed shut to the shelf. Bernice knocked hard on the hatch.

"Samantha, come on, love. I'm stuck in here and it's not funny."

There was no answer from the other side. Only the rustling, pattering sound of the rain getting louder. Bernice looked behind her at the small kitchenette window. The pane was unflecked by rain. Puzzled and irritated, Bernice hammered on the flap again.

"Samantha, please . . ."

And now she became aware of the other noise.

Someone was moaning; making a low, keening sound like a child in distress. There was an air of mounting panic and terror in that small, desperate sound, almost drowned by the ever-growing sound of the rain that was not rain.

Bernice realised at last that it was Samantha making that sound.

The terror and the fear had returned. Something bad was happening.

Bernice hurried back to the door, throwing herself at it now with both hands flat on the wood, shoving hard. She rattled and twisted at the doorknob, shouldered the door and felt the thin wood bulge, but still it remained fast—and the keening sound was rising in volume.

"Samantha! For God's sake what is it? What's happening?"

Samantha began to scream then; screams of utter terror as the rustling, pattering, hissing sound swelled until it sounded like a fast-running river. And Bernice felt a scream rising to her own lips as she pounded at the door; finally whirling away back into the kitchenette, looking for something—anything—to batter down the door. Frantically, she seized one of two kitchen stools and whirled back to the door, slamming the stool hard against it. Paint flaked under the impact, as Bernice swung hard again and again, crying out loud as Samantha's screams continued, rising above the bizarre hissing and rustling in the living room.

A wood panel in the door cracked.

Bernice heaved the stool back, took a deep breath and swung it around hard at the door. But it was as if someone holding the door closed from the other side had suddenly let go. Even before the stool connected, the door was suddenly hurled open—and Bernice was caught off balance, her swing carrying both the stool and herself over the threshold of the door and collapsing to the living room floor.

The air was filled with hissing, swirling life.

Bernice had fallen to her hands and knees, the stool clattering away from her.

And the carpet was alive.

For a second, Bernice thought that she was still dreaming; that all she had to do was will herself awake, to find that the letter had never arrived, that Samantha was lying quietly next to her in bed, that she still had her job, that Gideon had never been—and that everything would be normal again. Because only in a nightmare could this be happening.

The living room floor was a twisting, undulating carpet of squirming insects. A revolting mass of centipedes, slugs, spiders, earwigs, woodlice and cockroaches. Her hands were buried deep in that seething movement. She was kneeling in it. Insects swarmed over her hands and forearms, crawled on her nightdress and this . . .

. . . was not a nightmare, as Bernice recoiled, staggering back to her feet; frantically brushing insects from her hands and forearms, uttering cries of revulsion. The air swarmed with flies; a thick, buzzing cloud. Bernice felt them in her hair as she flailed back into the kitchenette.

Somehow, the threshold between the kitchenette and the living room was a barrier to the seething horde of insects. Bernice finished clawing the last from her legs, looking up wildly now as Samantha's screams were cut off.

Samantha was standing on the upholstered chair, her eyes wide in horror. Beneath her, a living sea of squirming life. One fist was clenched to her mouth now as she looked at the horrifying swarm all around her from her small "island." Every other piece of furniture was covered in insects; the sofa was a crawling mound, the lampstand beside Samantha swarmed with life. Insects dropped on to the orange bulb under the lampshade, popping and crackling in the heat, making wild, squirming shadows. The pelmet and curtains at the window were completely obscured by a writhing, glistening mass. Flies swirled madly. The drinks cabinet and walls were covered by a seething horde. And the rustling, hissing, rasping of that squirming nightmare filled the air. Samantha looked up at last, and saw Bernice in the doorway.

"Ber . . . nice . . . help . . ."

"Run to me, Samantha!" shouted Bernice over the hissing, rustling horde. "Jump down and run to me. I don't . . . don't know how, but they won't . . . they can't come in here."

"I . . . can't . . ."

Bernice stepped to the threshold, making ready to dash back across the living room so that she could grab Samantha and drag her back to the kitchenette. Instantly, a wave of woodlice and spiders swept up her leg. She stifled a scream, stepping back into the kitchenette, slapping them from her flesh. The uncrushed insects scuttled back across the threshold into the living room. Bernice braced her hands on the door-frame and gritted her teeth. She could do it. It wouldn't be pleasant but she . . .

. . . and Samantha screamed again as insects surged over the rim of the seat cushion and on to her naked legs. She flailed back against the chair.

It tilted.

Bernice watched, frozen in horror, as Samantha clawed at the air to regain balance, her hands clutching the seething mass which had been a curtain. The curtain tore free from the pelmet with a loud ripping sound as the chair went over backwards. Samantha fell heavily to the floor, and the curtain—with its undulating, glistening covering of insects—enshrouded her. Uttering wild, muffled cries of terror and disgust, Samantha thrashed beneath the curtain to regain her feet.

"Sam!"

Bernice launched herself into the living room, slapping at the flies which buzzed around her face, feeling a crawling mass on her legs as she blundered forward. She dragged the chair aside, knocking the table lamp over. Instantly, it was enfolded by the living mass on the floor. There were living things in her mouth and crawling between her legs now as Bernice scrabbled downwards at the thrashing mass on the carpet. Samantha was completely covered by the curtain which, in turn, was completely covered in glistening, squirming bodies. Bernice tore at the curtain, grabbing the fabric and tearing it backwards in a shower of living things. Bernice's face was covered. She staggered back, dragging at the curtain, and Samantha began to unwind from it, whirling wildly with her arms flapping. She tore free from the curtain, thrashing at the air and . . .

. . . Bernice screamed aloud as she threw down the seething curtain, when she saw that Samantha's entire body was covered in glistening, squirming, living things. Her face was completely masked by them, her red hair alive with horrifying movement; only her mouth open and screaming, now choking as things squirmed into it and . . .

. . . Samantha thrashed wildly backwards, hands clawing at her face, as Bernice lunged towards her, ready to grab Samantha and drag her back to the kitchenette where she could tear those things from her face so that she could breathe. But Samantha's wild impetus carried her backwards out of reach, and Bernice froze in terror as Samantha flailed backwards against the floor-to-ceiling window.

The glass exploded outwards around her in slabs of cracking, sparkling ice. The exploding spray of glass enfolded Samantha.

And then she was gone into the night.

Bernice tried to call Samantha's name, and her mouth was instantly filled with fat, buzzing flies. Spitting and tearing at the myriad, filthy things which swarmed on her body, Bernice staggered towards the ragged gap in the window, through which chill night air was now gusting. Her legs were completely encrusted in a glistening, black mass. Her hair was a living nest.

The room began to tilt before her eyes.

And at last Bernice embraced the nightmare, submitting to unconsciousness in the hope that there would be an awakening from it.

She turned and fell, face first, into the glistening mass.

* * *

Hands were lifting her.

She did not have the strength to lash out, to scream. There was light now, too bright for her to see properly. But those hands were lifting her and putting her on to something. Her flesh was no longer alive and crawling with living things.

The nightmare was over at last.

"Take it easy," said a man's voice.

There were other voices now: low, barely audible voices.

Someone was strapping down her arms, and she was able to open her eyes wider now to look around.

It was her living room. In a state of disarray, with chairs overturned. She saw men's legs, felt strong hands tightening the straps.

There were no insects. No crawling, living mass. The walls were as they'd always been, not blanketed with filthy glistening things. Just as she'd thought, it had been a very, very bad dream. And that was all.

The lampstand was lying on the floor next to the window—and a man in a police uniform was pushing a large wooden board up against the shattered gap in that window, broken glass crunching underfoot as he did so.

"Samantha . . . ?"

A flashbulb popped.

"She's awake," said another man's voice.

And Bernice was being lifted, realising now despite her curious enervation and inability to interact with what was going on, that she was being lifted on a stretcher. There were policemen in her living room, lots of them. And men in ambulance crew uniforms were carrying her towards the door.

Mr. Fenner, the caretaker, was standing in the doorway. A police constable pushed him out of the way as he twisted his face at her and said, "She killed her. No doubt about it. I heard them arguing and fighting like a couple of cats, and she pushed her out of the window . . ."

"Stand back please, sir," said the constable—and Bernice was carried out through the doorway and on to the main landing.

But there was no need for her to worry.

Just as she'd thought, everything so far had been a nightmare. There were no insects. And no letter. And no Gideon. And Samantha was fine.

She just hadn't woken up yet.

Bernice went back to sleep, prepared to wait for her proper awakening to a world of reason.

Chapter Twenty-Two
Shapiro

Shapiro took the turning for Swarwell Beach and followed the sand-swept coast road along its ten-mile reach.

On his left, grit-covered sand-dunes surmounted by coarse grass formed an undulating barrier to the flat grey expanse of the sea. The vast stretch of water looked depressingly cold and desolate. On his right, there was a heavy engineering industrial plant which seemed to have seen better days. He knew that the area was in economic recession, with unemployment at an all-time high for this decade. Many of the factories were derelict, their windows pockmarked by stone-throwing youths. Skeletons of dead cars and lorries littered disused junkyards, rust growing on their bones. That rust seemed to have drifted with the wind across the coast road, colouring the first stretches of sand that led to the dunes. No healthy, bright yellow sand here. Just the brown-red ashes of decay.

Shapiro looked for a break where he could turn the car. How on earth could he find Paul here? For a moment, he was filled with despair. Could he really be sure after all that the "feeling" he had experienced in hospital could really be a desperate plea for help from Paul? He gripped the wheel tight as memories of that day nineteen years ago overwhelmed him once more.

There are more things in heaven and earth, Horatio, than are dreamed of in your philosophy . . .

A wind-beaten, salt-corroded enamel sign at the side of the road told him that the Beachcomber Café was only half a mile further down the road. From the clear stretch of the coast road ahead, Shapiro could see a building set back off the main road amidst the dunes. Beyond that, the beach just kept on going until it came up against a jutting headland. This was the end of the beach, and it seemed that the café was the only place that he could pull in.

The Beachcomber Café had seen better days, too. A wooden shack, raised on eight-foot stilts against possible sand-drift, the external walls had once been painted blue, but the salt air had all but flaked it away. The windows were fly-stained and cobwebbed, and a six-foot piece of hardboard had been nailed across the door. No chance of refreshment here. But there was a rutted car park of sorts, and a path beyond the café which seemed to lead down through the dunes to the beach. It was not possible to take the car all the way down there, but at least he could leave it on the other side of the hut, out of sight from the main road and hidden from anyone passing by.

Why do you want to hide? What do you expect is waiting for you?

"Gideon," said Shapiro aloud as he swerved the car into the car park.

He hadn't said that name in nineteen years. It sounded guttural and threatening to him now, and he wished that he hadn't spoken.

When he finally swung the car behind the shack, he sat for a long time with his hands on the wheel, breathing deeply and steadying his nerves. The pain in his back and shoulder burned like an acid spill but they had stopped bleeding, and he was grateful for that. Steeling himself, he climbed gingerly out of the car. This time he could feel a dampness, and uttered a small prayer as he felt inside his shirt.

It was sweat. Not blood.

There were also stairs at the back of the café leading to another back door. Obviously so the punters could pile out with their families, straight down on to the path leading to the beach. Shapiro stiffly climbed the stairs. Another board had been nailed over the back door. He peered into the café. There was no furniture—only a decrepit wooden bar of sorts, and faded seaside scenes painted on the walls. Paint had been spilled in the centre of the floor. But there was no one in there.

What did you expect? First building on the beach—and you expect to find Paul there? Oh Christ . . . why didn't you just tell the police you thought you knew where he was? Why didn't you just tell them about Swarwell Beach and let them follow it up? Because . . . because Paul would be dead by then. And this is something that you have to finish. It began nineteen years ago, and you were too afraid to do anything about it then. This nightmare has lived with you ever since. And how many people have died since that time? How many people who could have been saved if you'd had the courage of your faith? No . . . that . . . that thing . . . has got Paul. And it's all up to you now. To do something you should have done then.

Shapiro descended to the rough, sand-strewn path and looked out through the gap between the bristling dunes to the sea. Grey-white water churned at the beach, and damp chilled air swirled through the gap to envelop him. *Cold as the grave*, came an unbidden thought.

God alone knew where Paul was on that vast expanse of beach. And Shapiro prayed that God would guide him today. Perhaps there was some kind of habitation in the dunes. He had felt nothing since that first desperate call and he controlled the inner anguish when the thought came to him that perhaps Paul was already dead, and that he had been called here simply to find the body. A last act of cruelty from the thing that called itself Gideon.

Shapiro walked back to the car, opened the back door and took out the Gladstone bag.

He headed for the gap between the dunes, and the first lap of his search.

And as he walked—he remembered.

Chapter Twenty-Three
Gideon

It's twenty years ago, almost to the week.

One o'clock in the morning.

And Veronica is lying in bed, watching the shadows of tree branches against the bedroom window. A wind has risen in the night; it moans and soughs around the eaves of the vicarage. She prays that he'll be coming to bed soon, and then realises that a prayer in the circumstances is less than appro-

priate. Tony has been working late again; on a sermon, she presumes. And it's about an hour now since she made him a cup of tea before coming to bed.

An hour.

The liquid she put into the tea should be taking effect soon, and she writhes in bed impatiently. She has less than an hour herself, because Veronica has an appointment.

At two o'clock in the morning.

In the church.

And she must be there.

A door opens and closes downstairs and a shadow creeps up the stairs. At last, he's coming to bed. Veronica closes her eyes and feigns sleep, listening to Tony as he comes up the stairs. She hears him yawn, and knows that the liquid must be having its effect.

Quietly, so as not to disturb her, the Reverend Shapiro lets himself into the bedroom, pushes the bedroom door carefully shut and begins to undress. She listens to the rustling of his divested clothes and wills him to hurry. Then a great and sickening fear falls over her. She does not want to go where she has been ordered to go, and yet she is reacting to his instruction as if it's the most important thing in the world. There is no pleasure where she's going; only pain, humiliation and a lingering sickness in her soul. Why is she doing this? Why can't she stop herself? Out of sight, Veronica grips the bedclothes tight, promising to fight, determining that she will not be keeping her 2:00 a.m. tryst . . .

. . . and wills Tony to hurry up and come to bed; wills him to fall asleep as quickly as possible. It can't be long now.

The old mattress tilts as the Reverend Shapiro slides into bed next to her. There seems to be a pause, and Veronica can feel his eyes upon her in the darkness, looking at the "sleeping" face. He exhales, and it sounds preternaturally loud in the bedroom, a sound full of weariness. Poor Tony. A young

*man, new to the parish. He works too hard and takes it all so
seriously. Finally, he pulls the quilt up around himself and
turns over.*

The wind sighs and moans around the house.

*The tree branches wave their spidery shadows over the
window.*

*On the dressing-table, the illuminated green alarm clock
shows 1:35 a.m.*

And the Reverend Shapiro's breathing is deep and regular.

In trepidation, Veronica asks, "Tony?"

There is no answer.

"Are you awake?"

*Still no answer. With sick anxiety in her stomach, Veronica
eases herself carefully out of bed, trying not to disturb the
mattress too much. She watches Tony all the time in the darkness, watching for any sign that her movements are disturb-
ing him. "Tony?" she asks again; this time a little louder. But
there is still no response; just the Reverend Shapiro's deep
and regular breathing.*

*Veronica slips quietly across the room in her nightdress.
She opens the bedroom door stealthily, catching the interior
sneck of the door-lock to make sure that it doesn't make a
noise; all the time watching her husband. Finally, she slips out
of the bedroom, across the landing and into the guest room.
There are wardrobes in here, too. And she opens one now,
quietly taking out the clothes that she transferred from the
main wardrobe in her own bedroom earlier on that evening.*

She dresses quickly and without noise.

*Her throat is tight, her chest constricted. She can feel her
heartbeat. And there are tears there, too; along with deep self-
loathing. But above all, she is desperately afraid. This is not a
clandestine meeting with a lover. She loves Tony deeply and
would never betray him. There is no pleasure for her in these
meetings; above all, no sexual pleasure. The stranger that she*

met in the middle of the street on her way home from work takes his own pleasure, and leaves her degraded and ill with anxiety at her motivations. Because she has no motivation for what she is now doing. Has she lost her mind?

She looks into his eyes—he tells her what to do—and she does it.

The fear has never left her, but now there is a new and hideous dimension to the nightmare; something which challenges everything she knows about the world. On three occasions, that terrible feeling of being "drained" has overcome her. The first time: in the High Street, with people recoiling from her as she staggered across the main street asking for help. Veronica remembers leaning against the supermarket window while people stepped aside to avoid coming near; remembers seeing her face in the window reflection; a haggard, white face of a woman who was herself, but somehow also forty years older than she should be. With heart hammering, Veronica remembers staggering home, praying not to be seen; remembers sitting in the bathroom looking with agonised horror at the old face that stared back with red-rimmed eyes and wattled neck. She remembers hanging her head over the washbasin, crying soft and bitter tears. She remembers looking up again to see that the nightmare was over.

But the nightmare had continued.

A motel.

A hotel.

A derelict building site.

And two more of those horrifying experiences, leading her to believe that her sanity had been irrevocably lost for ever.

Veronica struggles to control the tears. She crosses the landing again and looks in on her husband. He is still sleeping soundly.

She tiptoes downstairs in the darkness, takes her keys from the handbag in the hall, looks back once more up the stairs *and feels like bursting into tears. Somehow, she does not. Biting her lip, and feeling the dread within, Veronica lets herself out into the darkness.*

And when that door closes quietly—the Reverend Shapiro opens his eyes.

He waits for one minute by the alarm clock dial and then throws back the quilt. He moves quickly and silently across the bedroom to the window and sees his wife hurrying down the drive in the moonlight. She casts a look back at the vicarage and he manages to duck back behind the curtain out of sight. He quickly throws on his clothes, looks only briefly at the vicar's collar on the chair, and then also hurries down the stairs.

He opens the door an inch and looks out into the darkness.

Veronica is nowhere to be seen, but must have turned out of the drive and on to the side road. Pulling an overcoat from the coatstand, the Reverend Shapiro slips out into the night, quickly closes the door behind him and hurries down the drive after his wife.

When he reaches the gate, he looks through the railings to see a human-shaped shadow moving hurriedly down the main road towards the church. Ash-coloured clouds cast moonlit shadows across the church's crag-like spires and Gothic turrets. It does not look a comforting place. Could this be where she's going? He strains to keep track of that figure, making sure that he is well back in the bushes of the front garden so as not to be seen. The shadow seems to hesitate at the main gate of the church. Shapiro shrinks back further into the bushes, then watches as his wife's shadow disappears into the grounds of the church.

Shapiro follows.

The street is deserted. There are no lights in any of the windows. He hopes that there are no beat policemen out tonight, patrolling in their panda cars. How would he be able to ex-

plain?" "I'm following my wife, Constable. At almost 2:00 a.m. in the morning, on her way to church. Why? Well, I have a feeling that she is meeting someone there. And no, I don't know who or why. I also don't know why they're meeting at 2:00 a.m.—but I'm sure that she's meeting someone. Do I think she's having an affair? Yes, I'm afraid that I do—but there's so much more to what's going on than that. Other things that are preventing me from approaching her directly and asking the question. She used to be so full of joy, now she's changed so desperately for the worse. She looks haggard and ill. I've tried to suggest a doctor, but she ignores me or refuses to listen. And I've caught her at odd times, either going to or coming from a secret meeting. Yes, I know it's a secret meeting, because some of the excuses she's given me over recent weeks have subsequently proved to be lies. The friend she was supposed to be visiting; the same friend that I know has been on holiday in Greece for over a week. The old schoolfriend who doesn't exist. So here I am, at 2:00 a.m. skulking along the street after her. And what am I going to do if I find her with someone else? Honest to God, I just don't know. Maybe just seeing them together will be enough. Maybe I'll be able to leave and then confront her about it tomorrow. Or maybe I will confront them both now. I just don't know . . ."

Shapiro finishes his fantasy conversation when he reaches the church gates. He is just in time to see shadows moving by the main door, hears the creak of the ancient door (how many times had he meant to have that thing oiled?) and sees a deeper darkness appear in the shadows as the door opens and then closes. Veronica has spare keys for that front door in case of emergencies, and tonight she appears to be putting them to good use. He refuses to believe that their choice of meeting place is any kind of reflection on him.

"They?" whispers Shapiro to himself as he flits down the tree-lined entrance-drive to the church.

He pauses at the entrance, remembering the noise that the great oak door makes when it's opened. He feels for the keys in his pocket, considers his choices and then skirts around to the side of the great building. There is another door at the rear of the church, leading directly into a room that had once been a vestry but is now used for storage. The wind has risen again. The trees around the church hiss and thrash, reminding him of the sound of the sea. The clouds overhead in the night sky seem a strange colour. Moonlight has given them a strange, ashen quality; like ripped and shredded veils caught by the wind and scudding through the sky.

He can feel no righteousness about what he is doing, no sense of the avenging husband about to catch his wife in the arms of another man. He can feel no anger. Somehow, all that he can feel tonight is a dark, cold and unreasoning fear. Steeling himself, he opens the storage room door and lets himself in.

He knows the layout of the room fairly well, even if the room is little used. In truth, there is little to store here: only two old pews that have been removed from the main church and replaced years ago, and which the previous vicar has somehow neglected to throw away. Sentimental attachments, perhaps. Shapiro steps carefully through the darkness, not switching on the electric light lest it be seen when he opens the interior door. Despite his familiarity with the room he barks his shin on one of the pews and suppresses a cry. Hobbling to the interior door, he holds his breath and carefully lifts the latch.

Moonlight is gleaming through the stained-glass windows into the church; shafts of red, green and white light spear across the two ranks of pews and the aisle. The shadows of the trees outside swaying in the wind make those shafts of *light waver, filling the church with unnatural movement and shadows. Two figures seem to be silently swaying from side to side against the opposite wall. Veronica and her lover? No, it is two statues: Christ on the Cross and the Virgin Mary. Shapiro looks first to the left and the entrance lobby of the church through which Veronica must have come; then scans the aisle all the way down through the drifting shafts of moonlight to the altar and the pulpit. But there is no sign of his wife. Shifting position, Shapiro looks again.*

The church is empty.

But there is a sound; low and barely audible beneath the soughing sound of the wind. Shapiro strains to listen.

It is the sound of weeping.

And now at last, he can see a figure; sitting in one of the pews, head bent and hands clasped in prayer.

Veronica.

Shapiro cannot bear the sight or the sound. He pulls back the door and steps into the church. The sound of the hinges echo, and the shadow in the pew sits up, startled. Shapiro hears her intake of breath. She rises quickly to her feet, backing off defensively into the aisle.

"It's all right, Veronica. It's me."

Shapiro sees his wife freeze, and as he hurries down the ranks of pews to meet her, she begins to weep again; this time louder than before. They are bitter tears.

"Don't," says Shapiro as he comes to her. "Please don't . . ."

He rushes along the pew to her, grabs her roughly by both arms and embraces her. She embraces him in return, her body racked by a deep and profound distress; the sound of sorrow so grief-stricken that Shapiro cannot hold back tears either.

"It doesn't matter," says Shapiro, his voice hoarse. "Whatever is wrong doesn't matter. We can work it out, make it better . . ."

And Veronica suddenly pulls back from him, wiping tears from her eyes.

"*Oh God, Tony. You shouldn't have followed me. You've got to get away from here. You've got to leave!*"

"*What's wrong? Why . . . ?*"

"*If he finds you here, I don't know what he'll do.*"

"*Who, Veronica? Who are you meeting?*"

"*Please, Tony. For my sake, you've got to go away.*"

"*I followed you because I love you. And whatever is happening to you, whatever is terrifying you like this has got to stop. I'm going to stop it.*"

"*Nothing can stop him. Believe me, you've got to get away.*"

"*Who is it, Ronnie? Please, for God's sake, what's his name?*"

"My name is Gideon," *says a voice from the darkness.*

Shapiro whirls in alarm at the sound of that voice, just as a tall shadow steps from the darkness around the altar. The voice is deep, its sound seeming to fill the church. Veronica's hands tighten on Shapiro's arms, the nails digging into his flesh. And that shadow—a man, a very tall man—walks around to the front of the altar, standing there as if about to deliver a sermon. He is still in deep shadow and he stands there, waiting.

"*Don't look into his eyes,*" *says Veronica, in one terrified intake of breath.* "*Whatever you do, don't . . .*"

"*Be quiet, Veronica!*" *snaps that voice, and she is instantly silent, her arms falling to her side.*

Shapiro reacts in fury. The fact that this man is somehow in his church (And how can that be? asks a small voice. The front door was locked, you saw Veronica open it. And you unlocked the side door yourself); the fact that his wife is so terrified of him; the fact that he commands his wife's silence; the very fact that he speaks her name in familiar terms; all of this stokes Shapiro's anger.

"*What the hell are you doing to my wife?*" *demands Shapiro, and his voice rings in the church.*

"*Such language for a man of the cloth,*" says the shadow at the altar. "*What would your bishop say? And as for your wife—I'm not doing anything that she doesn't want me to do. Isn't that right, Veronica?*"

Shapiro hears his wife whimper and is again enraged.

"*Isn't that right, Veronica?*" demands the shadow.

"*. . . yes . . .*" she replies in a voice choked with tears.

"*Get out of here, Gideon or whatever your name is!*" shouts Shapiro. "*Get out of my church!*"

The shadow begins to laugh; a low, deep-base sound. "*So it's your church, priest. Interesting.*"

Shapiro turns back to his wife as he feels her hand on his sleeve again. Her fingers clutch at the fabric, as if the effort of touching him is causing immense pain. In the darkness he can still see tears streaming down her face.

"*. . . his eyes . . .*" says Veronica in a small, pain-filled voice, "*. . . don't look at . . .*"

"*VERONICA!*" The shadow's voice is filled with rage. "*Come here!*"

Angry and astonished, Shapiro feels his wife pull away from him. She steps into the aisle.

"*Veronica . . .*" Shapiro steps after her, grabbing her arm. She pulls away from him, face turned towards the shadow at the altar. "*Ronnie! Don't . . .*" But now she pulls away roughly from his grasp as if she now cannot bear his presence and begins to walk slowly through the shafts of moonlight, down the aisle.

"*No!*" Shapiro hurries after her, this time pushing her to one side. She reels against a pew. Shapiro continues on down the aisle, towards the shadow.

The shadow steps forward, as if to meet him, still shrouded in darkness.

And Shapiro halts in mid-step as his anger suddenly gives way to another, purely instinctive emotion. As if some inner

*mental or spiritual switch has been engaged, Shapiro knows
that he is in the presence of someone or something that is
purely evil. He has fear now, the anger which would have led
him up to this man in a physical confrontation now quickly
ebbing away.*

*The shadow cocks its head in the darkness, affecting child-
like curiosity; as if knowing what has happened to the priest,
and that simple action serves to fuel the fear which has
gripped Shapiro. Veronica is at his side now, pushing past to
reach the figure—but despite the fear, Shapiro grabs her arm
again, halting her progress. Veronica moans in fear, and
Shapiro knows with profound distress that she is afraid of dis-
obeying this man. She pulls away from Shapiro easily, and
walks to meet the tall shadow. Shapiro feels with horror that
he is present at some terrible kind of wedding. His own wife,
in his own church. Walking down the aisle through the moonlight to be with her new husband, who waits for her at the altar. The fear immobilises Shapiro. He cannot move forward.*

The shadow chuckles again. The sound is vile.

"Don't you believe in vampires, priest?"

*Veronica is standing right before the shadow now. The fig-
ure towers over her. She looks up at its still-hidden face. The
shadow laughs again.*

"Your wife most certainly does."

*And then the shadow hits Veronica hard across the face
with a blow so fierce that it flings her bodily back against the
front pew. She collides with it, falling heavily to the marble
floor, the sound of the blow still ringing in the church.*

*Shapiro roars in rage; no longer immobile, he hurls himself
at the shadow.*

*But before his fingers can fasten around that throat, his
hands are suddenly seized in an ice-cold grip. The darkness
sways and tilts, blood-red rage clouds his eyes, as Shapiro
feels those hard, stone-cold hands pull both of his hands to-*

gether in front of him. Like an adult with a struggling child, the shadow is now using one hand-grip to hold both of Shapiro's hands together by their wrists. Shapiro cries out in rage and pain as the shadow uses its free hand calmly to reach for his throat. He struggles and twists to be free from the shadow, but although he tugs and strains backwards the tall shadow does not move an inch, as if carved from stone.

The ice-cold hand fastens on his throat.

His hands are suddenly released, and Shapiro clutches at the single hand that now holds him aloft, his legs kicking and lashing. He cannot breathe, his throat is constricted. His eyes begin to bulge. He claws at the hand, but it is like stone. He kicks at the figure, but it is like kicking at a statue.

As his eyes cloud, Shapiro hears the figure chuckling again; a horrifyingly unnatural and hideously powerful sound.

The figure makes a half-turn, holding the priest from it at arm's length, as if he weighs nothing at all. Then it flings him across the church with careless disdain. Shapiro hits the church wall twelve feet away, his flailing legs knocking over a Nativity display, made by pupils from a local school. A papier-mâché stable and figures are scattered to the floor. Tinsel glitters in the moonlight. Shapiro lies there, gasping for air. The mists clear from his eyes, but there is terrible pain in his side and leg; his throat feels crushed. Still lying on the marble floor beside the pew, Veronica tries to crawl to him, weeping.

And the figure is still standing in darkness by the altar, laughing at them.

Shapiro blunders to his feet, the balance between fear and rage shifting again. He lunges at the shattered Nativity display, pushing aside the broken papier-mâché stable and seizing the wooden cross that formed a backdrop to the birth scene. He tears it free and limps forward to Veronica. She holds up a hand to him, and he takes it, still staring in rage at the motionless shadow. Gritting his teeth, whispering a prayer, he limps forward again, thrusting the wooden cross out before him in his right hand. He lets go of Veronica as he moves forward.

The shadow does not move as he approaches.

"Leave us ALONE!" shouts Shapiro. He lunges at the figure, thrusting the cross out before him.

The figure steps forward to meet him. A shaft of tree-shadowed moonlight falls on its face and Shapiro looks directly into Gideon's eyes.

"Whatever made you think this would work?"

Gideon takes the wooden cross from the priest's hand and crushes it in his stone-cold hands, letting the pieces drop clattering to the floor.

Terror fills Shapiro's soul. All he can see now are those eyes.

One of those hideous hands fastens on Shapiro's face, covering it completely like some huge and hideous spider. Shapiro screams, clutching at the hand, and when Gideon shoves him backwards, Shapiro collides with the front pew and sprawls beside his wife.

"Your faith is hollow, priest," says Gideon. "Let me show you mine."

And Shapiro can only watch from the marble floor as the figure beckons to his wife. Veronica rises from the floor, still weeping.

Can only watch as the dark figure sweeps her from her feet.

Can only watch as he flings her over the altar.

Can only watch as his wife is raped before his eyes.

And later, when it is over, Gideon sweeps Veronica from the altar like so much dead meat. Her semi-naked body falls to the floor on the other side. Shapiro can hear her moaning in pain, but cannot move, cannot go to help her.

Gideon steps down from the altar, towering over him. His eyes are like glinting fragments of ice in the darkness.

"It would be so easy to kill you," says Gideon. "So very easy. But I have a better plan for you both."

Shapiro looks up to that face in terror, and can only listen as the shadow continues.

"I have shown you that your faith is a lie. Killing you in that knowledge would be a mercy. But I want you to live with that knowledge for the rest of your life. I want you to know that my religion is the only way and the only truth. Evil simply IS, priest. Everything else is comforting lies, invented by your Church to hide you from despair. All you have to look forward to is death. And after death"—the shadow chuckled in the darkness—"after death, your soul will be meat for me and mine.

"Your wife will give birth to a son. He will be mine. And when he reaches manhood, my seed within him will flower. Nothing you can do will stop it. Each day you look on him . . . remember me."

One word passes through Shapiro's head as he lies there, and the shadow begins to laugh again.

"But abortion is an evil, priest! It's a sin! And in any event— she will not allow you. You are powerless. All your symbols, all your sacraments, all your communions and prayers and exorcisms are empty and worthless. This is what I leave to you and yours."

The shadow steps back into the darkness, laughing.

And is suddenly gone.

Tree shadows rear and loom in shafts of moonlight.

The serene and empty faces of plaster saints look down from the walls of the church.

From somewhere behind the altar, Veronica continues to weep like a lost and frightened child.

And Shapiro can only lie there against the pew, the cold creeping from the marble floor into his flesh. He can only lie and look at the shattered wooden cross on the floor, and his eyes are blurred with tears.

Chapter Twenty-Four
Jacqueline and Bernice

When the warder opened the door marked "Visitors," Jacqueline was instantly assailed by the smell of antiseptic.

It was the same smell that she had encountered in hospital corridors, and it never failed to make her feel apprehensive. It had been years since she'd been to a hospital; since the boys were born, in fact. But her latest visit, following the nightmare with the dogs in the library, had reacquainted her with that smell of fear. (Why was it that none of the antiseptic cleaners at home smelled the same way?) The doctors had wanted to keep her in hospital for observation after they had stitched the wounds in her arms, neck and shoulder. She had been lucky that a major artery had not been torn. But she could not bear the thought of remaining there. Far better that she be at home, with her husband and children and . . .

He's out there somewhere, Jacqueline.

. . . and not lying in a hospital bed in the middle of the night, waiting for the sound of someone's echoing footsteps in the corridor.

She was more than apprehensive now: a cold, sick wedge of anxiety had lodged somewhere deep inside as she tried to shrug off that odour—and then, prompted by the uniformed warder, she stepped into the visitors' room.

There were already four or five visitors in the room, which

had been divided in half by a counter and plexi-glass screen. There were individual sections partitioned off for each prisoner and visitor, and the arrangement looked just like a bank or building society office.

Only one prisoner was sitting alone at the far end of the counter. She looked up as Jacqueline entered. Unnecessarily, the warder said, "Booth twelve."

Struggling to control her anxiety, Jacqueline walked slowly along the counter. Slowly, because she needed every available moment to gather her thoughts and make some kind of sense of what was happening to her and to those around her. She looked at the husbands, fathers, brothers or sons as they talked to the women prisoners behind the plexi-glass, directing their voices to the round grille in the glass, just below face level.

All too soon, and still with no real answers, Jacqueline had reached booth twelve.

"Hello," said Bernice as Jacqueline finally sat down opposite her.

Her voice was slightly distorted through the grille; but carried a cracked and weary hopelessness. Her face was white and wan-looking.

Her hair, once so carefully arranged, seemed unwashed and had been pulled back fiercely behind her ears. Compared to the face which Jacqueline had seen on television, this face seemed to be worn and terribly, terribly old. The change both startled and alarmed Jacqueline. Bernice must have seen her reaction plainly enough. She laughed, one simple expulsion of air. "Yes. It's me. And you look as if you're going through your own kind of hell, too."

Jacqueline fingered the stitches on the side of her neck.

"You sent for me. Just one telephone call, and you asked for me—not for your solicitor."

"That's right."

"Would it surprise you to know that I was going to try and see you anyway?"

"No."

Jacqueline struggled for words. Finally, she said, "What the hell is going on, Bernice?"

"In a word," said Bernice wearily, "Hell."

"They say you killed your lover. Pushed her out of a window during a fight."

"That's what they say."

"And?"

"You know the answer to that question, I think. What happened to me makes just as much sense as what happened to you in the library."

"How do you know about that?"

"There are newspapers in here as well, Jacqueline. I'm in detention without bail on a murder charge. But they do allow me to read."

"None of it makes any sense. Why do . . . ?"

"There isn't time. I just want you to listen to what I say. Others are listening too, make no mistake. So let's not waste any time."

"All right, Bernice. I'm listening."

"You know who's behind all of this. In your heart, you know who it is. Someone who was ruining your life and who you thought was gone for ever. Well he's not. He's back."

"He can't be."

"He's *back!* And he wants revenge. Somehow, this is all his doing. And not one of us is safe. Listen to me, Jacqueline. He . . . he was never *found.* Do you know what I mean? Don't say you haven't been waiting for news, just like me. And that's because he was removed from that place. Someone came and took him away. Someone who I paid to follow him was made . . . was *made* . . . to come and find him and take him away to a safe place."

"But we . . . I mean, he . . . I mean, how could he *do* that after what we did to him? He was . . . was . . ."

"None of that matters, Jacqueline. The fact is, we didn't make him go away after all. And he had himself taken somewhere safe. I've been thinking about it for a long time. About what happened afterwards. About what happened to the man I paid. Now, one of the three has gone. And there's only us. But the most important thing now, Jacqueline, is for you to get away. I'm as good as dead, but you might have a chance if you just get away from here. Persuade your family somehow, but you've got to leave. Persuade them to leave! Because it's not just you he'll want."

"What do you mean you're as good as dead? You need a good lawyer, Bernice. You must be able to afford one."

"No, that's not the point. The best lawyer in the world can't help me now. Don't you see? He's got me where he wants me. Locked up. Trapped. I can never get away from him now. Believe me, Jacqueline. He can *do* things that seem impossible. I'll never live to see a trial. But you still have a chance."

"I came to you because I thought you had answers."

"No answers, Jacqueline. Just the best advice I can give you. Get away from here as fast as you can. And don't look back."

"Time's up," said a disembodied voice from somewhere behind.

The anxiety had grown to outright fear inside Jacqueline, but she was also filled with an overwhelming sadness as a warder appeared behind Bernice.

"Goodbye, Jacqueline."

Bernice stood up and was led away.

". . . goodbye . . ."

Part Three
Vengeance

Chapter One
Shapiro

Shapiro had been lying on the same sand-dune for more than an hour, looking down into the sandy depression below, surrounded on all sides by dunes and bristling crab-grass. He had no idea if there were other beach huts, but he had been walking for well over two hours, and because most of that walk had been on sand, the strain had been exhausting. He had begun to bleed again, and had taken to holding the dressing tightly into his side and back. More by accident than by design, he had veered into the dunes from the beach and climbed. Almost exhausted, he had been ready to rest but the sight of the chalet and the parked car had been incentive enough to lie down in the crab-grass to watch. The car looked as if it had travelled a long way; the windscreen was dirty, with two crescent patches of clear glass where the wipers had been at work. The wheels were mud-spattered and stained. There was no telling how long the car had been there. But clearly he had been wrong about getting car access to the beach. There must be another way in apart from the Beachcomber car park.

Shapiro peered through the grass down at the chalet. It looked as if there had been a fire recently. The end of the wooden shack seemed blackened and charred from this distance. The windows were boarded and there was a large black stain on the sand beside those windows. He fancied that he could still smell burning in the salt air.

Shapiro looked carefully at the other dunes around him. The wind hissed in the swaying grass, but there was no other sign of movement. Down at the chalet, he concentrated hard, trying to pick up any kind of psychic emanation that might tell him that Paul was alive and down there. But there was nothing. Shapiro suppressed a groan, holding his side again, pulling his coat tightly around him. The last thing he wanted was sand in the wounds.

The clouds overhead were racing inland from the sea. Again, the colour of those clouds depressed him; and then he realised that those clouds reminded him somehow of the shafts of moonlight that had illuminated the church on the night that . . . the night that . . .

The night that you lost your faith?

No, I never lost my faith. Never!

But you've spent all those years since, struggling with what happened on that night, haven't you? Watching throughout your wife's pregnancy, hearing the doctors remark on how well everything was going, how healthy the baby was, and knowing that as the pregnancy progressed, your wife was steadily losing her grasp on reality, steadily losing her mind.

I've spent the years since then consolidating my faith. I refuse to believe that there is only evil and emptiness.

The wooden cross, shattered and broken on the marble floor.

I've seen the Evil. But there must also be a God. If there wasn't a counterbalance, the universe would fall apart.

When he reaches manhood, my seed within him will flower.

And Shapiro knew, as he buried his face in his sleeve, that he had failed to confront what had happened twenty years ago. No one but Veronica and himself had known about the incident in the church. That they had been in the presence of something utterly evil and inhuman was beyond doubt and although he had been tempted to report the matter instantly to the police, Veronica had become hysterical at the thought. So the police had not been advised, and they had attempted to rebuild their lives. Comforted only in the knowledge that but for his intervention Veronica would surely now be dead, he had continued to care for his wife, had doted on her; only to watch helplessly as her mind had retreated. And hadn't he—God help him—thought about the possibility of abortion after all? Hadn't he raised this with Veronica? Didn't he remember how she had ranted and screamed? And hadn't he pushed the confrontation with Gideon to the back of his mind, relegating it to nightmare?

Paul had grown, strong and healthy. He was a normal boy with normal interests and in excellent health. Even though his mother's situation had deteriorated rapidly, there had been nothing about him to suggest anything unnatural. He had coped bravely with his mother's incarceration, necessitated by her wild and savage outbreaks of temper, and the secret abuse she had inflicted on her son when Shapiro was not around to see. It had almost broken his heart . . . and the shadow of Gideon seemed as always to be there: omnipresent and hovering.

By his inaction, Shapiro felt that he had failed. He had failed his wife and his son. But now perhaps—just perhaps—there was a chance for him to act. To do something that should have been done a long time ago.

The wooden cross, lying broken on the marble floor.

Shapiro refused to think of failure, and looked back to the chalet. There was still no sign of movement. Soon, he would stagger down that sand-dune and look inside the chalet. But in his heart, he knew that his son would not be there. Because the thing that was called Gideon must surely be behind his son's kidnapping.

And if Gideon was there, he would surely be able to feel it.

Chapter Two
The Other

"Oh Christ," moaned Paul. "It's starting again . . ."

Van Buren had been dozing on one of the scorched, ramshackle chairs beside the chalet door. The shotgun was cradled in his lap. Instantly, it seemed, he was alert, rising quickly and moving to the bottom of the bed where Paul was strapped.

"Are you sure?"

"How sure do you want me to be, you bastard? I can feel it coming—the Rage. That's all I know. For God's sake, Van Buren. Knock me out or something. I can't go through this again. I can feel it killing me inside and . . . and . . . the Other is coming! That's all you need to know, isn't it?"

"No. You're my barometer, boy. I can tell how close he is by the way you react."

Paul convulsed then, jerking and contorting against the straps that bound him to the bed. Through teeth clenched in pain, he hissed, "Oh Chrissssttt . . ." as Van Buren chambered a shell into the shotgun breech and moved back to the door, still with his eyes fixed on Paul. "He's . . . God, he's . . . tricked you, Van Buren." Paul convulsed again, giving vent to a cry that was some hideous parody of laughter.

"Tricked? What do you mean *'tricked'*?"

"He knows. Gideon knows what you're trying to do."

"Knows? What the hell do you mean?" Van Buren edged the chalet door open with his foot, looking outside. His face was grim. Quickly, he moved back to the bed where Paul was in spasm again, straining at the straps. *"What do you mean?"*

"I can . . . can FEEL HIM!" This time, the bed springs groaned in protest as he strained upwards to be free. As if this final effort had momentarily freed him from the pain, Paul slumped back to the bed, face gleaming with perspiration.

"What do you MEAN?" hissed Van Buren, shaking him by the shoulder.

"He knows, Van Buren. Gideon knows that something has happened."

"How? HOW?" And this time, Van Buren seized a handful of hair and shook Paul's head.

"He's *withheld* the Rage from me! He knows that I'm being kept out of the game. So he's withheld it because he knows that something is wrong."

"That's not possible. I've been following him for years. He can't . . ."

"Your barometer's fucked, Van Buren. Because the Other is here. *Now!*"

Paul groaned and began to struggle maniacally at his bonds again, taking fistfuls of the sheet beneath him. Van Buren whirled from the bed and hurried to the chalet door. Paul was groaning through clenched teeth as his captor burst out of the chalet, keeping low and with the shotgun ready.

It was late afternoon and the hollow in which the chalet lay was striped by long shadows from the surrounding dunes. A wind had risen, making the crab-grass on those dunes hiss and sway.

And from somewhere, Van Buren could hear the sound of a car engine.

That car engine was racing. And getting louder.

Still crouching low, Van Buren scanned the dunes. It was impossible for a car to reach the chalet over those dunes; the area beyond, stretching to the main road, was too rough and too undulating for any car to travel. He whirled to look through the narrow gap between dunes that led down to the beach. This must surely be the only place that a car could move so fast . . . and it could never get through to the chalet between those dunes at speed. In an instant, Van Buren had made his decision. He would follow the same strategy as previously. He would find a place at the top of one of the surrounding dunes, keep an eye on the gap to the beach and wait for the car to appear. Whoever was driving along the beach would have to stop, even if his Rage was directing him to where Paul lay, and then carefully manoeuvre the car through the gap, just as he'd done when he'd arrived before carefully erasing the tyre tracks. And when he appeared in that gap, Van Buren would emerge and finish the job. No matter how clever Gideon thought he was; no matter if he had managed to "withdraw" the Rage from Paul in an effort to trick him, this newcomer would die. And if this One was after Paul, having killed the other brother, then Gideon would have to emerge from his hiding place to find his last remaining son. And Van Buren could be patient. He had spent fifty years in his search and could wait longer. Time for Gideon was running out.

Van Buren hurried to the nearest dune and began to climb, grabbing at the crab-grass to aid him.

The car engine was roaring now. It was close, and the sound of the roaring engine seemed to fill the air. The acoustic effect within the hollow was shattering; the sound seemed to be coming from all around, filling Van Buren with urgency as he climbed, casting glances back towards the beach and climbing and looking, climbing, looking, and . . .

Only feet above him, something huge and snarling and black exploded over the top of the sand-dune like some massive roaring animal. The shock of it flung Van Buren awkwardly backwards in a spray of sand. Pain lanced through his lower left leg and the shotgun flew from his hand. Coughing and roaring, the thing passed over him, cloaking him for a split-second in its great, manta-ray shadow before hitting the sand-dune below with a rattling crash and another spinning flurry of sand.

Van Buren clawed the sand from his eyes as the car bounced to the bottom of the dune on its suspension, engine still roaring. For a moment, its wheels spun in the sand-grooves that its impetus had created, sending twin flurries of sand into the air, and Van Buren saw a figure behind the wheel of what he could now make out was a Ford Cortina. The figure was twisting wildly at the wheel in a frenzy, and then the car was free from its brief sand-trap, screeching around to the right . . . and trundling towards the chalet.

The car was in a bad way, its progress over the dunes having almost wrecked that suspension. As the figure twisted wildly at the wheel and the car coughed and roared, picking up speed, Van Buren lunged at the sand around him, hunting for the shotgun.

He could not find it.

And the car was picking up speed, now thirty feet from him but the tyres managing to find a grip on the relatively flat expanse of sand in the floor of the hollow.

Van Buren felt steel, and dragged the shotgun out of the sand. Shaking loose sand from the barrel, he swung the gun up from where he lay and fired.

The back windscreen of the Cortina imploded.

The car slewed to the right, engine screaming. Dirty black smoke began to gush from under the bonnet, providing an instant smokescreen as it shuddered to a halt. Cursing, Van Buren slid down the dune into the hollow, spitting out sand, and savagely slashing the smoke from his face. He braced his slide at the bottom of the dune with both feet and felt burning pain shooting from his left ankle to his knee.

"Shit!"

He heard a hollow *chunk!* and saw through the smoke that the driver's door had been flung open. A figure was struggling in the gap, and Van Buren fired again—but his aim was bad from this awkward position. The shot punched a hole in the wing of the car.

And now a figure had broken from the smoke, dashing from the driver's seat and across the sand. Van Buren struggled to rise, gritting his teeth at the pain as he hobbled as quickly as he was able out of the trail of billowing smoke. Coughing and gagging, he saw the figure running for the chalet, his feet kicking up sand. Van Buren's foot would not support him and he fell, now twisting from where he lay to load and aim the shotgun.

The running man was screaming as he ran towards the chalet.

And from within the chalet, Paul was also screaming—as Van Buren levelled the shotgun and fired again. The man staggered but still screamed and ran.

"Shit!"

Van Buren struggled and twisted on the sand for a better position, rolled and fired again just as the man reached the beach hut door.

This time, the blast hit the running figure squarely in the back, lifting him from his feet and hurling him against the chalet wall. He bounced from the woodwork and fell to the sand, arms and legs flapping . . . and was still.

Inside the chalet, Paul had suddenly stopped screaming.

Using the stock of the shotgun as a brace, Van Buren struggled to his feet. Spitting out sand and wiping the smoke away from his eyes, he hobbled around the burning car, keeping his eyes on the figure lying by the beach hut. There was a red splash on the chalet wall, and even from here he could see the slowly creeping stain in the sand around the body.

Don't you feel anything for the people you've killed?

Van Buren halted momentarily, wiping his face, surprised at this unbidden inner question.

"No," he said aloud. "I can't afford to."

The words tasted dry in his throat.

Van Buren hobbled slowly onwards, cursing at the pain in his twisted calf. Once inside the chalet, he would have to bind that leg tight. He could not afford to be lame for what lay ahead. Now that the last-but-one "son" was—hopefully—dead, he could feel something happening inside him, and tried to assess what it was as he finally reached the body lying on the sand.

Cold fire.

The phrase seemed to encapsulate it. It had taken him so many years to arrive at this point, with so many disappointments, so many near-misses and escapes over the years that now he should be feeling elation, or the hate which had pushed him on should somehow be reaching its peak. But all he could feel now was this "cold fire": a steady slow burn of something that was not heat, something that was curiously dispassionate. He looked down at the body.

It was a young black man.

He was staring sightlessly at the sky, his teeth clenched. His chest was a hideous, gleaming mess. Already the flies had found him. His blue-jeaned legs lay at an impossibly crooked angle beneath him.

Cold fire.

Van Buren's face remained expressionless as he arrived at the chalet door. Now, he would have to douse that car wreck and kill the smoke; just as he'd killed the smoke from the burning chalet after the previous attack.

"No one left, Gideon?" he muttered, as he pushed open the chalet door. "No more sons? If not, you'll have to come to me."

Paul was staring at him as he entered, still strapped to the bed, his face still gleaming with perspiration.

"Only a matter of time . . ."

And then a shadow loomed from behind the chalet door.

Van Buren never saw the blow coming, never felt the pain as the chunk of driftwood came down across the back of his skull.

Chapter Three
Faith

Van Buren dreamed of people arguing.

Vague, insubstantial figures flitted through gauze; some beckoning, some cajoling. Sometimes a face seemed to push close to his own to stare into his eyes, but those faces were also insubstantial, like ghosts. And because he could see right through them, at such close quarters the details of these faces were impossible to focus upon. They were made from cobwebs and drifted away again. But the arguing continued; muffled and distant, but still full of anger.

He was standing in a corridor now, a long dark corridor with mirrors on the walls. He could see someone standing at the bottom of that corridor with his or her back turned to him. He began to move forward now, drifting as only possible in a dream. And as he drew nearer to the figure he could see that it was wearing a nightdress; the same nightdress that he remembered from their wedding night. Now he wanted to run, but could not; could only drift at that slow and steady rate. She had her face buried in her hands, and although he wanted to call out, this too seemed forbidden in the dream place. A great and bitter hurt welled within him. It had been so long, so many years since he had seen her. So many years since the . . .

funeral

. . . and she was turning now, face still buried in her hands.

And in the certain logic of nightmare, now he did not want to see her face. A great and unreasoning terror had overcome him. But still he drifted on, and still she turned. He was able to struggle, but could not halt the slow drifting as at last she turned to face him. The sounds of argument from all around were clearer now, the anger in those voices rising in pitch and volume as she began to lower her hands.

Those voices were raised to shouting. The anger and the horror overwhelmed him . . . but he could not avert his eyes.

The corridor was filled with screaming as his wife dropped her hands and stared wildly at him.

And Van Buren was awake, shocked from his nightmare into the real world again. But the sounds of argument were continuing. His vision was still blurred, but now instinct told him that he was awake, and the confusion between waking and sleeping made him cry out. Somehow, he could not move . . . and his leg had been immersed in fire. The voices ceased as he tried to drag his leg out of the flames.

"Welcome back," said a voice he knew.

At last his vision focused.

Paul Shapiro was still on the bed, still strapped down but straining up to look at him. He was on the floor, beside the door where . . . where . . .

Someone had hit him as he'd entered the chalet.

And the memory made him twist from where he lay on the floor. But he could hardly move. His arms and legs had been tied, and when he looked he could see that it had been with twine from his own kitbag in the corner of the chalet. His legs had also been tied with the remaining leather strap from that bag; the same straps that had held Gideon's bastard son to the bed.

Another figure moved into view beside the bed: an older man, perhaps forty or forty-five years old, dressed in a sober dark suit which had been sand-stained by the beach. He looked weary, his hair wild . . . and he was busying himself at the side of the bed as the boy whom Van Buren had kidnapped twisted his head to watch what the man was doing.

Gideon!

Van Buren reacted in fury, writhing on the floor despite the pain in his leg. His rage gave him enough physical strength to brace his body against the chalet wall, but his arms and legs were securely bound and he knew that he could never break free. Despite all his plans, despite all his years of searching, it was all over for him now—and a great wave of hopelessness enervated him. He could no longer cry out or struggle.

It was over.

"No, it isn't," said Paul from the bed. The older man moved around the bed, apparently oblivious to both of them. He was carrying a Gladstone bag as he moved. His face was blank; Van Buren could read nothing there. "You think it's Gideon. But it's not. It's my father . . ." And the boy began to laugh then; a cracked and slightly manic sound. "Sorry, I mean it's *not* my father. It's only the man who I thought was my father. Isn't that right, Dad?"

The older man looked up at Paul. His face contained an expression of profound sadness.

And that expression convinced Van Buren beyond any doubt that the man before him could not be Gideon. There was something ineffably sad and human in that face, and Van Buren's gut instinct confirmed the man's humanity.

"The priest," he said from the floor.

"Vicar," replied Shapiro as he turned away.

"What . . . what are you doing?"

The sad man did not answer. Instead, he knelt on the floor at the foot of the bed and opened the Gladstone bag. Van Buren could not see what he was doing from this position and struggled to get a better vantage point.

"Untie me," Van Buren said as the priest rummaged in the Gladstone bag.

Still no answer.

"We're all in danger. Worse danger than you can imagine. And the only way we stand a chance is for you to untie me."

"Why should he untie you?" said Paul wearily. "He won't untie me."

The vicar looked up at his son. "I've told you, Paul. You won't be able to help yourself. You'll try to stop me."

"What do you mean?" asked Van Buren. He struggled at the bonds again.

And now he could see what the vicar was doing. From the bag, he took a Bible and placed it on the floor at the foot of the bed. Then he took out two silver candlesticks, a small bowl and a silver flask. The candles were placed on either

side of the Bible at the foot of the bed. Shapiro uncorked the
flask and poured water into the bowl. Van Buren heard him
mumbling a prayer . . . and then realised what Shapiro was
about to do.

"You bloody fool! You think an exorcism is going to
work?"

Shapiro kept his head down, still praying.

"Do you know anything about what you're up against?
Anything?"

"He knows," said Paul wearily. "He told me everything when
you were out. He knows about Gideon, and what he is."

"Then you know that none of this will do any good. So untie me now, and we'll all wait for him here. I know how
to . . ."

Shapiro lit the candles, crossed himself and said, "I exorcise thee, creature of darkness. I exorcise thee, creature of
night."

"Look, you idiot. If you know anything about Gideon,
then you must know that the old symbols and the old rituals
just don't work against him."

*A broken wooden cross lying on a cold marble floor in the
moonlight.*

Shapiro picked up the bowl and stood again. He seemed
to be in pain, leaning against the creaking bedframe and
holding the small of his back. Recovering, he moved to
Paul. Saying another quick prayer, he dipped his fingers and
made the sign of the cross on Paul's forehead. "For your protection: in the name of the Father, and of the Son and of the
Holy Spirit."

*I want you to know that my religion is the only way and the
only truth. Evil simply IS, priest. Everything else is comforting
lies, invented by your Church to hide you from despair. All
you have to look forward to is death. And after death, your
soul will be meat for me and mine.*

Shapiro walked over to Van Buren.

"Untie me, you ignorant, superstitious fool!"

"For your protection: in the name of . . ."

Van Buren twisted away from Shapiro, refusing to let him place his fingers on his forehead. "None of this will help. Why don't you just wave a bunch of garlic at the boy, or prick him to see if he bleeds?" Van Buren tried to lash out with his bound legs, but the burning pain in his leg made him cry out. Shapiro stood up again, expression unchanged.

". . . the Father, and of the Son and of the Holy Spirit." Shapiro splashed water down upon him as he lay, in the Sign of the Cross.

"You're wasting TIME!" yelled Van Buren as Shapiro moved back to the bed. The flame from the candles created guttering shadows within the chalet. "None of this will work. And all the time, he'll be getting closer to us. Don't you see that?"

" 'According to your faith, be it unto you,' " said Shapiro. He gripped the bed rail tight and looked hard at Paul. "God, the Son of God, who by death destroyeth death, grant that by the power entrusted to thy unworthy servant that this boy be delivered. Grant that by your power and yours alone, the deceits of the evil one be as naught; grant forgiveness to me that in the testing of my faith, I failed in heart. And in the power entrusted to me, I ask that this boy be delivered from all evil spirits, all vain imaginings, projections and phantasms, and all deceits of the one naming himself Gideon . . ."

Paul began to groan, twisting his head from side to side.

"It won't work, Shapiro!" snapped Van Buren. "None of this has an effect on Gideon."

"Be quiet!" snapped Shapiro in turn, his face suffused with anger as he turned back, his hands still gripping the rail tight. "I'm not exorcising Gideon . . . I'm exorcising *Paul!*"

And then Paul began to scream, twisting and thrashing at

the leather bonds. Shapiro hurried to his side, grabbed the Gladstone bag and took out a wad of cotton. Seizing Paul's thrashing head, he jammed the cotton between his teeth to prevent him from biting off his own tongue.

"It won't work!" yelled Van Buren. "It can't work! Gideon doesn't fear the Church, or the rituals or the Sign of the Cross or . . ."

The chalet was suddenly filled with sound.

Van Buren shook his head. It was the sound of wind; of a buffeting storm on its way. There was a heavy pressure inside his head now and he shook his head to clear it, as Paul lunged and jerked on the mattress, trying to scream but his mouth was gagged.

Instead, he gave vent to a long and muffled groan.

Shapiro lunged back to the bottom of the bed . . . and the storm was in the chalet now. There was no wind, no swirling, buffeting torrent of wild air, but only the *sound* of the wind; the sound of a raging tempest, drowning out Paul's cries. From where he lay, Van Buren saw Shapiro clinging to the bed rail and continuing his prayers and invocations, but he could hear nothing now as the sound continued to build. And all Van Buren could think, over and over, was:

It's not possible. It's just not possible. Fifty years I've hunted him. And I know that this can't work on him. It can't work, it mustn't work, because, because . . .

And Van Buren realised that if it somehow *did* work, then it would be all over. If the Rage was exorcised from the boy, Gideon would not come.

If there was no other son out there, Gideon would cease to exist when the last son was "removed."

And he would be denied the vengeance on the thing that had taken his wife.

Van Buren opened his mouth and tried to scream at Shapiro to stop, but the raging sounds of the storm snatched his voice away. He lunged and twisted at his bonds, just as the boy lunged and twisted on the bed. A bitter wave of helplessness and hopelessness robbed him of strength. The pressure swelled again inside his head and Van Buren rolled to the floor, tears streaming from his eyes as he lay helplessly looking at the ceiling.

The invisible storm raged on.

Chapter Four
Brian Brennan

Brian Brennan replaced the telephone receiver, and stood looking at it for a long time.

Next door, the sounds of Armageddon raged from a television set as the boys watched a Japanese cartoon on video. Brian walked to the front door and peered out into the darkening late afternoon as if, on cue, Jacqueline would be suddenly walking up the front path towards the house. But the street was empty. Brian kept looking, as if he could find some answers there. But the street remained resolutely empty and there were no answers forthcoming.

Jacqueline had gone out earlier for a "walk" and had not returned.

Brian walked back down the corridor and looked at the telephone again. He had telephoned the library to find out whether she had called in for any reason, but no one had seen her. Both Janis and she had been granted temporary leave of absence since the horrific incident with the dogs but, knowing as he did how much she loved the job, he had guessed that maybe she had paid a visit. But he had been wrong. It was pointless telephoning Janis; she had taken advantage of the paid leave to visit family at the other end of the country. (Even the staunch and supportive Janis had been badly shaken by the dog attack.) So there was really no point in telephoning her to see if Jacqueline had popped in. Brian continued on to the lounge, looked in on the boys who were lounging on the floor and on a sofa, lost in animated adventure. The noise was too much in there. He needed to think.

He entered the kitchen, sitting at the pine table and fingering his empty coffee cup.

He didn't want to think about what might have happened to Jacqueline recently; didn't want to concentrate on her strange comings and goings, her vagueness and listlessness over recent months. He had spent long enough worrying about that. It all seemed to have been put behind them, and when she'd given him assurances that she was okay now, he had looked at her face and had seen the curious relief there, and had believed her. But now? Well, now it seemed as if there had been a return to that bad time. God, he didn't want to lose her. He wondered now whether he should have been more direct in confronting her about what had been going on. But at the back of his mind, he had been afraid that in so doing, everything would have been brought out into the open—with consequences that could not be retrieved. Then that bloody weird business at the library had happened, where she had been lucky not to have been torn apart. The local media had taken an immediate interest, both local and national press trying to invade their lives and find out more about the heroines who had saved the kids from certain death. They had managed to resist all approaches, and Brian had been anxious, now that the initial shock was over, to get back to their lives again. They had successfully managed to convince them that the real hero and heroine of the day had been Mr. Gough (well known child-lover) and the schoolteacher, Mrs. Pooley.

But everything had changed again.

Despite his protestations, Jacqueline had refused to seek help from a doctor about the depression which had arrived after the terrible shock of her ordeal. She had been lucky from a physical point of view: the dogs had not inflicted any severe damage. Fortunately, there would be no physical scarring. But Brian wondered what other scarring had been done to her mind. The distancing had begun again, and he did not know what to do about it.

Could it be that she was seeing the same person again? The same person who . . . but Brian killed that thought. It simply wasn't possible. No, it was up to him to be as supportive as possible, to try and help her find a way out of this terrible situation.

The telephone rang in the hall.

Brian hurried from the kitchen, grabbing at the receiver.

"Hello?"

There was no answer from the other end; just a blank hissing of static, as if it were a long-distance call and there was difficulty with the connection.

"Hello, Jacqueline? Is that you?"

Again, nothing but the hiss of static.

"Hello!"

". . . *Mr. Brennan* . . ." The voice sounded far away and hollow. The words were strangled, gravelly; as if the very act of speaking was at the cost of great effort.

"Yes, who is this?"

"*Your wife isn't there* . . ." Blank, emotionless words. Neither a question nor a statement, but carrying with them a horrifying suggestion of threat.

"Look, who is this?"

There was no reply; just the empty, static hiss. But Brian could somehow sense that the speaker was still there, still listening.

"The hell with it!" Brian slammed the telephone down and headed back to the kitchen. Before he could reach it, the telephone rang again. For a moment, he tried to ignore it, then thought of Jacqueline out there somewhere unknown and strode angrily back to the telephone, snatching it from its wall mount.

Again, the hissing static.

"Yes?" It was an angry statement rather than a query.

"If you hang up again, it will be the worse for your wife." The words were cracked, but carried with them a force of such malevolence that Brian felt genuinely alarmed. He cursed, and moved to put the receiver back, to hang up on this crank or pervert, but something about the voice made him cancel the action. *"Do you hear me? If you want to see her alive again, then you will do as I say."*

"If you don't get off this line . . ." Brian was surprised to hear that his own voice was wavering.

"I'm the one she's been seeing, Brennan. I'm the one she's been fucking. And she's here with me. Now. And if you even think about the police, I'll know it. Believe me. And if you do—I'll kill her."

"Who are you?" Brian's mouth had dried. The common sense that would have told him to hang up had evaporated in the presence of this voice. His fingers were trembling on the receiver. Never in his life had he ever known such a churning and instinctive fear.

It was a long-distance call from Hell—and when the voice told him that he had Jacqueline, he knew beyond doubt that it was true.

"Leave the house. Take your children."

"I won't even . . ."

"I know that you have a car. In two hours drive to the North Road, and wait at the crossroads layby for thirty minutes."

"I . . ."

"At the end of thirty minutes, begin driving down the North Road. You'll know where to stop."

"And then?"

"You want to see your wife, don't you? Then keep driving."

"But where?"

"You'll know when to stop."

The click and drone of disconnection made Brian start in alarm.

Now, it really was a dead line.

He stood looking at the telephone for a very long time.

Chapter Five
Bernice

Bernice sat in the cell, staring at the stained pastel wall. The feeling of dreaming had returned, the same debilitating feeling that had overcome her during the police interrogations. Dimly, she was aware that someone was rocking her like a child—then realised that she was doing it herself. It was better for her in this dream state. On the occasions when she had tried to shake it off, the horror had returned with a vengeance, and there had been terrible pain inside. She had never realised it before—but fear was pain. It racked her body until it was unbearable.

Samantha was dead.

Gideon.

Bernice moaned and began to rock back and forth again.

She hoped that Jacqueline had escaped. That had been her last lucid departure from dreaming. That had been the *third* person inside her speaking to Jacqueline. There was the first Bernice, the newsreader, the media celebrity; the person she had created, the person whom the police officers had questioned with gleaming eyes. Wasn't it just *something* to have such a juicy incident to investigate? Bernice Adams: newsreader—and her lesbian lover. And the murder. Now, wasn't this a whole lot better than your average handbag-snatch or joyride?

What do you know about that? Bernice Adams the dyke.

Then there was the other person that she had become in this holding cell. And Bernice had a feeling that the person in this dream world was the little girl she had once been: Bernice Adams aged eight. This Bernice was able to keep the nightmare at bay, this Bernice could remember the childhood days so well, could bring forth delicious and forgotten times, and forget about the fact that she was trapped in this room, and could only wait for the bad things to happen . . .

And the third person: who was that? This was the person who had pulled herself out of the "safe" place, who had embraced the fear and the pure nausea of terror so that she could warn Jacqueline to get away. This was the person who acknowledged the reality of the nightmare, acknowledged the presence of . . .

Gideon.

Bernice moaned and rocked again. The little girl inside wanted to be *her* forever. That was the safest place to hide, the safest way to . . .

"No!" Bernice threw her head back as if cresting from

some dark, underwater place. "No, I'm not going to! No, I'm *not* going to give in." She lunged from her bench in the holding cell, ran across the tiled floor and slapped the palms of both hands hard against the wall. Once, twice, three times.

"I will not be a fucking victim! I will not just let him take me!"

The observation hatch in the door creaked open.

Bernice stood back from the wall, breathing hard. The knot of raw fear was back in her stomach again, but she would not give in to it. She turned towards the hatch.

"I want to speak to someone in charge. Now!"

The observation hatch remained open.

"I said NOW!"

The hatch flapped shut again, and Bernice returned to the bunk, still breathing hard. Head in hands, she forced herself to think back. Even now, she could hardly bring herself really to believe what had happened. Maybe something else had happened altogether, something similarly horrifying and bizarre? Something that had twisted her perceptions of the actual event. After all, *insects?* When the police had broken down the door, there hadn't been a single insect to be seen, not even one of the many insects which must have been crushed underfoot during that nightmare struggle. No, there couldn't have been any insects. They were only in her mind. But she knew that Samantha was dead. The feeling she had inside her about that could not be denied. No insects, no mad buzzing in the air, no crawling black glistening mass, no . . .

"Gideon. It's him . . ."

And she realised that she was fooling herself. She had known the truth, the reality of their situation, when she had warned Jacqueline. Rationalising things now, after the event, was only her way of trying to escape the terror and the knowledge that somehow, in some way, the man they

thought they had killed would be coming to take his revenge. Bernice remembered how the insects had not come
into the kitchen, remembered how she had fallen at last
into that horrifying, gleaming mass. By rights, she should be
dead like Samantha. But somehow, they had been prevented from taking her, and only Samantha had been horribly killed. She knew that somehow this was Gideon's way of
making her pay, of making her suffer terror before he finally
came to take her. Of the three who had conspired against
Gideon, Yvonne had been first to die . . . and for all she
knew, Jacqueline was already dead. Whatever, Bernice
knew that she was marked for death . . . but she was not going to sit in this bloody cell and wait for it to come to her.

Bernice heard bolts being drawn on the door and looked
back again as it opened.

A short, thickset man stepped into the holding cell. His
head was down, one hand raised to his brow as if he were
trying to solve a difficult crossword clue. He was flanked by
two police constables. At last, he looked up. His fair hair was
thinning, but was carefully combed. He looked like a carpet
salesman.

"Detective Inspector Fenton," he announced. "I'm told you
might feel like talking to us now."

Bernice nodded wearily, and one of the constables
closed the holding cell door.

Chapter Six
The Hiding Place

Van Buren awoke to the feel of cold, salt wind on his face. His leg ached badly; his arms were stiff and sore where he had been lying on them. He groaned, rolling over on to his front and then, through blurred vision, saw a figure standing by the fire-ravaged, shattered window-frame of the chalet.

It was Shapiro, and he had pulled aside the oily tarpaulin that Van Buren had nailed up there after the fire. Sea air swirled in the chalet now, cold and fresh. Shapiro turned when he heard the sound, and when Van Buren's vision cleared at last, he could see the careworn expression on the vicar's face. He also seemed in pain, holding his side and back as he walked carefully back to the bed.

The noise of the storm was gone. Now, only the sound of the wind and the susurrant hush of the nearby sea filled the chalet.

Paul too was awake, and when Van Buren struggled round to get a better view, he could see that the leather straps binding him to the bed had been removed. Shapiro stooped with a grimace to pick up the silver flask. The candles at the foot of the bed were no longer lit, the Bible was lying on the mattress beside the boy. Shapiro poured water on to a handkerchief and wiped it across Paul's brow. The boy looked as if he had been in fever and was recovering. His face no longer had the sheen of sweat, but was white with dark hollows under the eyes. His hair had been plastered to his head.

"It worked," said Shapiro simply.

Van Buren opened his mouth to protest, to deny . . . and then looked at the boy's face. There could be no denying the truth of it, even after everything he'd thought he knew about the man—the *thing*—he had been hunting for so many years. Again, the crushing and bitter disappointment filled his soul. He had lost Gideon again. This time for ever.

"Not much fun, is it?" asked Paul weakly, looking over to where Van Buren lay. "Being hog-tied all bloody day." Van Buren did not answer.

"I've told Paul everything about Gideon," said Shapiro. "And he's told me all that you know about what kind of creature he was. Like most truly evil things," said the vicar, wringing out the handkerchief, "Gideon was a master of lies. There *were* things that we could use against him. I served his purpose once, when he showed me that the old symbols had no effect on him. He . . . he broke a cross, smashed a wooden cross in my church, to show me that my faith was false. I put too much faith in the *symbol*, when I should have had faith in the faith itself. I don't know . . . maybe I saw one too many Hammer films when I was younger. Now . . . now . . . I'm ashamed of how weak I was. All those years, all the communions I've given, all the sermons I've delivered, all the confessions I've taken. And throughout all those years, what Gideon did to my wife, what he did to me, has always been there at the back of my mind, eroding what I was doing. All those people I let down . . ." Shapiro's voiced cracked.

"You didn't give in, Dad," said Paul weakly. He had felt a deep bitterness while Shapiro had been preparing for the exorcism and had told him of everything that had happened, of the unconscious "psychic" cry that he had somehow been able to transmit to his father under the influence of the Rage, and then . . . of Paul's true "parentage." That bitterness had overcome him while they'd talked and he had discovered that he had been lied to for all those years. The knowledge that something not human had fathered him, and that perhaps he too was something less than human had overwhelmed him. He had killed under the influence of his true "father"—the true son of an inhuman father. But then the Rage had descended, and this time the madness had resulted in oblivion. Upon awakening, that bitterness had somehow gone—along with the possession that Van Buren had called the "Rage."

But the commencement of the exorcism had been a new kind of hell for Paul, further torment in which he had seen . . . things. Now that it was all over, as he looked on his father's face, that bitterness was no longer there.

"I was weak," said Shapiro, hanging his head. "I let your mother down, when she needed me . . ."

"You didn't let her down," said Paul. "There was nothing you could do for her after Gideon. I was *there*, Dad. I grew up in that household, don't forget. And I know what I saw, what I experienced. I can see things as they really were now . . . the way that Gideon took Mother's mind, the way you stood by her and tried to make things better."

"And my parishioners . . ."

"You didn't let them down either. If you'd given up, if you'd stopped being what you are, then *that* would have been the victory for Gideon. Don't you see?"

"I don't know . . ."

"Why did you hunt me out? Why did you perform the exorcism?"

"The last act of a desperate man? I love you, Paul. I couldn't think of anything else I could do. But even then, all the time, I . . . I just wasn't sure that even if I did find you, that it would work. I thought Gideon had you. I thought I would be confronting him again. Even then, I wasn't sure whether I could do any good. But now the nightmare's over. You're free of him."

"There *is* one other son, Dad," said Paul. "I could feel it, could feel him."

"Pardon me while I puke," said Van Buren. There was nothing inside him now, no reason to live. "I don't know how the hell you found us here, priest. But I don't give a damn. All I know is that while you stand there pontificating, Gideon has escaped. For a so-called man of God, you make me sick. Aren't you supposed to be committed to ridding the world of evil? All right, that exorcism seems to have worked—but all you've done is for your own reasons. You've allowed something purely evil to escape. Do you know how many people Gideon has killed over the centuries, how many women have died to satisfy his lust? Now that you've 'exorcised' your boy, Gideon's free to escape and begin all over again. After that last boy, there is only one Other. When he'd been forced to come here, and I'd killed him—all we had to do was wait. When he'd died, Gideon would have been forced to come here, and I could have rid the world of him for ever. But now that you've rid your boy of the Rage, the rules will change."

"Rules?"

"Your 'son,' for sake of a better word, has had the Rage removed from him. If things had been left to run their course, then Gideon's sons would be forced to fight it out amongst themselves until only one was left. And then Gideon would 'embody' in the survivor. But now that your boy has been exorcised, had the Rage removed, he's been taken out of the game. As far as Gideon is concerned, he's as good as dead. Ruled out. Now he'll draw the last remaining son to him, wherever he is, and embody within him. Once that happens, he'll be able to live again and escape . . ."

"He won't escape," said Paul, wiping a hand across his face and trying to rise. Shapiro hurried to him, propping the stained pillow up behind him for support. Paul braced himself against the corroded bedframe.

"What do you mean?" asked Shapiro.

"Once . . . in a Rage . . . I called out and you heard me. I don't know how that was possible—something about Gideon's power in me, maybe. Something that I was able to use. While I was . . . 'tapped-in' to him . . . he had a kind of control over me. He couldn't see me, but he knew that I was somehow being prevented from hunting the Others. That . . . 'connection' . . . was a two-way flow, Dad. While you were exorcising me, I saw things."

"Things?"

"There's one Other Son out there somewhere. The Rage was also withheld from him while Gideon waited to see what was going to happen. He's clever, and God he's . . ." Paul shuddered. "I *felt* him. And he's pure evil. But that's not the only thing I saw."

"Go on, boy," said Van Buren, eyes glinting.

"I saw Gideon—and he saw me. He knows where we are. I *felt* him. Once he embodies within his last son, he'll come after us, and he'll kill us for having interfered. Vengeance is all that matters."

A new feeling flooded Van Buren. He could feel himself coming back to life as a mad kind of joy began to swell within. "You thought the nightmare was over, priest? You'll know what hell is when he finds us." For Van Buren, there was a reason to live after all. Gideon had not escaped, had chosen *not* to escape. He would hunt them down after all . . . and Van Buren would be ready.

"We'll have to get away from here . . ." began Shapiro.

"It won't matter," replied Paul. "Wherever we go, he'll hunt us."

"Vampires are vengeful bastards," said Van Buren in a tone approaching glee. "My guess is that he's already taken his vengeance on whoever killed him. We're next on that list."

"I know where he is," said Paul quietly. "When he saw me—I saw him."

"Then we have to find him first," said Van Buren. "Before he has a chance to embody in the last son. And then we can destroy him. Once he's embodied and comes to us, we won't stand much of a chance."

"Destroy him?" said Shapiro. "How do we kill something that's already dead?"

"There's a way."

"How?"

"I'm not going to tell you, priest. I've hunted the bastard for fifty years. I know of only one thing that can finish him and his kind, and it has nothing to do with your church."

"Tell us!" snapped Paul. "Don't we stand a better chance if we all know how to handle him?"

"Only one person is going to finish Gideon. And that's me."

"Then I won't tell you where he is."

"That's a stupid attempt at a stand-off, boy. You don't tell, and we'll just wait here until he turns up—and tears us apart, limb from limb. Listen, no one but me is going to destroy Gideon. And don't kid yourself, either of you. There is a way, but the chances of being able to do it, or of any of us surviving are minimal. We're probably all going to die . . . so tell me, boy. Where is he?"

Paul looked at his father, then back to Van Buren.

"I was in darkness, floating. Somewhere high. Looking down over a city. Neon-like stars. Buildings, factories. And then I began to drift down towards a building; a big, Gothic-looking place with spires. Everything became black as I moved on down, and I knew that I was inside the building now, still descending. And I knew that *he* was down there somewhere, aware of me; just as I was aware of him. I began to move down and saw boards of wood; like flooring planks. He was under there, I knew it. With his eyes open, looking at me straight through the wood, even though I couldn't see him. I could see scaffolding, and painted wood. Bright, garish colours.

"I didn't want to descend any further. I felt as if he would raise his arms and embrace me as I came down. I struggled to break away, to rise.

"And then I saw seats; rows and rows of upholstered seats.

"And then a sign: 'The Phoenix.' "

Paul paused. His face was gleaming with sweat again, despite the cool sea air.

"So what does that all add up to, boy?" asked Van Buren.

Paul cleared his throat. When he spoke, his voice was cracked.

"He's in a theatre called the Phoenix. In Newcastle."

"A theatre," said Van Buren. "I don't understand. Where in the theatre? Come on boy, where?"

Paul groaned again, wiping his face. He remembered the sheer malevolence and hate that had radiated from beneath those planks of wood.

"Under the stage," he said. "Someone hid him under the stage."

Van Buren rolled back to look up at the ceiling again, and laughed.

"Under the stage. Yes, right. Very poetic, Gideon. Very apt."

"Why apt?" asked Shapiro.

"A vampire that preys not only on sex, but on strong emotions. He also gets his strength from making his prey afraid, from others' intense emotions. So where else to rest while you're waiting for a new life to begin? Under a theatre's stage. Every night, actors and actresses are on that stage above him, creating raw emotion. And every night, hundreds of people are focusing their own conjured-up emotions on to that stage. All that projected emotion, all being sucked up by what's hidden beneath it. All giving him power. Perfect, Gideon. Perfect."

"So now what do we do?"

"We're going to that theatre. We're going to find him under that stage. And we're going to try and finish him."

"It may already be too late," said Paul. "The remaining son may already be on his way, may already have embodied."

"What other options do we have? How did you get here, Shapiro?"

"My car's a mile or so down the beach, parked beside the old restaurant."

"Good. We'll clear up here, and drive mine back to where yours is parked. Your car is bound to be in better shape than mine, and it's certainly in better shape than the wreck out there."

"I'll need to say some words over the body outside before we go," said Shapiro.

"You'll be wasting time."

"Whose time? His? It *means* something, Van Buren. Doesn't what's happened mean anything to you? All those people you've killed. Don't you feel anything about that? Doesn't the fact that the exorcism worked on Paul say anything to you? Doesn't it make you think?"

"No. All I want is Gideon."

"I feel sorry for you."

"Feel sorry for yourself, priest. Now come on, it's time to move. Untie me."

Shapiro looked at Paul. He nodded his head. Van Buren began to laugh again as Shapiro crossed the chalet and bent down painfully to loosen his bindings.

"Under the stage, Gideon? Always had a penchant for the dramatic, you bastard!"

"God help us," said Shapiro.

"Keep praying, priest," said Van Buren. "I may still be an atheist bastard, but we need all the help we can get."

Chapter Seven
Brian

Brian Brennan sat behind the wheel of his Nissan, clutching the rim tight and with an uncomfortable trickle of sweat in the small of his back. He shifted position, and the shirt stuck to his skin, making him feel even more uncomfortable and anxious than before.

The road ahead was clear. Only one station wagon had passed by in the last twenty minutes, and he recalled listening to that Bernice Adams on television reading out the latest news on complaints about this road. It was little used, a connection for a main motorway which had never arrived. Central government funds had constructed the linking road, but the same funds had dried up when it came to the motorway itself. So here was the road at the north of the city and leading nowhere in particular.

The perfect place to be at the disposal of someone who said they'd kidnapped your wife.

Jacqueline had not returned home, had not telephoned, and as time ticked by, Brian had become more and more nervous. He had been unable to dismiss the caller as a crank or pervert; the sound of that dead voice on the other end of the telephone line had conjured up feelings inside him that he'd never believed possible. There was an utter, horrifying *certainty* that Jacqueline was in very serious trouble, a dreadful conviction that the caller had his wife captive. And now that he was sitting here, what was going to happen? Brian's fingers were sticky with sweat. He wiped them nervously on the wheel and looked around. The sky was darkening, the sun was going down. Very soon, the night would be closing in.

"How much longer, Dad?" said Martin from the back seat. It had been a difficult twenty minutes, first convincing the kids to come with him when they wanted to watch television, and then having to fabricate excuses as to why they had to sit there for so long waiting.

"Not long."

"Can we have a different radio channel on?" asked James, still with his eyes glued to the Nintendo game on his lap. "I'm sick of that Radio 2 Muzak."

Brian switched channels, until a hard rock number blasted from the speakers. He turned it down.

"Oh Daaaaad . . ." moaned Martin.

"That's loud enough."

"Mum back at the library?"

"No."

"Then where?"

"Don't you listen, Martin? I told you, she's been to the doctor's."

"So why are we waiting out here, then?" asked James.

"Now listen, I've told you all this. She's been to see a

friend. I said I'd pick her up here." He could not disguise the tension in his voice this time, and could feel the boys shuffling uneasily in the back seat. Glancing in the rearview mirror, he saw them exchange a glance and knew that they were both getting worried, could sense that they both knew something more was going on.

Oh, Christ . . . Brian gripped the steering wheel tighter and looked at his watch again. Only five minutes to go.

What the hell am I going to do?

And Acting Detective Inspector McTighe lowered the infrared binoculars and smiled.

There was no pleasure in that smile; after all, the poor bastard sitting out there in the car was going through one hell of a time. The fear that Brennan was trying to contain was still plainly visible on his face, even through the binoculars. He turned to his driver, a plainclothes constable.

"Change from pounding the beat, Bob?"

Bob gave a weary smile and looked the other way. McTighe smiled again and lifted the binoculars.

This couldn't have happened at a better time. His predecessor, DI Farland, had just suffered a massive heart attack and even if he did survive it, there was no way that he would be returning to the force. McTighe had therefore been promoted to "Acting DI" until such time as the normal interviewing procedures could be arranged and suitable candidates lined up. What he really wanted now was something "big" to come along, something that he could act on immediately; something that could consolidate his position in interview.

And then, just at the right moment, the potential kidnapping had come along. Perfect. Although there had been less evidence than usual to mount a full operation, McTighe had jumped at the chance, revelling in the opportunity to take direct action. He had ignored queries from junior officers. Was the operation justified on the strength of a single telephone conversation? What about ransom? The caller hadn't asked for any cash. McTighe had "hung his hat" on a revenge motive. This was a nutcase. He didn't want money. He only wanted the Brennan family to suffer. Despite the intense interview with Brian Brennan after the telephone call had been received, and the husband's assurances that there was no jealous lover involved, McTighe remained unconvinced. He could sense a love triangle a mile away. Whatever—this was his chance to act, to show that he could mount an efficient and effective operation. Despite the reservations of others.

His car was parked in a screened layby on a side-road running parallel to the North Road. Another two unmarked cars had been placed at either exit after the surrounding area had been carefully and thoroughly searched. Again, these cars had been screened. At present, it was not possible to use the police helicopter for fear of alerting the kidnapper. Even at night, its presence could alert anyone in the vicinity. However, it was in the area, working on a six-mile circular flight pattern, and ready to move in when given the instruction. For the time being, there would be no radio connection between cars or helicopter in case the kidnapper had access to a CB radio band. The short-wave facility might well be able to tune in to the police radios. Again, McTighe's juniors had queried this action. Was McTighe being too careful?

No, you bastards, I just want this job.

McTighe scanned the Nissan again, watching as Brennan wiped perspiration from his face; then he moved to look at the two kids in the back. They were unaware of the situation, and McTighe gritted his teeth. Had he made a mistake here? He remembered shouting down his team when they had expressed concern at the kids being in the car, and at placing minors in potential danger. He had reminded them that the caller had been very specific; that the kids had to be in the car with Brennan. After all, what was likely to happen if, at some stage, the kidnapper saw that his instructions hadn't been followed to the letter? What was he likely to do to Mrs. Brennan? The kids wouldn't be in danger, neither would the father. After all, this was a major operation with the car under close surveillance at all times. No one was going to get them. And where the hell could they find two midget coppers to dress up in kids' clothes at this time of the day, anyway? As soon as the kidnapper made whatever move he'd planned, then they would move in. McTighe shifted uneasily. He didn't feel comfortable with this part of the plan now.

What if no one turns up? After all, what kind of crazy instruction was that to give Brennan? Just wait on the North Road for thirty minutes and then begin driving. Maybe he just wanted Brennan out of the house for some reason? Well, if so, there were officers staked out there. Perhaps Mrs. Brennan was already dead? Maybe the whole thing was just a hoax?

Hoax or not, McTighe would still have been able to show his superiors that he had been capable of mounting a streamlined and effective operation.

McTighe watched Brennan engage gears, watched him check behind him on the deserted road—and then pull away.

"Half past," said the DI unnecessarily, and watched as the car moved off down the North Road.

Exactly three minutes later, he followed.

Chapter Eight
Jacqueline

And Jacqueline pushed the key into the door lock.

In the living room, a policewoman and constable jumped up from the sofa and moved quickly towards the door as it began to open.

Jacqueline stepped into the room, and then froze as the two uniformed officers suddenly appeared in the passageway.

"Oh Christ," she said, "Oh Christ . . ."

"Mrs. Brennan?" asked the policewoman.

"Yes, what's happened? Where's my husband, and the kids?"

"They're fine," said the constable. "It's you we've been worried about."

"But where *are* they?" Panic was seizing Jacqueline now. Involuntarily, she had stepped forward and seized the policewoman's sleeve.

"Someone telephoned. A man who said you'd been kidnapped. Just a cruel hoax, Mrs. Brennan. So just take it easy, your husband and children are safe and well."

"Where?"

"They were told to meet your 'kidnapper.' But don't worry, they're under full police protection . . ."

"I've been walking," said Jacqueline distantly. "Just walking, wondering what to do, wondering what . . ."

And now, the police constable was guiding her into the

living room, guiding her to the sofa and looking guiltily at the two coffee cups and the plates of remaining food that they'd taken from the fridge.

"I didn't know what to do after I saw Bernice. I couldn't come straight home, I needed time to think things through. I needed time to think, time to work out what I was ... *They've gone to MEET him?!*"

The policewoman tried to restrain Jacqueline as she lunged from the sofa again.

"Take it easy, Mrs. Brennan. They're perfectly safe. Billy, you'd better radio in and ..."

"But you don't understand. They're *not* safe. They're in terrible danger. Please, I've got to go to them. Please ..."

"Alpha-Delta, this is 'Home Alone.' Mrs. Brennan has arrived home safely; repeat: Mrs. Brennan has arrived home safely. Instructions, please. Over."

"For Christ's sake!" shouted Jacqueline. "Stop whatever's happening. Get them back, get them ..."

The room dimmed.

Fear welled upwards within Jacqueline, out of control.

She reached for the living room door, saw it sway and tilt. Then nothing.

Chapter Nine
Bernice

"This is DI Fenton, in the presence of Police Constables Ainwright and Baron. The time is 8:23 p.m. and I'm interviewing Bernice Adams. So . . . Ms. Adams. What would you like to tell us?"

"I didn't kill Samantha."

"So what *did* happen?"

"Someone else killed her."

"And who exactly is that someone?"

"If I told you, you wouldn't believe me."

"Try me."

"His name is Gideon."

"Yes?" Fenton opened his hands, inviting more comment. Bernice finished lighting a cigarette, squinted as the smoke curled in front of her eyes. She had been taken from the cell to an interview room, almost as plain as the place she had left, with the exception of a barred window in one wall with frosted reinforced glass.

"That's all I know about him. Except that he isn't human."

"Not human. Right."

"He killed Samantha because he wants me to suffer before he kills me as well."

"Look, Ms. Adams. Would you like to start from the beginning? Who is Gideon?"

"I don't know. All I know is his name."

"He was in the flat with you when Samantha died. Is that what you're saying?"

"No."

"No," said Fenton and breathed out a long sigh. "He wasn't in the flat with you, but he killed Samantha."

"That's right."

"And just how did he manage to do that?"

"He sent things to do it."

"Things?"

Bernice inhaled from the cigarette again, blowing smoke straight up at the ceiling. "Look, if I told you exactly what happened you'd just dismiss me as being insane. I didn't kill Samantha, Gideon did. And I'm not going to tell you how it happened. He simply *sent* something, and Samantha died as a result."

"You're copping a plea of insanity, is that it, Bernice?"

"No, I'm not."

"You're sitting there, telling us a load of garbled nonsense. And you think that if you can keep it going for long enough, we'll start thinking you need a shrink. Well, I'll tell you what I think. I think you killed her. You were heard arguing in your flat . . ."

"Fenner," snorted Bernice derisively.

"Heard arguing," repeated Fenton. "And we know just exactly what you were arguing about."

"What do you mean?"

"We found the note, Ms. Adams. The note from Gideon."

Bernice felt the cold fear curdling in her stomach again, took another draw on the cigarette and struggled to keep control.

"You were having an affair with this man," continued Fenton. "He sent his note to Samantha. You fought about it. And you shoved Samantha through that plate-glass window to her death."

From somewhere beyond, somewhere in the police station, Bernice heard raised voices; as if some kind of altercation was taking place.

"That's not the way it was," said Bernice. Her throat had tightened, making her voice sound hoarse. "I tried to save Samantha, tried to protect her . . ."

Somewhere in the police station a man began to shout at the top of his voice. Fenton looked up, irritated. Taking the irritation as a cue, one of the police constables rose from the table and opened the interview room door. The sounds of commotion were louder now as he opened the door and slipped quickly outside, closing it behind him again. Probably a bunch of drunks resisting arrest.

"Look," continued Bernice. "He killed Samantha. And he wants to kill me. I need your protection from him. He can do things that just don't seem possible. I never want to be left alone, do you understand? Even *here* in this police station. I'm not just going to sit here and wait for him to come for me. I want you to protect me, to help me."

"And that's just what we'll do, Ms. Adams. If you cooperate with us and tell me everything. I want to know exactly what happened, exactly how . . ."

Somewhere beyond, there was a juddering crash of furniture.

Someone began to scream.

"Jesus Christ!" snapped Fenton. "What the bloody hell is going on out there?" The other police constable hurried to the door as Fenton switched off the tape-recorder. "How the hell am I supposed to . . . ?"

And then Bernice saw the look on the constable's face as he turned back from the opened door. That face was ashen.

"Sir? You'd better . . ."

Angrily, Fenton strode to the door, shoving the constable ahead of him. Angrily again, he swung the door closed behind him. Bernice heard him say, "All right then, what the *fuck* is going on . . ." just as the interview room door slammed shut.

Bernice stubbed her cigarette out, and then lit another.

Another crash from somewhere in the police station startled her. She looked back at the door. Now there were more men shouting. And something about the desperate, frightened tone of those voices was bringing back all of the fear.

Again, someone screamed—and the ululating, terror-stricken sound of it brought Bernice to her feet. The chair flapped over behind her.

Something was dreadfully, terribly wrong.

The screaming went on and on—and Bernice spun in the interview room, looking for some way out. But there was only the door and the barred window.

"Why doesn't someone stop it?" said Bernice aloud, now moving nervously around the room, looking from door to window. "Why doesn't someone come *back?*"

From beyond the door came the unmistakable sound of a window breaking.

"Come back!" shouted Bernice, desperately trying to remember the detective inspector's name. "Fenton! Come *back!*"

And then the interview room door flew open.

Bernice recoiled in alarm as Fenton burst into the room. Turning quickly, he slammed that door shut and threw his back against it. Bernice looked at him, mesmerised in terror. His face was cut. There were blood streaks on his left cheek. His hair was awry, the sleeve of his jacket torn and he was breathing heavily. For a second, he just stared ahead past Bernice, as if gathering himself. Then he looked directly at her. His former composure had vanished.

"What . . . ?" asked Bernice, her voice choked with fear.

"It's all right," said Fenton, holding out a hand to her. He seemed unsure of what to do or say. Bernice could see the mental turmoil there as he tried to rationalise what was happening. "All right . . . all right . . . Ms. Adams."

Something else beyond that door shattered and there were more screams. Suddenly, a fire alarm bell began to ring, sharp and frightening in the interview room. Fenton spun away from the interview room door at the sound, and now Bernice clutched at his arm.

"What in God's name is happening?"

Fenton seized both of her arms, looked around in confusion and then steered her back to the desk. Flipping the chair upright again, he put her into it.

"You've *got* to tell me. Please . . ."

Fenton put a hand gingerly to his cheek, looked at the blood on his fingertips.

"I don't believe it. Just don't . . ."

"*What*, for Christ's sake?" shouted Bernice.

Fenton looked at her with sheer disbelief in his eyes.

"Rats," he said simply. "Hundreds and hundreds of fucking rats."

The fire alarm continued to clatter. Bernice heard running feet in the corridor outside, then the sounds of a desk overturning. Someone began to yell for help.

"They're all over the station. Must have come out of the sewers or something, and they're just . . . just . . . *all over the fucking place*."

"Oh Christ," said Bernice. "It's Gideon."

"What?"

"It's him. He's come for me."

"It went for my face," said Fenton, still disbelieving. "I went out there and they were all over Jimmy Grantham. All *over* him. He was screaming, and thrashing . . . and one of them just flew straight at my . . ."

Fenton seemed to rally then, seemed to emerge from his disbelief and his horror.

"Stay there!" he snapped at Bernice and strode back to the interview room door. There was a coatstand next to it. He knocked it over and kicked the pegged, circular top-piece from it, then yanked out the pole from the base. Hefting it like a club, he moved back to the door. Somewhere in the police station, Bernice could hear a rustling, scampering sound that reminded her with horror of what had happened to Samantha in their flat.

"Where are you going?"

"I've got to go back there and help . . ."

"But it's him! It's Gideon, and the only reason that . . . that . . . *this* is happening is because of me. He's come for me, Fenton. You have to protect me!"

Fenton turned back then, just as another window shattered beyond the door, and the fire alarm went on and on and on.

"Nothing or no one is going to get you, Bernice. I promise you."

Fenton braced himself, lifting the pole with one hand and closing his other hand around the door handle.

"I'll close it behind me. Make sure it stays closed until I . . ."

Beyond the door, someone screamed and then began uttering short, hoarse cries of terror as he blundered away.

". . . until I come back for you."

"But I . . ."

"Stay here until I get back. You'll be okay. You'll . . ."

And then something exploded in the interview room.

Bernice cried out, reeling from the desk as a cloud of shattered glass filled the air. Fenton recoiled from the door, pole still held high, eyes wide in alarm. The insistent, piercing sound of the fire alarm added to the confusion as he whirled to Bernice. There was another impact, and more glass flew into the room. At last, they could both see what had happened.

Someone had smashed the frosted window from outside. And even as they watched, Bernice saw the shadow of something being withdrawn and brought back with savage force on the other side of that window, recoiled again as more glass was punched into the room.

"What the bloody hell . . ."

Fenton put himself between the window and Bernice, anxiously looking back to the door. Weighing the pole like a club, he waited for another blow to the window. There was none. And there was no sign of whoever or whatever had shattered the window. Practically all of the frosted glass had been smashed from the frame and was lying sparkling on the interview room floor. Four sturdy iron bars filled the window aperture, and Bernice could see over his shoulder that there was an alley or yard of some sort beyond. She could see a wet brick wall less than ten feet from the window.

Warily, Fenton began to move towards the window, still expecting another blow, or an attack of some sort from whoever was outside. Those iron bars could not be broken, so no one could get in.

"Fenton!" hissed Bernice. "If it's him . . ."

"Quiet!" Fenton reached the window at last, still warily straining to look from side to side, making sure that no one was lurking just within reach. Right at the window at last, he sneaked a look outwards and downwards into the alley or yard.

"Oh Sweet Jesus. I don't believe it."

"What, Fenton? *What?*"

"Rats. More of them. They're . . . they're just *swarming* out of a sewer grating down there. The whole alley's alive with them. Come on, we're going to have to risk it and get out of here. If we make a good run at it we should be able to . . ."

And a gnarled white hand clutched through the iron bars, seizing Fenton's hair.

He shouted in pain and shock, clutching at the hand and trying to twist away. But the hand dragged him back hard at the window-frame, his face connecting with the bars with a dull and bone-crunching impact. Fenton's legs collapsed under him as the hand jerked back again . . . and again . . . and again. Each time, Fenton's face was slammed hard against the iron bars.

And Bernice could only watch as, with each blow, a spray of thickening redness splashed the interview room wall. Fenton's body began to convulse and twitch.

The hand withdrew . . . and Fenton slithered to the floor, the bloody ruin of his face turning to Bernice with what seemed to be a hideous, mocking and shattered grin.

A shadow moved into the window-frame, behind the bloodied bars.

Bernice could not move, could only stand and look and feel the three personalities inside her fighting to hide.

The shadow stepped forward and braced its gnarled white hands on the bars. It leaned further forward . . . and at last, she could see its face.

"*Hello, Bernice*," said Gideon. The voice was hideous, guttural. "*Remember me?*"

Of the fact that it was Gideon, there could be no doubt. And now she knew that the three women had after all succeeded in their plan to kill him. Because the face that stared at her through the shattered window aperture was a dead face. It was a face that had rotted and decayed. Leprous grey-white skin was stretched tight over that skull face, the once immaculately groomed hair hung tattered and dishevelled in front of it. Where there had once been a right eye was now a deep and bloody crater where Jacqueline had shot him. In the half light of the interview room it seemed that there were living, moving *things* in that crater.

"What's the matter?" That voice was dragging, like a record running down, semi-liquid, as if some vile and poisonous fluid was in his lungs. *"Afraid to look in my eyes? Silly girl. Don't you know that I can't make you do things any more just by making you look into my eyes. No. I can't do that, can I? Because they aren't there any more."* The hideously decomposed face withdrew into the shadows again, and this time the voice was filled with a malevolent, chilling malice. *"Are they?"*

And then the rats swarmed through the shattered window-frame.

Huge, filth-encrusted rodents the size of kittens.

Glittering eyes, chittering teeth. Squealing, rustling. Leaping over each other to scrabble and claw through the aperture and into the interview room. Falling and scrabbling on to Fenton's bloodied corpse, swarming over his ruined, bloody face and leaping across the floor towards Bernice . . .

. . . who knew now that this was a nightmare, and that by interacting with it she would only make it real. She looked at the interview room door, and could not will herself to run to it. There were no screams out there now, no breaking windows or furniture, just the susurrant sounds of a multitude of living things on the other side, scratching and scrabbling to join their companions in the interview room.

"I will not be a victim," said Bernice, her words drowned by the rustling and squealing.

I wonder what the headlines will say? thought Bernice the newsreader. *Samantha,* thought the other Bernice, and felt herself being lowered for ever into that deepening well of sadness.

And at the last, only the child inside.

And the terror.

And the agony.

And the sound of Death, laughing on the other side of the shattered window-frame.

Chapter Ten
Brian

Brian had travelled along the North Road route before, on business. At a steady fifty miles per hour, he reckoned that he would reach the connecting roundabout in about a half hour—a view shared by the police.

He gritted his teeth as the kids started arguing in the back. Had he done the right thing by contacting the police, after all?

Of course you did the right thing! What the hell else could you do? Play straight into the hands of some bloody maniac . . . ?

And the thought that Jacqueline was at someone's mercy was almost too much to bear.

"Be quiet!"

The boys were instantly silent, unused to the severe tone of their father's voice. They settled back in surly mood.

The police were following, were all around. And as soon as someone made a move, it would be all over.

But what kind of move? "Keep driving and you'll know when to stop!" What kind of bloody instruction is that?

A large fly or wasp splattered against the windscreen.

Brian had seen the police action map, knew where the cars were stationed. He looked up into the night sky, knowing that there was a helicopter up there somewhere, just waiting to zoom in as soon as the instruction was given.

Oh Christ, Jacqueline. I hope you're all right. I hope that everything . . .

Brian cursed as several more nightbugs splashed across the windscreen. He operated the windscreen wipers, only succeeding in smearing their dead bodies across the glass in a crescent of milky fluid. He operated the water jet and kept the windscreen wipers on. But somehow, he was driving through clouds of the things now; clouds of flies impacting on the plexi-glass.

"Wow!" said Martin. "Look at that . . ."

James laughed. "Fly-tastic, Dad!"

Brian cursed, operating the water jets continuously. He'd never known flies to be around in clouds like this so late at night.

What if it's a bloody hoax? What if Jacqueline's safe and sound somewhere? You know she's been acting strange just lately. Maybe she just took herself off somewhere for a break?

And then Brian thought of the voice on the telephone, and remembered how he had felt.

But it was just a VOICE, for God's sake. It might just be a crank or a . . .

Flies were still impacting on the windscreen. There was a sludge of their compacted remains on the windscreen wipers themselves as the crescent swathes continued and the flies kept coming and coming and coming.

"This is ridiculous," said Brian aloud.

They were coming too thick and fast for the windscreen

wipers now. His view ahead was distorted and limited. Brian applied pressure to the brake, but the slowing of the vehicle served only to make the obstruction greater as masses of insects obliterated the windscreen. The plexiglass had become a great crawling mass of flies, and the boys were shocked into silence now as Brian cursed again and jammed down on the water jets and . . .

Someone suddenly strode out into the road, dead ahead of the car.

Brian saw the smeared image of a man through the plexiglass, saw him come to a halt directly in the path of the car, saw him turn and face the car as it came on towards him.

"Christ!"

Brian jammed his foot on the brake pedal. The flies on the windscreen were a buzzing crawling mass.

In the back, the boys screamed and clutched at their seats as Brian swung the wheel, trying to miss the tall shadow in the road.

And then the car overturned, smashing down on to its roof.

Brian saw a whirling mass before his eyes, an explosion of glass. The world had gone mad, had tilted into insanity. Something smashed into his head (*the roof of the car?*) and he spun away into unconsciousness.

"Christ!" exclaimed DI McTighe when the car headlights picked up the car in the road ahead. It was on its roof and had slewed to the other side of the road, right in the path of any other oncoming vehicle. Broken glass glittered on tarmac.

And someone was striding purposefully towards the car in the darkness. The tall silhouette of a man.

The time for radio silence was over.

"This is McTighe! Units Two, Three and Flying Man—move in!"

*   *   *

The agony in his back and legs brought Brian back to consciousness. His hand was dangling right before his face. It was cut along the forefinger and dark red blood gleamed on the flesh. He watched, fascinated, as a bead of blood collected on his fingertip and then dropped away into space. He followed that dripping trail, and then realised that he was hanging up in the air somehow. He groaned and tried to move. There was faint illumination from somewhere, but everything seemed wrong, everything seemed upside down and distorted and . . .

He remembered . . . and then realised that the car had turned over. He was still strapped into his seat, and was hanging upside down. He tried to move his legs and the pain racked his entire body. He knew that they must be broken, and releasing the seat-belt would only send him plunging face first to the roof.

"Dad . . ."

It was James.

Brian tried to twist around to look for his sons, but the pain was too much.

"Jim?"

"Yeah. Dad, it's Martin. I think he's hurt. I think he's . . ." There were tears coming, tears and panic.

"It's all right, all right. The police will be here any second. Where are you?"

"I'm still in the back. Still got my seat-belt on. But Martin's on the floor, I mean the roof, and he's not moving, Dad. He's not moving. I think . . ."

"It's okay, Jim. Can you get free?"

"Yes, I think so."

"Release the seat-belt catch carefully and let yourself down. Then get Martin out of the car and on to the road. The police will be coming. It's all right."

Brian gritted his teeth in pain and listened as James released the belt, grunting in surprise when it released him.

"You okay?"

"Yeah . . . yeah . . ."

Brian heard his son lower himself to the roof, heard him fumbling. He twisted his head around and at last could see James from the corner of his eye.

"Open the door, son. That's it. Just turn the handle and push."

A draught of cool wind filled the car as the door swung open, and Brian saw James crawling gingerly through to the tarmac.

Now Brian could hear the sounds of footsteps crunching on broken glass.

"They're here, Dad," said James. "It's the police."

"Thank Christ . . ." muttered Brian as a pair of feet came into view. Brian saw James lift up a hand for help.

Then he saw the look of horror on his son's face when a gnarled white hand reached down for his hand.

James gave a small cry of utter terror.

The hand seized his wrist, and Brian saw his son yanked out of the opened door and lifted aloft out of sight.

Then he remembered the shadow that had walked out into the road, in front of the car.

"James!"

The boots turned and walked away from the car, crunching broken glass underfoot. James was screaming now, and Brian could see his struggling shadow being borne away into the night.

"JAAAAAMES!"

Someone was moving away from the overturned car as DI McTighe's own car slewed over to it, siren blaring. For a moment, as he kicked open the door and climbed out, McTighe thought that it must be Brennan. He must have managed to free himself and was rescuing the kids . . . but now McTighe could see that this man was much taller, dressed in black. And he was striding away from the car, holding one of the kids with one hand as he headed for the roadside embankment. The boy was screaming and struggling.

"Stop right there!" shouted McTighe as his constable driver also leaped out of the car.

"For Christ's sake, stop him!" came a muffled voice from the overturned car, and McTighe ran towards the striding silhouette. Already, McTighe could hear the sirens of the other two police cars as they raced to the scene.

The shadow strode purposefully towards the embankment, carrying the boy as if he weighed nothing at all.

The constable was closer and faster than McTighe. In a moment, he had closed with that tall figure, grabbed its arm and tried to spin it around.

McTighe saw the shadow lash out backwards with its free hand, without turning its head. The blow was hideously solid, connecting with the constable's face. It flung him to the tarmac, and he wasn't moving as the shadow finally reached the embankment bushes.

"Police!" yelled McTighe, wishing now with all his heart that he had issued a firearms order for the operation. "Stop right there!"

He ran hard at the man, both arms straight out before him, intending to knock him down.

But somehow, the shadow had anticipated his move. Still holding the boy, it whirled just before McTighe could connect; seized one of his outstretched arms, side-stepped— and yanked.

McTighe was only aware of the terrible impact, at first almost believing that he had taken the figure down. He struggled to rise as night shadows crowded in, then realised that he could not brace himself against the embankment to stand.

The shadow stood above him, the struggling boy still held aloft. Now that shadow had something else in its other hand. And McTighe could only watch, at last able to understand why he could not move, as the shadow dropped his arm—wrenched from its socket—to the ground.

"Police . . ." said McTighe ineffectually, as the shadow loomed over him.

It stamped down hard on his head.

Once.

And then was gone into the night, leaving behind the blaring police sirens and the spinning lights.

Chapter Eleven
En Route

"How long will it take to get there?" asked Shapiro as the car flashed onwards through the night.

"An hour, maybe longer," said Paul.

Instinctively, Paul had climbed into the back seat of his father's car with Van Buren. Ostensibly, it seemed, they were all on the same side now, but Paul still didn't like the idea of Van Buren being alone in the back, behind them. Far better that he be there to keep an eye on him while his father

. . . father? . . .

. . . while his father was driving. Soon, Paul would take a turn with the driving. He knew that his back and side were giving him terrible pain, but had refused to let Paul drive on this first part of the journey.

Van Buren checked on the bandage that he had used to bind up his injured calf, and then leaned back in the darkness. He laughed softly.

"What's funny?" asked Paul.

"Gideon."

"Maybe I don't have a sense of humour—but I can't think of anything remotely funny there."

"The name," said Van Buren. "The fact that he should choose that name."

"I don't get it."

"It's probably only one of many names he's used through the years. In more modern times, he spends his time drifting from city to city, from hotel to hotel in search of . . . food, let's say. And you know what you'll find in the top drawer of most bedside cabinets in a hotel?"

"No, what?"

"A Gideon Bible," said Shapiro from the driving seat.

"Good," said Van Buren, laughing again. "Very good. Bet you that's where he got the idea from. It would satisfy his perverse sense of humour."

"Still not funny," said Paul grimly, looking out at the neon-blur of the city streets as they flashed by.

"Know what the name means, boy?"

Paul did not answer.

"It's Hebrew. It means: 'Brave indomitable spirit.' "

The car travelled on for a further five minutes, while none of them spoke. When Van Buren broke the silence again, there was no humour in his tone.

"It has another meaning. It also means: 'The Destroyer.' "

Chapter Twelve
Evan

His name was Evan, and he had been waiting for two hours.

He was content to wait, sitting behind the wheel of his Vauxhall Viva, for as long as it took. He did not switch on the radio, did not look to his left or right—just straight ahead at the dirt-track beyond the windscreen, with its overgrown shrubs and trees weaving in the darkening twilight. He had no need for distraction or stimulation. For the first time in his life, he was content in a way that he had never believed possible. He knew that the old person, the old self, the old *him* had gone for ever. There was a newness of life for him now, with a new existence that was not hidebound by rules, regulations and morals. All he had to do was wait and obey.

The feeling of Rage had driven him from home, but now it had disappeared. The Voice inside his head which had engendered that Rage had changed in tone and filled him not only with a cold resolve, but also had transmuted that Rage to Power. When called upon, he knew that he could use that Power, that Strength, to serve the Master's purpose—and thereby his own.

He had followed that Voice, and it had told him all. It had made him promises about his new life that he could hardly wait to inherit.

The Master was all-powerful.

The Father of Fathers.

But the extent of the Master's powers, and of his mobility, had become progressively more limited. Although he had the power to "send" those to do his bidding from his resting place, his own powers of mobility were now severely restricted. During the day, the Master had been able to rest and gain strength from the very nature of his hiding place; enough strength to allow him occasionally to venture out. But his corporeal existence, his physical shell, was being ravaged by the same things that ravaged the dead husks of those upon whom he fed. Since the whores had betrayed and killed that physical shell, the Master's awesome spirit had nevertheless continued to inhabit the decaying flesh until such time as the One Son could claim the inheritance. In the meantime, he had meted out his vengeance on those whores. Only one remained, and Evan smiled in gratitude at the great honour now being bestowed upon him.

He was the Master's chosen one.

The Master had confided everything in him, even though he had yet to be in his presence. Soon, they would meet at last and Evan could worship, as was only right. After he had assisted the Master to take his vengeance on the last whore, and the others who would conspire to thwart him, then Evan knew that the new embodiment would take place.

And Evan would be transcended. He would take his rightful place as an ultimate predator, and would live for ever.

Once, Evan had been a gentle and affectionate adopted son.

But now, he was already something more—and less—than human.

And even as he sat, staring ahead through the darkness at the swaying trees, Evan became aware of his presence and knew that he was drawing near. That awareness was a swirling texture of emotions; awe, elation and . . . yes, *fear*. He bowed his head at the wheel, heart hammering.

Somewhere behind the car, footsteps.

The power emanating from the Master was almost overwhelming Evan. Tears were streaming down his face now.

And then the back door of the car was yanked open, with sufficient force to make the car rock on its suspension. Something was thrown in across the back seat, and Evan had the impression that it was the body of a child. But he did not ask any questions, only sat with head bowed and heart overflowing with dark joy as that immense shadow climbed into the back seat after it.

Drive.

"Where . . . ?" Evan's voice was cracked with emotion.

The Phoenix Theatre.

Tears still streaming down his cheeks, Evan drove off into the darkness.

Chapter Thirteen
The Body

Leonard's car screeched down the ramp leading to the underground car park of the Grand Hotel, filling that car park with roaring echoes.

The car hit the bottom of the ramp hard and bounced. Leonard fought to retain control of the car, but the front wing clipped a concrete stanchion set into the wall and the headlight shattered. Twisting wildly at the wheel, Leonard swung the car around frantically and stamped down hard on the accelerator pedal. The car streaked on ahead through the shadows, and he prayed that no one would reverse out of one of those parking bays.

Here!

Leonard slammed on the brakes.

But the car had been travelling through a slick of oil on the concrete, and when Leonard slammed on the anchors, the car skidded sideways and to the left. The agonising screech of the tyres was quickly followed by a rending smash as his car slammed sideways into a parked Saab. The impact shattered the Saab's side windows, gouging a massive tear along the car.

Leonard flung open the car door. When he clambered out, his legs would not support him and he collapsed to his knees.

He did not want to be here. He wanted to be back home in bed, the place he had been ever since the man in the back of his car had showed him the true terror that lived in the world. Leonard had been held by those eyes in the rear-view mirror, could only sit and look at them as first he had obeyed the man's instructions and told him everything about Bernice, everything about how he had been hired to follow him and find out just who he was. And then he had been made to sit and listen as the man talked, and talked, and talked.

Gideon had told him of hopelessness and despair and horror. He had told him to despair.

And Leonard had done just that.

He began to sob.

Here.

Leonard staggered to his feet and looked frantically around for the source of the Voice that had awakened him from his nightmare-ridden bed. At its commanding insistence he had hastily dressed, had flung himself into the car and driven

*through town like a maniac. The Grand Hotel was the last
place on earth he wanted to be, but he had to obey that Voice.
Life as he'd known it had ended with those eyes in the rear-
view mirror.*

*Filled with a terror that could liquefy his gut, Leonard saw
the familiar black Mercedes.*

*And then the indeterminate, shadowed mass that lay on
the concrete beside it.*

Here!

*Leonard's mouth filled with bile. He swallowed hard and
staggered towards the Mercedes, footsteps echoing. Part of
him hoped that someone would come. Anyone! Then he
would have to leave, would have to get away from there . . .
and then he realised what would truly happen if someone
came. Gideon would make him kill. And he would have to
obey that Voice.*

*At last he had reached the Mercedes. He forced himself to
look down at what lay before it. This time he could not control his stomach. Leonard vomited, bending double and turning away. He fell to his knees again, and retched until there
was nothing left.*

"Oh my Good Christ . . ."

Get up!

Leonard stumbled awkwardly to his feet again.

Take me.

*He forced himself to look at that shattered face. The hair
was matted with blood. Black-red rivulets seeped from the
mouth. Where there had once been a right eye was now a
ragged hole, a glutinous mass glinting within. But somehow,
the overhead lights in the car park were making that remaining right eye glitter—and that eye held Leonard as he
reached down for the body.*

*One of those claw-like white hands slowly clenched and
unclenched.*

The mouth began to work; a dark rivulet streamed from one corner, spattering on the concrete.

Stomach in revolt, fear almost robbing him of strength, Leonard took one of Gideon's arms and began to drag him across the concrete towards his car. The body seemed incredibly heavy, and Leonard could see that it was leaving a glinting trail on the concrete as they moved.

Hurry!

Leonard finally reached the car and pulled open the rear door.

"I can't . . ." He clutched at the rim of the door, sobbing for breath.

YOU CAN!

Leonard stooped and grabbed the corpse under the arms. Whimpering, he heaved it up and pushed it into the car. Utterly terrified of the thing that he was handling, revolted and horrified at the cold feel of its flesh, Leonard's mind recoiled from the task. Time for him had lost its linear direction, its immediacy. Even now, as he slumped back against the car, it seemed as if what he'd just done had been a series of still, black and white photographs.

The blood-streaked face.

The one glinting eye.

The twisted, white hands.

And the blood.

His hands were covered in Gideon's blood, and when he held them up in horror, he could see that the blood was also on his raincoat. Uttering a hoarse, strangled cry, Leonard wiped his hands on the raincoat lapels. Then he pulled off the raincoat and looked back at the glinting trail that led back to the Mercedes. Bunching up the coat, he stooped and began to wipe up the blood. Following the trail all the way back to Gideon's car, he crumpled up the bloodied raincoat and mopped at the pool in which he had been lying. There was *too much blood. He could never hope to cover it all up. But maybe down here in the perpetual, man-made darkness of the underground car park, no one would notice. He'd skidded in a pool of oil back there. Maybe it would be mistaken for that.*

"What should I do . . . ?"

Hurry!

Flinging open the driver's door, he climbed in.

"Where . . . ?"

A place I've heard about. A place where one of the whores wants to live out her dreams. A place I can rest and grow strong.

"But where . . . ?"

The Phoenix Theatre.

Leonard's car screeched up the car park ramp.

Soon, it was lost in the night.

Chapter Fourteen
Enzo

Enzo Castelano had been a prisoner of war in England.

Native of Palermo, he had regarded his capture in North Africa the biggest single stroke of luck that had ever happened to him. He had been sixteen years old then, a farmer's son swept up into the nightmare generated by Hitler and Mussolini. Since his enlistment he had been waiting every hour for the bullet or the sliver of shrapnel or the tank shell that would finish his life before it had started. But being captured so early on in the war had been a blessing from God. His transportation to a prisoner-of-war camp in England had been God's second blessing. The war had been taken away, and working on the land was the next best thing to working on his father's farm in Palermo. Never once had he complained about the inhospitable English weather. Come rain, hail or snow—he loved being here.

And when the war had finished, he had met Isabelle. They had fallen in love, and he had decided to stay. Since that time, they had raised three kids, had four grandchildren and he couldn't be happier.

He had held down many jobs since that time and he reckoned that if he had made one mistake, then it was not having the foresight to get himself a good pension plan. Long past the age of retirement, Enzo still had to work to pay the bills. Hence his current job, a position that he had held now for three years: stage door manager and general handyman at the Phoenix Theatre. And during those three years, he believed that he was no nearer to understanding "show" people.

When the knock came at the stage door, Enzo rustled his newspaper angrily and said, "Yes?"

There was another knock, but no reply.

Enzo closed the newspaper and looked at his watch. The theatre was currently "dark"; closed while essential maintenance took place. The Royal Shakespeare Company's production of *Romeo and Juliet* had finished last week, and a local theatre company would be starting the new season with a thriller. However, the general manager had agreed to rehearsals taking place on stage during the dark period while the company designed and built the set on stage (an unusual course of action, necessitated by a fire at the drama company's warehouse). Enzo did not understand the true "professionals" in the theatre business one little bit, but he certainly understood the bunch who were rehearsing this new play. They were local "celebrities," desperate for the glamour of showbusiness, wearing their egos for all to see and, as such, were king-size pains in the arse. Enzo had been having more trouble with this lot than any of the other touring productions. He had told them before: the general manager did not want them to use the stage door during rehearsals. The security people didn't like the idea of it being used during the "dark" period.

Irritated that his brief "rest" down here in the stage door office was being disturbed, annoyed that someone else was trying to use the stage door, Enzo again said, "Yes?"

There was still no reply, just another knock.

Angrily, Enzo flapped his newspaper closed with a dramatic flourish, kicked his feet from the desk, strode out of the window-fronted office and headed for the stage door. The company members were complete pains.

Enzo unlocked the door and began to open it, ready to give a lecture.

And then someone on the other side slammed that door savagely inwards with such force that it knocked Enzo from his feet. He tumbled to the floor, crying out in shock and surprise. He struggled to rise, outraged—but whoever had burst through the door was standing astride him as he turned. Enzo clutched upwards at his assailant.

And then the world reeled away from him as that someone kicked him in the head.

Enzo awoke to find himself looking into a face from Hell.

That face was a dead face; spectrally white and smeared with blood. Instead of a right eye, there was a bloodied crater. And in the remaining eye, a tiny but incandescent light. That light was like the centre of the universe . . . and Enzo became lost in it.

How many people are here?

"Myself. Two security guards. The deputy manager. The general manager has gone home . . ."

Tell me everything about this theatre. Who manages, who staffs it. Security arrangements. Everything.

And afterwards, when it was over, Leonard pulled the corpse that was not a corpse away from the prostrate form of the stage door manager. Had the old man's hair been white when Leonard had kicked in the door and knocked him out? He couldn't be sure now.

That old man was just lying there, looking up at the ceiling. Leonard recognised the look of abject horror in his eyes.

"Help me . . ." Leonard's voice was a hideous croak. He did not recognise it as his own.

The old man fumbled to his knees, his eyes still staring and unblinking.

"Where?" asked Leonard.

Inside. The auditorium.

"What's your name?" asked Leonard as the old man ineffectually attempted to help him with his burden as he dragged the body to the inner door.

". . . Castelano . . ." said the old man distantly. For some reason he was looking at the ceiling as he spoke. As if his name and identity were lost and floating somewhere in the ether.

"Where are the security guards now?"

"Upstairs. On the third floor. Drinking coffee."

"Where is the auditorium?"

The old man pushed open the inner door and began to hobble down a corridor. Gritting his teeth, Leonard hauled the body up by one arm, dragging that arm over his shoulder. He began to "walk" it after the old man. There were framed prints of previous productions on the walls. Laughing faces from stage farces seemed to mock Leonard as he dragged the body after the old man. Castelano pushed open another door. Beyond lay utter darkness. The old man leaned out past the door and flicked a switch. And now, Leonard could see the ghost of an auditorium, barely illuminated by the overhead light above the Emergency Exit door. He could see the thinly sketched details of the seat rows; the gilded theatrical escarpments leading to the circle and the box seats. He had been to this theatre only once: over twenty years ago. And even though he was almost suffocated in folds of terror, Leonard fancied that he could see himself sitting with his late wife in the stalls, watching as the old man hobbled into the auditorium; watching himself as he followed, dragging this hideous thing after him.

The stage. Under the stage.

"How do we get under the stage?"

The old man was still looking around him, as if he had never been in the theatre before and it was a new and bewildering experience. He waved vaguely at the stage.

"The orchestra pit. There's a door down there."

"Show me."

Enzo hurried to the black-painted barrier and flipped open a door in it which was almost invisible. Leonard watched him descend the three wooden steps into the pit, and then followed, dragging his burden. The descent down the wooden stairs was awkward and difficult. Leonard reeled, grabbing at the barrier and almost falling. And then the old man had switched on another dim light which barely illuminated the orchestra pit, but gave him enough light to see where he was going. Enzo opened another door set into the foot of the stage itself, leaned through and switched on another, brighter light. He held that door open as Leonard staggered through with the body.

The space under the stage was about forty feet square. Dusty shelving, the tubular frame variety, stood against the side walls. Leonard saw the reels of electrician's wiring and tape, ancient "super-trouper" lights gathering cobwebs, and the unknown, forgotten detritus of bygone productions. Wicker baskets lay scattered randomly. Set into the wall next to the orchestra pit was an old-fashioned console with valves and dials that wouldn't have been out of place in a 1930s Frankenstein film. As he watched, Castelano moved to the console and flicked more switches, lighting up the deeper recesses of the understage area.

"All the auditorium and stage electrics are controlled from here . . ." said Enzo weakly, as if looking for something to say.

Hold me up. Let me see.

And Leonard held up the corpse's head, as if he were the ventriloquist and this was some hideous, oversized dummy.

The brighter lights now revealed that the stage floor above their heads had been subdivided into squares with chalked numbers on each. Leonard remembered with hideous and inappropriate clarity how one of the performers he had seen on stage all those years ago had dropped through a trapdoor in the stage. Obviously, each of the above squares could be converted into an appropriate trapdoor if required.

The beams.

And when Leonard looked, he could see the massive criss-cross beams supporting the stage floor.

Show me.

Leonard dragged the corpse nearer, until they were directly beneath a criss-cross intersection. There was a space up there: a hollow gap where the beams met at this point.

There. Put me there. Face upwards. But first . . . look at me, Leonard.

And Leonard turned that hideous face until it was staring directly into his own. He was unaware that he was whimpering as he was told what to do when Bernice came to him again, as she surely must. Tears were running down Leonard's grizzled cheeks when it told him exactly what he must do and exactly what he must say.

While Enzo held the wicker basket, Leonard was able with great difficulty to hoist the body up on to the beam at its cross-section point. He had no idea how long it took to secrete the body into the gap. Gasping, wheezing, weeping. Finally, he was able to push the body completely out of sight. The exertion had been enormous. Leonard staggered and almost fell from the basket. Climbing down, he could see that the old man was on his knees, still staring upwards.

Bring him.

Leonard pulled the old man to his feet and brought him to the cross-section. This time Enzo did not want to look up. He stared at his feet, eyes glazed. When the Voice spoke again, it was addressed directly to the old man.

Castelano.

It was the first time he had heard the Voice, and its sound made him cringe visibly.

You will say nothing of what has happened. You will protect me while I rest and grow strong. And you will do everything I say. Do you understand?

Enzo nodded his head vigorously.

Leonard.

"Yes . . . ?"

Look.

Leonard looked up at the cross-section where he had hidden the body. There was movement there now. A slow, scuffling, dragging movement. That hideous face emerged from the shadows, turning with the awkwardness of death to look down on him.

Go now, Leonard. I have no further use for you.

Blood leaked from the thing's mouth, spattering directly

into his face. Leonard recoiled in horror, but was still transfixed by the dead glint in that remaining eye.

Go and despair.

With wide eyes glazed in horror, Leonard staggered backwards to the under-stage door. He saw the old man kneel by the wicker basket, as if in prayer; then turned and blundered back into the orchestra pit.

Outside, the streets of Newcastle had become the streets of Hell.

Chapter Fifteen
En Route

"Dad?"

Shapiro seemed hunched over the wheel of the car, and Paul twisted around to get a better look at his face as they flashed onwards through the night.

"What's wrong?" said Van Buren.

And Paul just had time to see the grimace of pain on Shapiro's face before he slumped forward over the wheel and the car slewed screeching towards the motorway barrier. Paul tried to grab for the wheel, but was flung back into his seat by the sudden, dangerous swerve. Car horns behind were blaring as Van Buren lunged forward, grabbed Shapiro by the shoulders and hauled him back. Holding him around the neck with one arm, he managed to grab the steering wheel with the other, shoving it hard to the left and away from the crash barrier. Paul quickly recovered, shoving himself between the gap in the front seats and grabbing the other side of the wheel.

The car screeched back into its lane again as Paul clambered over the front passenger seat.

"Keep the wheel steady!"

"For God's sake, get a move on!" snapped Van Buren. "I can't hold the wheel like this for ever."

In the harsh motorway lights, Paul saw that his father was unconscious; his face a ghastly blue-white in those sodium lights. His eyes seemed hollowed; his breathing harsh and ragged. Sweat was dripping down the sides of his face. His foot had slipped from the accelerator pedal and the car was beginning to slow, but they were still travelling dangerously fast. The car wobbled as Van Buren tried to shift position.

"Van Buren!"

"Just get into the front, damn it!"

Paul finally managed to struggle into the front passenger seat and leaned across to take the wheel. "Hold him back."

Now, he was able to get his foot to the brake. Carefully, he steered the car into the hard shoulder beside the motorway barrier. When the car finally slid to a halt on the gravel, Paul leaned back and breathed a long sigh of relief. Quickly recovering, he turned to his father, gently bringing his head forward to look at that pale, bloodless face.

"Right!" Van Buren kicked open his door, wincing at the pain in his other calf as he hauled himself out of the car. Hobbling to the front seat, he yanked open the door and seized Shapiro by the coat lapels. "Out!" He began to drag Shapiro out of the car.

"Leave him alone, you bastard!" Paul struck out at Van Buren as he finally managed to haul him out of the car and on to the gravelled hard shoulder.

"Enough is enough. You're both a liability, and I can't afford to have any dead weight." Van Buren laid him down, but now Shapiro was beginning to recover. Groaning, he reached out for the motorway barrier and was able to pull himself into a sitting position.

"Paul, I'm sorry . . ."

"A priest on his last legs," continued Van Buren. "A boy half-battered to death. And me with this blasted leg. The odds are bad enough without . . ."

"Stand back, Van Buren!" snapped Paul. Van Buren looked up at the car to see that he had taken the sawn-off shotgun from the holdall. It was levelled at him through the open driver's door. "Leave him alone."

"Look, boy! Don't you appreciate what's happening? There's hardly any time—maybe none at all. Your father needs medical help. You're hardly in a fit state yourself. Just let me go after him . . ."

"And if Gideon kills you? What then? He'll come after us, and we've no way of knowing how to protect ourselves. No way of knowing how to fight back. You're not kidding anyone, Van Buren. You thought you'd be able to dump us somewhere along the way and go on yourself, didn't you? Well, you're fucking not. You think you're the only one who has a score to settle, the only one who's lost someone close? Well, who gave you the only right to vengeance? We're *all* in this, Van Buren. Whether you like it or not. And we're all going to see it through. I've *felt* Gideon . . . and he's waiting for us. He's allowing us to come to him, because he wants us dead. He thinks that we present no threat, and all he wants to do is kill us for interfering. So . . . it's time to tell us how we can destroy Gideon, time for us to work out some kind of plan. Otherwise, you really *are* going after him trailing a couple of liabilities."

"Look at him!" snapped Van Buren, pointing down at Shapiro. "How far do you think we'll get with him in this state? How far do you . . . ?"

"I'm all right," said Shapiro, using the motorway barrier to clamber to his feet. "I can make it, Paul. If you drive for a while."

"Are you sure?" asked Paul, still levelling the shotgun at Van Buren.

"I'm sure. You're right about one thing, Van Buren. We have no time. But Paul's right, as well. The sooner you tell us everything you know, the better."

Van Buren cursed under his breath, turning away from them both and staring at the traffic which passed them in the night. He moved to the boot of the car and sat on it, still studying the passing cars. They watched as he rubbed at the pain in his calf. Suddenly, he slammed his hand down on the boot of the car angrily, swearing again. He turned back to them.

"All right, damn it! All right! But let's get moving, for Christ's sake!"

"For who's sake?" asked Shapiro, with a wan smile.

"For *our* sake," said Paul. "Come on, let's get in the car."

"I'll drive," said Van Buren, yanking open the rear door as Shapiro moved to the car. Paul nodded his agreement. "But take that thing out of my face."

Paul lowered the shotgun, shoving it into the holdall but keeping it by his side. When Shapiro had eased himself into the back seat, Van Buren climbed into the front beside Paul. In seconds, they were back on the motorway.

"So?" asked Paul, after a long silence.

"The Witches of Salem," said Van Buren, matter-of-factly.

"What about them?"

"What happened to them?"

"They were burned at the stake," replied Shapiro.

"What?" Paul shifted uneasily, still keeping the holdall at his side. "You mean we have to *burn* Gideon?"

"Yes. But we have to burn him completely, until there's

nothing left. We have to scatter his ashes. For once, it seems your Church had the right idea about *something*, Shapiro."

"But how do we . . . ?"

"Well, it won't be easy. For one thing, Gideon may be dead, but he'll still have gathered sufficient strength since then to be able to tear us all limb from limb. And then there's the power he has over lower orders."

"You said that before, Van Buren. What the hell does that mean, 'lower orders?' "

"In its incorporeal state, in that period between physical death and its 'rebirth' in a younger body, the vampire has enhanced supernatural powers. It has the ability to summon, to direct, to control 'lower orders.' Animals. Cats, dogs, rats, insects . . . even children, if they're young enough not to have developed mentally. So God knows what's ahead of us."

"Are you *sure* about this?" asked Shapiro, holding his shoulder.

Van Buren laughed: a dry, humourless sound. "Fifty years tracking this thing. And millions of pounds spent in that pursuit. Yes, I'm sure."

"You must have some sort of plan," said Paul.

"Yes, I've got an idea. It's in that holdall that you're making such a point of hanging on to."

"Three have got to be better than one," said Paul, unzipping the holdall and removing the shotgun.

"Keep that bloody thing pointed *away!*" snapped Van Buren.

Paul took out what was left in the holdall and then turned back to Van Buren, puzzlement on his face.

"Like I said, boy." His face looked spectrally white as the headlights from an oncoming car swept the interior of the car. "It won't be easy . . . and the odds are all against us."

Chapter Sixteen
Jacqueline

When the weeping had ceased, and the words of consolation from the police had become a hollow and impotent refrain, Jacqueline at last allowed herself to be taken from Brian's bedside. He was pumped full of drugs to kill the pain of the multiple fracture in his leg, and their shared grief had pushed his own nervous system to the point of mental shutdown. A room had been prepared for Jacqueline here in the hospital for her to stay the night, and however many nights it might take.

Jacqueline had been talking to the police for three hours since the police operation had gone so disastrously wrong, and had resisted attempts to give her sedation. But gleaning actual facts from them had been surprisingly difficult. Quite how the whole operation could have gone so disastrously wrong was unclear and in an unguarded moment, she had managed to find out that someone fairly "high up" had been killed.

The kidnapper had escaped. Again, the police details on that seemed vague at the moment.

And James was still missing.

Even in the immensity of his pain, Brian had joined with her as they raged at an anonymous detective inspector and a superintendent. And when their shared grief had collapsed into distress, she had wanted to tell them about

Gideon, but could not. She had wanted to tell them every-thing that had happened, but didn't know where to start, or what to say. She was helpless.

"Coffee?" asked the policewoman as they left Brian's room. "Can I get you some coffee?" Her voice seemed to be coming from far away, from down a distant corridor.

"No, no . . . I need to see Martin again."

"Okay . . . okay . . ." said the policewoman, aware of the massive police cock-up, and eager to please. She was still busy conversing with a passing doctor as Jacqueline made her way to the children's ward.

Martin was still unconscious, still on a drip.

He had been that way since he had been pulled from the overturned car, with his father. X-rays had revealed concus-sion but no brain damage, and the experts were confident that he would make a full recovery.

Jacqueline sat at his bedside, stroking his hair. His face was white, with a thin sheen of sweat that made it seem as if he were made of porcelain. So fragile, so easily broken. In that moment, Jacqueline remembered in quick succession the ailments of childhood; the times she'd nursed him, first as a baby, then a toddler, then a boy. The same way that she'd nursed James. And those memories crushed her from within, and those damnable tears began again.

There was no comfort in giving in to these tears. They made matters worse, did not help. But the grief, and the knowledge that she was completely helpless, completely unable to save James, was soul-crushing.

Her attendant policewoman hovered uncertainly behind her. The time for comforting arms on shoulders was long since over. Dimly, Jacqueline heard the door open and close softly as she was left to the privacy of her grief.

Jacqueline became aware that she was unconsciously

squeezing Martin's hand too tightly. She replaced it gently on the quilt.

"Oh God, what am I going to do . . . ?"

It was too close here in Martin's room. There seemed to be no air. Jacqueline took a handkerchief out of her handbag and wiped her face. There was a buzzing in her ears now. Was she going to faint? Unaccountably, there was a new and unhealthy atmosphere in the room. She could feel it in her spine, down her arms, bristling at the nape of her neck.

A cold, creeping fear.

Jacqueline looked around. There was no one else in the room. Why should she be feeling this way?

The window at the far side of the room was misting over. Why had it suddenly become so warm? Why did she feel this way? Jacqueline stood up, trying to shake off the sudden fear, deliberated whether to move to the door and ask for assistance. But she did not want to leave Martin alone, not for a second. She turned in a circle, walked around the bed defensively, trying to locate the source of that slowly growing fear. And all the time, all she could think of was her conversation with Bernice Adams.

The most important thing for you now, Jacqueline, is for you to get away. I'm as good as dead, but you might have a chance if you just get away from here. Persuade your family somehow, but you've got to leave. Persuade them to leave! Because it's not just you he's after.

There was nothing to be seen. No movement . . . other than the moisture running on the window. And Jacqueline looked at the window to see that . . .

Letters were appearing on the fogged glass.

Sprawling, spidery letters were forming as if someone out there—behind the glass—was writing on the window. But this window was eight storeys high, and there was no one out there. Frozen in terror, Jacqueline backed up to the bed, instinctively moving to protect Martin and watching as dripping, running words began to appear.

Jacqueline.

Jacqueline held her breath, bit her lip, refused to give in to the fear.

I have your bastard.

The air was thick with that horrible, familiar smell that she had come to associate with Gideon. As she stood and watched that lettering run, she gripped the quilt on the bed behind her in two bloodless fists.

Come to me. Alone.
Tell no one or he dies.

"Where?" Her voice seemed unnaturally loud. It startled her, and horrified her to hear the sound of fear so obviously etched into her one word.

The Phoenix Theatre.
Let no one see you.

"But . . . but *where* in the theatre? How . . . ?" The words on the window were running into each other now, running and blending.

I'll find you.

And as the stark, running words dripped and blended and merged like liquid cobweb, Jacqueline could only see in her mind's eye the blood that had flowed and run from Gideon's shattered face.

The Reverend Colwell performed the last benediction of his late night service and turned back to the altar.

St. Lawrence's was the only church in Newcastle to perform such a late service on a regular basis, and the Reverend Colwell was pleased to maintain it despite the less-than-unanimous approval of his peers. This service always drew a scattering of attendees: of the homeless (who were sometimes politely but firmly told that they could not "doss down" on the pews overnight), of vagrants, of the lost, the lonely and the drunk. If one person took spiritual comfort from the service that was performed, then Colwell considered it worth while. This was a justification in itself.

The church was mid-nineteenth century and sadly in need of refurbishment. But there were no funds forthcoming for a city-centre church without a resident congregation.

The lost children of the night are this church's congregation, thought Colwell as he turned back from the altar, expecting to see an empty church now that the service was over, and seeing instead a young woman sitting in one of the pews. She was sitting far over to the left, at the end of a row and right next to the small inlaid cross that was set into the wall: a gift from a forgotten benefactor. She seemed to be studying that cross intently.

Colwell stepped down from the altar, and moved quietly towards her. She could see him approaching and bowed her head as if in prayer.

"Can I help you?"

Jacqueline did not look up. Instead, she asked, "Is there a God?"

Colwell studied her, waiting to see her face lift. When it

was obvious that she was going to keep her face down, he said, "I believe so."

"You believe. But do you *know?*"

"We aren't meant to know. That's the nature of faith. If we knew, we wouldn't have the free will to choose him or reject him. Then it wouldn't be the same, would it?" The young woman did not respond, head still down. "Are you a Christian?"

"I was born a Roman Catholic. I used to be . . ." And the young woman laughed. A low, derisive sound. ". . . devout."

"Until when?"

"My first period."

"Is that significant?"

"No . . . I mean, yes. I don't know. When I was a teenager, it didn't seem important any more."

"And it's important now?"

"I don't know. But I need help."

"Do you want to tell me about it?"

"It won't help. I don't have time. What I have to do . . . has to be done straight away. Do you believe in evil? In the powers of darkness?"

"Yes, I do."

"And do you believe that good will always triumph over evil?"

"In the long run, yes. Although sometimes it does seem to take a long while for the scales to balance, and people do get badly hurt along the way."

"Why do they have to get hurt?"

Colwell could not see the young woman's face, but he could feel the pain in her words. Nothing but an honest answer would be adequate. After a long pause, he said, "I don't know."

"Where I'm going, nothing in this world can help me. I

know that. I've come to the only place left I can think of that might help . . ."

Unaccountably, without knowing anything about this woman or the trouble she was in, Colwell felt the bitter grip of sorrow in his own throat for her. "I can't give you answers in five minutes. Won't you let me help you?"

"Where I'm going, I have to go alone."

"Then take God with you. Trust him. Believe in the power of the cross."

Colwell turned back, aware that the candles on the altar were still lit. Picking up the extinguisher, he quickly began to snuff them out until the church was only dimly lit by the ceiling lights set behind the altar.

"Come back with me. We'll talk some more and I'll see if I can . . ."

When he turned back, the young woman had gone.

And so had the inlaid cross from the church wall.

Still unable to lose that feeling of sorrow, Colwell said a quick prayer.

"I hope that it helps you."

Chapter Seventeen
The Familiar

Enzo used the theatre's master keys from his belt to open the communal dressing room door, reached in and flicked on the light switch.

The theatre had individual dressing rooms for principal

performers, but the communal room was for the "hoofers" and "spear carriers" as the general manager liked to call them. The room was long, like a miniature dormitory, and set back against the far wall was a twenty-foot dressing mirror with individual swivel seats that the manager had procured cheaply from a bankrupt typing agency.

Enzo crossed to the mirror, reaching behind its left-hand cornice and flicking the switch that was there. The dozen or so individual light bulbs placed directly above the mirror came on and Enzo skipped back to the main light switch again. Turning, he switched off the main lights—and smiled. The light over the mirrors was much better now. Much more theatrical.

Enzo's smile was a hideous, cracked expression; completely alien to what had once been a benevolent and gentle face. Once a popular man, over recent weeks people had been avoiding him in the theatre. Something about that smile unnerved them. He had still undertaken his job well enough, but the change in Enzo had not gone unnoticed. No one knew that Isabelle had left him for certain, had gone to live with friends for a while. He hadn't done anything to her, hadn't laid a hand on her, but had spent more time than usual at the theatre; had taken to sleeping there overnight, despite Isabelle's pleas. After all, he wasn't being paid to assist with overnight security, so why was he doing it? And all the time, Enzo would just look at her and smile with that horrible, cracked smile; would just sit and look at her and say nothing, with that horrible glint in his eye. She couldn't take it any more.

Enzo was no longer Enzo.

And the thing that Enzo had become had something important to protect.

He must attend to the Master's comings and goings.

My familiar, the Voice had said, as Enzo looked into the dying last gleam of that remaining eye. And although the light in that eye had long since gone out, the seed of control had been planted in Enzo's mind. Tonight, the Master had given Enzo, or the thing that Enzo had become, new instructions.

You are death, the Voice had said.

And sitting in front of the make-up mirror, Enzo rummaged in the nearest top drawer until he found a jar of white foundation cream. Face cracked in that insane rictus of a grin, Enzo scooped out a handful of that cream and began to plaster it on his face. Soon, his entire face was covered. His smile widened, heightening the hideous death's head appearance. Standing again, admiring his handiwork, Enzo walked quickly across the communal dressing room to the racks of smocks hanging in the corner, used by the performers like barber-shop smocks when they were putting on the more elaborate make-up. Feverishly skimming through the smocks, he finally found something that approximated what he wanted.

It was a black smock, quite long, hanging down past his knees like a cloak.

Perfect.

Enzo moved to the telephone on the side-table near the door.

He dialled the security number.

"What the hell do you want, Enzo?" asked Packard, cramming a sandwich into his mouth as he talked. Across the table from him, Charlie Newton stopped dealing the cards. Both security men were the same age, fifty-eight, but it was the only thing they had in common.

There was no reply on the other end of the telephone.

Packard kicked his feet off the desk and straightened up, swallowing hard.

"Enzo?"

"Better come down," said Enzo at last.

"What is it?" asked Charlie.

Packard waved at him impatiently, finished swallowing the sandwich and said, "What's wrong?"

"Nothing wrong. But you'd both better come down."

"We got intruders?"

"No."

"Security problem?"

"No."

"Then it's not our job, Enzo. It's yours. You see to it." Packard hung up and turned back to Charlie. "Okay, keep dealing. This time I'm going to thrash you for all the pennies in your money belt, Charlie."

"What's the matter with Enzo?"

"You tell me. Reckon the guy's ready for the funny farm. Don't know what the hell's happened to him these last few weeks. Used to be a really nice guy, but now . . ." Packard gave a mock shudder. "Now he just gives me the creeps."

"I heard his wife's left him."

"Could be that, I suppose. Always was a family man. Maybe that's what it is. Now, deal . . ."

And then the internal security alarm began to ring in the office.

"Shit!" Packard slammed his cards down on the desk. Startled, Charlie jumped to his feet and crossed to the security console set into the wall. Every door and window was represented on that console in a diagram that looked like the London Underground network. A red light was flashing on one of the access/exit points.

"Where?" asked Packard, pulling on his black cap and jacket.

"Communal dressing room," said Charlie. "The window."

"Shit!" Grabbing his unofficial night-stick, Packard threw

open the security office door and started down the marble stairs, closely followed by Charlie. Packard kept silently cursing all the way down the side staircase. How the hell were you supposed to creep up on someone in a place like this, with so much marble and so many echoing passage-ways? Whoever was down there was bound to hear them coming long before they arrived.

On the landing below was a set of fire doors. Packard and Charlie pushed through, Packard gnashing his teeth at the screeching sound that the door made as they passed. There was a carpeted corridor beyond, but there was no point in tippy-toeing now. Packard hit the next set of fire doors with both hands, and whirled left as they flew open. At the end of the next corridor was the communal dressing room.

The door was closed.

Packard was well ahead of Charlie now as he lunged to-wards the door. He could hear Charlie behind him, huffing and puffing. He'd lost count of the times he'd nagged him about keeping fit.

Charlie saw Packard burst into the room, thought, *Bull in a china shop*, and then saw the door slam shut instantly be-hind him, as if someone had been waiting there behind it all along, just waiting for someone to come through. Charlie heard a brittle *click*! as the door was locked, just before he hit that door hard himself. Beyond the door, Charlie heard Packard breathlessly say, "For Christ's *sake*, Enzo . . ."

And then Packard screamed.

"Packard!" Charlie threw his full weight against the door, but it would not budge.

Something in the dressing room overturned and smashed.

"Enzo, Enzo, Enzo, Enzo . . ." Packard's voice was desperate, terror-stricken. Charlie knew that he was trying to get away. *"Enzooooo!"*

His scream was cut off by a heavy *chunking* sound. Charlie recoiled from the door, sweat gleaming on his face. That noise came again: a heavy, grunting, wet-sounding impact. Packard was making no more noise.

And fear enveloped Charlie now as he backed away from the door. That noise continued; steady, slow, rhythmical. Like some slow-moving piston. Charlie didn't want to hear it any more, didn't want to break through that door and find out what was happening to Packard. The flesh seemed to be crawling along his arms, up his back. His hands were sweating. He felt sick . . . and why the hell was he in this job, anyway?

The telephone.

Charlie kept backing off down the corridor, as that dreadfully unknown sound continued. Someone was putting effort into whatever was happening, because Charlie could hear a small grunt of effort just before each stroke of that wet piston. And then the sound stopped.

Charlie turned, heart hammering, and ran for the fire doors.

Just as the door to the communal dressing room burst open behind him, slamming hard against the wall.

The thing that had come through the door was screaming . . . and Charlie was screaming too as he hit the double doors with both hands the way he'd seen Packard do it. But Charlie was overweight, too bulky and too out of condition. The impact winded him. Worse, a crippling pain enveloped his chest and set his left arm on fire. Choking in pain Charlie fell to his knees and pitched forward. He saw his widowed mother at home, preparing his meal, waiting for his shift to end.

There was no air in his lungs. He could not breathe as he rolled over.

But he still screamed when he saw the hideous white-faced nightmare standing above him.

Still screamed when it wielded the blood-stained fire axe high above its head.

Chapter Eighteen
Jacqueline

Jacqueline stood in a shop doorway on the pavement opposite to the Phoenix Theatre—and watched.

The Phoenix was one of four theatres in the city centre. The Theatre Royal and New Tyne Theatre and Opera House had been built first—the Phoenix had followed at the turn of the century. The Playhouse, not far from the city's Haymarket, was a more modern construction. Considerably more Gothic than its companions, the Phoenix stood on the east boundary of the city centre, its grey stone walls almost black from traffic pollution, its mock turrets stabbing the sky. Martin had once called it a haunted castle, and the irony was not lost on Jacqueline tonight.

It had begun to rain on her way from St. Lawrence's Church. Her hair was soaked and lay lank across her forehead. With her white face and burning eyes, she stared from the shop doorway like a drowned person.

It was late, very late. But the main reception doors of the theatre were still open, and orange light glowed within. The streets were glinting black, the late night revellers now only a straggle of nightclub survivors looking for taxis. Jacque-

line listened to them as they passed her in the shop doorway, listened to their laughter and remembered the way that
she had laughed with Brian and Martin and . . .

And James.

Jacqueline felt for the inlaid cross in her pocket. It was
nine inches long, sturdy and made from some kind of non-
precious metal. The touch of that cold metal reminded her
of Bernice's Webley service revolver, reminded her of
Gideon's face as she'd pulled the trigger. Jacqueline screwed
her eyes tightly shut and gripped the cross. It was the only
thing she had left. She hadn't prayed since teenage days, but
she prayed now. She looked back at the theatre, at its dripping arched windows, at the billboards fronting the weathered building. The next performance would be *Strangers*
and even from here she could see that Bernice Adams's
name had been papered over. She'd known that Bernice
was supposed to be appearing here, guessed that her re-
placement would be required by present circumstances.

Her present circumstances.

Jacqueline wondered if Bernice was still alive.

Bernice. The Phoenix Theatre. And now Gideon. Did that
mean something?

James.

Steeling herself, Jacqueline crossed the black-glinting
street towards the theatre. Her shadow on the street
stretched long before her, as if anxious to reach the building
before she could. Jacqueline felt sick with fear, clutched the
inlaid cross in her pocket, paused on the glinting street outside the theatre . . . and then entered.

The reception area had been built principally from marble. Tall columns supported a high, vaulted ceiling. The box
office was directly ahead, and to its left—a door marked "Auditorium." At either end of the reception were two flights of
marble staircases leading up to the circle and grand circle.

Jacqueline's footsteps were brittle and echoing on the marble floor. She stopped in the middle of the reception and waited. Apart from the dying echoes of her footsteps there were no other sounds. She resisted the urge to call out, not wanting to hear the lost echoes of her voice in this place.

I will find you.

She knew that he was here. She could feel his presence in the cold marble walls, in the stillness of the theatre.

James.

Jacqueline moved quickly to the auditorium door, and pulled it open. The sound of that opening door seemed gigantic in the empty auditorium beyond. Jacqueline entered, letting the door close softly, not wanting to hear its echoing slam. She stood for a long time, just watching and listening.

The fire curtain had not been lowered. On stage, there was a drawing room set from *Strangers*. Pattern-papered walls and a window looking out on to a painted summer backdrop. A chaise-longue, chairs, a French window looking out on to more of the same painted backdrop.

Jacqueline walked down the centre aisle, looking from left to right at the empty seats. The carpet swallowed all sound. She scanned the box seats at right and left as she drew nearer to the stage. They were also empty. Now, she had found her voice and could call out.

"James?"

She clutched the cross in her pocket even tighter. The wounds in her neck and shoulder from the dog attack seemed to throb with pain.

"James?"

There was no reply.

Jacqueline scanned the drawing room set before her. Its emptiness served to fuel the sickening atmosphere of watchfulness, of waiting. As if the stage furniture itself was sentient and waiting for human—or inhuman—players to begin a final enactment. Jacqueline swallowed hard, fought down the urge to vomit . . . and then anger began to override that fear. It seized her, made her tremble. The cross was biting into the flesh of her palm as she yelled at the stage, "Gideon, you bastard! Give me back my *son!*"

"Catch your boy, whore!"

At the foot of the stage, Jacqueline whirled back to the auditorium in alarm. And what she saw above, on the circle balcony, released the inner terror in a flood.

A young man in denims was leaning forward over that balcony, dark straggling hair hanging in front of an insane grin.

And he was holding James over the balcony by one outstretched hand.

James was unconscious, turning slowly in the air, as the grinning man held on to his hand.

"JAMES!" Jacqueline started forward.

"Careful, missus," said the grinning man. "Give me a fright—I might drop him."

"Please . . . for God's sake . . . don't . . ."

"Why do people always talk about God when they're in deep shit?"

Fear was a living thing, lodged deep within Jacqueline's breast; alive and squirming, and desperate to be free. She edged forward further. Could she get directly beneath James? How high was that balcony? God, could she catch him if . . . ?

The grinning man feigned a slip over the balcony. James twitched in the air.

"DON'T!"

"Oops," grinned the man. "Butterfingers."

"Please . . . who are you? Look, don't . . . don't . . . just pull him back . . ."

"Time to die, whore!" snapped the man, the grin now vanished. Quickly, he yanked James back over the parapet and out of sight. Jacqueline cried out, and ran up the centre aisle towards the auditorium door. Fear gave her extra strength as she burst out into the reception area again, feverishly looking from side to side before dashing to the left-hand staircase.

"*James James James James.*" Her son's name came with each tortured exhalation of breath as Jacqueline ran up the staircase. On the first floor was a bar area and another main door leading into the circle. Hurling herself around the marble column at the top of the stairs, Jacqueline ran full tilt at the door.

It crashed open in an explosion of sound, and she tottered to regain her balance at the top of the carpeted stairs leading down to the balcony.

The grinning young man was gone.

But someone was sitting down there, his back to her, facing the stage.

In the seat next to that figure, Jacqueline recognised a curly mop of hair.

"James!"

She started down the stairs . . . and then halted halfway. There was an unmistakable aura emanating from the shape sitting next to James. She recognised it of old. Now, the terror had returned in all its sickening intensity. Breathless with exertion and fear, Jacqueline felt in her pocket for the cross, and continued down the stairs towards that figure.

Somehow, there was movement in that shape's hair. Even from twelve steps up, she could see that there were living things in it. As she watched, a writhing maggot uncurled and fell to the collar of that horrifyingly familiar long coat. Jacqueline swallowed hard . . . and pulled the inlaid cross from her pocket, holding it out before her as she descended.

And then the figure turned in its seat to look at her.

"Oh, *Christ . . .*"

"Your handiwork, Jacqueline," said Gideon.

His voice was a liquid thing; a regurgitation of noise from somewhere deep within the thing that he had become. Jacqueline saw that the same movement in his hair was also taking place in the ragged hole that had been his right eye. The torn flesh and bone had decayed and crumbled further around that hole. The leprous grey skin had completely peeled away from a shattered cheek and jawbone to the thing's neck. The left eye had rotted and shrunk into its cavity. The skin around the lips had shrivelled and peeled back, giving a perpetual death's head grin to that hideously decayed face.

Jacqueline had involuntarily retreated back a step, but stopped herself from giving in to the panic—and stood firm.

"What *are* you?"

"I am what you made me," grinned that hideous face, and more squirming things fell from its lips.

Jacqueline held the cross out before her, forcing herself slowly to descend.

"Our Father, who art in heaven . . ."

The figure still stared at her, grinning, as she descended.

". . . hallowed be Thy name. Thy kingdom come, Thy will be done . . ."

Beside it, James was still. Was he dead? *Oh God, please don't let him be dead!* ". . . on earth as it is in heaven. Give us this day . . ."

"How touching," said the thing, death's head grin widening even further.

And then Jacqueline was suddenly seized from behind.

She shrieked, lashing out backwards as two arms encircled her, pinning her own arms to her sides. But that grip was immensely powerful, and she could not break free as she kicked out backwards, twisting and trying to overbalance whoever had taken her. Suddenly, another blurred figure had appeared from nowhere and had taken the cross out of her hand. Still shouting in fear and anger, Jacqueline felt her heel dig deep into a shin, but there was no cry of pain. Instead, her captor threw her heavily into one of the seat rows.

Jacqueline scrabbled to her feet again, bracing her hand on the seats.

The grinning man who had held James over the balcony was standing on the centre stairway, casually tossing the cross end-over-end in his hand. He was still grinning. Now she could see the bizarre figure who had grabbed her from behind and thrown her down. It was a grotesque sight. The man, whoever he was, had smeared white paste or paint all over his face and was wearing a black smock which hung to his knees. There was an identical, insane grin on his face.

Gideon had not moved from his seat.

"I can't love you to death the way I wanted, Jacqueline," said the death's head. "So these two will do it for me."

Evan and Enzo moved towards her.

Chapter Nineteen
Vengeance

"Taxi?" mumbled the drunk, knocking on the car window.

There was no response from within the car.

"Come on, want the trade or not?"

The rear window wound down.

"Not," said Paul, and the drunk recoiled from the sawn-off shotgun pointed at him.

"Okay, okay, okay," mumbled the drunk, staggering back and holding up his arms in drunken exaggeration, like an extra from a western film. Weaving to the front again, he staggered off into the night.

The window wound up again . . . and they turned their attention back to the Phoenix Theatre. Nothing had moved in there since they had arrived. The main reception doors were open; orange light glinted on the pavement from the interior. They had not expected the theatre still to be open at this time of night and had planned to break in. Those open doors seemed to mock them, seemed to want them to enter as soon as possible. They had discussed at length their strategy for entering the theatre. Main reception? Or stage door?

"Van Buren?" said Shapiro at last.

"Yes?"

"Something happened back there in the chalet, at Swarwell."

"Lots of things happened."

"I'm talking about the exorcism. The fact that it worked."

"So what?"

"Doesn't it prove to you that there is a good as well as an evil?"

"What the hell is it with you, priest? Are you trying to convert me or something?"

"I just want you to think about it before we go in there. You've done a lot of killing in your search for Gideon."

"Fine. Is the sermon over now?" said Van Buren, grabbing the holdall and climbing out of the car on to the rain-washed pavement.

Paul looked at his father's pale, haggard face in the back seat. Shapiro saw him looking and tried to smile. Paul placed an arm around his shoulder and tried to speak, but could not. His throat was too constricted with emotion. Shapiro gripped and patted Paul's knee. Memories of his son's childhood overwhelmed him.

"Right through . . ." Paul found his voice at last. "Right through this nightmare, I've never . . . never had a chance really to think about Mother."

"I know," said Shapiro. "I know . . ."

They both knew what lay ahead of them . . . and wept.

Van Buren turned from them, walking away from the car with the holdall, looking up and down the deserted street. Somewhere, a train whistle echoed from the Central Station; a lost and forlorn sound. When the car doors opened again, he turned back.

Paul helped his father out of the car, and then moved to the boot. Opening it, he took out the can of petrol they'd bought from the motorway service station en route. He wrapped it in the burlap sack and slammed the boot.

"All right," said Van Buren, in a voice that was somehow too ordinary, too commonplace. "Let's go."

They crossed the deserted street and entered the theatre.

In the marble-floored reception area, Van Buren took the sawn-off shotgun out of the holdall and checked the breech. Snapping it shut, he handed the holdall to Shapiro. "Remember, Shapiro. Any night staff, or security people or cleaners. We have to tie them up, get them out of the way."

"With the minimum of force . . ."

"Never mind that. Just make sure the knots are tight."

Van Buren moved to the auditorium door as Paul pulled out the petrol can, discarding the burlap sack over the ticket counter.

Steeling himself, Van Buren pulled open the door.

Paul could feel the *stillness* of the auditorium closing in as he followed Van Buren down the aisle towards the stage. He turned back to check on Shapiro, who nodded at him as he gently closed the auditorium door. In that ordinary act, it seemed to Paul that he was truly seeing his "stepfather" for the first time. Not simply a gentle and sad man of the cloth, but a man of extraordinary strength who had endured the agonies perpetrated by the thing that called itself Gideon. He had hunted Paul out after that desperate psychic call for help . . . and had saved him. He had known just what he was up against in Gideon, having once failed to stop him. But he had still come, intent on saving the boy he'd called son. Paul waited for him to catch up, took an arm and helped him as they followed close on Van Buren's heels.

Paul tried to recall some small part of the Rage that could tell him that Gideon was near. But the exorcism had completely eradicated it. He remembered his father's words to Van Buren in the car, and realised that there were bigger questions to be asked about what had happened. But the immediacy of their hellish danger obliterated the ability to ask those questions now as they approached the stage.

"He's here," said Van Buren. He had stopped in the middle of the aisle, his attention centred on the stage. "And he's waiting for us."

Paul and Shapiro followed Van Buren's gaze. It took them some seconds to work out what they were seeing.

There was a drawing room set on the stage, with French windows and stage furniture. But what they had assumed to be a stage dummy nailed to the wallpapered drawing room wall, another hanging by its feet from the lintel of the French window and a third lying across one of the chairs . . . were not stage dummies at all.

"Oh, God . . ." said Shapiro.

There was blood smeared on the plasterboard walls; scrawled, bloodied handprints. Someone had been finger-painting like a child.

"There's a door down there," said Van Buren. "Leading

down into the orchestra pit. We might be able to get under the stage from there . . ."

"There are *people* up there, Van Buren!" hissed Shapiro. "We have to see if there's anything we can do for them."

"Are you joking? One of those poor bastards has been *nailed* to the wall. They're dead, Shapiro. And we can't afford to waste any time . . ."

From the stage came the sound of someone groaning.

"The hell with it!" snapped Shapiro, with an anger that surprised Paul. "*I'll* go and see."

Shapiro moved quickly and with obvious pain to the stairs at the side of the stage. Van Buren cursed, hobbling to the barrier overlooking the orchestra pit and scanning it, before turning back to the auditorium, keeping the shotgun ready and levelled for any sign of movement. Paul followed his father.

The drawing room set on stage had been converted into a butcher's shop. Shapiro had already examined the ghastly remains of the two uniformed men on the wall and hanging from the French windows. Despite all the horror that Paul had endured, despite the killing that he had himself been forced to commit, he could not look at those hideously butchered bodies. They had been security men by the look of their stained uniforms, and they had obviously been put here to be found.

But there was also a woman lying across one of the chairs, and she was moving as Shapiro hurried to her. Paul moved to help.

"Get a move on!" hissed Van Buren, still scanning the orchestra pit and stalls for any sign of threat.

The woman had been badly beaten. There was a huge purple bruise emerging under her eye. Her clothes had been torn, and Paul could see that she had been badly bitten on the neck. More like an animal bite than a human bite. There was a gash there, crusted with dried blood. Shapiro tried to lift her, but groaned when the agony in his shoulder and side began again. Paul lifted the woman away from him, laying her down on the fake chaise-longue.

"She may be concussed, but I think she's all right. We've got to . . ." And then Shapiro moved behind the chair, his attention taken by something lying on the floor. "Paul?"

"What is it?" Paul hurried to his father again and looked.

There was a small boy lying behind the chair in a crumpled tee-shirt and blue jeans. He was about nine years old.

"Not a child, too . . . ?"

"No, he's okay," said Paul. "He's breathing. He's all right . . . I can't see anything wrong with him."

"Come ON! hissed Van Buren again.

Paul lifted the boy, made room for him on the chaise-longue and laid him down next to the woman. She was stirring now, as if trying to wake from some terrible nightmare.

"Look, Dad," said Paul. "You stay here and look after these two. Van Buren and I will go on. We'll finish what's under this stage—if he's there—for good. Just let me . . ." And then Paul saw the look on his father's face, and knew in that moment that he would not be venturing under the stage with Van Buren, after all. The look on his father's face told him everything that he needed to know. It was a look that spoke of nineteen years of agony, nineteen years of hell, nineteen years of a tested faith. And now, it was vital—it was imperative—that Shapiro himself should finally face that thing again and try to end it. "All right . . . all right . . ." said Paul. "I'll stay. You go."

Paul walked to his father, handed him the petrol can.

They embraced.

"Boy!"

Paul turned back to Van Buren, just as he threw something up to him on the stage. Paul snatched it out of the air.

It was a handgun. An automatic pistol.

"Better keep that by you for protection."

"How long have you had *that?*" asked Paul.

"Long enough to have blown your head off when you started waving the shotgun in my face. Now come on, we've got a job to do."

Shapiro descended to ground level again as Van Buren opened the small hatch in the orchestra pit barrier. He descended first, and the vicar followed. Paul moved to the edge of the stage, watching them as Van Buren found the door leading to the under-stage. It was locked. Using the butt of the shotgun, he knocked off the lock and hasp. He didn't look back at Shapiro, or up at himself, as he pushed on ahead under the stage. Shapiro paused at the entrance to look up at his son. Paul held up his hand, and his father returned the salute. Then he was gone.

Behind Paul, the woman began to moan.

He turned back to her.

Van Buren had stepped into utter darkness under the stage.

"Give me the torch from the holdall."

Shapiro fumbled in the holdall, found it and switched it on. The light swept over tubular frame racks as Van Buren took it from him and played the light on the nearest wall. In a moment, he had found the first interior light switch. He leaned over and flicked it on. The bare bulb lit up the first twenty feet or so of the under-stage area, but the furthest recesses were still shrouded in darkness.

It was impossible to see if anyone was lurking under the stage. Shapiro took in the shelving and the dusty, strewn items of stage equipment, the packing cases, the wicker baskets.

"Come on," said Van Buren. He was studying the stage overhead, keeping the shotgun pointed up at it as he moved out of the light and towards the shadows.

"Careful with that gun, Van Buren. I don't want you blowing Paul's foot off up there."

"That's the least of his worries," muttered Van Buren as he pressed on ahead, studying the criss-cross beams above their heads which supported the stage. Shapiro followed, waving a cobweb away from his face.

A wooden cross lying broken on the marble floor of the church.

Your faith is hollow, priest.

After death, your soul will be meat for me and mine.

"Where?" muttered Van Buren, standing on the periphery of the light thrown by that bare bulb and staring ahead into the darkness. "Where . . . ?"

"Behind you," said Shapiro. "There's another console in the wall."

Van Buren turned, saw the console and moved quickly to it, still keeping his eyes fixed on the stage above. Glancing quickly at it, he finally located an under-stage bank of switches and flicked them all on. Instantly, the deeper recesses of the under-stage were lit up. He pressed ahead quickly.

The pain in Shapiro's shoulder and side was crippling.

No, please. Not now, he thought, as he followed Van Buren. He did not want to pass out again, as he'd done in the car. Gritting his teeth, he forced himself erect and followed. Now, he became aware that Van Buren had frozen in his tracks and was staring intently ahead and up at the stage. He was nodding his head, almost imperceptibly. "Got you, you bastard. *Got you!*"

Shapiro drew level at last, to see that Van Buren was staring directly ahead and up at the stage, where two beams intersected.

Hanging over the vee of that intersection was a gnarled, white hand.

". . . got you . . . got you . . . got you . . ." Van Buren muttered over and over again as he stepped cautiously towards it.

"Now what?"

"Take the cap off that can. *Now!*"

Shapiro quickly screwed off the cap. It clattered to the
concrete floor.

Van Buren stepped forward again, holding the sawn-off
shotgun with one hand and reaching for that bloodless
white hand with the other.

"James . . ." mumbled the woman, and Paul moved back to
her again. He had been moving nervously about the stage,
keeping the automatic pistol pointed at the floor. The memories of that "vision" he had experienced during the exorcism were still horrifyingly vivid. The thought that he was,
even now, standing just above Gideon brought him out into
a cold sweat.

"It's okay," he said, holding her gently back as she struggled to be free.

"Where is he? Where's James?"

"Who's James? You mean the boy?"

And Jacqueline saw her son at last, lying at the bottom of
the chaise-longue. She pushed Paul away and struggled to
him, seizing him in a crushing embrace. He groaned, and
the relief burst inside Jacqueline. She washed his face in her
tears.

And far above the stage, on the gantry just below the
vaulted ceiling of the theatre, Evan looked down on them
and smiled his insane smile.

"Get ready," said Van Buren.

Shapiro took a step back, holding the can ready.

And then Van Buren seized that white hand and yanked
hard.

Above them, a body began to slide out from its hiding place. Van Buren tugged harder, and there was the sound of ripping cloth as something snagged on a nail in the beam.

"Look out!" Van Buren jumped back, cursing at the pain in his leg, as a body fell out from the hollow above the cross-section. It fell lifelessly to the concrete floor with a wet and horrifying impact.

Van Buren exclaimed in disgust, and Shapiro had a glimpse of a completely shattered and mangled face as he stepped forward with the petrol can. The thing was dressed in black, its gnarled hands frozen in a clutching spasm. And Shapiro was frozen in horror at the hideous sight.

"Do it!" snapped Van Buren. "Come on, Shapiro!" Angrily, he snatched the petrol can from his hands and upended it over the bloody ruin on the floor. The air was filled with the acrid fumes as the petrol sprayed over the body.

And then something laughed behind them.

It was as if the under-stage area had suddenly been flooded with cold air.

They turned away from the hideously mangled body of Enzo Castelano and looked back at the doorway to the orchestra pit.

"I've been expecting you, priest," said the thing that stood there.

The figure was tall, very tall, and looked as if it had clawed its way out of its grave. It was shrouded in a long dark coat hanging down to its ankles. The face was horribly decayed, there were no eyes, and the flesh had all but rotted away from the right side of its face down to the ragged neck. Semi-skeletal claws clenched and unclenched at its side. The figure was so badly decayed that Shapiro could not recognise it as the thing which he had confronted in his church. But even though the voice was a sibilant and rasp-

ing distortion, he recognised it immediately. *"I saw you
through the boy's eyes. When you took him from me. And believe me—I'm going to make you pay for that."*

The thing took a step forward. It was an awkward and un-
gainly movement.

Rigor mortis, thought Shapiro in horror. Despite the dete-
rioration of the thing's physical frame, he could still feel the
terrifying power emanating from it.

Shapiro suddenly became aware of Van Buren, stepping
forward to join him, could feel the tension and the cold fury
in him.

The thing laughed: a hideous, liquid sound that seemed
to fill the under-stage with unnatural echoes. It cocked its
head to one side in a way that Shapiro remembered from
twenty years ago.

"Have we had the pleasure?"

"Not yet," said Van Buren quietly, in a voice like ice.

"Such hate. Who are you?"

Shapiro heard Van Buren grind his teeth. "Death," he said.

*"No. I don't think so. You are not acquainted with it in the
way I am. You have no understanding . . ."* Living things
squirmed from the death's head mouth and scurried across
its shredded chest, finding dark folds and recesses in which
to hide. *". . . no understanding of the pain involved. Let me
acquaint you."*

"You filthy . . ." began Van Buren.

And then the stone and concrete walls of the under-stage
area began to hiss. It was a noise like escaping steam, or the
sudden onset of rain. And as the thing laughed its horrifying,
liquid laugh again . . . something began to happen to those
walls. There was movement there now, from the cracks in
the walls, from the shadowed corners.

Within seconds, the walls had become a seething, squirming mass of insects. The brickwork was entirely covered in a glistening mass of spiders, cockroaches and centipedes.

"Let's call it a"—the thing laughed again—*"a stage-managed effect."*

Shapiro felt the old terror seize his soul.

"Time to die," said the living corpse.

It advanced on them.

On the gantry, Evan moved carefully along the iron-strutted gangplank, examining their handiwork. It had taken Enzo and himself a long time, and he had bowed to the Italian's practical skills. Not only had he been skilled at repair, but he had also been very skilled at *unrepair*. Evan looked down again at the figures on the stage, and smiled once more. Reaching the service door in the theatre wall which gave access to the gangplank, and thereafter to the stage gantry, he turned carefully to look back.

Perfect.

He knew that Enzo had performed his last service for the Master down below; but knew that he—Evan—was destined for a great inheritance.

Bloody perfect.

He picked up the fire axe that he had left lying on the service ramp, being careful so as not to be overheard from below. There was great power in it. It had already been bloodied for the Master, was now to be the instrument for the final killing. Evan raised it carefully with both hands, turning to his left and looking down at the thin metal rod which Enzo had connected to the gangplank. Bracing himself, he brought it down with as much force as he could.

The fire axe bit through the metal.

Beyond, the entire gantry squealed, groaned . . . and tilted to the left.

Below, Evan saw the bastard and the woman suddenly look up.

Then he whirled and brought the axe down hard to his right. It only half sheared the metal rod. The gantry juddered and tilted again. Evan cursed, drew back the axe, screamed and brought it down again. This time, the rod was sheared right through.

And the two-ton gantry, completely severed from its moorings in one wall, crashed downwards to the stage.

Above them, something exploded on the stage.

Shapiro and Van Buren reeled as two of the great beams supporting the stage cracked and shuddered overhead, showering them with dust. The concrete walls cracked and split, and the entire under-stage area seemed to tilt like a ship's hold in a storm. Insects showered their hair and shoulders. They flailed at the squirming rain, as the lights sparked off and then came on again. Many of the bulbs had shattered, suffusing the under-stage in a grey half-light of groaning beams and swirling dust. The squirming mass of insects on the cracked walls seemed instantly driven to a renewed, hissing frenzy.

Gideon had stopped and was looking up at the cracked and splintered beams, shrouded in clouds of billowing dust. Shapiro had the fleeting impression that Gideon was disappointed that the stage had not collapsed on top of them.

The living corpse turned back to them . . . and came on.

But Van Buren had recovered now. Calmly, still holding the petrol can, he raised the sawn-off shotgun in his other hand. Hugging the stock tight under his armpit, he fired.

Shapiro was deafened by the blast, saw the shot hit the Gideon-thing squarely in the chest, saw part of a rotted ribcage explode away as the corpse was flung back against a supporting beam. But Gideon did not fall. Pushing himself away from the beam, he came on again.

Van Buren knew that the shotgun would not stop him. But he had waited so long, and this was his way of venting the anger and the bitterness which had gradually destroyed him inside during the time he had hunted for this thing.

"Fifty years!" yelled Van Buren—and fired again.

Gideon staggered, his long coat flying. And Van Buren took advantage of the momentary delay in the thing's momentum to thrust the shotgun into Shapiro's hands . . . and then jerked the petrol can again and again in Gideon's direction, spraying the corpse with the acrid liquid.

"The holdall!" yelled Van Buren.

Shapiro knew the plan, but the immediate horror of what was happening had robbed him of initiative. "Shapiro! NOW!"

Gideon recovered and came on.

Shapiro fumbled in the holdall, and Van Buren yelled again as he hurled the petrol can at the advancing figure. Gideon lashed out, shattering the can in mid-air; spraying all three of them in petrol.

At last, Shapiro had found what he was after—the thing Paul had taken out of the holdall in the car, with a less-than-convinced look on his face.

It was a single-shot, distress flare-gun.

Shapiro dropped the holdall and raised the squat, heavy metal. But he was too late. Gideon closed upon Van Buren, seizing him by the shoulders. In his rage, Van Buren struck out at the hideous thing with both hands, still yelling his anger directly into its face. Effortlessly, the Gideon-thing threw Van Buren head first up at the stage. He slammed into it with sickening impact, falling back again as limp as a life-size rag doll.

Shouting in rage, Shapiro squeezed the trigger.

But Gideon took him by the throat, lifting him instantly

from his feet just as he had lifted him twenty years ago. The flare pistol was prised from Shapiro's grasp and dropped on the floor.

The face of death breathed directly into Shapiro's own.

A wooden cross lying broken on the marble floor of the church.

Shapiro did not resist the claw which was gradually constricting his windpipe, crushing his larynx.

The thing laughed.

Shapiro did not claw or thrash for air, did not beat at that hideous figure, did not resist.

Twenty years. His wife. His son.

And somehow, Gideon was no longer laughing. The corpse-thing stood, holding Shapiro aloft like a child; sightless, ravaged eye sockets fixed intently now on the priest's face and seeing . . .

That there was no fear on that face. No terror. No desperation. No pleading for life. Only a steady and direct condemnation of the very essence of Gideon. A condemnation of the anathema that he represented to all human life. Gideon could see in that face that the long years of suffering which he had inflicted had not broken the man, had not destroyed his faith. The priest's presence here—now—served to confirm only one thing. Far from destroying the man, Gideon had served to forge a deeper faith . . .

Gideon began to moan.

The priest's eyes were sharp, vital and radiant.

And the utter certainty and condemnation in those eyes caused the most hideous, psychic pain. Shapiro had damaged Gideon—*was* damaging him—in a way that no other human, both in and out of death, ever had.

Screaming, Gideon hurled Shapiro against the far wall.

The priest slammed into the lighting console.

It exploded on contact . . . and Shapiro's shattered, petrol-soaked body instantly ignited and fell to the concrete floor. The console sparked, burned, and then the lights went out. Now, the only illumination was provided by the burning body of the priest, sending guttering shadows crawling and lunging on the undulating, hissing walls.

Paul and Jacqueline froze, staring up from the stage as the theatre was filled with the sounds of screeching iron. The screeching became a chaotic jangle of steel, as if a dozen church bells had torn free from a dozen belfries all at once, pealing their gigantic one-note discord as they fell. An explosion of concrete high up in the vaulted ceiling sent great slabs of masonry and twisted metal plunging into the theatre as the gantry tore free from its moorings.

And Jacqueline was suddenly alive again as Paul stood and watched the chaotic rending of metal above. Seizing James, she whirled from the chaise-longue, yelled, *"Come ON!"* and Paul had broken from that horrified inertia as the severed end of the gantry swung down like a gigantic pendulum, its other end still embedded in the opposite wall.

"It'll miss, it'll miss, it'll miss . . ."

"No it won't!" yelled Jacqueline. "Come on!"

And then the gantry tore free from the other wall in an explosion of shattered concrete and gushing clouds of dust. Chunks of masonry were already falling at the back of the stage as Jacqueline ran. The gantry hit the backstage area, shattering an internal wall and punching a hole clear through to the rehearsal rooms. For a long second, it seemed to stand on end. Paul heard Jacqueline cry out, looked around to see her falling to the stage with the young boy in her arms . . . and then looked back as the gantry began to fall towards them like some toppling factory chimney forged from steel.

Paul ran towards the woman, feeling the gigantic shadow

of the toppling steel above him. He grabbed her arm, dragged her to her feet again, leaned down to help with the boy . . . and then saw the terror in the woman's eyes as she looked up past him.

He knew then that it was too late.

The shadow enveloped them like a roaring, nightmare storm.

Paul was smashed to the stage floor.

He had no idea how long he had been unconscious, or whether he had been unconscious at all. There was a great ringing sound in his ears, the remaining internal echo of the gantry as it fell and disintegrated. Clouds of plaster dust gushed around him, into his lungs. He felt as if he must choke as he tried to cough his lungs clear. The sound echoed back to him, as if he were in an enclosed space.

Somewhere, he could hear the rustling patter of masonry dust still falling. He was still alive. God knew how, but he hadn't been smashed to a pulp. Paul feverishly checked himself out, still unable to see anything other than the gushing dust. He seemed undamaged, although the old pains in his ribs were hideously renewed. His hands were scratched and bloodied, but he could find no serious damage. He twisted around on to his back and raised his hands carefully. They connected with metal both above him and on all sides. He seemed to be in a cage. He tried to turn over, felt something snag on his jerkin and rip it. He waved the choking dust from his face, and heard the sound of a child crying. It was a small, frightened sound. Paul tried to speak out, but the choking dust filled his lungs again and made him gag.

He felt a movement beside him, reached out towards it; and then heard the woman say, "Is that you? Are you all right?" Her voice quavered with fear.

"Yes, yes . . . you okay?"

"I think so. But my son . . . James . . . I can hear him."

"He's over here. I think I can . . ."

And then the swirling dust began to dissipate. Paul could make out a distorted mass of metal, tangled wiring and twisted scaffolding above and around him. He waved at the dust, cleared it further and looked for the boy as the small, distressed sounds came again. A hand connected with his arm—the woman. And Paul could see the boy now, lying not far away, covered in white dust.

At last, the gushing dust had settled.

"Jesus Christ." It was neither a prayer nor a blasphemy. Just a statement of incredulity. Now, Paul could see what had happened.

The gantry had fallen diagonally across the stage, right on top of them. But it had hit the false wall of the drawing room set and knocked it over on to them first. The collapsing wall had fallen over them, splitting in half and forming a protective arch as the gantry had finally smashed to the stage. Impossibly, the wall had protected them and they had survived.

"Where is he?" asked the woman again, and Paul reached for the dust-whitened body, snagging his fingers in the boy's collar. He dragged him slowly towards him through the maze of twisted metal, bent scaffolding and shattered plasterboard. Paul could see beyond that twisted mass of metal, wiring and scaffolding now; could see the auditorium and the rows of empty seats. The woman suddenly cried out from behind him.

"What's wrong?"

"My leg," said Jacqueline simply. And now Paul could see her face as she crawled to him. "There's something sticking in it."

"Look, your boy's all right. Christ knows how, but we're all okay."

"Can you get out? I can't see . . ."

"Yeah, yeah. I think so." Paul seized a twisted aluminium rail over his head and pulled. It seemed sturdy enough, not likely to bring down further detritus on their heads. Grabbing it with his other hand, he heaved himself up through a gap in the twisted metal, pushing aside a knot of electrical wiring. He was standing now, looking back across the fallen wreckage of the gantry, lying directly across the stage.

Dad! Had the stage caved in somewhere on top of them? There was a new urgency now as Paul began to pull himself out of the wreckage.

Somewhere in the wings, someone was whistling.

It was a light, jaunty tune. As if the whistler didn't have a care in the world. In this nightmare tangle of wreckage on the stage, the effect was bizarre. Paul's trouser leg snagged on something below.

"I'm caught . . ."

Beneath him, Jacqueline reached for his leg, began to twist at the trouser fabric to free him.

And then Paul saw a man his own age walk out on to the stage from the wings. A young man dressed in denims, still whistling, and tossing something end-over-end in his hands. It looked like a crucifix. There was a fire axe over his other shoulder. The whistling stopped when he saw Paul. He began to grin.

"All the world's a stage, eh?" said the young man.

Below, Jacqueline heard the voice.

"Oh Christ . . ."

Paul looked down. "What's wrong?"

"Him!" hissed Jacqueline, tearing to free his snagged trouser leg.

"What?"

"He's with Gideon!"

The Other!

Paul snapped his head up as the young man screamed at him. It was an inhuman, animalistic sound. Holding the fire axe in a two-handed grip, he began to stagger over the wreckage towards them.

Below the stage, Van Buren scrabbled in the darkness for his coat pocket. There were living things on his arms and legs; things that crawled and squirmed and hissed. He could feel them on his face as he groped for the pocket. The shapes and shadows before his eyes were doubled-haloed, and he knew that he was concussed. The pain behind his eyes and at the base of his skull devoured like acid. He had "woken" with the sawn-off shotgun still in his hand, did not know what the thing called Gideon had done to him but knew that he was badly hurt somehow. All he could remember was the savagery of his own hate as he had screamed directly into the thing's face. Now, the lights had gone off, and the only illumination came from something that burned beneath the console panel on the wall.

Van Buren found his pocket at last, fumbled in it for a shell. God knew what had happened to Shapiro and the flare-pistol. Even though a shotgun blast could not stop him, Van Buren could only hope that somehow another shell might ignite Gideon's petrol-soaked body.

The burning pile beneath the console cast guttering, rearing shadows in the under-stage area. And suddenly, a tall shadow detached from the surrounding darkness and began to stride towards him. Van Buren snapped open the breech of the shotgun, twisted up on to one elbow, felt the pain eating his brain at the movement.

The shadow filled his vision as Van Buren levelled the shotgun from where he lay, and pulled the trigger.

The noise of the detonation stabbed excruciating pain behind his eyes. He screamed; saw the shadow stagger backwards as the gunshot passed straight through it, hitting the console directly behind. It exploded in great fizzing arcs of blue fire.

But the shadow was untouched by the flame. It came on . . . seizing the shotgun and smashing it across Van Buren's head. Then it flung the gun aside into the deeper recesses of the under-stage, and turned back to him. Seizing Van Buren by the lapels of his torn coat, it dragged him to his feet.

Shrieking, Evan brought the fire axe down on Paul.

Paul dragged his leg clear, the fabric splitting to the knee, and threw himself backwards over the shattered gantry rail.

The fire axe clanged against the rail, sending echoes chasing in the theatre as Paul fell awkwardly to a bare part of the stage. A cloud of dust engulfed him as Evan pulled the axe back, still shrieking. He was clambering up on to the shattered part of the gantry from which Paul had come, eyes wild, as Jacqueline shrank back further into the protective, twisted cage. He swung the axe up and down again as Jacqueline grabbed James protectively to herself beneath the steel. The axe rang on the iron directly above her. And this time, Paul lunged back, grabbing the axe by the head. Evan lashed out at him, knocking him back to the bare, cracked boards of the stage again. He began to clamber after Paul.

There was dust in Paul's eyes, and he frantically tried to rub them clear. He saw the silhouette of their attacker standing on the wrecked gantry, swinging the axe around ready to jump down directly on top of him. Crying out, Paul twisted to one side . . . just as the axe embedded in the stage boards an inch from his head.

"The gun! The gun!" Paul had lost it. When Van Buren had thrown it to him, he had jammed it into his jerkin pocket.

Now, it had fallen out . . . and Paul lunged at the axe again, seizing it once more by the head as his attacker jumped down to the stage and tried to drag it free from the wood. Paul lunged at him, the force of his move throwing them both heavily back against the shattered metal of the gantry. The axe remained embedded in the stage. Evan clawed for Paul's eyes, and the nightmare had come full circle again. Paul was no longer fighting for his life in this theatre. He was at home in his father's living room, fighting to wrest control of a shotgun from a young man, his own age, who had blasted through the French windows and almost killed his father. This was Paul's chance to turn back the clock. In his desperation, something inside filled him with the absolute conviction of instinct that he must overcome this attacker . . . and everything would be the way it was before.

No Rage.

No insanely murderous half-brothers.

No Gideon.

And now, no half-hearted measures, no self-protection. He must kill this attacker and . . .

Evan headbutted Paul over the left eyebrow. The impact and the shock hurled him back to the stage floor. Blood spattered into Paul's eyes as Evan lunged back and seized the axe. He began frantically to lever it free from the stage.

"Here!"

And Paul twisted to see that the woman was reaching through the cage of twisted metal towards him. She had something in her hand, slapped that something down hard on the stage . . . and shoved it spinning across the floor to him.

Jacqueline had found the gun.

Paul scrabbled for it, blood streaming down his face.

Evan twisted the axe free, shrieked, and raised it above his head.

And Paul screamed too, as he pulled the trigger. Again and again and again.

The first bullet shattered Evan's jawbone, tearing the lower part of it free from his face in a spray of shattered tissue and blood. His shriek was instantly silenced. The next shot smashed his shoulder, the impact flinging him back against a shattered part of the plasterboard set wall. The axe clattered to his feet. The third shot punctured Evan's stomach and as he slid down the tilted plaster-board wall until he was sitting in his own blood, he tried to say *This isn't supposed to happen. What about my inheritance . . . ?* but had no mouth. He wanted to cry, looked up at the fire curtain hanging loose far above his head . . . and then a different kind of curtain came down behind his eyes.

Beneath the stage, Gideon howled in pain and rage.

Dropping Van Buren to the floor again, the corpse-thing turned the decayed remnants of its face up to the stage above.

It raged.

And then flew back through the guttering shadows to the under-stage door.

Paul finished dry-heaving where he sat. This was not the same as before. The Rage was not upon him. He was human. And he was not in the vicarage living room. He had not cancelled the nightmare, had not turned the clock back. A great and bitter sorrow threatened to enervate him.

"Come on," said the woman. "Help me."

And Paul dragged himself over to the woman, wiping blood from his eyes.

From somewhere below, he could hear what seemed to be a wolf howling. That sound struck some kind of chord inside Paul. It seemed to mirror something deep in his soul as he finally reached the tangle of wiring and twisted aluminium that had both protected the woman and her son, and had imprisoned them. Staggering to his feet, Paul began to twist a gap in that tangled wreckage.

"I can do it," said the woman at last. "I think . . . think I can get through." Paul leaned in as she shoved the boy through the gap. Paul pulled him the rest of the way. He was semiconscious now, still groaning but with his eyes closed; as if not wanting to wake into a worse nightmare. Paul gently put him to one side, reached back in for the woman. She took his hand and began to pull herself through. Halfway through the gap, her grip on his hand tightened and she drew a hissing intake of breath. Gritting her teeth in pain, she reached back to her leg. Paul looked through the gap and saw that her leg was trailing blood.

"Are you all right?"

"I'll be okay. Just help me to . . . *oh Christ!*"

Paul jerked back, following the woman's gaze.

Smoke was beginning to creep up over the rim of the stage.

And something was ascending the steps at the side of the stage.

Something that surely could not be alive, could not be moving slowly up towards them.

"It's *him!*" said the woman—and Paul knew that she meant Gideon.

The tall, ragged, living corpse reached the debris-strewn stage and stood looking at them; not thirty feet away. Smoke swirled behind it. Paul had seen death and horror, had been a part of it, had himself been forced to murder. But nothing could have prepared him for the sight of that tall and hideously decomposed nightmare. He could feel its power as it walked awkwardly towards them. Without realising it, he had raised the gun.

"It won't do any good," said the woman quietly, with desperate resignation in her voice.

Gideon stopped beside Evan's body, looking down. The corpse-thing reached for him with one hand, taking his body by the lapel of Evan's denim jacket and lifting him as effortlessly as a parent would lift a newborn child. It held him before it, now lifting him high with both hands towards the vaulted ceiling of the theatre.

Gideon howled again. It was a long, ululating howl of rage and pain . . . and sorrow.

And then it dropped him to the stage, discarding the bleeding flesh as if it suddenly meant nothing at all.

Gideon advanced on them.

Paul fired. Once, twice . . . the second shot screaming away into the theatre with an endless ricochet. But neither shot had any effect, and now the hammer was falling on an empty chamber. Gideon stopped, ten feet from where they lay. The corpse-thing watched as Jacqueline crawled to James, cradling him and defiantly staring back. The gun fell from Paul's nerveless fingers as he stared at the thing. So this was Gideon? This was the source of the nightmare.

This was his true father.

"You're mine," said the corpse-thing. *"You are my flesh."*

"Never," said Paul, surprised at the sound of his own voice. "You may have sired me, but you're not my father."

"I can give you eternal life, Paul. You know that."

"You can't make me do anything any more. You can't make me kill. You can't make me . . . make me *be* you!"

"Free will. Isn't that the dictate of your priesthood? The ability to choose between your dead and forgotten God . . . and me?"

"I'm exorcised from you, Gideon." There was a purity in the anger which welled within Paul. In Gideon's presence, that anger was focused and vital. Paul was trembling with that rage when he spoke. "When I see what you are, how you've survived . . . and what you've *done* . . . I could never be you. And thank Christ, my father has reclaimed me."

"Yes, the priest has removed you from me. But you can still claim your inheritance, Paul. Use your free will! I cannot forcibly embody within you . . . but if you want me, if you want to be me, then it is still possible. You have no idea of the glory, the liberation, the power . . ."

"Death," replied Paul. "Everywhere you go you bring death. You feed on the innocent, Gideon. Your existence is at their expense. I could never be you. I deny you. Do you hear me? *I deny you!"*

Gideon was silent.

"Where is my father? My *real* father?"

Gideon laughed. The sound was horrific. A statement of hideous intent. Paul could see the bullet-shattered ribcage, could see living things move within it when the thing laughed.

"The priest is in hell."

And even as Gideon spoke, smoke began to curl through the cracks in the stage floor.

The wolf was howling again. Paul could hear it. But this time, it was not coming from beneath the stage, not coming from the thing called Gideon. Suddenly, he realised that the ever-building sound was coming from himself.

Paul flew across the stage at Gideon.

The corpse-thing seized him effortlessly by the neck and threw him hard over its shoulder. Paul collided with a tangle of plasterboard, wiring and torn scaffolding, falling limply to the stage. Gideon turned slowly, and Jacqueline could sense the rage within him.

"I will not die. I will not allow you to let me die."

Paul moaned, struggling to rise again, coughing as the smoke from the stage floor began to thicken. "You're . . .

you're going to die, Gideon. I'm the last . . . the last son. And I deny . . . deny you. You're going to die . . ."

"Then you will die too, Paul. And believe me, you'll beg for my forgiveness of that denial when your free will no longer matters."

Gideon advanced on him.

Jacqueline hugged James tighter from where she knelt on the floor. She did not understand what was happening, did not know who the young man was; but she knew that Gideon was finally, for reasons she could not fathom, on the verge of extinction.

"You're beaten, you bastard!" she shouted. "You're beaten, and *you're* the one who's going to rot in hell!"

Gideon turned back. *"Not before I've really made you suffer, bitch."*

The living corpse strode awkwardly from Paul towards her.

The death's head grin widened. Maggots squirmed and writhed behind those teeth, in the one remaining eye socket and in the horrific crater which had been the other side of its face. It raised semi-skeletal claws as it came on. Behind it, Jacqueline heard the young man say, ". . . no . . ."

And then Gideon reached down for her.

At last, this was the way it would end.

Gideon's leering, decomposed face filled her vision.

And somehow, the inlaid metal cross that she had taken from the church was in her right hand. Jacqueline was not aware that she had picked it up, knew indeed that she had *not* picked it up. When she'd last seen it, the other young man—the one who had so hideously abused her and now lay dead on the stage—had taken it from her. But, impossibly, it was in her hand. And as those skeletal claws reached for her and that no-face grinned its hideously evil grin, Jacqueline saw Brian and Martin and Bernice and Yvonne.

And James.

Holding the crucifix like a dagger, her fist clenching the upper half tight, Jacqueline stabbed it deep into Gideon's remaining eye socket.

Gideon reared back, roaring. The cross was embedded deep in his face. The corpse-thing thrashed away from her, clutching at the dagger and Jacqueline screamed her defiance as . . .

Paul hurtled across the stage with the blood-soaked fire axe, whirling it heavily above his head and bringing it down with all of his remaining strength. The axe embedded deep in the corpse-thing's decomposed, shattered chest cavity, and Gideon staggered back under the blow, still clutching at the cross embedded in his face, tearing the axe from Paul's grasp. Paul collapsed to the stage, breathless with exertion and fear as . . .

Gideon staggered backwards . . . and fell against a protruding rail of scaffolding. The tubular rail impaled him, bursting from his chest by a good six feet, and dislodging the axe to the stage floor with a bloody clatter. Gideon's claws flew to the impaling rod, clutching at it; decayed head shaking from side to side to dislodge the cross-dagger as . . .

Van Buren reeled up the stage stairs and yelled, "Paul, get her out of the way!"

Paul clambered to the woman, dragged her and the boy backwards away from the thrashing figure impaled on the scaffolding as . . .

Van Buren raised the flare-pistol that he had found beside Shapiro's burning body, and pulled the trigger.

Gideon, still soaked in petrol, instantly exploded in a roaring man-shaped ball of flame. A great howling, that was somehow much more than the sound of those raging flames, filled the air. The burning shape thrashed and squirmed, and Paul cried out aloud as . . .

Gideon began to pull himself off the scaffolding. Step by

step, the blazing shape was walking itself along the scaffolding pole. In seconds, that blazing, howling monstrosity would be free again. Free to take them with it to its own blazing hell.

"He won't die!" screamed Jacqueline. "He'll *never* die!"

"Ashes to ashes, you bastard," said Van Buren. And Paul looked back at him just as . . .

Van Buren hurled himself across the stage, his own roar of defiance and rage matching the howling hatred and pain and insanity of the burning, thrashing mass impaled on the scaffolding. Paul shouted at him to stop as . . .

Van Buren threw himself on to the scaffolding pole and was instantly impaled, the force of his headlong rush slamming him hard against the burning mass. His arms encircled it, just as his own petrol-soaked body also erupted into a fireball.

"No!" Paul looked on in horror, still dragging Jacqueline and the boy away from the hellish scene as the burning shape of Van Buren wrestled with the thing that had been Gideon. And as Paul and Jacqueline watched, Van Buren *walked* down the impaling pole; pushing the thrashing, burning mass that was Gideon before him. The scaffolding pole protruded twenty feet behind them when, at last, their joint silhouettes vanished and were consumed within the inferno. *"Oh Christ, no . . ."*

Smoke was gushing from the stage floor as Paul pulled himself to his feet, helping the woman. She cradled the boy and they staggered to the stage stairs, still looking back at the blazing mass amidst the wreckage of the fallen gantry. At last, they turned to descend . . . but flames were leaping up before them, from the open door leading to the under-stage. Paul looked desperately around, saw the other set of stairs at the far side of the stage. Waving acrid smoke from their eyes, glancing back at the fiery mass on stage, they clambered over wreckage and fallen masonry until they had reached those stairs. The fire both beneath the stage and on top of it was spreading rapidly to the rest of the theatre.

They staggered down the stairs.

Paul looked back at the stage, only once, as they limped down the centre aisle towards the Exit door.

Smoke gushed into the cold marble reception area with them when they burst through the door. Not pausing, they staggered out through the main entrance and into the night.

It was raining again. A light drizzle that would never put out the inferno that was to devour the building. The feel of that rain on their bodies was cool and cleansing.

The dark-glinting streets were still deserted, with no one around to raise the alarm until the fire had well and truly engulfed the building, and the horror within.

They crossed to the other side of the street and looked back at the great Gothic building. Smoke gushed from the main entrance. From within, they heard the crash of more masonry falling on to the stage.

"Is he dead?" asked Jacqueline.

"Ashes to ashes," said Paul. He felt as if he should weep, but could not. "This time he's really dead."

"I can't believe it." Jacqueline's voice was hoarse. She held James tight as he moaned again. "Can't believe that I'm still alive."

"Come on," said Paul . . . and they limped into the night.

Epilogue

They walked in silence, letting the rain wash them clean.

Neither of them asked questions of the other. Neither asked what part Gideon had played in their lives.

When they reached the Quayside and looked out over the glinting black troughs of waves on the River Tyne, and the myriad ripples caused by the rain, Jacqueline said: "I'll be able to get to the hospital from here. There's an all-night taxi rank not far from here."

"Your leg?" asked Paul. "Maybe you should get an ambulance."

"No, it's stopped bleeding. And I don't want to draw any attention to us. I'll be okay."

The child in her arms moaned and pushed his face into the crook of her shoulder, still asleep. Despite the horrors they had all endured, his face seemed tranquil and serene.

"How's your son? Is he all right?"

"I don't think he's hurt. I think his mind has been . . . switched off. At least, I hope it has. Kids can do that sometimes. I just pray to God that he hasn't been aware of anything that's happened." Jacqueline stroked James's hair, looking back at Paul's battered and ragged silhouette. "What are you going to do?" she asked at last.

"I'm not from this neck of the woods." Paul looked up at the railway bridge which spanned the river. "Maybe a train from the Central Station. I think I've got . . ." He rummaged in his jeans pocket. ". . . yeah, I've got money."

As if in answer, they heard the mournful sound of a train whistle somewhere in the night. The train whistle was suddenly joined by the distant sounds of fire engines somewhere in the city.

"Will you be all right?" asked Paul.

"Yes." Jacqueline held James tight. "I've got my family to go back to."

"My family died back there in the theatre." Paul moved to the quayside edge and looked down into the rippling, dark water. His silhouette looked back up at him. He remembered the way his reflection had looked back at him from the glass doors when he'd visited his mother in hospital. Remembered the way his hideous, blood-stained reflection had thrown a tyre iron at him in that abandoned, wrecked petrol station. And he remembered how alien those reflections had seemed to him. Somehow, the silhouette down there in the water didn't look at all alien to him now.

"I'm so sorry . . ."

"No," said Paul. And Jacqueline could not tell whether it was tears or rain on his face. "Don't be. We won. That's the important thing. That's all that matters."

"Are there more like Gideon out there somewhere?"

Paul turned back to her. "Yes, I'm sorry to say. But there's one less now and that's for sure."

"I don't understand how things like him can exist. How do we protect ourselves?"

"I don't know. By having faith in ourselves, maybe. By

changing the way we look at things that we call Good and Evil."

The train whistle mourned again in the night.

"Where will you go?" asked Jacqueline.

"Well, I don't know if I can go back to where I came from. There are too many questions that can't be answered. But for the first time, I'm my *own* man. You won't know what that means, but for the first time in my life I know who I am. I'll take it from there."

Jacqueline looked towards the taxi rank and then out over the Swing Bridge that would take her to the hospital where Brian and Martin were recovering. She didn't have answers to the questions which were bound to be asked either, but they were together again and the nightmare was over. Brian had been right in quoting the Noël Coward play, but he had no idea just *how* far away Jacqueline had been.

Paul tightened his ragged collar, looking at the railway bridge.

"What's your name?" he asked, and held out his hand.

Instead, Jacqueline embraced him with her free arm. He hugged her in return.

"Jacqueline," she said as she stood back.

"My name's Paul."

At last, they turned from each other . . . and limped into the night.

Away from the Nightmares, and into new Futures.

THE WYRM

STEPHEN LAWS

Something hideous is about to happen to the small town of Shillingham. Why does a madman shoot at the workers tearing down the old gallows at the crossroads? Why are the children drawn to play in its shadow, as if by a silent command? What is the eerie, thickening fog that surrounds the village, cutting off the inhabitants from the outside world?

Beneath the ground, something stirs. As the workers continue working and the bulldozers roll on, a dark and unimaginable evil, imprisoned beneath the gallows for centuries, slowly awakes. It is alive. It is powerful and cunning. And it wants revenge.

Dorchester Publishing Co., Inc.
P.O. Box 6640   5219-9
Wayne, PA 19087-8640 $6.99 US/$8.99 CAN

Please add $2.50 for shipping and handling for the first book and $.75 for each additional book. NY and PA residents, add appropriate sales tax. No cash, stamps, or CODs. Canadian orders require an extra $2.00 for shipping and handling and must be paid in U.S. dollars. Prices and availability subject to change. **Payment must accompany all orders.**

Name: _____

Address: _____

City: _____ State: _____ Zip: _____

E-mail: _____

I have enclosed $_____ in payment for the checked book(s).

CHECK OUT OUR WEBSITE! www.dorchesterpub.com
_____ *Please send me a free catalog.*

STEPHEN LAWS
DARKFALL

A massive storm is raging, filled with lightning, power . . . and terror. But inside one high-rise office building, all is silent. Moments before, the building was filled with Christmas parties and celebrating employees. Now it is empty. Everyone has vanished, disappeared into thin air. The only thing left behind—a severed human hand.

Detective Jack Cardiff and his squad are about to discover the living hell that is Darkfall, where the impossible becomes all too real, and where things that were once human become living nightmares. As the investigation proceeds, the full extent of the horror emerges, a horror more fearsome than the howling storm that spawned it.

Dorchester Publishing Co., Inc.
P.O. Box 6640
Wayne, PA 19087-8640   __5218-0
                         $6.99 US/$8.99 CAN

Please add $2.50 for shipping and handling for the first book and $.75 for each book thereafter. NY and PA residents, please add appropriate sales tax. No cash, stamps, or C.O.D.s. Prices and availability subject to change.

Canadian orders require $2.00 extra postage and must be paid in U.S. dollars through a U.S. banking facility.

Name_____
Address_____
City_____ State_____ Zip_____
E-mail _____
I have enclosed $_____ in payment for the checked book(s).

Payment <u>must</u> accompany all orders. __Check here for a free catalog.

CHECK OUT OUR WEBSITE! www.dorchesterpub.com

THE HOUSE ON ORCHID STREET
T.M. WRIGHT

"A country charmer," the ad calls it. "Secluded but accessible." But this white bungalow is no ordinary house. It may look perfectly nice, with its picket fence and quaint path, but within it lurks a horror few could imagine. Behind its neatly painted white walls, the house conceals secrets far better left unrevealed.

Katherine Nichols thinks the house will be perfect for her. She's looking forward to a little seclusion, to being able to work—to living alone. It isn't long, though, before she realizes she isn't alone after all. Soon she discovers the evil that lives in the house. Evil that has survived for nearly a century. Evil that lives—and hates.

Dorchester Publishing Co., Inc.
P.O. Box 6640
Wayne, PA 19087-8640

_____5090-0
$6.99 US/$8.99 CAN

Please add $2.50 for shipping and handling for the first book and $.75 for each additional book. NY and PA residents, add appropriate sales tax. No cash, stamps, or CODs. Canadian orders require $2.00 for shipping and handling and must be paid in U.S. dollars. Prices and availability subject to change. **Payment must accompany all orders.**

Name: _____

Address: _____

City:_____ State: _____ Zip:_____

E-mail: _____

I have enclosed $_____ in payment for the checked book(s).

For more information on these books, check out our website at www.dorchesterpub.com.
_____ _Please send me a free catalog._

MESSENGER
EDWARD LEE

Have you ever wanted to be someone else? Well, someone else is about to become *you*. He will share your soul and your mind. He will feel what you feel, your pleasure, your pain. And then he will make you kill. He will drive you to perform horrific ritual murder and unimaginable occult rites. You are about to be possessed, but not by a ghost. It's something far worse.

The devil has a messenger, and that messenger is here, now, in your town. He has something for you—a very special delivery indeed. It's an invitation you can't refuse, an invitation to orgies of blood and mayhem. Don't answer the door. There's a little bit of Hell waiting for you on the other side.

Dorchester Publishing Co., Inc.
P.O. Box 6640   ____5204-0
Wayne, PA 19087-8640 $6.99 US/$8.99 CAN

Please add $2.50 for shipping and handling for the first book and $.75 for each additional book. NY and PA residents, add appropriate sales tax. No cash, stamps, or CODs. Canadian orders require an extra $2.00 for shipping and handling and must be paid in U.S. dollars. Prices and availability subject to change. **Payment must accompany all orders.**

Name: _____

Address: _____

City: _____ State:_____ Zip: _____

E-mail: _____

I have enclosed $_____ in payment for the checked book(s).

CHECK OUT OUR WEBSITE! www.dorchesterpub.com
____ Please send me a free catalog.

ATTENTION
BOOK LOVERS!

Can't get enough
of your favorite **HORROR**?

Call **1-800-481-9191** to:

— order books —
— receive a **FREE** catalog —
— join our book clubs to **SAVE 30%!** —

Open Mon.-Fri. 10 AM-9 PM ^{EST}

Visit
www.dorchesterpub.com
for special offers and inside
information on the authors you love.

 We accept Visa, MasterCard or Discover®.